ZHERO

FICTION

Kraftgriots

Also in the series (FICTION)

ZHERO

FICTION

Vincent Egbuson

Published by

Kraft Books Limited
6A Polytechnic Road, Sango, Ibadan
Box 22084, University of Ibadan Post Office
Ibadan, Oyo State, Nigeria
℃ 0803 348 2474, 0805 129 1191
E-mail: kraftbooks@yahoo.com

ISBN 978-978-918-037-0

= KRAFTGRIOTS =
(A literary imprint of Kraft Books Limited)

First printing, October 2011

Chapter One

'Odedekoko! Odedekoko!'

The woman by the speaker looked at her, shocked by her childish delight in the simple song of a bird. Zhero suppressed his amusement at the speaker's neighbour's frown.

'Odedekoko!' the happy speaker repeated, while her neighbour deepened her frown and Zhero struggled to suppress his laughter at what was happening. 'Sing on, sing your happy song,' she said to the bird, as if it was by her.

To Zhero's surprise her neighbour guffawed.

'A happy song! You call that a happy song? My mother used to call herself Odedekoko anytime she was crying over the death of a child.'

'For me it is a happy song. I used to ask my mother, "Why does Odedekoko's name resemble its song?" My mother used to answer, "Because its song resembles its name."'

The women laughed together. Zhero searched for a stone, went near the tree in which Odedekoko was singing and aimed it at the bird — a bird he had loved since he was in Primary One, the meaning of whose song he had never thought any adult would argue about. Odedekoko flew away.

'Zehroh!' one of the women shouted. 'Winch!'

'Jero na winch!' the other woman affirmed, in pidgin English too, and in her happiness unconsciously pulled off her *adire* scarf and unwittingly showed that her hair had been dyed black beyond the hairline. She quickly restored the scarf. 'Jero na original native winch.'

All the people in the waiting shed, except one man, laughed heartily. Since he came to Mabo Waterside the boy had not ceased to engage his interest. In fact his interest in him started when at the Mabo Motor Park he ignored a woman who wanted him to carry her large sack and came to him.

'Sir,' he had said respectfully, 'I go carry your load.' The boy laughed when he saw that all his 'load' was just a briefcase and a life jacket. 'I think say you bring good business, na only that you carry? Sho! Make I go where money dey.'

'Where's the way to Mabo Waterside?' he had asked him.

The boy turned sassy.

'Follow the people. Anywhere you reach na waterside,' he answered as he walked away.

He went to the woman he had ignored and heaved her sack of beans onto his head. The woman laughed.

'Zeehero, you no dey shame?'

'Person wey dey shame for money, im head correct?'

The woman laughed again, adjusting her happy *adire* headscarf. 'Zeehero, today na only twenty naira I go give you.'

'Plus de normal fifty naira,' he had replied and the woman had laughed once more. 'Ma, dis load heavy. Make we dey go. Me and you no go fight because of money.'

The woman insisted on paying him only twenty naira. Without a word he started to move then stopped and called out.

'Sir, please follow us. We are going to Mabo Waterside.'

As he came up to them the woman greeted him with a gap-toothed smile and after a minute or so said gratuitously, 'Dis Zeehero, he like money too much o — no money, no help. No matter how you beg am.'

A woman who was about to pass them in opposite direction stopped and said to him, 'Zhero, my van go soon come o. As you go, come back quick. Na only you go touch my things.' She turned to the woman by Zhero. 'Mama Yagi, good day o.'

'Good day, Mama Susan,' Mama Yagi replied and they resumed walking.

As his friends greeted him they variously called him as Zeehero, Zehroh, Jero, Zorro, so he had to ask him what his name was. He had first spelt it then pronounced it the way Mama Susan had done. The pronunciation reminded him of a former girlfriend whose name he was never able to pronounce properly — Zera, a girl from Dahma, a girl he had looked out for everywhere he went.

When he asked Mama Yagi why Mama Susan would insist on the services of a person who liked money too much she had laughed.

'Dat na de thing nobody understand. Zeehero no dey do anything free, but if you put Zeehero in charge of your things, even if one million naira dey inside, one kobo no go miss when you come back. Any other porter here, dem go disappear with your money.'

After he finished carrying Mama Susan's goods to Waiting Shed 3 he had carried things for several other people before coming to Waiting Shed 1 where the women had jokingly called him a 'witch'.

6

A boy who had been somewhat rude to him suddenly turned very respectful, and when he introduced himself as Engr. Bati Bazi and asked him to pronounce the name he baulked at doing so, only saying 'Thank you, sir.'

Four twenty-five-seater speedboats were coming. Bazi stopped thinking about Zhero. Mabo Waterside which had been somewhat quiet for about thirty minutes after the last speedboat left for a village suddenly came alive: porters, some of them shouting to their friends, as they rushed about unsure of which jetties the boats would land at; touts for taxi drivers shouting out the destinations of their taxis even though the boats had not landed; some traders in stalls far away from the jetties packing their trays with goods and noisily hurrying to the jetties; intending travellers now unable to sit, some of them on edge, loudly wishing the boats were for their destinations, some of them cursing the government for not building roads and bridges in the riverine areas to make travel easy for the people.

All the boats were for Waiting Shed 3. To beguile the time Bazi went there to watch the travellers. An old woman was begging Zhero to carry her bunches of plantains into one of the boats.

'Mama, I tell you say I no come watch video here, na money I come find.'

'So because I no get money nobody go help?' she asked, looking left and right, as if for a compassionate ear in the universe.

Zhero was slightly offended because he felt she had spoken as if in virtue of her old age she had the right to free service from him, but he only shrugged and started to walk away. Bazi smiled and asked him to carry the bunches into the boat. He frowned, Bazi smiled again, and he did as he was requested to do. The old woman thanked Bazi profusely. As she went into the boat and sat down, she shook her head and wiped her tears. Two women who knew what had happened comforted her, while they cursed the owner of the boat who had refused to employ a boat assistant to load and unload passengers' goods and luggage into and from the boat — a miser whose life and physical appearance the money he loved so much had not impacted on positively.

Mama Susan had agreed on a price with the driver of the fourth boat, who signed his assistant to moor a little away from the jetty. With the commanding voice of wealth she shouted, 'Hey Zhero! Come!' He rushed to her, and each of them made three rounds to the boat with her goods, wading barefoot through the shallow water.

She obviously paid Zhero handsomely — he was happy as the boat pulled out and he waved back to her. He then brought his rubber flip-flops from the side pockets of his trousers, wore them, rolled down his khaki trousers and went towards the Motor Park, humming a tune and swinging his head from side to side, reminding Bazi of the moments during Sunday worship service when the keyboardist Otiossa, his happy keyboard, and his celestial tune seemed to have no separate identities. Zhero was obviously happy.

It was after the third boat had left that the intending travellers around knew what had happened — one woman had selfishly chartered a twenty-five-seater boat and left in it. They cursed her variously. Bazi silently prayed to God not to grant a woman's prayer for the waves to swallow the boat Mama Susan had deprived them of while some people said amen. May Susan embrace her mother in welcome soon, Bazi prayed.

He saw Zhero returning from the Motor Park. A woman, who had been staring vacantly at the river for a long time, removed her attention from the objects of sorrow floating on her mental stream, went to him and called him to a corner within earshot of Bazi.

'My pikin,' she said to Zhero, 'you fit help me make me and my daughter eat something when we go home?'

'How I go help you? How about the *ogogoro* wey you dey sell?'

'Zhero, you know say since government begin say make drivers no dey drink alcohol, market no dey move for me, and de small small provision wey I dey sell, I don eat de money finish . . . Zhero, my pikin.'

'Mama, I no get anything for you.'

She glanced at Bazi. He appeared not to be listening to them, so she said pathetically, 'But dat woman give you plenty money na. Zhero, pity me and my pikin,' she begged in a tone that had desperately emanated from the gnawing image of her daughter going to bed tonight without food since afternoon.

'My money na for me and my own mama. Bye bye,' Zhero replied, as if to a friend he had stopped to briefly chat with in the road, and walked away, swinging his head to the rhythm of an Efik song coming out from Madam Afang Special's eatery to share its delicious beauty with all and sundry.

Anamo, a porter who was behind her and within earshot, was glad about what Zhero had done to the woman who was fond of insulting porters and never tired of telling them how untrustworthy

8

they were and how honest Zhero was — 'All of you, na only Zhero I fit leave for my shed and go out.'

The middle-aged woman was rooted to where she was for a long time, then she unwillingly plodded towards the Motor Park, fighting back her tears, nearly every step of her sorrow-sodden feet raising dust from the ground. Bazi went to her and pressed five thousand naira into her right hand. When she realized what had happened she dropped on her knees.

'No, madam, please get up.'

'So you been dey hear wetin Zhero say?'

'Get up, madam, please get up,' Bazi pleaded, stung, inexplicably, by the tears his kind action had drawn from her eyes.

As she weakly tried to get up she fell on her hands and her tight well-worn dress cruelly tore at the backside revealing her brownish white slip. He held her up, told her to stop weeping and walked away. For a long time she could not move . . . If someone told her that the receding stranger was an angel in human form her heart would join her mouth, which was now agape, to sing praises to God . . . .

Bazi laughed at the inscription on the wooden wall of a shack: ILLEGAL STRUCTURE, STOP-WORKS ORDER NOT APPLLICABLE.

Twenty minutes or so after he returned to Waiting Shed 1, two boats arrived for the people there. He did not have to rush because they would not fill the two boats. After the first boat left, the remaining twenty or so passengers leisurely went into the second one. The driver counted the passengers — only twenty-one, he needed four more. Luckily two men soon came, and the passengers requested the driver to start the engine. Without a word he left the boat and went into the Waiting Shed and shouted for a hawker to bring him *akara*. She walked leisurely to him and put her tray of *akara* and loaves of bread on the floor in front of him.

'How much?' she asked. 'You want bread too?'

'Give me *akara*,' he gruffly replied.

She bent forward and started to fork the *akara* balls into a nylon bag.

'How much own?'

He did not answer her. She raised her face and realized that his eyes were glued to the décolletage of her blouse which was generously showing him her breasts. She straightened up, frowning, even though she subconsciously liked the power of her body over him.

'Give me one hundred naira own.'

She forked one more piece into the bag and gave it to him with her left hand, adjusting her décolletage with the right hand.

'You no go eat am with bread? Fifty kobo bread.'

'One hundred naira *akara* with bread? I be millionaire? And na wetin you take make the *akara*?' he playfully asked.

'No be beans dem dey take make akara?'

'Dis breasts — I mean, balls — wey big like dis, you sure say you no add garri?'

'I beg, pay me make I go, Amin,' she sternly replied.

He gave her a two-hundred naira note. 'No, no, keep de change. Ah,' he sighed, 'Sarah, Sarah,' hoping that Cupid's arrow would pierce her heart.'

She sniggered at his heart-sigh, as if it was a toddler's missile which had hardly touched her skin, took up her tray and left without a thank-you. He sighed again and started to eat his meal without relish . . . She had firmly told him a relationship with him was impossible: How much was his income? To live in his waterfront shack with him and raise a family? To produce children who would end up as hawkers and boat drivers? Her ambition was to go to secondary school and then to university — 'If your primary school certificate is enough for you my own is not enough for me o. I don't want my children to hawk for a living' — she was right, but he loved her . . . he loved her and he wanted her to be his wife, even though she had said love was not enough reason for marriage . . . .

A man wearing only khaki shorts and rubber flip-flops stopped her and she started to attend to him. His naked enormous potbelly and his happy face made Bazi think of him as a porter carrying a rich merchant's heavy load on his stomach, very proud of his porterage. Amin ate only two balls and went into the boat. Some of the passengers had been quarrelling over the boat driver's behaviour. Some said he was disrespectful, some said his I-don't-care attitude was insulting — leaving them in the boat without a word. When a man said he was simply greedy a woman stoutly defended him: how much would he make in total from the trip? Minus the owner's rent, minus the cost of fuel, minus the assistant's pay, minus repairs if the boat developed any fault. Bazi quietly paid for the two vacant seats, the driver said 'Thank you, sir' and started his engine. Then he realized that the boat assistant was not in the boat.

'Oh damn it! Wey dis boy? Maiko!' he shouted. 'Maiko! Maiko!'

The passengers who hated him felt triumphant. One of them laughed. 'Una see de driver wey una dey support?'

He saw Zhero coming and eagerly called him. Zhero, whose dirty sky-blue shirt was now draped over his left shoulder, sauntered to the end of the jetty and stopped. Bazi half envied him — a monarch in his social milieu.

'Zhero, you see Maiko?'

Zhero laughed happily and revealed the secret he had kept for so long. 'Maiko don reach im house by now. He say your pay too small.'

All the passengers, except a woman, laughed.

'Zhero, please, you fit help me?' Zhero shook his head. 'Just to help de people wey dey go down carry their loads.' Zhero said no. 'Only three villages between here and Amabra.'

'You fit pay me how much I go make before I close today?'

'How much?'

'Six hundred,' he answered impassively.

'How about de free transport to Amabra?' Amin reacted with shock.

'I tell you say I wan go home today?' he offhandedly riposted and made to walk away.

There were some Amabra women in the boat but they did not dare to interfere lest Zhero should tell his mother that they prevented him from making money.

Zhero going to Amabra? Bazi eagerly told him he would give him the amount. Zhero put on his shirt and walked down the stairs of the jetty onto the boat. The woman who had not laughed now laughed alone in her gravelly voice.

'Greed done jam greed today! Driver want money for empty spaces, boat assistant charge six hundred for one trip!' she happily remarked, her voice, Zhero felt, like that of a constipated frog and not that of Odedekoko.

Locked up in his lovelorn universe the driver did not respond to her — her words only glanced off the windows, his ears which had desperately yearned, day and night, for Sarah's 'Come into my heart, Amin, the door is open,' not her derisive laughter at his gifts of love.

Giving Zhero a frog-might-croak-in-the-presence-of-humans stare, the woman spat out, 'The love of money is the root of all evil.'

Zhero only dropped his eyes. His mother had brought him up to respect all his elders. Conscious of the odour of his shirt he felt uneasy. But he felt relieved when the boat started to move. Soon the wind would neutralize all possible human odours in the boat. Bazi was one of the few passengers wearing life jackets. As he noticed Bazi's eyes on him he responded to a feeling in him to tell Bazi to take off his life jacket. It was a whisper no one else could hear but Bazi felt a strong compulsion to obey him, and he did. Then when the waves turned violent he felt himself a prize fool for obeying the words of a boy who would probably have passed the night in a wooden waiting shed at the waterside. He contemptuously regarded the dirty shirt, the dirty khaki trousers, the dirty rubber flip-flops, and the probably dirty skin the boy was wearing, and unconsciously looked at his own grey safari suit and sparkling black Italian Bali shoes.

A man wondered aloud. At the landlubber speed the boat was running would night not meet them on the river? Several passengers turned and looked at the driver. Jolted out of his reverie, he looked at his wristwatch — the boat recklessly accelerated like a woman brutalized by the man she loved and who therefore no longer cared for life. There was a silent agreement by the passengers not to utter a word — if a boat driver was angered he would capsize the boat.

Bazi in the middle seat took up his life jacket from his lap and looked at it questioningly. When he raised his face his eyes locked together with those of Zhero who was sitting in the small bow seat and facing the passengers. Bazi dropped his eyes, he dropped the maroon life jacket on his lap, he confronted himself — even the women looked unruffled, why was he so fearful?

The woman who had called the driver and Zhero greedy people before the start of the journey spoke: 'Amin, na beg I beg you. Drive small small. E be like say piss wan fall from my . . . Amin, no disgrace me.' She removed her *alari* headscarf and slapped it on her lap. 'Amin, I be woman o!' she pleaded, her voice and her gestures portraying fear as a ridiculous thing.

The passengers laughed and their hearts turned calm. Only Amin did not laugh but as compassion flowed from his heart to the fibreglass speedboat she turned calm too and she ran more and more smoothly, deftly maneuvering between or through the waves until two boats she had passed in opposite direction made a fast U-turn.

'Eh we are finished!'

'Those must be pirates — see how fast their speedboats are!'

12

'Allah, what will happen to my family!'

Bazi felt like asking Zhero if what his fellow passengers were feeling was right but he decided to be silent. Nobody, not even the young men wearing life jackets, looked like his social equals — he had to behave with dignity.

'Yeh!' many voices shouted and some passengers appealed to Amin to stop, it was better to have their property taken than for the boat to capsize, if they didn't stop the pirates might kill all of them out of anger, life was more important than any earthly possessions. Amin slowed down and the boats came up to them. From each boat they fired a shot into the air and a stentorian voice told them to switch off their mobile phones. Hands shaking, those with mobile phones brought them out and switched them off. The speaker noticed that some people did not bring out their phones. He hoped, for their own sake, he hoped they had not lied, he hoped they truly had no phones. An old man apologized and trembling like the leaves of a plant in a windstorm switched off his own too.

The pirate laughed, 'God has saved you today, Papa.' He stopped laughing. 'Now, if anybody phones or if the phone rings that person is dead — *instanta!*'

One boat moved and Amin was ordered to follow it. The second boat watched Amin from behind him. Each capacious Yamaha fiberglass boat had ten masked men each holding a formidable gun at the ready. They went through a canal, debouched into an expanse of water and drove for about ten minutes to arrive at a run-down hamlet from which the inhabitants had been expelled by fear of the Anti-Terrorism Force and dread of the militants fighting against the economic exploitation of the region by the federal government. They were welcomed by other armed men who ordered the captives to be absolutely silent and to get out of their boat immediately. The captives obeyed without a word and two youths rummaged their property for money, jewellery and other valuables in the boat while two other youths dispossessed them of the valuables they were carrying or wearing.

'Right,' the masked owner of the stentorian voice said, 'you will go back to your boat — no talking, no talking, I say! You will go back to your boat. Except you . . . you . . . you . . . and you.'

Two youths shoved the four men wearing life jackets towards a thatched mud house.

'Hey!' an elderly woman wailed. 'People wey dey travel together with us.'

An armed man slapped her venomously and she shut her mouth. As he walked away from her the tears rolled down her face . . . A boy who would never measure up to her son's achievements even if he lived for one hundred years more . . . her son, a professor of mathematics . . . .

No one said a word, and it was as if the unnatural action had taken place in a world peopled only by the armed man, the elderly woman, her hurt and her smothered anger until Amin protested. 'This na evil una dey do o!' he suddenly shouted. Two men pounced on him with the predatory speed of a lion but he continued to express his mind: 'This thing you people are doing is not good o! Una dey give our people bad name.' They continued to beat him but he did not stop. 'Kill me, am ready to die. You people are evil beings. You are animals. You are not human beings. You are not from this region, das why. Kill me. Is better to die fighting than to die of shame. Go on, shoot me. They are my passengers. Am responsible for their safe arrival to where they are going. Shoot me!' he shouted in a try-something-else-I-have-broken-the-pain-barrier tone.

The stentorian-voiced man told them to take him far away from the others for him to be shot, his voice flat like that of a judge sentencing to death the umpteenth criminal before him in the year. Some of the passengers wailed, they begged, some went down on their knees, a woman clasped the legs of the man who gave the order and begged him, 'If our driver is killed, how do we go back? You have killed us too. Please, sir, have mercy,' she wept, as if the father of her children, her husband was being taken to the gallows and she was about to be widowed.

A forty-something-year-old fair-skinned woman, her brain reeling, dashed a few metres away from the group, lifted up her blue lace wrapper and black slip, parted her legs and started to urinate in full view of the pirates and her fellow passengers. No one gave a thought to her smooth-looking buttocks and shapely legs except Bazi, who silently prayed that the pirates would not be aroused to rape her, and then he wondered how such a beautiful woman was travelling without wearing panties. The woman, a diabetic, returned unabashedly to the group, deeply grateful to God that her urinary urgency had not disgraced her this time.

Zhero was not happy that he was afraid to help a friend in need . . . All he needed was to kill his fear and fight for his friend . . . His

mother once said to him, Sometimes fear is better than courage . . .
Perhaps he should tell Amin to beg for mercy?

Bazi firmly told Amin to stop talking and he did, and for the sake
of his passengers he was not killed. Without a word Amin and his
passengers went into their boat and they were led back by the two
boats to near where they had been captured. Even after the kidnappers
had departed nobody spoke. Amin stopped the engine and wept.
Only the old man and the old woman joined him in weeping without
saying a word. To Bazi, the natives were in collective denial of the
humiliation they had experienced, but in reality the Niger Delta
indigenes were feeling too bitter to talk — the death of tribal love
was too bitter for them. After a few minutes Zhero persuaded Amin
to start moving. As he was starting the engine a bird sang from the
top of the mangrove they were close to.

'Odedekoko,' the old woman sighed and she wept afresh, 'life
goes on.'

A man explained that the men wearing life jackets were taken to
be either oil company workers or non-indigenes of the region. No
one responded, and the silence continued.

Bazi could not believe that what happened to him was real: for
no reason he had obeyed Zhero to pull off his life jacket; the pirate
youth had patted him down several times without discovering the
wallet in his trouser pocket, the boy who had roughly pushed his
hand into the pockets of even the two young women wearing trousers
and turned their pockets out. Most wonderfully, the youths omitted
to search his briefcase in the boat — one of them looked at it and
pushed it aside. Then another youth took his life jacket, which he
had left on a seat, without asking for the owner. He looked at Zhero,
intending to say thank you but Zhero pointedly looked away from
him. He understood Zhero's language — he might be accused of
complicity if it was known that he advised him not to wear a life
jacket.

At Yinbara, Daama and Yamusu villages some of the passengers
wept as they received their goods or luggage from Zhero, making
the onlookers or the people that knew them curious, but in each
village the travellers could not recount their experience immediately,
they could only pray tearfully for the departing travellers not to
meet further danger on their journey.

Only four passengers were going to Amabra — three women and
Bazi. Bazi wondered aloud why the air around Yamusu was so warm

15

as if the sun was shining. The woman by him pointed to the gas flare beyond the village, the fire that burned day and night, whether it was raining or shining, whether the people of the village were cold or hot. She paused, and then explained that it was the reason many indigenes of the village had left for other places, the remaining few fighting with various types of disease. In a tearful voice Amin added that if the four kidnapped people were oil workers they were probably coming to Yamusu.

Bazi turned his head and looked at the orange/yellow/red/white flare for a long time. He called it a kaleidoscope of colours and felt it was beautiful . . . but it brought the people disease, suffering, death — not multicoloured joy.

They remained silent until they reached Amabra.

'Hey! Hey!' the woman by Bazi suddenly yelled clapping her hands and stamping her feet.

Bazi jumped to his feet then sat back. Zhero rushed to the woman and looked at her feet thinking that a snake had bitten her. The others were about to jump into the water but Amin had the presence of mind to accelerate and beach the boat.

The woman answered her neighbours' interrogative eyes: 'Cant you see? Not a single boat. Only canoes. And not a single person at the waterside. Is something not wrong? At this time of the evening.'

'Hey, Amabra, you have fallen to your enemies,' the second woman lamented, her eyes absently roving over the impassive wooden canoes moored to stakes in the river.

'So it was laugh the juju priest was laughing at us, when he said something good was coming to Amabra soon,' the third woman said, more to herself than to the others.

The first woman faced Zhero and gesticulated interrogatively. 'If only three women remain to repeople a village shall they open their thighs to strangers?' Zhero did not look to have been dramatically spoken to. 'Hey, Amabra! Amabra!'

The women took their luggage and left. Zhero stopped Amin from pushing out his boat.

'Won't you pay me before you go away?'

Amin was stunned by the sudden dart of negative energy from Zhero as Zhero grabbed his right arm and yanked him away from the boat he was about to push out. Bazi wondered at the boy whose primary concern was for money even in the present situation.

'Let him go,' he said to Zhero, 'I'm the one to pay you.'

16

Amin thanked him, pushed out the boat, jumped into it and started the engine. His eyes roamed the riverbank. He wondered what had happened to Amabra. He shrugged.

'Zhero!' he shouted genially. 'Don't cheat the man oh! Am going to Ibozi — ten minutes only!'

He waved to Bazi and zoomed off.

Bazi laughed. 'Let's go.' Zhero did not move. 'Oh, your money.' He gave him one thousand naira. 'Take it — one thousand naira.'

'We agreed on six hundred.'

'Now I've made it one thousand.' Zhero thanked him, bending his knees slightly as he did so, then started to walk away. 'Hey, my friend, are you leaving me alone here?'

'Where are you going, sir?'

'Chief Kulokulo's house.' Zhero looked shocked. 'What's the matter?'

'Nothing,' Zhero shrugged his shoulders, but on the way he told Bazi that the village regarded Chief Kulokulo as an evil man: all the money the oil company regularly gave the village went into his pockets only. If any chief or member of the Amabra Development Union accused him of 'eating' the money that should be used for the whole of Amabra, strangers would beat the person either at night or in the forest where the person went to farm or hunt. Whether the person was a man or a woman the strangers would beat the person mercilessly. The people of Amabra had always prayed for the militants who were fighting the government of the country to come and save them but they would not because he regularly gave them big money. Chief Kulokulo lived in the city but every weekend he came to Amabra in the oil company's helicopter.

Bazi was not moved by the boy's anger, rather he was happy that if Chief Kulokulo was so powerful his word to the State Governor would clinch the contract he wanted for him.

There was a large crowd outside Chief Kulokulo's concrete-walled fence. In the distance some of the people around looked subdued but as they reached the place they saw that while a few people were straining to appear sad the majority of Amabra people around Chief Kulokulo's house were happy at the tragedy that had befallen the family. A youth gleefully told Zhero that Chief Kulokulo had just been killed by a group of militants who told his family that they regarded him as a federal government agent working against the interest of the oil-producing region.

Bazi followed Zhero through the massive iron gate which had remained open since the death of the owner of the compound. He was instantly shocked by the splendour of the mansion in contrast with the mud and thatch houses he had seen on the way to this place. He heard some women saying that since Kulokulo's house was built they had never come inside the compound until today.

A woman remarked, 'House wey be nearly twenty years old, see how new e be!'

A younger woman responded, 'Dem say every year he dey change de paint and plenty plenty things, whereas other men no fit give dem wife one new wrapper.'

The women laughed.

A youth said to his colleagues, 'All these fine fine things — the house, the swimming pool, that big generator — which of them go follow am go inside grave?' He shook his head. 'He spoil im name for de sake of de things other people go enjoy now. And even before dem bury am some friends go forget am.'

They laughed and the philosopher pointed out that there was even a place for a car. A carport, it was called a carport, one of them said, and the philosopher said the carport was in anticipation of the motor road the oil company planned to build.

'Greedy man,' one of them, a student of a secondary school in Port Harcourt, said, 'is it not because of him that road has not been completed? Ten years, a small road has not been completed. His company is the one doing the road but every time the oil company gives him money he does small work and says the money is not enough.'

'A man who stoked his happiness with the sorrows of Amabra, ta!' the headmaster of the primary school bitterly said. 'Our road shall be built.'

A woman remarked, 'His own journey has ended. Road or no road our own journeys continue.'

Bazi appreciated the woman's remark, but he had heard enough. He tapped Zhero. Zhero asked if he would like to meet the family whose wailing inside the mansion did not seem to affect the people outside at all. Bazi shook his head and they went out of the compound.

'My friend, how do I return to where I came from?' Zhero laughed. 'What's funny?'

'I'm sorry, sir.'

'Please tell me how I can leave Amabra. Any hotel . . . or guest house here?' He knew it was a silly question, a hotel in this run-down village of thatched mud houses. He modified his question. 'Anywhere I can sleep tonight?'

'You can pass the road that has not been completed. But there is deep water in two places in which there should have been bridges. If you are lucky the boys who carry people on their shoulders will still be there. Let me show you the road, sir.'

Bazi wondered at the number of people, children and adults, walking barefoot . . . and quite a number of children were half-naked, wearing only ragged shorts or pants. He had also seen about three bare-chested girls whose breasts were beginning to peep at men.

Instead of taking him to the road Zhero took him along the riverbank and they walked towards Otutubiri Quarter. Bazi admired the undisturbed river in the twilight. No humans in it, no boats on it, it was calm and beautiful — ah, like the traveller who had no time to stop and smell the roses he regretted that he had to walk on. After five minutes or so he saw something dropping from a pier latrine into the water.

'What's that, Zhero?'

Zhero did not mind the foolishness of the question. 'Shit,' he answered in a you-should-know-what-shit-is tone. 'Someone is shitting.' In the city Bazi would have been offended by the boy's diction, but it was the pollution of the river he loved that offended him. Zhero added, 'That's why my mother and I, we don't fetch drinking water here. I take a canoe, go far far to fetch drinking water.'

'Always?'

'Some people who are too lazy to do so just walk into the river, dip their buckets inside and carry the water home. Some people put alum in the water to purify it. In the night people sometimes carry shit home.'

To their left a naked child of about two years squatted in front of a house and started to . . . Bazi laughed because he nearly used Zhero's word.

'Zhero, it isn't what you said, I'm laughing at something else, don't mind me.'

Two teenagers called Zhero aside, asked him what he had been doing at Mabo Waterside for three whole days — three whole days they had waited for him — and they told him that they too had decided to become militants. Kuroakpo's group was ready to admit them. Would Zhero go with them? It was far better than a porter's life of suffering. Zhero looked at them contemptuously then went back to Bazi.

'Sorry, sir,' he apologized for having gone to his friends without saying excuse me.

'How far is the road to this place?' Bazi asked him, a little suspicious of his brief meeting with his friends.

'It's not the road we're going to.'

Fear gripped Bazi. He tightened his grip on his briefcase. 'This boy where are you taking me to? Where are you taking me to?' he asked, dreading that the Niger Delta boy could erase him from the earth for the sake of his briefcase.

'Sir, there is one upstairs building at Otutubiri Quarter. It's not as big as Chief Kulokulo's own, but it's good.'

'Upstair building — a storey building. How does that concern me?'

'It's only Christmas time the owner comes. But the people guarding it, if they are given money they allow people to stay there for a short time.'

Bazi burst out in laughter. 'This boy Zhero, I can't understand you. You change our plan without telling me? In any case how am I sure some militants won't cut off my head before the morning? What did those boys say to you? Zhero are you honest?' Zhero laughed. 'What is the name of your own quarter?'

'Eko Quarter. We are not going there.'

'That's good. How about Chief Kulokulo?'

'Kulokulo Quarter.'

'I mean the name of the quarter his family lives in.'

'It's Kulokulo Quarter. He changed the name from Lewai Quarter.'

'And the people allowed it?'

'He wanted to change Amabra to Kulokulo City but the government did not allow him.'

Bazi laughed widely, thumping his chest with his right fist to stop himself from coughing — the door within opened and fear flew away from his heart. He was happy.

'Zhero, where are you going?'

It was a woman in a group of five women and a man returning from their farms. Bazi followed him to where the women had stopped, curious about the woman's voice — he had heard that voice before! Or something like it.

'I'm taking this man to . . .' He looked at Bazi. 'I'm taking him to —'

'Zera!' Bazi exclaimed. 'I'm sorry, I'm sorry, I'm Bati Bazi.'

The man who was carrying nothing except his machete quickly dropped it and held the woman's basket with his two hands to prevent it from falling off her head. Zhero too was quick: he held her firmly until her faint dizziness was over.

'I am alright now. Let's go.'

The man gave her basket to Zhero. 'Help your mother to carry her yams home.'

Bazi's legs would have turned into yam tendrils that needed stakes to stay upright if he had not shored them up with his mind until his brief spell of dizziness was over.

'Zhero!' he called out in a pleading tone as he trotted towards the fast-walking group. Zera did not look back. Zhero looked at his mother, who ignored him, and he stopped. Bazi came up to him.

'She's your mother, ish, is she your mother?'

'Yes.'

He stopped Zhero and mused on his face, which he did not see as distinctly as he did at Mabo Waterside. He shook his head. He noticed that the boy felt embarrassed, and he apologized to him. On the man's suggestion the group slowed till Bazi and Zhero caught up with them. They were discussing Chief Kulokulo's murder which they had heard about before they met Zhero. Every time Zera spoke Bazi compared her voice with the past — when was it sweeter, now or then? He wished she didn't stop speaking, he loved to hear her voice, the voice that couldn't qualify for the choral group of her former secondary school, but it was Zera's voice, and Bazi was hearing it again, with the ears of fresh love, and it was enthralling like the Ishaku Stream gurgling through the Yankari Botanical Gardens of his former university, he wished she wouldn't stop speaking, but because she was conscious of his presence her statements, which made the group laugh, were laconic. He was glad when he heard her saying good night to the man. Zhero told him they had reached Eko Quarter, where their house was. In less than one minute they got home.

Zera went into their thatched mud house while Zhero took the basket to the thatched bamboo outhouse kitchen at the backyard where he dallied, expecting his mother to do something about Bazi who was standing at the front-yard not knowing what to do or say.

21

Zera came out of the two-room house holding a kerosene lantern and without looking at him went to the backyard. He noticed that she was wearing very thick rubber flip-flops, the type made from discarded motor vehicle tyres.

'Zhero, what are you doing here?'

'Nothing.'

'Won't you go and give your friend a seat? By the way, how, where did you meet him?'

'He came in Amin's boat. He came to see Chief Kulokulo.'

'Now! Go and tell him immediately to go away. Kulokulo's friend must not be seen with us.'

Zhero went and told him to go away for the reason his mother had given. He rushed to the backyard.

'Zera,' he begged. 'He isn't my friend. No one knows that I came here to see him. Only your son knows . . . Zera please let me stay ... If you say no I'll walk about the village till morning and come back to see you.'

'To see me or to shoo me away?'

'Oh, Zera, Zera.' He fell down on his knees. She quickly turned the light of the lantern down. Zhero went to the front-yard to continue to think about the night's mystery. 'The moment I heard your son's name at Mabo Waterside, because your names are close, I prayed to God to forgive me so that I could meet you again in this lifetime. Oh, Zera, God has granted my prayer.'

'Please get up.' Still on his knees he thanked her profusely. 'Please get up and sit on that stool.' He thanked her again as he sat down. 'I want to cook and then have a wash.'

She spoke as if she did not want him around until she finished.

'Can't I stay with you while you cook?' he half pleaded.

'No you can't,' she replied emphatically. As she turned the light up he wiped his wept face with his hands. She shrugged and called Zhero. 'You have to walk about with your friend till I finish cooking and so forth. One hour.'

He gladly followed Zhero, who did not ask him any question. They walked in silence along the breezy riverbank which was deserted tonight due to the unrealistic fear that the murderers of Chief Kulokulo might return. He thought back to the rainy Sunday morning he terminated their affair . . . She wept copiously, to his annoyance for believing him a fool, he pushed her out of his house and banged his door. A wicked girl — she came with pregnancy into their relationship! She intended to foist a bastard on him! Pumped up with pain and anger he had his bath, dressed, ate in anger and went to church. When he closed his eyes and prayed to God not to lead him into temptation anymore — Zera was on the altar! He opened his eyes. For a moment he thought the priest was Zera and he nearly shouted her name . . . If only he had gone to her that day! He didn't, but when he did the next weekend her friends told him she had left the school — just yesterday . . . 'Oh Bazi!' he groaned.

Zhero was frightened. 'Sir any problem sir?'

'No, Zhero, no, don't mind me, Zhero. Where are we going, Zhero?'

'We are just walking about.'

They heard wild shouts of 'Goal! It is a goal!'

'What is that?' Bazi fearfully asked.

'It's from the Naija Video Viewing Centre.'

'On a night like this?'

'Goal! It is a goal! Goal!' the Amabra night replied, unwilling to be defined in accordance with only one person's feeling.

'I think they have scored again,' Zhero explained and pointed to a place in the distance, where the love of football left no room for any thoughts about social issues. 'That's the video centre.'

'They have electricity?'

'It's a small generator. We call it I-pass-my-neighbour. You want us to go there?'

Bazi laughed. 'My goal is different, Zhero. What's your goal, Zhero?'

Zhero did not answer him.

They continued walking.

'Ahh Zhero o.' It was his great-uncle, the middle-aged man who had prevented his mother's basket of yams from falling off her head. 'Zhero.'

'Uncle.'

'Where are you going?'

'I am showing my mother's friend the village.'

'Your mother knows him well?'

'Yes.'

'If you say so then I will go back. I was going to see if all is well.'

Zhero laughed. Bazi and the man shook hands and greeted and he went back. Zhero liked the silence because his mind was full of thoughts. After two minutes or so he suggested that they sit on a four-feet high bamboo platform near the edge of the bank.

'If it is safe.'

Zhero assured him it was and they sat on the platform. He noticed that Zhero was still but his own legs had been swinging forward and backward. He called them dangling participles, smiled and stopped the swinging. When, about ten metres in front of them, a man rose from the water he jumped to his feet and would have run if Zhero had not quickly told him it was a man who had probably been relieving himself or bathing.

'Zhero, is it your voice I am hearing?' the man half shouted.

'Yes, it is my voice, Yari.'

'Is there a woman with you?'

Zhero laughed. It was when the naked young man came to where they were that they saw his towel was on the platform. He tied it around his waist and peered into Bazi's face.

'Ahh Zhero, this your friend, I have not seen him before o.'

'He is my mother's friend.'

'Oh?' the man stepped back respectfully. 'Good evening, sir.'

'Good evening, friend,' Bazi responded, offering him his hand which the young man took respectfully with both his hands after quickly wiping them on his towel, his civility a sharp contrast to his leviathan size.

He advised Zhero not to stay out too long considering the murder of Chief Kulokulo and he left them. Zhero launched into a description of Yari's wrestling prowess, but when he noticed Bazi's lack of interest in what he admired he stopped and reassured him that the night was safe.

Now and then the odour of Zhero's shirt made him feel uneasy but he did not see any reaction from Bazi. Probably, he thought, the fresh river breeze drowned the odour before it could reach Bazi.

Only in the Nollywood films he had watched at the Naija V.V.C (Naija Video Viewing Centre) had Zhero seen men go down on their knees and beg women to forgive or to marry them, never in real life before that moment when Bazi fell on his knees before his mother. What could that mean? . . . His mother who had never talked about any man before except to mention that his father was dead, could she have been intimate with Engr Bati Bazi? . . . All his life he had never known her to leave Amabra for long — where could she have met him? When she was a student in the city? But that was so many years ago . . . .

24

Bazi was thinking of the remoteness of Amabra from government presence and protection: no police, no soldiers, no motor road, no public power supply — if a disaster should occur tonight, from where would help come to Amabra? . . . Because he abandoned Zera she was languishing in Amabra . . . If she forgave him he'd make it up to her . . . What could she be doing now? Still cooking or looking forward to his return?

She had finished cooking, she had had a wash and she was now lying on her old wooden bed which Zhero had frequently held together with nails, her mind on the past as fresh as yesterday . . . .

The Federal Government scholarship was delightful not just because she was the first girl in the region to get it, but especially because even Christopher who used to beat her in all examinations from primary one to primary six did not pass the scholarship examination . . . And she was the first girl in Dahma to go to Queens College where learning was a very happy experience . . . Rev. Sister Mary Keelson, the principal, was fond of telling the students 'My dear girls, the primary duty of Queens College is to make you rounded human beings' until one day in the morning assembly Mrs Asamoah cut in, 'Like your principal's round voice' — oh the joy of the students that day because for so long they had admired the principal's liquid voice when she sang Christmas carols and no one had had the boldness to say to her that her voice was sweet! . . . Her own happiness wasn't total, because her parents were too poor to supplement the scholarship and she lived almost like a beggar, until she met a man who relieved her condition, but he abandoned her after he impregnated her . . . Then came Engr Bati Bazi, to whom she confessed after a few months of their relationship that she was pregnant.

'How many months old?' he asked her compassionately.

'About four months.'

'Then it can't be mine.'

'Yes.'

'Mine? Are you saying mine?'

'No.'

'Then why are you telling me?'

'I want you to help me,' she naively told the man she had loved deeply.

He contemptuously told her to forget that she ever met him, because he was a family man. She cried, reminding him that he had several times said he loved her — was it only sexual love? He pushed her into the rain and banged his door, and it was as if her tears were the rain drenching the earth. Her friends told her to do what all of them were doing — abort the pregnancy and move on. She told them she didn't fall from the sky, she had parents, she'd go to them . . . But her father too, her father too drove her away from his house . . . So her mother brought her to her own village, Amabra, and she took her mother's maiden surname, which she gave to Zhero too when he was born . . . When her mother died three years ago her father didn't care about her burial, so she hadn't seen him since the day her mother brought her to Amabra . . . .

After primary school, Zhero couldn't go to school because there was none in Amabra and she didn't have the means to maintain him in any of the towns in the region where there was a secondary school . . . .

Her thoughts went back to Bazi, who at that time put his right arm around Zhero's shoulders, the shoulders of the child of the woman he loved. For a minute or so he was silent.

Then he said: 'Zhero, I want to say two things. One, when you taught me how to pronounce your name I thought about your mother, because she too had taught me how to pronounce her name. Two . . . .' He paused for a long time, and then continued. 'Two, someday, perhaps, someday you'll know how I wronged your mother . . . But meanwhile . . . for now . . . I only want you to do one thing for me and let me come back into her life.' Zhero was silent. 'I think I should have first asked: Is she married? Is there any man she's thinking of marrying?'

'No, sir.'

'Then will you help me?'

'Yes, sir.'

'Ah, Zhero, thank you . . . Do you know, Zhero, why you told me not to wear a life jacket?' He answered his own question. 'Because God didn't want me to be kidnapped. Because God wanted me to meet your mother tonight . . . Because the stories of our lives — your mother's, yours and mine — are one . . . Zhero, life is a series of becauses.'

Zhero laughed — he'd never heard 'becauses' before. 'Let's go home, sir?' he suggested when he stopped laughing.

'And home is your mother's heart.'

'A house inside a person's heart?' Zhero asked him.

26

Bazi laughed. 'Someday you'll understand, Zhero. And you'll speak better English. By the way, Zhero, why do you carry loads on your head? Why not use a wheelbarrow?'

'People steal wheelbarrows a lot. This year alone I've lost three wheelbarrows. It's better I use my head. At night thieves steal wheelbarrows. But they can't steal my head.'

Bazi's belly laugh amused Zhero. Then they walked in silence until a woman who bolted out of a thatched wooden hut nearly ran into Zhero. She fell to the ground as he sidestepped her.

'Wooh wooh wooh!' she continued to shout on the ground. 'Good people of Amabra, Egberi wants to kill me oh!' Her four-year-old twins came out and joined her in weeping. 'Oh my father! Oh my mother! Why did you leave me with Egberi whose only job as a husband is to beat me? You said he was a good man — is this what a good man is? Oh my father! Oh my mother! Come and take me to the land of the dead. Please come tonight let me go and rest with you. If the people there work too, let me marry a man who would add his own yams to my fish to feed our children,' she wailed to the silent neighbourhood which heard her call but could not respond because all compassionate hearts were confined to their houses by the monster, fear of the lamenter's husband.

As she beat the ground with the flat of her hands her children yelled, as if they were feeling the pain of the earth. Bazi felt like scooping up the family and pressing them to his chest — the woman's family ethic made him feel like the object of her quest, a co-worker to raise a happy family.

'Sir, let's go,' Zhero said to him. 'If you try to help her and her husband sees you he will turn the fight to you. People are hearing her but no one will come out. If anyone tries to help her he will use the things the person's father and grandfather did to form a story.'

Bazi shook his head and they left the place. Zhero told him about Egberi: he used to be a good husband and one of the best storytellers in Amabra until he fell down from a palm tree and broke a leg which took about two years to heal. After he recovered he refused to go back to palm wine tapping or to do any other work, saying that his wife had a duty to feed him and to take care of him because he paid a big bride price to her parents in order to marry her. Now the only thing he did was beat, beat, beat his wife anytime he wasn't drinking ogogoro, the ogogoro he started drinking as a pain reliever after he fell from the palm tree.

Immediately they got home Zera laid the brown plastic table she had brought to the front-yard and told them food was ready. She went into her room and lay on the bed.

'Zhero, how can we eat when your mother isn't here?'

She heard him. She came out and sat at the table.

'I forgot I ought to first taste the food I prepared in case it was poisoned.'

Bazi laughed — oh, she hadn't lost her sense of humour!

'Zhero, please thank your mom for me.' Zhero's response was to take his plates and stand up. 'No, Zhero, please stay with us, otherwise the atmosphere will be awkward.'

Zera and her son laughed, and they all started to eat happily.

'Pounded yam in so short a time, Zera?'

'Yes.'

'Thank you.'

'Thank you too.'

'The soup is sweet. *Ogbono*, bitter leaf and dried fish only?'

'Made sweeter with crayfish — crayfish pounded smooth.'

'Someone told me crayfish is highly nutritious, and this fish, and the *ogbono* — the African bush mango.' She smiled. 'I don't know about bitter leaf.'

'Everything created by God is useful. Like life, the bitter part too is useful.'

'Oh, Zera, not that, not yet.'

He was worried that she was frowning. He followed her eyes to a ragged woman approaching with a plastic bowl. Before she could speak Zera told her she had nothing for her tonight. The woman stood speechless for some seconds then said thank you and slowly walked away. Bazi got up, called her back and gave her ₦5000.

'Hey! Tamara! Tamara!' she called out, her eyes raised to the sky, 'You are always good to me.' She turned her wet face to Bazi. 'I do not know how old you are. I should have gone down on my knees to thank you.' Bazi told her it wasn't necessary and she left, her voice rising to a crescendo. 'God is good. As she created poor people she also created good people. She created rich people to take care of the poor people. Hey, Tamara, thank you, Tamara!'

Zera suppressed her anger, but she had to explain her behaviour.

'Sometimes one gets tired of giving, especially to such people. Her husband doesn't do anything except to impregnate his two wives. How his wives and children feed isn't his business. This one has eight children, small rats. The other woman has five. One of her daughters, at fifteen years, already has three children. Can you imagine that? The boy that impregnates her is just sixteen years. A jobless boy. The last time, both mother and daughter were pregnant at the same time.'

Bazi thought, Strange forms of human abuse. But not by the people themselves, caused by the government which has neglected the people, which hasn't given the people education, which hasn't taught the poor how to avoid producing children they can't take care of — people abuse.

Zhero was surprised — his mother had not behaved that way to anyone in need before. What he did not know was that his mother had subconsciously transferred her anger at life and its agent, Bazi, to the poor woman, she who had always said to her son to love life no matter what.

Bazi noticed Zera's eyes on him. As he resumed eating he told her about their encounter with the kidnappers and she told him she and her son had decided not to entertain fear of militants or kidnappers because they believed nothing could harm them unless they gave it permission through their actions either in a past life or the present one — they believed in karma. Bazi said karma was a strong traditional belief of his tribe too.

After the meal Zhero took the plastic plates to the backyard and sat there, leaving his mother and Bazi facing each other, the plastic dinner table between them. When Bazi realized that he had softly tapped his eight fingers and two thumbs on the dinner table for too long he placed his hands in his lap. Because he did not sit upright as he removed his hands from the table his action had given him a stupid stoop. When he saw her face he asked her if he looked laughable. She burst out in laughter.

'Oh, Zera, to confess, I'm not at ease. I don't know what to say. I don't know if I should say anything. And you're not about to help me.' She laughed again. 'You're not about to help me.' She laughed again. 'That is it,' he sighed. 'Your ability to laugh. What I called your UHQ. Do you still know the full meaning of the abbreviation I coined for you?'

'What does it matter?'

'Unique human quality. Your ability to laugh is your unique human quality.'

'Engr Bazi, please —'

'Bazi? Engr Bazi?'

His pained voice, his tears brimming over as if from a geyser behind the eyes — she changed her mind about reminding him of how he pushed her out of his house while the rain was falling from her eyes, and the heavy rain from her eyes mingled with the rain from the sky as she stepped outside his door . . . What did it matter? For years after that she had laughed, and laughter had sustained her.

'Since you came,' she confessed, 'I had struggled in my mind not to call you Bazi, and yet I couldn't say Bati. But what's in a name? Bati, I have to go to bed now because I must wake at 4am. My friends and I are going somewhere. We're starting at 5am. By canoe.'

'Over my dead body, Zera,' he protested as he wiped his eyes. 'You're not travelling by canoe in the night. Whatever it is I'll give it to you — now.' She laughed. He wiped his face and called Zhero. 'Zhero, please tell your mom she can't travel in a canoe at night.' He did not like her frown. 'Zhero, please beg her for me, please.'

Zhero did not know how to respond. His mother laughed at him.

'Obey your friend, Zhero.'

They all laughed.

'Ah, Zera, thank you.'

'For what?' He was silent. 'For my "unique human quality",' she air-quoted.

'For everything, Zera. For the laughter.' He asked tentatively, 'Is there a place for me to pass the night? Here per —'

She told him Zhero was his host. Where he should sleep should be his host's responsibility. After all, Zhero was taking him somewhere before she saw them.

Zhero suggested that Engr Bazi could sleep in his room while he went to a friend's house.

'You are a foolish boy. You want the whole of Amabra to feast on gossip about me?'

'I'm sorry, Zera,' Bazi quickly apologized, to mitigate the boy's embarrassment.

'You'll sleep in his room. He'll sleep on the floor in my room.' She smiled slightly on seeing Bazi's happy face. 'Zhero, go and tell Ebido to tell everyone that we won't travel tomorrow, because I have a visitor.'

Zhero gladly left them together. Bazi requested to see where he would sleep. Immediately they entered the room he fell on his knees on the earthen floor and begged her to only listen, to say nothing even if she didn't like what he was going to say. First he asked her why Zhero was a porter when he should have been in school. She was silent.

'Zera?'

'You said I should say nothing.'

He laughed, she joined him, and they sat on the bed. She wiped the stain of the floor on his trouser legs with her scarf.

'Thank you . . . You haven't answered my question.'

'He'll go to secondary school when we have enough money.'

'Why are you living alone . . . with Zhero?'

'My mother died three years ago.'

'I'm sorry.'

'Thank you.'

'This is between me and you. I'm not Kulokulo's friend. He promised to help me with a contract. I came with a large sum of money to say thank you. The money is in my briefcase. The kidnappers did not open my briefcase, as I told you . . . Zera, if you can promise to say nothing now . . . Zera?'

'Go on.'

'Thank you. I want to leave part of the money with you. I want to come back in two weeks' time because . . . because I want Zhero to go to school in Port Harcourt.' A small rat which was emerging from a hole in the base of the wall opposite them quickly withdrew into its house when it saw humans in its foraging field. Neither of them reacted visibly. 'Zera, did you hear me?' Bazi asked.

If he had said he wanted her to come with him to the city she would have vehemently told him not to come back, but Zhero, for Zhero to go to school, for Zhero to have an education, to go to secondary school, to go to university . . . .

'Zera, why are you weeping?' he tearfully asked.

In his happiness Zhero did not knock on the door before entering his room, and he saw his mother and Bazi sitting side by side, their faces profusely wet. Zera stood up, said she was going to pass the night at Ebido's house, and she left, slowly as if she was a non-swimmer paddling in water whose depth she was not sure of.

'Zhero.'

'Sir.'

'Where is my briefcase?'

'It's in my mother's room.'

'Make sure it's safe. No, don't go yet. Zhero, I promised your mom I would come back in two weeks' time to take both of you to Port Harcourt. I had told you before to beg her to forgive me. Now it doesn't matter whether she forgives me or not. All I want is for you to go to school and for her to do something better than farming with a machete and a hoe or canoeing in a dark night. That's all I want for both of you. Your mom is a very good woman, but because I can't be easily forgiven I depend on you to persuade her to accept my offer. Will you help me?'

'Yes, sir.'

'Thank you, Zhero. Going to school . . . education, let that be your goal. Good night. It's nearly 10pm.'

'Good night, sir.'

Thinking about school, Zhero could not have slept for up to two hours before his mother knocked on the door at 7am or so. She called him to the backyard and mildly scolded him for not having washed the plates and swept the compound — was it because they had a guest he wouldn't do his morning chores? Bazi heard her voice and came out. He gave Zera the key to the briefcase and told her to bring him his toilet bag because he wanted to brush his teeth. When she opened the briefcase the amount of money in it frightened her. It should be more than enough to see Zhero through secondary school! All this money he had wanted to give Chief Kulokulo? She took the toilet bag to him and told Zhero to give him water.

Zhero! You're using your left hand to give your elder something? And your knees are stiff, aren't they?' Zhero transferred the plastic cup to his right hand. 'That's better.'

Zhero apologized then gave Bazi the cup, bending his knees slightly as he did so. Bazi smiled at the genuflection, the people's culture, and thanked him. Zera told Zhero to go to the waterfront to see if boats had started to come. He came back after about thirty minutes to say it did not seem any boat would come to Amabra today. It must be because of the piracy incident and the murder of Chief Kulokulo. Zhero suggested that Bazi might have to go through the uncompleted road but he said he would neither wade through water nor be carried by a fellow human being.

'Meaning?' Zera asked.

'I'll stay here until there's a boat for Port Harcourt.'

Zera noticed that her son did not dislike the idea, and she shrugged. But about an hour after they had eaten their breakfast of *okodo* (yam and smoked-fish pepper soup) they had a problem in their hands — Bazi could not use the fly-infested outhouse latrine. The place was not only uncomfortable. The big flies, some of them greenish in appearance, frightened him and after he had run back to the front-yard their humming continued inside his ears for some time. (Would he use the pier latrine at the waterside?) For the people of Amabra to stare at the droppings from his anus? They laughed and Zhero offered to canoe him to the other bank of the river. He preferred Zera to help him. In fact he could have a wash there.

She took soap, her towel, gave him a pair of flip-flops to wear, told him to carry the paddle and they went to the waterfront. There were few people. Zera explained to the two women close to her canoe that she was taking her visitor across the river for him to relieve himself. The two women, who were crouching and were neck-deep in the water, stood up, not minding their naked breasts, and laughed.

One of them said, 'So if he wants to shit six times today you will paddle him overside?'

Zera told them to cover their breasts and not embarrass her friend. The second woman spread her hands, pushed out her chest and replied.

'My breasts big pass my hands. How I go fit cover them?'

'You no fit go inside water?'

A serious-looking woman washing clothes agreed with Zera — the women should not have exposed their breasts to a man from the city. They should know that in the city men never looked at women's breasts, covered or uncovered, with a pure mind but with lust, especially big bouncing breasts like theirs. The women laughed, beating the water with the flat of their hands, splashing Zera and Bazi with water.

Bazi who had now sat on the middle seat of the canoe smiled at the speaker's deadpan humour and consciously looked away from the women. They turned the boat and gave it a vigorous push far away from the shore and Zera who was sitting on the rear seat playfully called them shameless women and started to paddle towards the opposite bank.

The river was calm because there were no speedboats running on it. The birds in the sky reminded Bazi of Odedeko. He felt like asking Zera what Odedeko's song symbolized for her but he decided he would not be the first to speak . . . The river made him think: He who had jeeps and cars, a woman was transporting his life in a wooden canoe, a BC mode of transport, across a river, a river which at that moment was more important than the familiar six-laned roads and spaghetti flyovers of Abuja and Lagos . . . What did it matter whether a person spent their life on the topmost floor of the Burj Khalifa in Dubai or in a thatched mud house in Amabra? What mattered was happiness . . . The simple joy of life in a pristine village — he dallied with the idea of coming back to live in Amabra after marrying Zera. He had enough wealth for the rest of their lives . . . He admired the way she was paddling — the born-with-it grace with which she dipped the paddle into the water, pulled the paddle backwards and brought out its round flat end again, the splashes of water glistening in the mild morning sun enhancing the beauty of her action. It was the second time he had glanced at her over his shoulder but she did not react in any way. What could she be thinking of?

After thinking back to how he cruelly pushed her out of his house she felt that her reaction to his return into her life was wrong . . . But would it have been good to send a fellow human being who needed her help away from Amabra last night? . . . Of all people, it was through Zhero he came to her — she saw the hand of God in what was happening . . . Hand of God! Wasn't she rationalizing her hope for relief from her present condition? . . . She tried to push the image of the money in the briefcase out of her mind, but it persisted and she concluded that it was because of Zhero, she was sacrificing her honour for Zhero, for Zhero to have a better life, to be away from a village of poverty and morally demanding hardships, to have an education . . . Rev. Sister Mary used to say self-sacrifice was the noblest human quality — for her son she would sacrifice her very life . . . .

The canoe was rocking slightly. He turned his head. The paddle was across her lap and with her right hand she was scooping water from the river and washing her face. Could she have been crying? She smiled wanly at him. Her reaction to a log that loomed up in front of them frightened him — in panic she roughly steered the canoe rightwards and accelerated to avoid being hit on the left side by the floating big log. After she steadied the canoe he gently turned on his seat and faced her.

Smiling at him, 'I'm sorry,' she sweetly apologized.

'I thank you for . . . .'

'For what?'

'For who you are . . . for what you are.'

She smiled. After a few seconds a question he had not thought about dropped out of his mouth.

'That woman who talked about city men and women's breasts, is she your friend?'

'Hnnh . . . not really . . . not a close friend. We both belong to the same age group, Zuzuna Ogbo. Why did you ask?'

'Her sense of humour.'

'She has known sorrow. One night in Lagos, because she did not return in time from the hair salon the gate of her family's compound wasn't locked. Armed robbers went into the house . . . They raped and killed her two daughters before her husband gave them the money in the house. Her husband had a stroke some days after and died. After losing a long battle over his property with his mother and his two sisters she left Lagos and came to live in Amabra.'

'Human evil.'

'Her in-laws said she went to her lover's house that evening, not to the hair salon. Because the houseboy said a man brought her home in his car.'

His stomach lurched as the canoe she had purposely accelerated hit the beach. He turned back — they had reached their destination. To their right, in the distance a lone man standing in a wooden canoe was punting away from them, so he felt the river could not be too deep.

Slapping his buttocks he asked her, 'Where can I do it? It's about to fall.'

She told him he could do it in the bush or in the river. As he started for the bush that looked too thick for comfort she asked him how he would wipe his anus. He had to do it in the river. She assured him the river was safe — no crocodiles at this time of the year — and advised him to pull off his clothes.

'I'll close my eyes.'

'No, no, no. Close your eyes and not see if something is happening to me? Suppose a crocodile's around unseasonably.' She laughed. He looked across the river. 'Can they see us?'

'Not the details.'

Her English — Not the details. He felt sorry that he abandoned her when she needed help to complete her education . . . And the man who impregnated her — may God forgive him and the man.

She asked him what he was thinking about. He shrugged, pulled off his clothes and went into the water. After he finished he told her to close her eyes while he used his hand to wash his anus. She only smiled. When he stood up she behaved as if she did not see his erection. He turned his back to her, and had to look at his pieces of excrement which were bobbing up and down on the river as they moved away from their producer. He suddenly said, 'Everyday leveler.' She went to him with a sponge and soap, which he took without facing her. He felt the sponge which was made of coconut fibres was too rough and hard, so he used only the soap to wash himself. By the time he faced her his erection had gone, so he walked to her and took the towel which gave him a romantic feel because it was her towel. His erection was threatening to return as he went back to her by the canoe, took his clothes and quickly put them on.

'In Amabra when men and women are bathing in the river we only see them as humans. And there's no erection.'

He looked at her intensely. 'Zera, must we go back now?' He looked at the opposite side of the river. 'There's nobody at the waterside. Can't we stay here a little?' he asked, like a pilgrim who did not want to go back to where he came from — where he was at the moment was the home he had searched for all his life.

'If you don't want to be marooned, get into the canoe now.'

Marooned! He couldn't have ever used that word, and he couldn't remember when last he heard anyone use it. He got into the boat.

'Why are you looking at me that way?'

'The word "maroon". I admire your English.'

'Does the word rhyme with abandon?'

'No. Zera, you can't fill me with guilt now. On the contrary I'm so full of admiration for you.'

'There's nothing to admire in a simple word. I studied *Lord of the Flies* in secondary school.' She averted her face from his amorous gaze. 'If you want me to take you back safely, please turn around.'

Instead of turning on his bottom he stood up, the canoe rocked from side to side, in panic he bent forward and gripped a side of the canoe with both hands — the canoe capsized. Fortunately the water was not too deep where they were — just above his navel and up to her breasts. But he had involuntarily swallowed some water. When she saw him gulping for air she waded towards him but he pointed to the boat and the paddle which were drifting away. She swam vigorously, retrieving the paddle first, and then pushing the overturned canoe with her hands as she swam vigorously against the current, using only her legs. When she reached the shallow place he was standing in he pulled the canoe to the shore. They turned it upside, pulled it up the sand and turned it on its side to empty it of the water in it. He appreciated what she had done when she said if he had not alerted her promptly the canoe could have reached the whirlpool which was not far away.

She remembered the title of a song, 'Knock on Wood', and she asked him, 'If you had died — knock on wood — who would believe that I didn't bring you here to kill you?'

'Motive,' he answered breathlessly. 'Finding no motive, no one would say you killed me.' He sat by her on the sand. 'Zera, I lack the words to tell you how sorry I am.'

She burst out laughing. 'Oh Bati!'

He went down on his knees before her, pushed her down on her back and kissed her with the passion with which he had kissed her in his daydreams and his night dreams for years, oh he was full of gratitude for her yielding to his hands, his lips, his mouth and his tongue in her mouth, so full of gratitude that he would implode if he did not intermittently say thank you, Zera, thank you, thank you. He continued to thank her after she pushed him away.

'It's not because I want you back in my life. It's because I haven't forgotten how deeply I loved you . . . That's why it pained me when you refused to help me . . . I didn't have the money to go to a good doctor for abortion. But when you drove me away, I took it that I shouldn't abort the pregnancy. And I vowed not to abort it even though I agreed with my friends that aborting my education was a foolish thing. In any case who would have given me the money to do it? Prostitute myself to raise the money? I chose to leave school, Bati.'

They wept together.

'Oh, Zera, I'm sorry.'

'I don't know why I'm weeping. Many many years ago I had concluded that I was foolish to expect you to help me. How long had we known each other? Just a few months. And I told you to take care of a pregnancy another man had implanted in me before I met you.' She laughed. 'Sheer foolishness, isn't it, Bati?'

'Even then I'm sorry I failed you. I failed a fellow human being.'

'I think something more than the two of us has brought us together in this lifetime.'

'That's how I feel too, otherwise how could I have recognized you so easily in the dim twilight after so many years?'

His reply impressed her like a revelation.

'Come,' she said thoughtfully and walked into the water, her movement as graceful as that of a mermaid in Izon folklore going back home after sunbathing on the beach. 'Come,' she said again to him and he went into the water too, gingerly, like the human invitee of the mermaid. 'Let's wash off the sand and go home.' It took some time to remove the sand in her hair. 'Just like life. The woman is always worse off than the man. Even from a simple kiss in the sand,' she remarked.

'Zera, you'll make me cry again.'

'I'm sorry. Let's go.' Feeling that it was wrong to admit him back into her life she said out loud, 'Our Indian teacher was right. She said, "If you sleep with a man or a woman just once you have created a karmic tie as strong as an iron chain. Therefore practise chastity." That's what one of our teachers often told us.'

He felt guilty. They did not speak until they got to the other side of the river. She moored the canoe far away from where people were, in order to avoid questions from them. No one paid attention to her and her friend because the people had seen an unusual number of speedboats coming at the same time and at a furious speed.

Bazi drew her attention to it and they stopped to see if they were transport boats. As the boats came close to the landing spot the huge waves they raised seemed to be a deliberate show of police power. When Zera said the police must have come in connection with Chief Kulokulo's death Bazi reacted fearfully.

'Bati, where are you rushing to?'

'Sorry, sorry. As if I know the way to the house. Zera, we must look for Zhero immediately. No one must know that I came here to see Chief Kulokulo. Come let's go.'

Several people were hurrying to the waterfront. Zera saw her son among a group of teenagers. She shouted for him to come and he ran to her.

'Zhero, you must not tell anyone that I came here to see Chief Kulokulo.'

'Yes, sir.'

'Enh? You will? Have you told anyone?'

Zera laughed. 'Bati, leave my son alone. Zhero, go and play.' She noticed his look of surprise at their wet clothes. 'The boat capsized.'

Zhero laughed. 'Does he know how to swim?'

'Get out of here, Zhero.'

'Yes, sir.'

They all laughed. Zhero went back to his friends and Bazi and his mother went to the house. She gave him a wrapper to tie around his waist and he pulled off his clothes which she washed and hung on the clothesline at the backyard. When she returned to him in Zhero's room he told her he felt like a village husband, and as if they had never been separated. He believed life in Amabra could be sweeter than a dream. She laughed and thought, Outside this door for how long would he be able to love Amabra? But she had no time to say her thoughts to him. They listened. There was commotion in the air. She opened the door and stood in the doorway. Some people were running past. She wanted to go and see what was happening but he begged her not to leave him alone. Not in his present state — just a wrapper, no underwear. She laughed at the man who said life in Amabra could be sweeter than a dream but was afraid of the monster in broad daylight. He laughed too and she assured him that she would be in her room. She went out, closing the door behind her.

Alone, he wondered why he suddenly felt like he hadn't found what he wanted even though he loved her so much . . . For years he had thought about her and looked out for her everywhere he went, yet he was now feeling like he was at the beginning of his quest . . . Perhaps for the thrill to come . . . .

An hour or so later Zhero came and told them what had happened: Chief Kulokulo's son was arrested last night in Yenagoa following the report of one of those who took part in the killing. They were six and it was Chief Kuloulo's son, Oweiebi, who led them to his father's house to rob him of the ₦10 million he had in his safe. It was Oweiebi who shot his father several times and killed him because his father had recognized his voice. The one who reported to the police did so because Oweiebi refused to share the money equally with them. It was their practice to always share any money equally but Oweiebi said the ₦10 million was his father's money and he could only give each of them ₦100,000.'

'Why were people running about and making a lot of noise?' Bazi asked him.

'The police said they wanted to take the body to Yenagoa. As some people were carrying the corpse out of the compound people started to throw sand at the corpse and some people even spat at it. As the police were struggling with the people one policeman's gun went off and killed Angelica who was standing far away and just watching.'

'Hmmh . . . hmmh . . . hmmh . . .' Zera moaned, her lower lip between her upper and lower teeth. Then she jumped to her feet and yelled, 'Eh Angelica!' She wept bitterly. 'Angelica, Angelica, Angelica . . . .'

'Who's Angelica?' Bazi asked Zhero.

Zera answered him. 'Angelica is the woman whose sense of humour you admired. Angelica is the woman whose daughters were raped and killed in Lagos. And her husband died of stroke. And her in-laws dispossessed her of her husband's money and property. Angelica is dead, Angelica is dead, Angelica is dead, Angelica is dead. Eh! Eh!'

'Zera, you're making me cry,' he said tearfully, stood up from the bed and went to her.

'Thank you, thank you, cry for Angelica, thank you, Bati, thank you,' she cried, tightly holding his arms and shaking him, her flooding face raised to his.

Zhero left the room, crying for the first time since Angelica died. Bazi realized that instead of crying he should console her and make her stop crying. He wiped his face and begged her to stop. Between sniffles she told him that Chief Kulokulo was a selfish head of the village. When Shell wanted to build a secondary school in Amabra he told the oil company that there would be land acquisition crisis in the village, so they gave him a part of the money they had intended to spend. And that was why Zhero had not been able to attend secondary school. There were many many other instances of greed, she said. Tired, the few chiefs and elders who refused to be on his payroll secretly approached Oyinkuro, a most powerful juju priest to help Amabra. But he told them there was nothing he could do. The ritual Chief Kulokulo killed his daughter to perform gave him power above any other juju power. She sniffled once more and then continued. The juju priest said only the daughter Chief Kulokulo killed would set Amabra free from the evil man, because she had come back to him as a boy. Eh! Tamara, Tamara, Tamara, the juju priest was right. Amabra was free. But how about Angelica? Angelica, Angelica, she burst out in tears . . . and she sang.

40

It is not night yet
But where is Angelica?
Before Odedekoko's home call
To the children of the soil
You have left your farm, Angelica.
Is it because you despaired of the harvest?
Odedekoko, singer of life's song
Sing to me about Angelica.

Zera's lyrics, her music and her love-laden voice drew fresh tears from his heart, then he realized again that he ought not to be crying. After a lot of cajoling, mild scolding and begging, he succeeded in stopping her from crying. Then she remembered that she ought to prepare food for the afternoon. He begged her not to do anything. Whenever they were hungry Zhero could buy bread, sardine, cocoa and things. She went outside to tell Zhero she had stopped crying. He only raised his tear-stained face to her. She drew him up, wiped his face and told him to go back to his friends. She watched him go, then went back to Bazi.

'How old is Zhero?' he asked her.

'Fourteen . . . You don't believe me?'

'Counting from when we parted, yes. But he looks bigger than fourteen.'

'He grew fast and strong for the life he has come to.'

Zera's friends kept away from her because of her important guest, about whom they hoped she would soon come and tell them. In spite of the past the hours passed companionably for her and Bazi, and in spite of the village tragedy when she and he sat in front of her little house to the admiration or the envy of some adults who passed by, the evening was as quietly happy as a resigned other-mother who had returned from the farm, prepared food, had a bath, eaten supper, and was expecting some children in the quarter to come around for a story or two in the moonlight while her husband was in a fruitful concubine's house.

Zhero came back a little after 8pm to say his mother's uncle, Kenitari would soon be coming to see her and her friend. Zera knew it was his way of rebuking her for not going to tell him about her visitor, so the three of them immediately left for his house. A woman carrying a big sack on her head overtook them, crying and lamenting her fate.

'Other women,' she said in a tear-ringed tone, 'let a man touch them just slightly, they would be pregnant. But me, eight years of three marriages, my womb is like land in which no man has tried to plant seeds. So I am going back to my father's house again. The bad fate Tamara gave me.'

'What's happening?' Bazi asked Zera.

'She's barren. Her third husband has just driven her out.'

'When day breaks,' the woman continued, 'Amabra will have something to laugh at. If a woman bears children and dies early, people will see her children and speak well of her. But my fate is to live for people to laugh at. Did I ask for long life? Bad fate . . .' her voice trailed off.

It was obvious Zera's uncle had no intention of going to her place because a number of children were gathered at his feet listening to the story of Tortoise who had everything in life, but helped no one since he wouldn't need anyone's help.

'Uncle,' she said to the bare-chested storyteller, 'soon you will be totally naked.'

He pulled the top part of his wrapper up to nearly his navel and continued.

'Egberi o!'

The children chorused, 'Yah!'

'Egberi o!'

'Yah!'

He asked his audience if they liked to know the consequences of Tortoise's wickedness. They said yes and requested him to tell them. He deliberately paused, roamed his gaze over his expectant audience, and then continued.

He sorrowfully said sick people died, because Tortoise would not help them. The widow watched her children die one after the other because Tortoise said he was not their father. When the widow wailed Tortoise danced and sang, 'I am not their father/I am not their father.'

The children took up Tortoise's nasal singing: 'I am not their father/I am not their father/I am not their father . . . .'

Kenitari raised his hands after about a minute and they stopped, some of them feeling their noses with their fingers.

When a pregnant woman begged Tortoise to lend her money till her husband's return from Onitsha Market where he had gone to sell his goods, Tortoise danced and sang, 'I am not your husband.'

The children sang the sentence in a nasal voice for about a minute before he raised his hands.

'Egberi o!'

'Yaaah!'

One day Tortoise died. And the boatman that ferried people across to the land where there was no suffering was a man Tortoise had refused to help in his lifetime. There was no way for Tortoise to cross the river. Tortoise begged and begged but the man would not listen to him. Then Tortoise remembered that he had come with a load of money. But it was only one type of coin people were using to pay the boatman — a gold coin which the man collected from them and gave back to them. The boatman went and came back, went and came back, still it was as if he had neither known nor seen Tortoise before.

In frustration Tortoise asked a woman why the boatman would take a coin he would not spend and not his own load of coins and ferry him across to the land where happiness had no beginning nor pause nor end — why? How much was that coin worth?

The woman showed him the one in her hand. 'This coin is kenitari (one love),' she said in a proud tone. 'It is the only coin you should have brought from earth life. If at nightfall you are not ferried across you will be taken to a place where you will suffer for some time, then you will return to earth to be a poor person or a rich person, to work hard and honestly until you find this coin, which you will give to people, and they will give it back to you, like those people going to the land of happiness.'

The woman did not like the way Tortoise was looking at the coin in her hand, so she put it inside her bra.

The children laughed. The girls called the boys Tortoise and Zera and Bazi joined in the laughter. A mischievous boy said aloud, *Kenitari*! and the children laughed because the name of the coin was the name of the storyteller. Kenitari laughed too.

After advising the children to make out the moral of the story before sleeping tonight Kenitari told his eldest wife to tell them another story, and he got up. As he was going inside the house with Zera, Bazi and Zhero the wife protested that tonight was not a night to tell children stories and laugh *yakataah*.

The children laughed repeating her word, *Yakataah*!

In the living room Kenitari and Bazi sat together on the cane couch and Zera and her son sat in plastic armchairs. Kenitari asked his niece what drink her friend would take and she explained that they had just eaten before coming to see him.

'But if I did not tell your son that I was coming to see you —'

'No, Uncle, we would have come to see you before he leaves.'

'Yes, Zera is right,' Bazi said. 'It was our intention to come and have your permission for Zera and her son to go with me to Port Harcourt. For Zhero to go to secondary school, and then university.'

Zera's mouth was agape — Zhero was afraid she might contradict Bazi. But when her uncle looked to her for confirmation she nodded. Zhero was relieved.

Kenitari forgot the reason he had wanted to see Zera — for her to confirm or deny the rumour that her visitor was the father of her son. He only expressed his joy.

'I am glad for Zhero. Eh, Zhero, I am glad for you. This village life of ours makes a man feel like an impotent man looking at the woman that used to be proud of him. He pities himself because he cannot perform his duty anymore.'

Bazi and Zera laughed.

'The other day, when I was at Onitsha Market, when the radio said a seventy-seven-year-old man had climbed the tallest mountain in the world, some women laughed that some Nigerian men at forty cannot even climb their wives.'

'Uncle, a small boy is here oh,' Zera playfully protested as the adults laughed.

Zhero admired his great-uncle's sense of humour. He had probably invented the joke to make Bazi laugh. A man who for years had not travelled out of Amabra, yet he said 'the other day'.

'Zhero,' his mother said, 'I hope your ears are not open. Please close them.'

Zhero smiled.

'What does it matter?' his great-uncle replied. 'A child must learn how to make people laugh . . . Zera, I know how clever you were before you came here. Then you gave birth to Zhero and the boy grew up as clever as you because you were teaching him at home better than the teachers in the school. Such a boy finishes primary school and nobody in his family can help him. Zhero, listen to what I want to tell you now.' He paused before he said it. 'You are going there not for yourself alone. You are going there for your mother's family. You are going there for Amabra. Go and bring what will make us great and proud. Any Amabra person who goes out for success is doing so for Amabra. . . Even if he does not come back. At least he will not be a burden to Amabra.' He paused. 'My grandfather used to say that the things a man gathers on the road may be more important than the thing he set out to find.' He paused for a longer time, then he said to Bazi. 'Your name is . . .?' Bazi told him. 'Thank you, Bazi. When Zhero finishes university and comes back we shall be proud that we too have a man in our family. Thank you, Bazi.'

'Sir, what you were doing for the children when we came here, I don't know which word to use for it. It is invaluable.'

'Thank you, Bazi.'

Bazi did not like the look on Zera's face. Lest she should say something contrary he told Kenitari he would come and see him tomorrow before they left.

'That means I will not go to the farm. Aha, Zera, what will happen to your farm?'

'We'll discuss all that tomorrow, sir,' Bazi replied and stood up.

Kenitari looked for his motor-vehicle-tyre flip-flops which his feet had pushed away while he was speaking. Zhero took them near him. He slipped his feet into them and stood up.

'Remember what I always say, Zhero. When you set out to search for something what you learn on the journey is equally important as what you are searching for. In fact, without your knowing, the things you learn are the reason for the thing you are searching for.'

Zera responded on behalf of her son, 'That is true.'

'Tomorrow your journey starts, Zhero. You too, Zera.'

'That is true, Uncle,' Zera said again to the man she regarded as loquacious.

'Zhero,' he said and paused, looking beyond the boy who was waiting for his words. It was as if his eyes had penetrated the wall and were seeing something in the distance. At last he spoke. 'Zhero, the storm will blow in your path but the dust won't blind you, and the falling branches of trees won't harm you.'

'Amen, Uncle,' his mother responded. 'Say thank you, Zhero.'

'Thank you, Uncle,' Zhero said to his great-uncle whose turn of phrase had always enthralled him and made him wonder if he too would someday be able to speak so expressively.

'Zhero.'

'Uncle.'

He changed his mind about advising the boy to keep away from guns. He only said, 'Go well, Zhero.'

'Thank you, Uncle.'

When they went outside Kenitari roamed his eyes over the place before he spoke.

'Zera, do you see what Agnes has done? She has driven the children away, leaving the mats they sat on for me to take into the house.'

His visitors laughed and he wished them a good night. Zera went to Ebido so that Ebido would accompany her to Angelica's paternal family house in which she had lived since she came from Lagos. After that she would suggest an emergency meeting of Zuzuna Ogbo, no matter how late in the night just in case she would leave Amabra tomorrow.

Bazi and Zhero went home and sat together in the front-yard like a father and his first son. In fact some people seeing them together in the moonlight now believed the rumour that Zhero's father had come for the woman with whom he had quarrelled when she was pregnant with his son.

Zhero was happy he was going to get a good education — secondary school, university . . . His uncle said to get it for Amabra . . . .

Bazi was happy that God had given him a chance to make it up to the girl he ill-treated when she needed him to see her through her problem . . . He had known her for only a short time and yet he had not been able to get her out of his mind since that day . . . The way he saw her on the altar that day and repeatedly thereafter in his dreams, and the way he had felt since last night — there must be something more than this lifetime binding them together . . . .

Two boys passing by saw Zhero and called out his name. Zhero asked them why they were so rude, didn't they see he was with their elder?

'Jero, no vex. We jus' wan know whether na Mabo Waterside or Swali Market for Yenagoa you go go tomorrow. You know say boats dey come.'

Zhero answered them, 'Make we see how tomorrow go be now.'

Dumbfounded the boys walked away without a word.

Bazi asked him, 'If Amin hadn't made you come home yesterday where would you have slept in the night?'

'Maybe the waterside. Maybe the motor park. Anywhere.'

'Why not farming? Why don't you go to the farm with your mom?'

'Sometimes I do. But not much money in farming. When the

yams or cassavas are growing, no money at all.'

'So you chose to be a porter?'

'Yes. Every day small money comes in. Unless I'm not well.'

'You like the life?'

'It's better than armed robbery. And kidnapping,' he pointedly added.

'That's true, that's true,' Bazi readily agreed. He had not thought of it that way before. He silently hoped he had not offended the boy — his tone was defensive.

'The dilemma of modern society —'

'Sir?'

'No, I wasn't talking to you. I was only thinking.'

He had to think silently: We look down on menial jobs, we say some menial jobs devalue human beings, we feel it isn't proper for a human being to scavenge rubbish for a living, but when a person is absolutely jobless what should they do if not a menial job? Take to armed robbery or kidnapping? Or let hunger kill them?

He thought Zhero said no. 'What did you say? Did you say something?'

'Nothing, sir.'

They were silent again for a long time. Bazi felt like telling the boy that his mother unknowingly made him a rich man . . . Not to the boy. He might think that was the reason he wanted to be good to her . . . The true reason was that he realized after he couldn't find her that he had never loved any girl the way he had loved her . . . .

His mind shifted to Zhero: He admired the boy's desire to escape the poverty, degradation and violence of the Niger Delta region.

'By the way, Zhero, won't you go about and tell your friends that you are leaving them tomorrow for a long time? On a long journey?'

Zhero smiled. 'When I've gone they'll know I'm no longer here.'

Bazi laughed at the boy's logic. A clever boy, he thought, but he did not know that the boy was reacting to the years of humiliation he had experienced from his friends. One or two of them had called him a bastard in angry moments, but he knew that nearly all of them freely called him that word behind his back, and they were happy that in spite of his cleverness at primary school, like them, he could not go to secondary school. If he corrected their bad English they would ask him, 'How mush good Englis fit fess porter?' And so he too had descended to the level of pidgin English.

Thinking about what Kenitari said about Zhero, Bazi wondered if the many children he had seen walking naked or half-naked in the village went to school at all. He asked Zhero. Zhero explained that it was impossible for some children to be properly cared for because their parents had too many children. Some men had too many wives and they wanted each wife to have as many children as they could, he added, shaking his head.

'But they are happy, aren't they? There's so much laughter here, much more than in the city . . . Perhaps we overestimate formal education. Perhaps happiness doesn't depend on it. Many highly educated people aren't as happy as many of the people I have seen here . . . I don't know,' he sighed.

Zhero wondered how he should respond to what he had said — life in Amabra a happy life? With all the poverty and suffering around? He remained silent. Bazi did not expect any response from him, he was only trying to resolve the confusion in his mind.

'Zhero,' he said, 'your mother should have been here by now.'

'Yes, I'm here,' she replied. 'But I want to go back. I only came to tell you that we're going to have a meeting soon — Zuzuna Ogbo.'

'In that case . . . I mean . . . Shall we go in and discuss?'

'Whatever, say it here.'

'It's not so confidential. When Zhero and I were coming home, I thought instead of tomorrow morning we can say our goodbyes tonight . . . Hmm . . . I'm thinking . . . If you don't say no, we could give your uncle ₦500,000 and Zuzuna Ogbo ₦500,000 too. You can take it to them.'

'How about my friend Ebido? Things are rough for her.'

'I have thought about her too. You said apart from your son she's the only true friend you have in Amabra, and each of you can lay down your life for the other.' He paused then continued. 'You can give her ₦7 million to rebuild this house and take the balance for herself.' She was silent. 'Zhero, tell your mother to say something.'

'Thank you, sir.'

She looked at her son, who dropped his face. 'Thank you, Bati.'

He was glad. 'Please go about it now while Zhero tells me a folk tale in the moonlight.'

They went in, he gave her the money and she left. She changed her mind about attending the Zuzuna Ogbo meeting. Immediately after giving her uncle his share of the money she hurried to Ebido in order to meet her at home before she left for the meeting. After the joy, the weeping, Ebido's dancing, the sorrowing over how life had treated them, and then gratitude, gratitude to God for always being with them even when they were not aware of his presence, Ebido insisted on coming to thank Bazi personally, and so Zera came home with her. The ten minutes or so Ebido stayed with them was very pleasant because Bazi made light of what he had done, yet when he was out of earshot Ebido said to her friend to listen to her words.

'Zera, open your ears. If a hunter fails to find an animal in the forest he returns to his home and feasts on the chicken in his backyard. If the brave man the community sends out fails to find what he was sent out to bring he does not kill himself out of shame, he returns to his people and tells them about his journey. If the community profits from his experience then he is not a failure . . . Zera, know that I am —'

'I know, Ebido, I know you are always here for me. If you repeat it, it is as if you don't believe that I trust you. Thank you, Ebido.'

Ebido spoke loudly for Bazi's benefit. 'Zera, be careful in the city. When members of other age groups go to the city they come back with happiness. But our own age group, we have not been lucky. Amabenumo went to the city and a lorry killed her. Rita's marriage was not up to one year — she came back with a new-born baby and her husband has never come to see her and his daughter. Doweni's own is not something to talk about. Her husband said she went to the market and never returned. In less than one year he married another woman.'

Zera, who was feeling embarrassed, told her to shut up and talk of happy things and they laughed, but she immediately had the sense that life was a whirlpool spinning her and her canoe round and round and pulling them down . . . but with her strong son they would paddle through and away from it.

They escorted Ebido part-way to where the Zuzuna Ogbo meeting would take place and returned home. As early as around 6.30am the next day Zhero went to the waterfront to charter a speedboat and they left Amabra before the waterfront would become busy.

Chapter Two

'For your sake, I will swallow my bitterness, I will swallow my pride and go with Bazi, because I want a better life for you, because I want you to have a good education, I will go with Bazi, for your sake, my son, for your sake . . .' She had sniffed for a long time before she continued. 'If you succeed in life then all the suffering you have gone through will not be for nothing, my son.'

Whereas at Amabra he would have lunged across from his bed and touched the wall, here he had to feel his way across the big space between his bed and the wall and, not yet used to the position of things in the commodious room, he had to find the switch by feel. He turned it on. He blinked at the sharp brightness of the fluorescent light before he looked at the wall clock: just after midnight. He switched off the light and went back to bed.

He knew that if he did not have enough sleep he would not be strong and lively at school tomorrow, his first day at school. The image of himself and his mother sitting on her bed returned once more. They had finished packing and would leave Amabra very early the next day. He said good night to her and lay on his mat on the floor to sleep. After about an hour of sleeplessness she told him to come and sit by her. He did, but for about a minute she said nothing, then she burst out, 'For your sake . . . for your sake . . . .' When her voice and her sniffing were becoming too loud he begged her to stop, otherwise Bazi might hear her through the thin mud wall . . .

In the morning they left Amabra before the waterfront would become busy. At Mabo Motor Park Bazi chartered a taxi which took them to Second Home Apart Hotel in Port Harcourt where he and his mother stayed and Bazi frequently visited them until he brought them to the present place, a three-bedroom flat. Bazi did not live here with them but he had twice passed the night in the third room . . .

His mother wanted him to wait till next year to start secondary school since he already had the Primary School Leaving Certificate, but Bazi said that instead of sitting at home for months and doing nothing he should go to Port Harcourt Metropolitan Primary School for primary six . . . Before he was taken to school Bazi had to get a sworn declaration of age for him. Bazi said because his name was too difficult to pronounce they should change it. He was given his mother's grandfather's name, Adonkia as his first name, and Bazi as his surname. In the school he would be known as Adonkia Bazi. Bazi told his mother, 'I want to be his father.' Bazi said he should call him 'Dad' and his mother 'Mom'. In the beginning it wasn't easy not to say 'sir', but he was now getting used to Dad and Mom . . .

Tomorrow he would start school, the reason his mother agreed to come to Port Harcourt . . . For your sake, Zhero, for your sake . . .

He could not have slept up to four hours but he woke up at five feeling fresh with happiness. He went to the bathroom to relieve himself and to brush his teeth. Then he took a broom from the store in order to clean the flat, starting with the living room. About fifteen minutes later their neighbours in the second flat on the upper floor of the storey building started their unfailing matutinal prayers, noisy as ever, but this morning Zhero did not frown or feel negative about them — he worked happily to the rhythm of their loud singing or speaking in tongues. His mother's room was the last place to sweep because he did not want to wake her so early, but when he went into the kitchen to sweep it she was there. She smiled.

'Good morning, Zhero.'

'Good morning, Mom.'

'You're surprised? I must prepare food for you to take to school. Your dad says you are not to buy unhygienic food in the school. The Ugbuson family's noise woke me. I think we've found something good in their early morning noise — it will wake us, and you'll never be late to school.'

They laughed, he went to her room and swept it, had his bath, dressed, and went to the dining room for his breakfast. She was waiting for him there. She told him to stand still for a moment. He did and she admired his school uniform — white short-sleeved shirt and claret trousers. But he hadn't tucked in his shirt. He said he would do so after eating.

She left him, hurriedly had her bath and feverishly dressed like a village girl whose husband-to-be and his family had come to pay her bride price and were waiting for her in her father's sitting room. She caught herself.

'Hey, Zera!' she said, 'As if you are the one going to school.' She laughed then turned solemn. 'It's another stage of life for you too, Zera.'

They were both ready when Bazi's driver came upstairs.

'Where's Bati?' she asked.

'He's in the vehicle,' the driver answered and made to take Zhero's school bag from him.

'No, no, no!' Zera protested. 'Foolish boy,' she said to her son, who should not be allowed to forget his origins, 'is it too heavy for you?'

They went to where the Mercedes Benz jeep was parked in the street. Zera opened the left back door and entered. While she was exchanging pleasantries with Bazi the driver opened the front right door for Zhero before going round to his own side. Zera made a mental note of scolding her son for allowing the driver to open the door for him.

'Good morning, Dad,' Zhero half shouted, as if 'dad' were a crowd of people — his pitch had to match the magical morning.

'Good morning, Zhero. First day in school — any butterflies?' Zhero looked left, up and right, but did not see any butterflies. Bazi and Zera laughed. 'I mean, are you nervous? Frightened?'

'No! I'm happy.'

They all laughed. The driver was happy for his master— his master wasn't *important*, as some of his workers thought. Traffic was light until they came close to a junction where there was a build-up of vehicles due to the contraflow as a result of the construction of a flyover. Zhero tried to recollect the name of where they were. Bazi had told him the name of the place before. Traffic was now at a standstill but they did not feel uncomfortable because the jeep had airconditioning.

'I hope you are taking note of the route.'

'Yes, Dad,' Zhero answered, the butterflies suddenly flapping in his stomach — suppose he was asked the name of the junction!

'Because,' Bazi continued, 'Michael will drive you to and from school for only one week. After that you're on your own. You'll go by public transport.'

Zhero would love to be on his own. As he watched the opposite streams of pedestrians on the road he ached to go down and embrace the spaciousness of the city and the beauty of its people moving about with a sense of purpose — ah, the difference between Port Harcourt and Amabra, the village whose length he could walk in fifteen minutes, where most people walked sluggishly in the morning. Once he started going to school on his own he would sometimes do so on foot.

After about thirty minutes around the junction it took them less than five minutes to reach Port Harcourt Metropolitan Primary School. Zera smiled as her son walked jauntily to the Primary 6 classroom block.

Bazi remarked, 'It's as if he's been in this compound for six years.'

Zera smiled but she did not tell him that that wasn't Zhero he was seeing — it was joy.

Bazi smiled . . . Zhero at his age in primary school . . . He thought about the world's oldest school pupil, Kimani Maruge, the former Mau Mau fighter, who went to school at eighty-four when his country started a free education programme . . . Kimani Maruge demonstrated the importance of education to the children of Kenya.

They went back to the house and the driver went to the office from where he would go to the school in the afternoon and bring Zhero home. Out of happiness she complimented Bazi on his grey suit, dark blue tie, sparkling black shoes and his six-foot height. He complimented her back — her trouser suit was as beautiful as youth in a thriving corporate organization. She told him he was more money-minded than Zhero and they laughed. She went to her room to change into an orange blouse and claret shorts, and when she came back to tell him she was going to the kitchen he drooled over her shapely legs. She smiled and left him.

While he stayed in the sitting room and speed-read some pages of the novel he had bought for her yesterday, she prepared his favourite dish of plantain porridge for breakfast. Since Zhero did not like unripe plantain it had to be the quantity two of them could finish.

In the days of their first affair he would have stayed with her in the kitchen and admired her panache as he watched the way she put the ingredients together or the way she ladled the boiling soup and put it in her half-cupped hand for both of them to taste, blowing on the soup and saying that it was burning her hand, it was burning her hand, he should lick up everything quickly. (Must she put it in her hand?) She'd tell him to shut up and just lick the soup . . . But now there was an unspoken gulf between them which he was looking upon time to fill, and so he had to read the novel until she invited him to the dining table.

He sniffed the steam rising from the plate as he sat. 'The smell of love.'

'Scent leaves,' she smiled.

He eagerly dug into the plantain dish . . . A simple dish yet so delicious, because of the love she'd put into it. So much sweeter than the expensive dishes in his house . . . Time had honed her culinary skills . . . In those days he used to say everything she prepared was moreish, and now even before finishing what was before him his appetite was craving more of Zera's love.

'What are you thinking of?'

He did not answer her immediately. Her radiant face, her orange blouse, her claret shorts, her happy voice, the fragrant dish — the ambience of the dining room made him feel like a seeker who had come to the end of his wanderings.

She asked again, 'What are you thinking of?'

'Remember I called you a perfect cook then? Because everything, *anything*, you cooked was — remember the word? — moreish.' she smiled. 'I don't know what to call you now.' She smiled again. 'It means in everything there's a plus factor.'

'Bati, please stop talking and eat.'

His reaction surprised her. 'Since I saw you in Amabra I've been feeling that you didn't know how old your pregnancy was when you told me you were pregnant.' She waited with bated breath. 'We explored our bodies in those days. I saw no such sign in you.'

'So?'

'It means I could . . . I may be Zhero's biological father.' She was silent. 'His face is a masculine copy of yours.' She laughed. 'So there's no way to know from looking at his face.'

'Bati, don't be silly. Zhero isn't your biological son. However I'm glad you love him like a son.' She noticed that he had stopped eating. 'Bati, I'm hungry. But if you don't eat I'll stop too.'

He said he was sorry and they resumed eating. After they finished eating she asked him if he liked the food.

'Yes,' he answered, 'I'll eat some more before I leave. Thank you, Zera . . . Ah, Zera, I've been married for about fifteen years but no child. I told you my wife is German . . . She's barren.'

'I'm sorry, Bati.'

'It's not words I need.'

She breathed in deeply and out loud. The close-mouthed sigh was more eloquent than a dozen statements of wariness. He decided not to go on with what he had in mind.

After she put the washing-up in the sink they went to the sitting room. He expected her to sit by him on the couch but she sat in the armchair opposite him. After a long silence he spoke.

'Zera, if I hadn't abandoned you . . . If I had helped you to terminate the pregnancy, you should have finished secondary school, and university . . . and then . . . .'

'And then?'

'I wouldn't have been out of your life all those years.'

They fell silent again.

'Is that the novel you bought for me?'

'Yes.'

'What's the title?'

'"I Have Loved Glory Too Much".'

She took the book from him. 'Why this photograph — a man in chains?' He shrugged. 'I think I'll go to my room and read it.'

'In that case I'll take a taxi and go to the office. Tell Michael to come to the office after dropping Zhero.' His jacket and his tie in the crook of his left hand he made for the door. 'Bye for now,' he said to her in a deliberate tone of disappointment, his face pointedly unhappy too.

Without a word she saw him to the street door downstairs, stayed there till he had taken a taxi, and she went back to her flat. She flopped down onto the couch and wept — how was she going to handle the oncoming problem? She suddenly felt like an adolescent girl who needed her mother's guidance, but she no longer had a mother, and Ebido wasn't around.

When she started to blame life for what was happening to her she stopped crying. She told herself she was in charge of her life, she had always been in charge of her life, she *would* make her life what she wanted it to be. She had been a victim of her own foolishness, but she should be thankful for the experience — it had made her as wise as she needed to be.

She washed the crockery, cleaned the kitchen, took the copy of the novel and went into her room to read it. But she only lay on the bed and searched the jungle of possibilities for Bati's true reason for bringing her and her son here . . . Everything he had said, everything he had implied, everything she had inferred was as valid as the others . . .

She visualized herself and him romping about in his house in those days . . . She said, because her soulmate's house was richly carpeted she walked about barefoot and a blade slashed her sole . . . She needed to tread carefully this time . . . .

She had a dream she had occasionally had for many years: She was a dashing male lawyer who was having an exciting affair with a girl whose elder sister he wanted to marry. Both girls deeply loved him. When both sisters became pregnant for him at the same time he fled the African country in which they were to London . . . .

When she woke up she thought about the dream. It started when The Home Stretch taught the interested people of Amabra how to inquire into one's past lives through the use of spiritual exercises to prove the reality of karma and reincarnation . . . The people of Amabra had always believed in karma and reincarnation but it was thrilling to know that one could consciously inquire into one's past lives . . . This dream had come up now and then on its own after the first night she did a spiritual exercise. What was it telling her? . . . She was a wicked man in a past life . . . What did Bazi want from her? To be his secret wife, to bear him children? . . . .

When she woke to the sound of the doorbell it was nearly 3pm. Like a person returning from a failed quest she walked wearily to the door and opened it. On seeing her son she remembered today should be a happy day — she immediately sloughed off her sad look.

'Good day, Mom.'

'Welcome, Zhero.'

'Madam,' the driver asked, 'you were sleeping?'

'Yes, Michael.'

He took it that Bazi was sleeping. He happily said, 'I have to wait till Sir wake. Or will you wake him?'

'He isn't here. He says you should meet him in the office. He left here since morning.'

'In dat case we go see tomorrow.'

'Bye for now, Mike.'

'Thank you, ma.'

In his room Zhero was savouring his scores in classwork.

'See,' he said as his mother entered, 'I scored 8 over 10.' She took the English Language exercise book from him and looked at the exercise on subject-verb agreement. 'Some people who have been in that class since the beginning of the year scored less than 5 over 10.' She smiled. 'In Maths I got 6.'

She did not remind him that he had passed the Primary School Leaving Certificate exam before. He looked and sounded like a person who had already returned from a successful quest. She rejoiced with him and advised him to take off his school uniform, eat and rest a little before going over his schoolwork. He obeyed her, but while eating he had to tell her about some of his classmates when she came to see what he was doing. She smiled — whereas in Amabra he had behaved like an adult, since he came to Port Harcourt he had become almost like a child again. She would make him grow fast.

'They have no food and no money to buy food. Boys who have not known me before, see the way they were begging me to share my food with them.'

She smiled again. 'You can't share your food with too many friends, but did you help anyone?'

'No oh. I went to hide in a corner to enjoy my food.'

His mother laughed, and the next day she packed his lunch box with enough rice and stew for three. In his hiding corner at lunch break he felt ashamed of himself when he opened the box — so much rice, and three big pieces of beef! His mother's advice to share — he went to where someone could see him. He invited a hungry-looking boy with his eyes and they ate together, he using the fork and the boy using the spoon. He told the boy his registered name in the school was Adonkia Bazi but his friends and his parents called him Zhero. He spelt it, taught him to pronounce it, and the boy told him his own name was Oyinnijesu Peter. Though Oyinnijesu was his junior — in Primary 4 — they felt like agemates and Oyinnijesu told him a lot of things about Port Harcourt Metropolitan Primary School.

On his return home his mother did not give him the chance to tell her his experiences but the next morning again she loaded the lunch box with food for three. Zhero invited a classmate, they both looked for Oyinnijesu and the three of them went to a corner to eat the lunch. Oyinnijesu said yesterday's rice and stew was sweet but today's beans, *dodo* and fish was super! Zhero and Oyinnijesu laughed heartily, Israel just for form's sake, because he could not see any reason why Zhero should invite their junior to eat together with them, but he gradually loosened up as he enjoyed the meal and in the end he positively liked Oyinnijesu.

At home when he saw that his mother was not interested in how he ate his meal he changed the subject.

'Our teacher said there's no such word as "housegirl". We can say "houseboy" but not "housegirl".'

'Your teacher is right,' she replied. 'I've never seen the word in any dictionary. But in Nigeria we use the word. So we can say it's accepted in Nigerian English. You shouldn't use it, but don't try to correct anyone who uses it.'

He silently wondered, houseboy but not housegirl . . . .

On Saturday Bazi took them to One-Stop Store to buy better clothes than they were able to get in his friend's boutique which he had taken them to two weeks ago. To his annoyance Zera was more interested in the books' section, and she was the only one there. Persuading himself to be patient he decided to take Zhero to the snack bar upstairs. He guided him onto the escalator without appearing to do so. Smart shop assistants, happy-looking, affluent-looking customers, nearly everybody soft-spoken, and these stairs carrying stationary people upstairs — to Zhero the tony store had the indescribable feel of a holy place to a first-time pilgrim . . . Could life ever be as sweet as this in Amabra?

They went to a vacant table and sat down. A young woman who had not seen Bazi for some years stood up from where she was sitting alone and walked towards his table. Zera was approaching too, smiling. Bazi felt he was going to black out. Zera drew out a chair, sat and started to tell them to see what a wonderful book she had found. The young woman sashayed past without a sign. Zhero looked at her in amazement — a Nigerian, not the Indian women he had seen in videos, wearing a sari! Bazi was grateful to her, in his heart, he blessed her. She was a table dancer he used to be intimate with . . . more than five years now, but she still recognized him.

While Zera and her son relished the sauté prawns he ordered for, he only drank iced pineapple juice to cool himself down. Zhero's eyes roamed the bar for the source of the atmospheric music. He decided to ask his mother. Just then Bazi remembered that he had not said anything about the book Zera was so proud of.

'What's the title?'

'"Knowledge is Power".'

He did not say that it was a trite title. 'Who's the author?'

She gave him the book and he pretended to be interested in it. 'Foreword,' he read out loud.

'Haven't you seen the name of the author? She's a woman,' she proudly said. 'Zainab Shettima.'

'Who reads it first?' he asked, without any intention to read it.

'You'll pay for your own copy downstairs. Come, let's go downstairs.'

They went downstairs where they selected a lot of good clothes and he paid for them, but not a copy of the book for himself. Zera was happy that he dropped them at home and went away. After examining and putting away the clothes she had bought, she had a cold bath and then set about finishing the 158-page book before dusk, but because she had to eat dinner around 6pm she was able to read only 141 pages, and after dinner she felt an urgency to explain a chapter to her son —The School of Life.

She said to him: 'Since you were born you have been in the school of life. This means that as long as you are living, every day, at anytime, you are learning something. You go to school from Monday to Friday to learn, but whether or not you are in school you are learning things. Even at school it's not everything your teachers teach you. From what you do with or to people, from what they do to or with you, you learn lessons. From the good things you do and from the good things others do you learn lessons. From the bad things you do and from the bad things other people do you learn lessons. You learn lessons from what happens to human beings as a result of the good or bad things they do.'

She stopped because she had talked too much. She was happy when he responded with a question.

'Sepp Blatter, the president of FIFA, last week he said that football is a school of life. What does he mean?'

'Now you are going to use my explanation to answer your question. What does Sepp Blatter mean?'

He did not think for long. 'If a player cheats he may get the consequence on the field or later in life. At the Video Viewing Centre in Amabra when we watched the World Cup we said France did not do well because they used Henry's handball to beat Ireland and qualify for the World Cup.'

Zera laughed. 'That is life! Also, when a team win does their victory make them too proud? When they lose are they bitter? Do they hate their opponents? Do they blame the referee? Or do they find out why their opponents were better than them and make necessary corrections? A lot, a lot of things to learn in football too. Especially honesty. People should learn not to cheat.'

'Also not to give up in life.'

'How?' she asked him.

'For example, if Manchester United are some goals behind their opponents, do they give up? Or do they continue to fight hard, believing that they can win? In life we shouldn't give up.'

Zera was grateful to God for the son He had given her.

Around 10pm Bazi phoned to tell her that he would come and take them to church the next day, but when he came around 8am she told him she was not interested in going to church. (How about Zhero?) She forgot to tell him. (Zera forgot to tell her son to prepare for church on Sunday!) Why not? she fired back and they laughed.

'See how clean this sitting room is,' he said. She did not understand his drift. He felt the brown leather cover of the seat and the backrest of the couch he was sitting on with his middle finger. 'No dust,' he said showing her the inside of his middle finger. 'No dust,' he repeated, 'thanks to Zhero. A boy who is well-brought up should be nurtured in the church.'

'Hmph. If you say so he'll go with you.'

She called him and told him to get ready and go to church with his dad. He was glad for the opportunity to wear some of the fine clothes he got yesterday. His face lighting up like Bazi's rich white *agbada* he hurried away to have his bath.

After a long consideration Bazi decided to give another reason why she should attend church.

'Zera, you made me a rich man.' She looked at him questioningly. 'Yes, Zera. The day I pushed you out of my house you left a newspaper behind, a paper I had never bought before. When I read the paper some days after, I saw an advert calling for people to bid for a contract. It was a big contract. I won it and made big money for the first time. And because I took care of the people that mattered in the company I won many more big contracts, and I've grown richer since then ... Zera, you and I have to go to church together and thank God.'

'How about your wife?'

'She goes to a church attended mostly by whites. Besides she'll be returning to Germany soon.'

'Going or returning?' she asked, her phlegmatic tone muffling the expectancy in her heart.

'Returning. She said I could join her there whenever I liked. She's afraid of the kidnapping of whites in the country. She scarcely leaves the house.'

'Bazi, what nonsense is this? Why are you weeping?'

'Am I? I didn't know that I'm weeping.' To her surprise he wiped his face with his white *agbada* and got up. 'Please tell Zhero we'll go to church next Sunday.'

She did not call him back but at 2pm she phoned him.

'Bati, what's the sin I've committed? Food is ready, I'm hungry,

I've been waiting for you since you left.'

She switched off her mobile. Before 3pm he was with her, admiring the *banga* soup with which they were eating pounded yam. He wondered why her *banga* soup was so much sweeter than the *banga* soup of other cooks. What was the composition of hers? he asked her. The same as that of his other women, she answered. They laughed and she told him how to prepare it: Lightly pound the fresh palm nuts in a mortar to remove the skin without breaking the nuts; add water to the content in the mortar then sieve —

He stopped her. Henceforth, he said, they would cook together in her kitchen as they once did in his own. That was the best way for her to teach him. She was silent for a long time.

'What do you say, Zera?'

'Bati, I don't think I like what's coming.'

'Can I give you time?'

'Thank you.'

They finished eating and he left happily while she went into her bedroom and wept . . . .

On the day Zhero was to start going to school on public transport, she asked him if he was sure not to miss his way. She believed his emphatic yes; even then she gave him a lot of money, just in case he needed to charter a taxi.

'What is your address?' she playfully asked him.

'Rt Hon . . . no. No 13 Rt Hon Westwood Avenue.'

She saw him to the street and watched him for a moment. He knew she must be watching him, so he turned. They both laughed and waved goodbye once more . . . He looked to her like a seeker on a long journey, and she was the mother looking out for her hero's return . . . .

When he returned in the afternoon she immediately noticed that he did not have his lunch box. He explained that in the mad rush to enter the bus in the morning the box was knocked off his hand and the content spilled on the road. When people shouted 'Na who get this *moimoi* for ground? Na who get this rice? Na who get this dis sweet stew?' he pretended as if it was not his own. His mother laughed — thank God she had given him enough money.

Without taking off his school uniform he went into the kitchen, made *eba*, dished soup and went to the dining table to eat. His mother frowned when she saw him using his hand instead of a fork.

'You're eating with your fingers. How will you wash your hand?'

'I know the tap isn't running.'

'So how will you wash your hand?'

'I'll use bottled water. I used bottled water to make *eba*.'

'Instead of going to fetch water first.'

He caught her don't-forget-your-origins tone and frown. He looked at his hand. 'Immediately I finish, I'll fetch water.' She shrugged. 'Why is the tap dry?'

'Only on our side of the street. A broken pipeline somewhere.'

Immediately he finished eating he took a bucket and went to a compound on the street where borehole water was sold. The queue of buckets and jerrycans was extremely long and it would take more than thirty minutes to get to his turn. His bucket was directly behind the jerrycan of a housegirl with whom two other housegirls were discussing the cruelty of their employers.

'Beatrice, your own small,' one of the girls said. 'Any small thing I do my madam go cut my salary of ₦8,000. And upon dat she go first beat me. Listen, Beatrice, some time I dey feel say something wrong with dat woman because of de kind happy wey she dey happy anytime she beat me. She go buy hot drink and sing gospel song, one after the other.'

Her colleagues laughed and the one she addressed as Beatrice spoke.

'Dat kind woman dangerous o — she fit see vision one day and kill you o! Daba, after the third time your mama come talk with your madam she don change? She still dey beat you with iron rod?'

Daba pulled up her skirt and showed them her right thigh.

'Yeh!'

'Wetin be dis?'

'Dis na my life o. She know say I no fit leave am because she dey pay me well, and my mama need de money for my two brothers' school fees. If I run comot na beg my mama go still come beg am.'

'So na how dis one happen? Na wetin you dey take treat am?'

'Na hot iron my madam use o, because I no press her trouser smooth.'

'Na wetin you use?' Beatrice repeated the question, her face full of disgust.

'Na Gentian Violet I put.'

'See, your madam dey come o,' Beatrice warned and moved away from her, as if to avoid any closeness with her madam who she regarded as wickedness in human form.

Daba quickly went to stand by her jerrycan and hoped for the worst-case scenario. Her employer came up to her.

'Daba, what are you doing here?' she asked.

Daba bent her knees slightly then stood straight. 'Ma, I dey wait for my turn.'

'Your turn, Daba, your turn . . . ,'

'Yes ma, yes ma,' Daba cried as she tried to protect her head from her employer's blows.

'You see any queue in that front where other people are gathering? Because you don't want to work you are queuing? Come on take your jerrycan and go to the front.'

Daba took her jerrycan and trotted towards the front, her employer hot on her heels. As she tried to push Daba through the crowd to the tap several young boys protested and shoved her back. A boy she slapped pushed her violently and she fell on her bottom. The crowd jeered.

Daba wailed, 'My own don finish today! My own don finish today! My own don finish today!'

Zhero saw his mother. She had to call him because the tap had started to run again. On the way he explained what had happened and at home he told her about the housegirls' conversation.

'I hope you didn't contribute to what they were saying.'

'I didn't, Mom. How can I?'

'Thank you. I know you won't.'

She told him that Bazi was in the third room and he went there to greet him. He knocked three times and went in. Bazi was poring over a sheet of paper.

'Sorry. You're busy.'

'No, no. Just looking over my CV — curriculum vitae. You know what's a CV?' Zhero shook his head. 'My CV is my bio data.' The boy looked more confused. 'My date of birth, schools attended, educational qualifications, my achievements in life etc etc. Have a seat, Zhero.'

He expected Zhero to come to the sofa so he shifted to the right end, but Zhero sat in the armchair by the desk.

'Do you want to use it to go to school?'

Bazi's rumbustious laughter brought Zera into the room.

'Your son . . . Zhero wants to know whether I'm preparing my CV for school admission.' He continued to laugh. 'Oh Zera!'

She sat on the left end of the three-seater sofa.

'Why don't you tell him what a CV is?'

'Zhero, haven't I told you?' He gradually stopped laughing. 'A CV is for many things, Zhero. But this one is to enable a club to write my citation.'

The boy's mother came to his help. 'And a citation is . . . ?'

'The things the club will tell the public when they are giving me the award. They want to give me an award — a sort of card, a big card to say I've done great things for my country.'

Zhero had not yet fully overcome his pecuniary instinct. He asked, 'The club, the people giving you the award, what is their own gain?'

Bazi laughed boisterously again. 'Zhero! You were born to be a businessman . . . Well, to answer your question, the club gains nothing. The people receiving the award give them some money, though. For organizational expenses. I gave them only ₦5 million.'

'Five million naira! For a card, a sheet of paper!'

'Your concern should be what you want to become in life, Zhero. Not the money. When you've succeeded you'll see that money is just a piece of paper . . . Go to secondary school, go to university, get a PhD, do big things for your society — your reward will never stop coming.'

Zera advised her son, 'Whatever you do for someone, do it for love only. If you do anything because you expect a reward from it, in the eyes of God you haven't done anything.'

'So go to work and don't expect a salary?'

'Zhero knows what I mean.'

'Hey, Zera, let the boy go.'

Zhero went out.

'Can I stay here tonight?' he asked with a half-amorous smile.

'To stay or not to stay — the choice is yours. I have no objection, whatever your choice.'

'I shall stay.'

'Thank you.'

He could not understand her tone — was she happy or not? He phoned the driver and told him to come back for him by 7am the next day.

'Thank you, Zera.'

'It's too early to go to bed. Let's go to the sitting room.'

'First let me ease myself.'

A bathroom separated the room and hers, each of which had a door to the bathroom. He went into the bathroom leaving the door

64

ajar, intending to plump her mood. The stream of urine falling noisily onto the water in the toilet bowl — her mind struggled with what was coursing through her body . . . .

No, she told herself, she didn't even know yet on what terms she was here, no insurance of any kind against the future . . . Zhero was going to school but suppose something happened between them

Buttoning and then zipping his trousers he came back into the room and made to sit by her but because she immediately stood up they went to the sitting room.

'Get up and go to your room.' She had told Zhero not to use the sitting room anytime Bazi was around. 'By the way, have you cleaned the kitchen?'

'Zera, why are you so hostile to the boy?'

'He knows why?'

'Why, Zhero?'

'She says whenever you are here I shouldn't use the sitting room.'

'Zera, am I such an ogre? Come, Zhero, what were you reading?'

'It's the book Mom bought at One-Stop Store.' He showed it. "Knowledge is Power".'

'Come sit by me . . . What did you find useful in the book?'

He opened to chapter 2: The School of Life. 'Here it says life is a school.'

'Yes, that's right.'

'But the Yoruba song boys and girls sing in my school says life is a market where we have come to buy and sell. And yesterday Sunday, on the TV the pastor said life is a journey.'

Bazi smiled. 'Don't be confused. The pastor is right — Life is a journey: As we travel together we must help our neighbours with their load when they are too weak to carry it. Your neighbour is any person you come across in life. In life —'

Zera cut in. 'Today you help your neighbour, tomorrow your neighbour may help you. The load your neighbour is too weak to carry may be hunger. So if you share your school lunch with somebody you are helping that person along the journey of life. When you grow older you'll understand what that church Chief Kulokulo banned from Amabra used to teach us — that life is a journey towards God.'

The boy contemplated the ideas out loud: 'Life is a school . . . life is a market . . . life is a journey.'

Bazi laughed and he laughed too, but Zera felt like telling them to leave the sitting room, to leave her with the only companion she loved to be with at the moment — her thoughts.

Zhero imagined a journey of a sea of people walking on, like on the East-West Road from Port Harcourt to Yenagoa . . . A middle-aged man by him was flagging due to his heavy load . . . He took the load from the man, a porter of many years he had the strength to carry other people's heavy loads, he helped the man and the man was able to walk effortlessly until he became strong enough to carry his own load again . . . .

'Zhero.'

'Yes, Mom.'

'Go and clean the kitchen.' He left them. 'I have noticed that when you're around he slacks and doesn't want to do the things he normally does. Does he want you to indulge him?'

Bazi felt she was in a foul mood . . . but why?

'But he's a good boy,' he said.

'I didn't say he's a bad boy.'

They laughed.

'You said he was a good fisherman.'

'Yes.'

'And a good hunter too. At fourteen plus!'

She turned happy. 'Yes. Kenitari taught him how to hunt, how to use the gun . . . One day, in the forest, four people were about to capture Kenitari. Zhero shot two of them down and the other two ran away. The men didn't die and they were taken to the village and handed over to the police. They confessed that they were hired by Chief Kulokulo to kill Kenitari because of the types of stories he was telling the children of Amabra. The police took them to hospital, but two days after, they were kidnapped by some armed men and never seen again. Chief Kulokulo denied any relationship with them. Ironically Kenitari started to distance himself from Zhero. He told people that he feared Zhero because of the way he shot at the men, a young boy of his age.' Bazi laughed. She laughed more. 'The day Zhero told Uncle Kenitari that a former policeman, the militant who lived at Mabo Waterside in the shack called "ILLEGAL STRUCTURE, STOP-WORKS ORDER NOT APPLICABLE", when Zhero said the militant taught him to handle an AK-47, you ought to see Uncle Kenitari's face — it was as if Zhero was pointing the AK-47 at him!' They laughed together at the hilarious incident, Bazi visualizing the militant's shack. 'The only person Chief Kulokulo feared in Amabra was Zhero, because several times the people he sent to kill him couldn't succeed. And only Zhero could openly criticize Chief Kulokulo in Amabra.'

'Zhero?' Bazi marvelled.

'My mother used to say her mother boiled him in a pot of charms for seven days and seven nights in the land of the dead before he was sent to this world.'

They laughed once more. After the evening meal Bazi, who had taken a new and deeper liking to Zhero, wanted him around them, so he called him to the sitting room. While Zhero regaled him with stories about Amabra, Zera watched TV absently, her mind on the possibilities of the night. After Zhero described how he nearly ruined his former school's end-of-year play because he forgot his lines, Bazi told him that he too used to like acting, but his mother ruined his interest in drama.

'I played my part well that night,' he continued, 'and the audience clapped a lot for me. After the play my mother didn't congratulate me at all, and as we were going home she didn't say a word to me. But immediately we entered the house the volcano exploded: "You foolish boy, you good-for-nothing boy, of all the parts it is the part of a servant you had to play, and you invited me to come and watch you! Is it not the son of a woman that played the part of a king? Is his mother better than me? A servant! Is that why I carried you in my womb for nine months? To come to this world and be a servant? Servant!" She spat on me.'

The men laughed like palm-wine drinking mates together. Zera looked at them, and she laughed at them.

'It must be a very sweet story.'

'Zhero will tell you later.' They stopped laughing. 'But I learnt a lesson from it, Zhero: to be the star wherever I am.'

The star! Zera did not like his philosophy, but she did not want to upstage him. She would tell her son it was enough to be a star and let others be.

Only Zera's happiness was not total that night and when they went to bed, while the men soon slept off, savouring the feel-good hours of the evening, she changed positions several times to enable her to sleep off . . . On her back she thought, what should she do if he knocked on the connecting door? Pretend not to hear the loud knock? Tell him she wouldn't open the door? Was that possible? ... She changed to her right side . . . Demand a definition of their relationship? How about his wife? Even if she returned to her country

. . . She had made a mistake in following him to Port Harcourt, she could have remained in Amabra and if he wanted to help, Zhero could have gone to secondary school anywhere and he should have paid the school fees, no, no, she didn't make a mistake, she came to Port Harcourt so that her son could have a good education, she came to Port Harcourt for her son's sake . . . Even if she had made a mistake she wouldn't fill herself with guilt . . . She shifted to her back once more . . . She sighed, 'It's hard to be a woman.'

The next morning Bazi did not leave until the driver had taken Zhero to school and returned for him. Before he left she felt like asking him how he was explaining his absence from home to his wife, because she did not want to be responsible for the break-up of a fellow woman's marriage, but for no reason she did not ask him. She felt unhappy until Zhero returned from school. About two days ago she had decided to put more emphasis on inspecting his classwork and supervising his homework and discouraging him from telling too many tales of non-academic matters in school, but today she hungered for whatever he had to say. She sat with him at the dinner table and asked him to tell her, what happened in school today?

He told her the History teacher couldn't answer a girl's question. In every book they talked about Christopher Columbus, Amerigo Vespucci, Ferdinand Magellan etc, did each of these persons travel alone? Why were the people who accompanied them and the individual roles they played not mentioned? He said the class laughed when the girl asked whether those men were not even married. Zera laughed.

She remarked that he was looking unhappy. He said it was because he remembered a girl who started to cry when they were to leave the classroom and go home — she feared going home because almost every night her father forced her to . . . to . . .

'Oh, don't say it, don't say it. Oh poor girl. How about her mother?'

'Her mother has married another man.'

'Poor girl . . . poor girl . . . ah, it's hard to be a woman,' she sighed as she thought of the girl who had to cook her father's food after school and cool his bed at night.

After Zhero finished eating she asked him if he could go to the evening market at St Andrews to buy thyme.

'Don't pretend to be tired, because it's to make your school lunch super.'

'I'm on my way.'

She laughed. 'Won't you take money?'

'I have money, my pocket money.'

'Your pocket money is not for that.'

She gave him some money and he went out. As he stepped out of the compound he saw Daba on the other side of the street, as beautiful as the Nollywood actresses he liked very much. She was going in the same direction as he was. He wondered where she was going. His heart started to beat faster. He had never talked with any of the girls in the neighbourhood before. He crossed the street in obedience to a feeling for the poor girl. She was now in front of him. He was afraid yet he increased his pace till he came abreast of her. When he turned his face their eyes met. His face was instantly hot and his mouth dry. She greeted him. He wasn't sure of how he had greeted her back. The silence was awkward. He overcame his heart and asked her where she was going. He told her he too was going to the evening market. He asked her about her injury and before she could speak he said her madam was a wicked woman. Daba said no, it wasn't her madam's fault. She had lied when she told her friends that it was because she didn't iron her madam's trousers properly. It was while she was ironing the trousers that her madam had discovered what she had done and used the iron to burn her thigh. She asked him if he could keep her secret if she told him the truth. He said yes and she told him the truth. It was her practice to steal her madam's foodstuffs and sneak them to her mother and her siblings. Her madam had warned her against it several times before but she felt that what she was doing was better than allowing her family to die of hunger. Her pay was better than that of many other housegirls, still it wasn't enough. After a pause, she thanked him for giving her the opportunity to confess her sin and then she said her name was Daba, what was his? She laughed at her futile efforts to pronounce it properly then told him what mattered was his person not his name.

When they came to a chemist shop he said to go inside for her to take treatment. She did not say yes or no, she only followed him inside and he paid for the cost. The female nurse angrily shouted at a junior colleague who came in belting out a song, 'They are the heroes of life!'

'Agoba, is your head correct? In presence of customers!'

The young man stopped guiltily and slunk off behind the medicine showcase. The female nurse cleaned Daba's wound and gave her an injection, antibiotics for five days and instructions on how to clean and dress the wound herself. In case she might need to return to the chemist shop Zhero gave her two thousand naira, and they went to the evening market, bought their needs and returned to their respective homes.

That night Zhero hated himself for telling his mother about Daba, not because she advised him to be weary of being involved in such a girl's problem, but because he had failed to keep Daba's secret — oh, he had broken a promise in less than one hour!

The Ugbuson family's noisy song of praise unto the Lord at 5am woke Zhero and his mother for whom the devotees' praise and address to God was a call to early morning household chores. Zhero was sweeping the sitting room when his mother went into the kitchen. He knew she was in there but did not go and say good morning to her. When he was sweeping the room that might now be called Bazi's own she deliberately went to look for something in it. It was then he greeted her and she greeted him back. His face and his voice told her that he was not feeling in a good mood. She asked herself what could be responsible? The way she reacted to Daba's story? Was he in love with her? She shrugged her shoulders, scooped a little of the broth she was cooking in a bain marie and tasted it. After a while she could not remember her assessment of the broth at the time she tasted it. She shrugged again and turned off the gas cooker.

This morning the prayer session next door was insufferable to Zhero. When he remarked on the nuisance his mother asked him, without looking at him, when next door's problem started to be his problem, and continued to scoop the vegetable broth into his breakfast plate. He went away from her and had an unpleasant cold bath because he did not remember to turn on the water heater when he woke up around 5am.

When he was at the breakfast table they suddenly heard Mrs Ugbuson wailing for help. He was at the door when his mother rushed out of her room.

'Where are you going?' His face asked her if it was wrong to help a neighbour in need. 'Listen. It's her husband that is beating her.'

'Suppose he kills her?' he replied, as if to remind her that in Amabra they had seen men beat their wives to death.

Mrs Ugbuson was now banging on the door and begging them to

'Open, open, open the door before my animal husband kills me!' Zera shrugged and Zhero opened the door to let Mrs Ugbuson in. She begged him to 'Lock the door, lock the door before he comes and kills me.' She flopped down onto the floor and cried asking God to tell her why He made her a woman when He knows that womanhood wasn't a blessing. Zera burst out in laughter.

'You are laughing. You can laugh because your husband is not Ugbuson.'

Zera laughed the more and drew her up.

'Come let's go to the sitting room. You, Zhero, finish whatever you're doing and go to school.'

In the sitting room Mrs Ugbuson explained the problem. 'Just because I told him not to beat the boy. The bucket of water he wanted to use to wash his car, he saw Anderson take a cup of water from the bucket to wash his face. As he was pursuing the boy I went down and held him and begged him not to beat another person's son. After washing the car he came up and started to beat me saying that instead of supporting him I was supporting an outsider. My sister, to be a woman is not a good thing oh.'

'I know. It's hard. A woman's life is a hard life.'

'And the things he always says about me anytime he's beating me. Can you imagine? Telling me I'm a useless woman because I don't go to work and I don't contribute to the family income. If I say let me go to the Environmental Sanitation Authority for work, he will say how can his wife be a road sweeper? Let me go and sell *garri* at Mile One market, how can his wife be a *garri* seller? And yet, look for work for me, he can't.' She paused then wept bitterly. 'He hates his children too because they are girls. He says in his father's family he's the only one having only girls, so he doesn't know from where I got them.'

'Stop crying. It will be good.'

'It cannot be good, my sister, it cannot be good. I think there's madness in his father's family. The way he beats me, that's the way his elder brother beats his wife, because she's giving him only boys, boys, six boys no girls — so he won't collect any bride price?'

Zera laughed again. 'I'm sorry I'm laughing.'

'You are right, my sister. This thing is beyond crying. Head or tail the woman loses. I shall not cry anymore.'

Zera wondered where Zhero was. He had left, having locked the door from outside and thrown the key through the window.

'I wanted to know whether my son has gone to school. He has. Can I make you a cup of tea? Plus some sandwich?'

'You want to kill me? If he sees me eating in your house he'll say your husband is my boyfriend.' Zera shook her head. 'Your son is a good boy. I've never seen him angry. He'll be a good husband when he becomes a man. Have you seen him teaching Anderson? He's a clever boy. One day I heard him saying to Anderson that life is a market where we have come to buy and sell. Me, I have only come to buy beating from my husband.' Zera laughed wildly. 'My sister, it's good to laugh. It is the only way to cope with life.'

'But this laughter you've caused can kill,' Zera replied, still laughing.

'You haven't seen laughter yet. One day he was singing a song and I said to my husband and master that the boy's voice is as musical as his sweet song. He looked at me with disgust and said, "Is that music? Fela's song. Fela's worldly music is music?" I gave it to him, "It is better than the things we shout and sing every early morning disturbing the neighbourhood." If I had not run out of the house immediately I would not be alive to be talking with you now.' Zera laughed anew. 'My sister, continue to laugh. God has given you and your son laughter.'

Zera was proud of her son and she visualized him on a bus going to school . . . A loving son . . . .

She did not know that at that time he was resolving not to tell her things anymore. He had seen five of the boys living in the uncompleted building in the street hawking in the tailback. Two were hawking chewing-sticks, two were hawking boiled guinea fowl eggs and the fifth boy sachets of ice water. They did not know him. When one of the boys with guinea fowl eggs was humiliated by a man who called him 'hawker by day armed robber by night' because the boy would not reduce the price, out of compassion he bought five eggs from him. When the other boy saw that someone had bought a lot of eggs from his colleague he ran towards the bus, but then the traffic had started to move. He pursued the bus until the stop-go traffic stopped once more.

'Please buy from me too,' he begged the man in the window seat, 'help me make I eat breakfast.'

'You miss road today,' someone shouted and many of the passengers laughed.

The man in the window seat who had called his colleague an

armed robber gave it to him too.

'You use this hawking to deceive your neighbourhood. At night you are armed robbers, rapists, kidnappers.'

Nearly the whole bus laughed. Zhero in the window seat behind the man unabashedly bought five eggs from the boy who thanked him prayerfully.

'A primary schoolboy that is buying ten eggs at three hundred naira where did he get the money?'

A woman told the man not to overdo the joke. Didn't he see that what the boy had done was 'an act of compassion?

'Act of what?'

'Hoo!' some passengers shouted.

'Shut up!'

'Shut up, Mr Man!'

He stopped his attempt to reply. The bus was nearing Eke Bus Stop. A woman admired Zhero out loud: it required courage for a boy of his age to act publicly the way he had done.

Zhero said 'Thank you, ma', stood up and left the bus. In his heart he was grateful to his mother — she had always told him to act without fear if he believed that what he wanted to do was good.

In the evening he would have loved to tell his mother about the boys in the uncompleted building who hawked for a living, about the man who hated the boys, about the good people who didn't like the behaviour of the man, and about the eggs nine of which he gave to his friends, and his friends were happy. But after the way she reacted to what he did for Daba — oh, why did she react that way to a poor girl?

He told her he wanted to take a walk in the street and he went out. He strolled about in the general area in which Daba lived till he felt his mother might be concerned about his long absence, and he went home. She pretended not to notice his behaviour, they said their good nights and went into their respective rooms.

On Saturday he took a walk at noon and then in the evening in and around the street for a long time and deprived his mother of his companionship, but she did not complain. After he had told his mother good night and gone into his room he looked at the time. Just after 9pm. The chemist shop might still be open. He could go there and ask after Daba. He laughed at his folly. Why didn't he ask for her address that night? He looked at the time again — not yet 9.30pm. While he was encouraging himself to go out once more a loud wind erupted outside, people and vehicles screeched in the street as they hurried to beat the rain that might follow, but it came almost immediately. It was so heavy that he felt the roof of the sky had given way and a river was dropping down. He looked out of the window and told himself that even a fish shouldn't go out this night . . . The night would be cold. He brought out his duvet from the wardrobe and placed it on the bed. He didn't have to change into his pyjamas. He flopped down onto the bed and clasped the folded duvet to his chest . . . .

About two weeks later he was lucky. Daba came out of the house. She said she had seen him walk past her house to and fro in the past, and today about three times. He was tongue-tied. She told him to come in. He did and she locked the door. (How about her madam?) Her madam had just travelled to Dubai and she was home alone. They went in. He sat on the posh couch when she told him to do so, and she sat by him. After a minute or so she laughed and gave him a cold bottle of Coke. Then she laughed again.

'Zhero, can't you talk? Can't you say something?'

'There's nothing to say. I just wanted to see you.'

'Zhero, you wanted to see me!' He nodded. 'And you say there is nothing to say?'

'I just wanted to see you,' he repeated.

'Can't you ask about my wound?' She pulled up her skirt. 'Look, look, no scar. You can't know that there was a wound before. Touch it, Zhero.' She took his left hand and placed it on the healed spot. 'Thank you, Zhero, I will never forget you.' She put her right arm around his shoulders. 'Thank you, Zhero,' she said more affectionately.

'Thank you too,' he replied, appreciating the softness of her thigh . . . not rough like her hand, when she welcomed him into the house with a handshake.

When he gulped and removed his hand from her thigh she removed her arm from his shoulders.

'Sometimes I see you going to school. Port Harcourt Metropolitan.'

'Yes.'

'I too used to go to school. I stopped at junior secondary three.'

'Why?'

She made light of it. 'Isn't it the usual story? No money. Our father left our mother when we were very young. My elder brother is in Lagos. We don't hear from him. My mother married another

74

man who died. The two boys from that marriage are in primary school.' She paused then added, 'By now I should have been studying medicine in University of Port Harcourt.' After a long pause she placed her arm around his shoulders again, fondly hoping that he would aggressively pull her down on the couch. 'Zhero, you have not touched the Coke I gave you at all.' He gulped again. 'Zhero, I am glad for you — your father is a very rich man.'

At home that night Zhero was unusually happy so his mother called him and told him to listen to her words.

'I know you are a good boy. But any human being can forget. That's why I want to remind you of what I've told you several times. If you put a girl in the family way, you have ruined your future . . . Happy night?'

He laughed, 'Good night, Mom.'

'When Bazi came to the house the following evening he was surprised at what he heard.

'Zera, when did you buy a bird? Isn't that Odedekoko singing? It's inside this house.'

To his shock Zera burst out in laughter. She gradually stopped laughing and told him it was Zhero singing. Then she told him of the day Chief Kulokulo banned The Home Stretch: That day when they were talking about Soul, Odedekoko was singing in the big tree near the place. The Home Stretch people were saying every living thing is Soul and God loves all Souls equally. It was at the time Chief Kulokulo was passing and the bird was singing. The speaker said all Souls are equal and to God the bird singing was no less important than the biggest man in Amabra. After they finished that evening Chief Kulokulo called them to his house and told them to never come back to Amabra. Now he's dead and Odedekoko goes on singing. Bazi joined her in laughter.

'What's the name of the religious group?'

'The Home Stretch. I've told you before.'

He was about to get up and leave the sitting room for his bedroom when a sponsored programme came on on the TV. It was the celebration of the 60th birthday of Professor Otto Ozibo, a writer. The celebration started with an opening prayer said by a pastor and then the MC acknowledged the few dignitaries in the gathering of mainly students of the professor's university before announcing a slight adjustment of the programme. The citation and the launching of the Festschrift would be the last items, obviously a way of waiting for the moneyed invitees. Then the members of the Committee of Friends who had organized the celebration and the production of the Festschrift stood up one after the other as he slowly acknowledged their presence.

Bazi's interest was the citation which was not coming soon. Unaccountably he asked her about Zhero's father. She decided not to react emotionally. She intended for them to define their relationship tonight.

'I've told you I don't know. That's why I wanted you to help me to abort the pregnancy. Alternatively to help me to manage the pregnancy. Then I could have finished school.'

'You don't know the man?'

'No. But I told Zhero his father is dead.'

'You were in Form 5, you'd won the National English Language Essay Prize and a scholarship to the university, four months to the School Cert Exam and a bastard prevents you from finishing secondary school. Because you didn't have the money to do an abortion. What a tragedy!'

She was incandescent with anger. 'Don't call my son a bastard! Never ever!'

'Zera, I'm sorry. Please I'm awfully sorry. I love Zhero too. In fact I feel he's my son. Something tells me you made a mistake in your calculation. I've wished to say this for a long time: I would like him to do a DNA test.'

'He's not your son and he's not doing any DNA test!'

Zhero quietly left the dining table and went into his room. He heard it all, he heard it all. So he was a bastard! His friends at Amabra were right. He was a bastard, the son of a prostitute who didn't know who impregnated her. The only person he loved in his life, the only person who loved him was a loose woman, a prostitute who would have killed him in her womb if she had the money. He wept because she had lied to him, he wept because she had fought those who called him a bastard even though she knew he was a bastard, he wept because he had thought she was the best woman in the world whereas she was just a prostitute, a harlot . . . .

His mother used to tell him about a man — was it Tai Solarin? — who said that if the devil gave you a scholarship take it. In order to get an education he had to be patient, he would be patient, he would pretend not to have heard them . . . He had thought that after succeeding in life he would go to Amabra and help to develop

Amabra, but how would he go to a place where everybody knew he was a bastard? It was impossible, he wept afresh . . . .

They did not notice that he went to bed unusually early, because for a long time Bazi tried to explain the meaning of 'bastard' to Zera. Yes, it was derogatory but — look it up in any dictionary — it wasn't as bad as she was thinking. Even in it's archaic or old-fashioned sense it simply meant a person who was born out of marriage — what was so bad about that? In exasperation he told her she and her fellow Nigerians were too emotional about the word. He incensed her — did she know how many children in the Niger Delta region were born to women who didn't know the whereabouts of the men who impregnated them? In fact, wasn't she aware that her Izon language had no word for it? A few mischievous people used the imported word 'bastard' to hurt people, but does the Izon society look down on children because they had no known fathers? She told him to go to his German wife and he left.

The next morning Zhero's mother did not realize that he had not woken till after she had finished preparing breakfast and his school lunch. She half anxiously hurried to his room. When he did not answer the door she was alarmed. She tried the handle — the door was not locked.

'Zhero!' He did not answer her. 'What's happening to you?'

'I don't know,' he answered, shivering.

His forehead almost burned her palm. She shouted on the phone that Zhero was dying. Before 7am Bazi was in the house and they rushed him to a posh private hospital. He was discharged the next day because it was just malaria. When Zera learnt of the cost she felt herself a fool for involving Bazi in a thing she could have taken care of with less than one thousand naira. But Bazi was proud of his fatherly role — what was ₦57,000 compared to the life of a son?

'Thank you, Bati, thank you for the love.'

In the night she phoned and told him she hated him for not staying with her. He apologized — it was because Einfuhlung was leaving Nigeria for good at midnight.

She lied, 'I'm sorry, Bati.'

He had told her about the meaning of his wife's German name before: 'Einfuhlung' meant 'empathy'. Empathy . . . empathy . . . .

She shook her head and went to her bedroom.

Zhero did not have to go to school the next day because on that day all the private primary and secondary schools in the country were forced by the Nigerian Union of Teachers to join their public school counterparts who had been on strike for over three months over salary increase. Zera was not bothered because he already had the Primary School Leaving Certificate and was eligible for secondary school admission.

Zhero felt silent contempt for his mother for taking a man who did not pity her. She said it was for his own sake — for your sake, Zhero, for your sake. What type of self-sacrifice was that? He hated Bazi, whose reason for wanting his mother he could not understand. He used to pity Mrs Ugbuson but now he despised her too, for doing nothing but staying at home and depending on a man for her upkeep . . . Did the Civics Studies teacher know about his mother when he advised the girls in the class not to be a kept woman and explained the meaning of kept woman? His mother was a kept woman — that was what she was! He wept in self-pity, Oh, his mother who everybody in Amabra respected, what had she turned herself into? His own mother, it was shameful, he was ashamed of her . . . .

When she went into his living room and saw his pillows wet she was afraid for his health again, but he assured her he was well. She went out thinking, Could it be that girl, Daba the thief? In love with a thief? Perhaps she should encourage him to go out as he liked until he was finally well and strong and then start to restrict his movements? Once he was fully well she'd tell him the implications of falling in love with Daba, a thief.

For two nights she suggested that he should take a walk and remind himself of the outdoor beauty of Amabra. He was glad of her offer. The first night he returned home unhappy but on the second night he was the Zhero who loved to sit by her in the moonlight at Amabra. When he saw her watching TV he sat by her and enthused that in spite of the menace of crime the city had a feel of beauty. She was happy to hear that but when they saw an advert of the deluxe brand of a car driven by a man who the young women wanted everywhere he went because of his deluxe Toyota she wondered what had happened to her son — Zhero said, 'All women are like that.' She was shocked beyond description.

Two days later, out of fear for the state of her son's mind, she told Bazi about his behaviour. Bazi said the forced holiday was to blame. He needed to be occupied. For a start he would go with Michael to buy some bags of cement and take to his house. Zera liked the idea. She went happily to the market.

Bazi called him, gave him ₦50,000 and instructions on the price, the brand and the packaging of the cement. He told him to dress quickly and meet Michael in the car outside. He added that he was giving him the money to hold because Michael was not reliable over money. After Zhero finished dressing he went into Bazi's room without knocking. Bazi, who thought he had locked the door, was totally naked. He quickly slipped on his trousers.

'What is it, Zhero, what is it?'

'The name . . . the name of the cement you say we should buy.'

'You've forgotten the name of the brand! In how many minutes? Get out of my sight you bastard!'

'Bastard! . . . Bastard . . . Bastard.

Zhero ran out of the house. Michael asked him where he was going.

He replied, 'I'm coming,' and continued to run.

Zera returned about three hours later. After putting down the things she bought in the market, she went to Bazi's room to tell him she was back.

'Zera, I feel like a newly-wed.'

'I'm glad for you, Bati.'

'Tonight?'

'Is still far away.'

She smiled and went into the kitchen, resolving that their relationship must be clearly defined tonight. After about thirty minutes he came into the kitchen. She asked him where Zhero was.

'He's gone out with Michael. I think they'll soon be back.'

'Then they must have come back, because Michael is sleeping in the car.'

He phoned Michael, who said they had not gone to buy the cement. He shouted for Michael to come up and he did.

'Where is Zhero?'

'Sir, I saw him running away oh. When I call him he say he is coming.'

Zera looked for a seat. Bazi was sitting on the only chair. She sat on the floor.

'Bati, where is my son?'

The driver answered on his behalf. 'He say he is coming.'

'Shut up!' Bazi shouted at him. 'How many hours ago?'

Zera turned off the gas cooker and went to the sitting room.

'Bati, tell me the truth.'

He told her what had happened and swore to God that it was the truth.

'You called my son a bastard. You called him a bastard again . . . Odedekoko.' She snuffled. 'Odedekoko.' She snuffled again. 'Odedekoko.'

And her cheeks were deluged by the rain from her eyes.

'Michael.'

'Sir.'

'Let's drive around and look for him.'

'I will go with you.' He looked at her clothes. 'There's no time to change. If you'll be ashamed of me I won't go out of the car.'

'Madam,' the driver pleaded 'Just for five minutes. Change your dress. We fit go police station too.'

She agreed with him. She went into their bedroom for some minutes, came out and gave the key to the house to Mrs Ugbuson in case Zhero should return home in their absence. They drove about, Bazi and Zera peering through the tinted window glasses, even Michael looking left and right until Bazi told him to concentrate on his driving, they drove around the city for about four hours then went back home. Only Zera went to ask Mrs Ugbuson if the boy had come home. Not yet. She rushed downstairs.

'Neighbour, I hope there's nothing wrong.' Mrs Ugbuson called out from her balcony.

Not looking back Zera shouted 'Nothing! Nothing!' and rushed back into the car. 'Hey! Where does he know in this Port Harcourt?'

'Madam,' the driver comforted her, 'just put your mind say we will see him. We will see him.'

Bazi only squeezed her left hand affectionately. At dusk they went back to the house and Zera rushed up again. Her tearful voice confirmed to Mrs Ugbuson that Zhero was missing as she repeatedly cried out his name. Her husband who was about to beat her for taking other people's house keys — 'Suppose they accuse you of stealing something' — he came out too and said 'God forbid, it is not Zhero's portion to miss. You will find him.' Without saying amen Zera rushed back to the car and they went to GRA police station. The DPO (Divisional Police Officer), a casual acquaintance, was glad to see Bazi's face.

'An urgent matter, a very serious one.'

'Then let's go to my office.'

Bazi beckoned to Zera to come. Her pace confirmed to the DPO that the matter was urgent. He quickly led the way to his office. Bazi told him what had happened and dictated what should be done: No twenty-four hours' waiting, inform all police stations in the country, start announcing tonight, search every police station in Port Harcourt tonight in case he had been arrested by the police. The DPO asked for the required data and the boy's latest picture, which Zera brought out from her wallet, and he promised that the police would do their best. Bazi dropped a ₦100,000 bundle on the table because he did not want the police to be hampered by logistics and demanded for a policeman to go round all the police stations in the city with them. When he said he would personally take care of the policeman the DPO gave him a sergeant after his own heart.

At every police station they looked at the detained persons' list on the blackboard on the wall behind the counter and then looked inside the smelly detention room for males, sometimes calling out Zhero's names — Adonkia Bazi! Zhero Sai! — if the place was too dark.

Mr and Mrs Ugbuson were awake and waiting for them when they returned home without Zhero around 2am. Bazi said he would not have believed if someone had told him there was such love in this world. Mrs Ugbuson said in a tearful voice that it was for Zhero, it was for Zhero, for Zhero they could stay awake all night, and she hugged Zera, wept together with her and assured her that she would find her son — her heart told her so.

When Bazi said he had to go to his house for a change of clothes Mrs Ugbuson told him he did not have to come back and she volunteered to spend the night with Zera. He readily took the advice because staying with Zera's sorrowing might kill him before daybreak. When she started to call her son Odedekoko affectionately and address him as if he was sitting opposite her he quietly went out.

He came back the next day and for four days they went to the police station every evening in case there was some news, they searched the waterfronts, the marketplaces and the motor parks, they watched TV, they bought and searched through many newspapers, they listened to the radio, they drove around the city now and then — all for Zhero. And then the police advised that they should stop pushing too hard and trust in God and in the police. Every day the night would fall, then the dawn would break, and then the sun would start to shine, as if nothing had happened to Zera — it wasn't the business of the universe to bring her son to her, she must do something, she must do something more than hope for her son to come back home. With Oyinkuro, the powerful juju priest in mind she suggested that she should go to Amabra — Zhero might have gone back there. Bazi liked the idea especially because it would take her away from him for some time. He needed some sleep and some good food.

She left for Amabra the next day. Everybody, except Ebido, believed she had only come to tell them that she and her son had settled down in Port Harcourt, and because they were so very happy to see her they failed to see that her smiles were not the smiles of an Amabra-born girl, warm like the shimmying surface of River Niger in the noon sun in November.

At night Ebido, with whom she was staying, told her how much she had spent to build her house, why she rented it out to the Catholic priest who had started building a church in Amabra, and how much rent she had collected.

'This is the passbook. The bank manager agreed that whenever you come back you can come to the bank and sign the papers. The account is in your name. No one else can withdraw from it. The balance of the money I used to build this small house for myself as you told me to do. When my mother was alive she never for one day dreamt that her daughter would stop living in a mud and thatch house . . . The rain is falling heavily outside, yet not a drop of water on the floor, because the roof is not leaking. Since I completed this house I have loved the rainy season. Thank you, Zera.'

So much honesty — Zera started to weep.

Ebido gazed at her for some time with the penetrating eyes of love and friendship.

'Zera, that is not why you are weeping for so long. Did he ill-treat you? Did he send you away?' She started to weep too. 'If he has sent you away Zhero would have come with you. Tell me, is Zhero dead?' she asked, taking her friend's hands like a mother who wanted to know the truth no matter what.

'Oh, Ebido, Ebido, he is more than dead.'

Ebido violently dropped her friend's hands, as if they were pieces of hot yam from a boiling pot which had scalded her hands. "Zera don't! 'Zera don't tell me that my son is in jail! No, my son cannot commit any crime.'

'No, Ebido, no . . . Your son is missing.'

Ebido dropped onto the floor from the chair as if she had been thrown down from a height.

'Hey, Zera! You have killed me, Zera, you have killed me!' She addressed the clap of thunder. 'Oh thunder! Break down this house and let it crush me to death. It is not a good price for Zhero's life.'

'As you are seeing me so, as you are seeing me so, I'm dead too. It is my corpse that is walking about, it is my corpse that is with you.' There was another loud peal of thunder and a flash of lightning. 'You heard my friend, thunder, and lightning, you saw her saying it, punish me with death for my foolishness.'

After they stopped weeping Zera told her in detail what had happened. She omitted to say her real reason for coming to Amabra was for both of them to go to Oyinkuro, the juju priest — she had decided that it was a foolish idea.

Ebido approached the question in her mind warily. 'Zera, do you know him well?'

'I have had no reason to mistrust him.'

'Hmm . . . .'

'Speak your mind Ebido. Speak your mind to Zera.'

'No, nothing in my mind . . . since you trust him.'

'Ebido! Ebido! Don't ask me the question in my mind. I've refused to say it to myself — has Bati used my son for a money-making ritual?'

'Hey! Hey!' Ebido slapped the floor as she wept. 'I did not like the way things were happening. Too fast, too sweet, just like magic, but I did not have the courage to tell you. I wish I had warned you, I wish I had warned you. But I didn't, I didn't because it was sweet for me too.'

Zera joined her on the tiled floor and they wept for a long time, they asked God where His beloved son was, they told Zhero's grandmother it was not yet time for her to receive him where she was, they wept and wept and wept, because they did not know where Zhero was, they begged Zhero to tell them where he was.

'Odedekoko, where have you flown to?'

'Odedekoko, where have you flown to?'

Chapter Three

He had no place in mind when he ran out of the house. When Michael, the driver, called him and he said to Michael 'I'm coming' he had meant to go back soon for them to go and buy the cement, but he had continued to run until he felt it was strange that he was running when everybody else wasn't running, and he stopped running and started to walk about, aimlessly until he felt like a searcher who knew what he was searching for but not where it was — what he wanted was a safe distance from his mother and Bazi but he didn't know where that could be. So he scrambled to enter a half-empty bus when he saw a small crowd of people doing so. Because he looked like a lost traveller when only three passengers were left on the bus, the bus conductor asked him where he was going. The bus conductor, who was inwardly contending with his own personal problem, only told him to pay the fare when he answered that he didn't know where he was going. For a fare of fifty naira he gave the conductor a thousand-naira note. The conductor stared at him for a moment and went back to his seat by the driver. At the last bus stop the conductor rushed out of the bus and called him back.

'I hope you know whosai you dey go?'

He shook his head vigorously, 'No, no.' The conductor, who regarded him as if his head was a shell he was shaking to make sure there were seeds inside, gave him back his one-thousand-naira note and told him to go well. The conductor watched the aimless traveller for a moment, shook his head and went back into his bus. He too had his own problem — his rich younger brother who he thought would finance his wedding had failed him, and the date for the wedding was less than two months away.

Zhero walked on . . . He thought, bastard . . . bastard . . . There are many children in Amabra and the villages we go to who don't know their fathers but when people call them bastards it doesn't pain them, because their mothers don't lie about their fathers . . . When people call me a bastard it pains me because she has made me believe that my father died before I was born . . . and I used to blame my father for dying before I was born . . . The day Monday called me a bastard I broke his tooth for nothing . . . Why did she lie to me? Why did she lie to me? . . . If from when I was very young she had told me the truth . . . .

He fought back the tears. People shouldn't see him weeping. He placed his attention on the skyscraper to his right, wondering if such a tall structure could ever be built in Amabra. He stopped to count the number of storeys, losing count, starting again, losing count again and then starting all over again — he gave it up, his neck was paining him . . . There were so many storey buildings around . . . Bazi's office was in a two-storey building. He owned the building . . . If he took his education seriously he too could own a storey building where his office would be and he would be the employer of workers there . . . But it's a teacher he would like to be, he did not need big buildings like these . . . He sidestepped a girl hawking bananas, she called him 'foolish man', but he did not answer her . . . The unending streams of people in the road reminded him of what the pastor said about life as a journey . . . But all the people weren't going in the same direction; on a journey all the people should be going the same way, and it would be easy to help someone along the way —

A hungry-looking gangling boy much younger than him stopped him.

'You need wristwatch? See dis one. I give you for only five thousand.' He shook his head. 'Three thousand.' He shook his head again. 'Two . . . one thousand, last price,' the boy said with finality in his tone.

'I don't need a wristwatch.'

The boy told him in a loud minatory tone to buy the wristwatch but as he bunched his fists and frowned darkly the boy ran away. He relaxed and walked on, thinking, this can't be what the song means by life is a market where we buy and sell . . . How can a small boy force me to buy what I don't want? If he's hungry he should beg me to help him . . . .

When he felt the sun was too hot it glowed and burnt more intensely — a friend warning him to go back home. He reached inside his right back trouser pocket for a handkerchief but did not bring it out — no need to bother, no one was wiping their face. A car screeched to a halt. He swivelled around — he was the cause. He was dumbfounded. A six-foot-tall middle-aged woman came out of a snack bar in the frontage of a building and firmly but with motherly affection drew him gently to the sidewalk and thanked the driver of the car, who drove away without a word. Some passerssby advised him to be careful on the road, some told him to thank God for his life and to pray for the driver of the car, while some angrily said he was looking for someone to blame for his death. Shaking imperceptibly he went to the snack bar and sat on a stool under the tarpaulin canopy. The woman politely avoided him till he spoke to her.

'Thank you, ma.'

'Thank God. Can I give you ice water?' she asked thinking, some mother's son was probably lost in life.

He replied after a few seconds. 'Not yet. Let me buy . . . let me buy meatpie.' Lest the woman should feel that he had no money he brought out the one thousand naira the bus conductor had returned to him and which he had put inside the breast pocket of his shirt. 'Two meatpies and Coke.'

He went to the counter so that the woman, who was obviously older than his mother, would not come out and serve him, and he took the bottle opener from her and opened the Coke bottle himself. She thanked him. While he was eating, a hungry-looking dog in front of the neighbouring building came and sat a little away from him. He politely avoided the gaze of the dog several times before he decided that the dog was hungry. He asked for two meatpies and gave them to the dog who devoured them in a few seconds. He guessed the dog would need four more. The woman did not interfere. After finishing the fourth meatpie slowly the dog looked satisfied. He paid his bill of nine hundred naira, thanked the woman, who said 'Go well, my son' as if to a traveller starting on a long journey, and he left. He felt his pocket. The remainder of his pocket money, and the fifty thousand naira for the cement bags — the bulk assured him that he couldn't be lost in the city. He could charter a taxi at anytime and go back home. He walked about looking at the goods in the shop windows or going into the shops to admire the goods, especially the shoes and the jeans which he was more than once sorely tempted to buy. He felt like buying some fine shoes, jeans and trousers and going back to Amabra . . . But Bazi would call him a thief, and his mother would be very ashamed of him . . . .

When he felt hungry he went into an eatery and ordered a six-hundred-naira plate of boiled beans with stew, fried ripe plantain and fried chicken. It was a heavy meal and he felt tired and unwilling to get up and leave but a server who noticed his sleepy eyes contemptuously told him that the eatery wasn't a bedroom. He felt angry when his thoughts turned to home. He gave the young woman a one-thousand-naira bill and walked out without taking his change from the woman who did not despise the contemptible customer's money. In his anger he did not mind the sun but when he reached under the massive Boro Flyover he felt relieved, he liked the breeziness and the coolness of the place. It was also a very busy place and he could stay there anonymously for as long as he liked. He looked for a comfortable place and sat on the concrete floor. Vehicles were loading for Aba, Owerri, Enugu and other places. Hawkers of various goods were moving around, some of them shouting out their wares, as if everybody else was blind and could not see what they were hawking. A man with a pyramid of music CDs on his head and holding a ghetto blaster which was blaring out Christian songs of praise in Igbo unknowingly delighted Zhero with his air of freedom and joy as he and several people sang along to his CD player . . . Life was beautiful . . . .

When he woke up the place was empty — just one, two, three, four people. He wondered what the time might be. That boy was right — he needed a wristwatch. When the headlights of a passing vehicle illuminated the place he saw that one of the persons was gentle-looking and did not look much older than him. He went to him. The young man was shivering slightly. He was probably not well.

'Good . . . evening,' he greeted him tentatively. 'Please . . . where can I take to Rt Hon Westwood Avenue — no, don't worry, I'm not going there.' The young man looked at his wristwatch. 'What is the time?'

The young man knew his type — running from someone, maybe a wicked guardian. No, he didn't look il-treated. Must be from an offended parent.

He asked him point-blank, 'You are running from your father? What did you do wrong?' In spite of his shivering he smiled at Zhero's unconscious reaction. 'Dis place not for people like you o. Make you go home.'

'I don't want to go home,' he firmly replied and then shivered at the hooting of a car horn which resembled that of Bazi's jeep.

The young man stared at him and shrugged. 'Then what can I do for you?' Zhero was silent. 'Sit down naa.' Zhero sat by him. 'De night still long o. It has just started. You go fit survive here?'

Zhero silently wished he would drop the pidgin English.

'Is this place for people who are running from someone?'

The young man smiled at the boy's boldness. 'Or from something,' he answered him. Very soon you go see more people.'

'You sleep here too?'

'Yes. What's your name?' He noticed Zhero's hesitation. 'You don't have to tell me. My name is Rowland.'

After a pause he told Zhero his story: For over two years he had worked for a man who gave him goods to hawk and paid him a commission. It was good business because he could make something extra now and then by inflating the prices of some items. He came from Owerri every morning and returned in the evening, but four days ago, because he was making a very good sale he forgot to stop until he sold the last item. By then there were no more vehicles for Owerri — transporters now closed early due to fear of armed robbers and kidnappers on the route. He intended to sleep at the motor park but Satan told him to take a walk, and he did. He saw a beautiful babe, took her to a hotel and they enjoyed each other and they went to sleep. When he woke in the morning the babe had gone, all his money had gone too. Not even the transport fare to Owerri. She didn't leave anything for him. He had to go to Mile One market to carry loads and raise his transport fare. When he went back and told his master that armed robbers had stolen the money from him the man chased him with a gun. He came back to Port Harcourt to work as a porter, but since yesterday his body had turned weaker and weaker. Today he had eaten only one meal. After a pause he asked Zhero why he didn't laugh at him. Zhero's concern was his health. The way he had accompanied his words with his shivering showed that he was seriously sick.

'When I was sick like this the doctor said it was just malaria,' he suggested, 'simple malaria.'

'Yes, I know it is malaria, but it is money that cures malaria,' Rowland replied, a little offended.

Zhero laughed. 'It's malaria tablets, not money. Do you know where a chemist shop is? I have some money.'

Rowland was touched. 'When I was telling you my story I was wondering why I was telling a stranger everything about myself. Now I see why.'

They went to a chemist shop and Zhero paid one thousand and fifty naira for the tablets. Because the nurse said the tablets were to be taken after meal they went to an eatery where Rowland had a good meal for the first time in many days, and he joked that immediately the malaria saw the dish on the table it started to run away from him, like Usain Bolt of Jamaica. Even then he took the tablets and they left the eatery, Rowland walking with a slight rightward stoop which gave him an air of satisfaction with life.

Outside, he stood upright and gazed at the Port Harcourt night sky he had known intimately.

'Why are you looking up?'

'If it rains, under the bridge will not be good for you.' Zhero did not tell him that he was no stranger to open-air existence. 'If you can afford two thousand naira, plus transport fare we can go to a cheap hotel.'

'Where?'

'October 60 Hotel. Can you afford it?'

Zhero said yes, and they took a taxi to the hotel. The rain started to pound on Port Harcourt just as they entered the hotel, and Zhero remarked on Rowland's accurate prediction. In the morning Rowland felt he was strong enough to go to the market and carry loads for money but Zhero advised him not to be deceived by his body, and so they did not check out at midday. Rowland stayed indoors too, because after the night's rain walking in most of the streets in Diobu would not be a pleasurable experience. Around 8pm they went to a fee-paying video centre at Azikiwe Street to watch a UEFA Championship match and returned to their hotel a little before midnight. Wisely, they did not talk about the Chelsea Vs Manchester United match because at the video centre they had been on opposite sides, and the victory margin of three goals had caused a fist fight among some fans. Because they did not comment and argue about the finished game their enjoyment of it was not total — they returned quietly to the hotel.

Before they slept Rowland asked his friend, 'Jero, you have a lot of money in your pockets, but you are not afraid that I will steal it and run away.'

'If you do, I'll go into the market and carry loads.'

Rowland jerked up. 'You have carried loads before?'

'Yes.'

'I mean in the market.'

'In the market, at motor parks, at watersides. I used to be a porter.'

'Is that how you made the money?' He looked at Zhero's face.

'No, please don't tell me, don't tell me . . . Please don't cry.'

Zhero wiped his face. Now Rowland knew, now he knew why Zhero looked pensive whenever they were silent — there was an untold story. He remembered what his master often said 'Every manpikin na storybook. Unless you open am you no go know de kind story wey dey inside.' After a long silence he reopened his own book and read out another bit of his story.

'Jero, I left school at junior secondary two because I didn't like school. There was nothing my mother could do about it. By the way I don't have a father. I don't know him because my mother says she doesn't know who is my father. She married a Hausa man who was killed during a Jos crisis. She stayed with his mother to take care of her but two years after her husband's death there was another crisis. She says she became pregnant during that Jos crisis in which the old woman of about eighty-something-years old was burnt together with the house.' He paused as if to remind himself that the cold facts of history must not be read out in a cracked voice and then he laughed. 'I don't know whether the man who raped my mother is a Muslim or a Christian. So I have rejected Islam and Christianity till the two religions stop fighting in this world.' He looked at Zhero. 'Jero, why are you crying?' Zhero said he was sorry and wiped his face. Rowland continued, a little doubtfully. 'As I was saying, I left school, but my ambition is to succeed in life. My only problem is women. When I see a beautiful woman I can't control myself. But after that girl taught me a lesson I have decided to change. If you can trust me, you can loan me ₦20,000. If I pay my master his money I can get enough items for both of us to hawk. Then I can even introduce you to him. It's good business if a person can save.'

After he finished he felt like one who had told a hard-luck story, wondering whether his silent hearer regarded it as a true-life story or mere fiction. Without a word Zhero gave him the amount. Rowland could not believe what had happened. In fact he was visibly afraid. He laughed aloud and mirthlessly and looked at Zhero, not sure of the success of his bravado.

'Jero, this is big money! It's tempting for me to go and do something else with it. But if I don't pay my master what I'm owing him he'll kill my mother. The bastard, he loves money too much.'

When he saw the expression on Zhero's face he stopped short, thinking that he had portrayed himself as an unreliable person. He did not know that the cause of Zhero's facial expression was the word 'bastard', the word that had rankled with him since he left home.

The next day Zhero went to One-Stop Store and bought a short sleeve shirt, jeans and underwear so that he could change into clean clothes.

Two days later Rowland came back with fifty Chinese-made mobile phones and Zhero accompanied him to sell them not minding if anyone looking for him would see him. As Rowland's employer had advised him they did not hawk on roads but went from door to door at Diobu where they sold the phones for three thousand naira each instead of Rowland's employer's price of two thousand naira. The phones were a new brand introduced into the Nigerian market just a few days ago and were completely sold off before dusk. When Rowland refunded Zhero his twenty thousand naira Zhero felt he had found a trade that would enable him to pay his way in school. He agreed to go with Rowland and be introduced to his employer, on condition that he would be posted to another city, not Port Harcourt.

They went to Rumuokoro Motor Park where the touts and the bus conductors of a few mini buses were shouting for passengers for Aba, Owerri, and Yenagoa. They went into an Owerri bus which had more passengers than the other ones. In the din of the shouting for passengers Rowland chattered happily about a lot of things, to which Zhero only responded with silence or a monosyllabic 'hnnh', but when he said he saw a police announcement in a newspaper about a missing boy in school uniform when he was in Owerri, Zhero was agitated.

'What's the name? What's the name?' Zhero asked him.

'The boy looked like you. Wearing Port Harcourt Metropolitan School uniform. He has two names: Adonkia Bazi and one other name which I didn't see well. Someone was reading the newspaper in the bus. Jero, are you the one?'

'My name isn't Adonkia.'

Rowland felt the subject was not as important as their future. He told Zhero the most lucrative place for hawking was Lagos, and selling Nollywood videos was the most lucrative thing. That was where they should end up. Without waiting for Zhero's response he gave him the cards of two employers of video hawkers. His friend, who was doing well in Lagos, gave him several business cards of employers of hawkers, he concluded.

91

Zhero asked him after pocketing the cards unenthusiastically, 'Why haven't you gone to Lagos?'

'I don't know. I think it's fear. You know, a place you haven't been to before.' He laughed. 'My mother says am a coward because she conceived me in fear.'

Zhero wanted to be far away from Port Harcourt. He asked, 'Why don't we go straight to Lagos?'

'It's too late to get a Lagos bus.'

Zhero hated Bazi and his mother. He didn't want his schoolmates to see him in Port Harcourt as a hawker. And Daba, Daba mustn't see him as a hawker . . . Several reasons had coalesced into the call of adventure — alone, without a father, without a mother, he'd go to faraway Lagos and return to Amabra as a successful man, able to help his people . . . A man must stand on his own two feet — that was what his mother often said to him . . . Even though she lied to him about his father her teachings were very good . . . .

'We can go back to the hotel and go to Lagos tomorrow. Let's go down.'

Rowland thought for a moment. 'The problem is my master's money with me. If I don't give him his money he'll kill my mother. We can go to Lagos tomorrow. Jero, my only problem as I told you is women. I cannot steal a person's one kobo. Let it be tomorrow. My mother always says life is a very long journey. A traveller must not walk too fast. If he walks too fast he will be tired before the middle of the journey.'

Zhero was happy . . . He'd go back to his mother, he'd go back to Amabra after he'd made it . . . The journey of life could be interesting . . .

Tired from the hours of hawking during the day he slept off not long after the journey started. He scrambled to his feet before he knew that he had done so in response to an order for everybody to come out of the bus, and everybody was frightfully obeying the order. They obeyed the order to line up. They obeyed the order to face the forest. To be silent while they were frisked and dispossessed of their money and valuables. To remain silent until their bus was thoroughly searched. Except one person they all obeyed the order to go back into the bus silently.

'Agbulo,' Zhero said to the last giver of the order. He turned and faced Zhero. 'Even though your face is covered I know your voice, Agbulo. Are you an armed robber now?'

'Shoot him!' one of Agbulo's colleagues said.'

'Ogoun! You too?'

The two other bandits agreed with Ogoun.

'Ogoun,' Agbulo protested. 'You no know Jero? Kill Jero? Me I no fit stand by and see Jero die o.'

One of them solved the problem. 'He go join us. Simple matter. Put him inside the jeep.' He turned to the travellers inside the bus 'All of you are wretched people. Kidnapping you will be a waste of time and resources. Bye bye.'

He ordered Zhero into the boot of their jeep. Zhero obeyed without a word. They went into their jeep and drove off. After he had calmed himself so that he would not pass out he decided that the kidnappers had only two options — kill him or release him. He decided not to blame his mother for bringing this tragedy upon him. Rather he pitied her because she'd suffer a lot if she knew that he was killed by kidnappers . . . He didn't blame Rowland too. In his position he too might not utter a word? . . . Where would Rowland find ₦100,000 for his master? What would happen to his mother?

As the vehicle jolted along a rough terrain he struggled not to throw up. At last it came to a stop and a kidnapper opened the boot to let him out. Agbulo rushed to him to support him for some time before he could stand firmly and walk. They were on a track in the forest. He felt that he would not go out of the forest when the vehicle drove away. He silently prayed for God to take care of his mother. Agbulo pleaded with him not to try to escape and they started to walk through the forest, their immediate surroundings illuminated by the kidnappers powerful torches. The one who decided that Zhero had to join them answered his mobile phone and then announced that a minister and his driver had been kidnapped by one group and a lady by another group. Even Agbulo was excited. Zhero shook his head at what Ogoun and Agbulo had turned into, and thought of Chief Kulokulo's two baby tigers which grew big and nearly destroyed their cage one day. Chief Kulokulo told a hunter to shoot them.

After thirty minutes or so the ranking member admired Zhero aloud.

'Jero, you are a tough guy. You no look tired at all. Other people for don fall down, piss and beg. But you, as if you don use to dis type of life before.' He addressed Agbulo. 'Give am a good name.'

Agbulo explained to Zhero that he had to be given an alias so that the 'bastards' they kidnapped would not know his true name and identity.

'Which name we go give you naa? . . . Let me see . . . .'

'Jero,' the ranking member said, 'take a name for yourself, fast fast.'

Responding to his commanding tone Zhero spontaneously said 'Joseph' and the gang laughed at the meekness of his name.

'My name na Naija,' the ranking member said.

'Babylon,' Agbulo said.

'Rambo!' Ogoun half shouted, thumping his chest.

'I am Tarzan,' the fourth kidnapper said of himself, 'King of the Evil Forest.'

Naija remarked, 'Joseph the dreamer, dis our profession no time for bedroom sleep o. Our only dream na naira —millions, billions.'

Their destination was about a kilometre away from the track.

'Boss,' one armed kidnapper proudly said immediately Naija's group came up to his group, 'na de goods be dis o. Mission accomplished,' he added as a way of handing over the goods to his employer.

The woman, the minister and the driver were sitting on the ground, their backs against a tree, their legs in chains. It pained the minister, so deeply in a way he could not express himself, that the boy called them goods.

'Well done, Kilimanjaro,' Naija replied him after shining his torch on the abductees. 'Well done, all of you.'

'Thank you, Boss,' they chorused.

'Kilimanjaro, Rambo go give you de small cash we been collect. Add to de one you collect from dese people. We go check everything later. Now, who is the minister among you?' The minister thought the answer should be obvious. 'I say who's the minister! You want me to kill you?'

'I am, I am, please tell him to drop that gun,' the minister frightfully said, pointing to Rambo (Ogoun) who pretended to be waiting for the order to pull the trigger. 'Oh,' he sighed as Rambo (Ogoun) lowered his gun in response to a sign from Naija.

'Stand up, all of you.' The abductees scrambled to their feet. 'We are not murderers. We are only working for our daily bread as any other Nigerian. Forget whatever you were before you entered this forest. Life has a way of requiring everyone to be humble. So just do whatever any of us tells you.' After a brief pause he continued. 'Boys, shine your torchlights let them see us, let us see them.' The order was carried out. 'Your only prayer to God tonight is that your people should pay the ransom we shall demand.' He noticed the mistake in showing Zhero's face to the abductees. 'Babylon, take Joseph away from here. We'll settle his case soon. Kilimanjaro.'

'Yes, Boss.'

'Are their handsets with you?'

'Yes, Boss.'

'Good. Take the names and phone numbers of the people they want us to tell that they are alive. Rambo, come let's go to Babylon and Joseph.'

They met Babylon persuading Zhero to join them if he did not want to be a porter forever. Zhero said no. Didn't he want to make some millions and start a better life — build a few houses, establish a business, marry a fine girl, and so on? Zhero said no, not through their way. If that was the case, did he want to be killed? Because after he had known their identities it would be unthinkable for them to let him walk away.

Zhero replied, 'Agbulo, you know I cannot do such a thing.'

Naija who had been standing behind him, kicked him in the back. He jumped up and faced the person that had kicked him. Naija slapped him.

'What did you call him? You don't know his name is Babylon?'

Babylon (Agbulo) came in between them.

'Naija, please calm down.'

'You see what you are causing by breaking the rule?'

'I sorry. He go change.'

'Dis one no go change. Take him away. Let him join the others. Chain him. He's a kidnap victim too.'

'Nai —'

'Not one single word from you!'

Babylon took him away.

Immediately after they contacted the abductees' next-of-kin that night they unchained them and took them to another place in the Evil Forest. Several times Zhero and the driver had to support the minister on the about-two-hour journey. Feeling too hot the minister pulled off his jacket and flung it away. His white long-sleeved shirt made no effort to hide the ugliness of his potbelly. He removed his tie, flung it away too, and pulled his shirt out of the trousers. No one paid attention to the woman's plea to be allowed to stop to urinate. Zhero felt she urinated as she trudged along — he was sure he heard water lightly dropping on dry leaves. A good thing she was wearing a skirt. At last they reached their destination and even the kidnappers flopped down wearily as Naija announced that the abductees had two hours to sleep. The abductees were chained again. The stench of human excrement was thick in the air. Perhaps other abductees had been around here before.

The kidnappers brought out loaves of bread and tins of sardine from a hand-grip and shared among themselves only. If any of their victims was hungry they did not say, and they soon fell asleep.

They were woken up at 5am, given thirty minutes to relieve themselves and thirty minutes to eat their meal of bread and sardine, the loaves of bread in their hands, the tins of sardine on the ground. Taking a bit of the sardine from the tin and adding to a bite of the bread in the mouth was not as dignifying as Zhero's method. He had split the loaf lengthwise and spread the sardine inside. When the woman said she was going to do it his way he said no, the bottom of her tin must be sandy; if she tried to empty the content of the tin into the bread the sand at the bottom of the tin would go into the bread too. He carefully wiped the bottom of the tin and shook the fish out of the tin into the bread. He helped the minister too while the driver did it for himself.

They saw that they were allowed to talk. Having lit where their victims were with a torch the kidnappers had moved into a dark distance where they could see their victims without being seen.

'Young man,' the minister said, 'thank you for helping me. Thank you. What's your name?'

'Joseph Endu,' Zhero lied.

'Thank you, Joseph. I am Dr Kymer Odiza, Minister of National Development and Social Mobility. My driver's name is Coles. Madam, what's your name?'

The woman, who had laughed when she tried Zhero's action, burst into tears. The minister was confused.

'Ma, sorry. Don't cry.'

'Thank you, my son. Joseph?'

'Yes, ma.'

'I'm sorry,' she said. 'My name is Dame Valerie Onna. My husband is the cause of my problem. This is the second time I have been kidnapped since he announced his interest in the governorship of our State. What's in governorship? I told him to forget about politics, let's live in peace, he won't listen to me.'

The minister consoled her. 'I've never met Dr Onna. But I know

96

him by reputation. I think he'll win.'

'When he becomes Governor a thousand policemen will guard us. But what happens after he leaves office? Can't people see what Nigeria is turning into?'

The minister pointed at the sole of Dame Valerie's right shoe. She must have stepped on fresh human excrement where she had gone to relieve herself. Zhero took the shoe and cleaned it thoroughly. A tear of gratitude dropped from her left eye, and there was a long silence within which there were words of sorrow from her heart and the minister's.

Coles gave out a short sharp cry. Something had stung him on his right buttock. He quickly unbuttoned and unzipped his trousers and felt his left buttock with his hand. He stood up and started to pull down his trousers. 'No' he said, realizing that it was impossible to pull off the trousers, because of the chains on his legs. He only shook the trousers vigorously and pulled them up again.

'Coles, you don't wear pants?'

'Sorry, sir.'

Dame Valerie laughed. 'He reminds me of my husband. No pants even when he's going out. I tell him, suppose there's a free-for-all in your political rally, your nakedness will be shown on national TV.'

The minister laughed. Apparently the kidnappers were too tired to come and take them to the next place. Dawn was breaking through the branches of trees. When some birds perched on top of the tree they were sitting against, for the first time in many many years Dr Kymer Odiza paid attention to the singing of birds and he felt that the world was bigger than self-important humanity. He looked contemplatively at the big-girthed trees, which might be older than him, and which might outlive him . . . He did not draw away his left foot from the beetle that was crawling near it . . . As children, he and his friends loved to play with beetles, or crush them, or dismember them.

A kidnapper came and told them they would soon move to another place. Some minutes later he came back to take Dame Valerie and Zhero to the gang. After her husband was warned that the phone's loudspeaker was on she was told to tell him to pay the ₦100 million they had demanded from him. She shook her head. They beat her till she begged them to allow her to tell her husband to do as they had demanded. She could not speak, she only wept as she heard her husband cry where he was. Naija yanked the phone from her and insulted the husband for weeping like a woman instead of telling his wife when he would pay the ransom.

A kidnapper led her back and brought the minister. Naija peremptorily told him to direct his wife on how the ₦500 million ransom could be paid within forty-eight hours. The minister knew the consequences of disobedience having heard Dame Valerie shouting as she was being beaten.

'Princess, please tell the president.'

Naija was infuriated. He shouted, 'Tell the president what? ₦500 million! ₦500 million! You're saying tell the president!'

Princess begged, 'Please don't touch my husband, please don't beat him, let me talk to him, we'll see what can be done.'

Naija switched off the phone, called the minister's wife again and told her to listen to her husband crying. As he cried and begged for leniency his wife and his children cried too, begging for mercy. Naija switched off the phone again, and told the minister to get away. A kidnapper helped him away while he continued to weep, acutely hurt that a low-life like Naija and his fellow armed robbers and kidnappers had so much authority over him — the power of the gun, the power of evil, the power of violence.

Naija turned to Zhero. 'Joseph, are you joining us or not? I give you twenty-four hours to say yes or no. Get away from here.'

When Zhero returned to the minister, his driver and Dame Valerie they regarded him with suspicion. He confronted them frontally.

'You are thinking that I'm a spy. I'm not. They kidnapped me too and they want me to join them.'

Babylon (Agbulo) came to him.

'Joseph, for de last time. If you say no, na there our friendship end o. Bye bye.'

He angrily walked away.

'But you said you were kidnapped.'

'Yes, sir.' The minister sniggered. 'After they robbed our bus they said no big man to kidnap so we should go. But because I recognized the voices of my two friends they wanted to kill me, but one of them begged them not to kill me, and they said I must become their member.'

Dame Valerie wept. 'Oh, my son, so they will kill you?'

'Ma, don't cry.'

They were taken to another place where they were given water to drink on arrival. Then at midday they were given bread, sardine

98

and water. The abductees knew that negotiations were going on but they were not told the details. In the evening Naija announced that Dr Onna was going to be taught the lesson of his life for offering them a bait of ₦50 million. The place he promised to drop the money was suddenly swarming with people who did not resemble poor villagers in anyway! People with fat cheeks! People with smooth and shiny skins! His punishment would be the gang rape of Dame Valerie, the photographs of which would be sent to him. Zhero, who they had inadvertently not chained, jumped to his feet.

'No!' he shouted, 'No! It's not good, it's not good. Babylon, please tell them not to do it. Babylon, you Rambo, have you forgotten the things we used to say when we were suffering together as porters? We used to say that in any place God puts us we should not make people suffer the way we were suffering . . . we should make life better for people . . . that we should show people how to love one another instead of just talking about love. Have you forgotten? Babylon and Rambo my friends, please don't forget.'

He was weeping. Dame Valerie told him to come to her, come to her and be embraced by a mother before she was killed; he went to her on the ground and she hugged him and wept with him. Naija walked away. His boys followed him. Ten minutes or so later he came back alone and told Dame Valerie to ask her husband how much he could pay tomorrow — not beyond tomorrow. She begged for her husband to pay ten million. Naija agreed and phoned her husband. Dr Onna apologized and promised to do his best.

'Provided your best is ten million,' Naija told him. 'And now wey you don tell de police, dem go dey watch for see if you go withdraw big amount. So how you go do am?'

'My friends will help me. Please, don't torture my wife.'

Naija mused on the abductee's chains. 'You are in chains. Do you know how many Nigerians are in chains of poverty? How many millions in chains of illiteracy? Chains of unemployment, like mine. Chains! Chains!' he shouted insanely as he walked away.

When they were alone Dame Valerie told Zhero to sit by her.

'Joseph, come sit by me, so that if they come to carry me away when we are sleeping I can touch you before I go to my death . . . Joseph, Nigeria is a good country. Because you are Nigerian . . . Come, Joseph, come sit by me . . . Thank you, my son.'

The minister did not bother to wipe his tears.

Coles thought about his own situation: Though he was a kidnapee too they had not asked for any ransom for his release. Was it because they considered him as a fellow deprived Nigerian, or because he was insignificant?

Dame Valerie was released the next day. From the newspapers the kidnappers had learnt that the police had requested for a human-heat-sensing device from Israel to track them in the forest. They told the minister so and he was given the phone to tell the police and then his wife that the irreducible amount of ₦100 million had to be paid before 6pm the next day. While he was talking with his wife Naija maniacally fired six shots into the air. The minister's wife who had nearly passed out was relieved to hear his warning.

'Mrs Odiza! This is for real: 6pm tomorrow or come to Onija Market thereafter for your husband's naked corpse.'

Babylon and Rambo pleaded with the minister to persuade the federal government to pay the ransom because they really needed the money. There was a long pause while they puffed their marijuana wraps, then they explained to the minister that they wanted a new life, a better life — they couldn't live like this forever. The minister and Coles pitied them. Kilimanjaro came and called Rambo away. Babylon's manner turned conspiratorial. He bent forwards towards Zhero and spoke in Izon.

'Zhero, if this man's money is not paid he will be killed. As for you, Naija has said even if you agree to join us he cannot trust you. So he will kill you before we leave this place and go and operate in our State for some time . . . Naija is from your grandfather's village and he knows you. I think I should tell you the truth. Naija is your grandfather's sister's son. That is why he did not kill you that night, but now it is a matter of killing you or being killed when you tell the police and the police arrest us . . . Tell these people that in the night I will come and open their chains. You people should go this way, straight, do not turn left, do not turn right until you reach the motor road.' As he saw Rambo returning he addressed the minister rudely. 'You want to say all the money you don make from our oil money is not up to ten times ₦100 million?'

'Babylon, de boss say make you come.'

When Zhero told the minister about Babylon's plan and the kidnappers' resolve to kill them if the ransom failed, the minister's immediate reaction was to stand up, turn his back to Zhero and Coles and urinate. Zhero noticed that he had started to develop rashes on his buttocks. As he was about to sit down Coles pointed at his trousers. He thanked Coles and zipped, buttoned and belted the trousers which were dropping. Endlessly, absently he wiped his face. The more he wiped his face the wetter it was with sweat and silent sad tears from his thoughts about his wife and children . . . So Princess would be without a husband at her age . . . His children who loved him so much . . . Why did he procrastinate over making his will? Now it was too late. His brothers and his sisters would deprive Princess and her children of his wealth — he had sowed for his lazy relations to reap . . . .

'Joseph.'

'Sir.'

'Joseph, suppose you call your friend, let me tell them to let me speak with my friends who can bring the money immediately. They are businessmen, contractors, suppliers, consultants — they have a lot to gain by my being alive. And the president to tell the police not to attempt to rescue me. Joseph do you have pen and paper for me to list them?'

Zhero said no. Coles suggested that he should wait till the next day.

'Yes, sir.' Zhero agreed. 'Tomorrow, sir.'

'If you say so, Joseph, if you say so. You said you trust your friend? My life's in your hands, Joseph.' He listened to some night birds in the tree. 'Joseph, if we were birds would life not be sweeter?' Zhero laughed. 'Don't laugh, Joseph, don't laugh. See how free they are in the night — no fear. And when death is coming no long agony like this.'

Zhero pitied him. 'We shall not die, sir.'

'Thank you, my son.'

A mobile phone radio was on and the kidnappers were enjoying a Nigeria-Ghana match. When Nigeria scored the first goal they were wild with joy, but when Ghana equalized their sorrow affected the abductees too. Then Nigeria scored the winning goal, and the kidnappers loudly called for more brandy — they were proud of their country! A country to love in spite of the selfish and corrupt politicians and leaders! The minister felt guilty. Coles behaved as if he had not heard them. Zhero said to himself that if football could make even kidnappers love their country, footballers were doing a good job. He regretted his inability to play football well.

After the gang, except Rambo and Babylon, had caroused and slept, Babylon plied Rambo with marijuana and Rhemmy's brandy until he fell into a deeper sleep than the others. He quickly unchained the captives and told them to reach the motor road in not more than two hours, because he would pretend to wake up, discover their escape and raise an alarm. He called Zhero back.

'Zhero, you sure say you no go betray me? But even if you tell de police about me I no go fit vex with you. After wetin you don do for me, Zhero.'

'Trust me, Agbulo.'

'Dem been take all the money inside your pockets. Take this one. Na twenty thousand naira. Una fit use am for transport.'

'Thank you, Agbulo.'

'Bye bye.'

Zhero ran and caught up with the minister and Coles. The minister asked him why his friend called him 'Jayroh' — was that his nickname? Zhero did not answer him. In less than one hour the minister was tired. Several times Zhero and Coles had to support him until he could walk faster on his own. He regretted his potbelly out loud, calling it a symptom of poor health fools delighted in as a sign of wealth. Zhero advised him on the need for silence and he was grateful. They were just about fifteen minutes to the road when they heard voices in the distance. Coles told his boss and Joseph (Zhero) to go on. He would stay until they were near, and he would make a noise to attract them away from his boss and Joseph. After about five minutes Zhero and the minister heard several gunshots and Coles' wailing for a few seconds. Zhero stopped, contemplated the silence and shook his head. The minister drew him roughly — did he want all of them to die? After some minutes the sound of heavy footsteps on dry sticks, of someone brushing through plants, and of heavy breathing came nearer and nearer. The minister fell, and Zhero could not pull him up.

'Joseph . . . Joseph . . . .' the minister puffed.

'Sir, let's keep quiet.'

'Yes, yes,' the minister agreed but he was not in control of his heavy breathing.

'Joseph! Joseph!'

It was Coles but the minister told Zhero not to answer.

'Sir, it's Coles.'

'Suppose they are pursuing him.'

'Joseph! It is me, Joseph! Sir, it is me! Can you hear me?'

'Coles!' Zhero shouted in defiance of the minister. 'Coles. We are here.'

Coles came up to them, puffing for breath.

'I . . . I . . . I shouted as if . . . they shot me . . . I heard them saying . . . saying . . . saying they would spread . . . out and search the area . . . I think the police are also inside this forest. As if I heard the police saying 'Drop your weapons! Drop your weapons!' He stopped talking for a long time. 'Sir, let us go. I am hearing the sound of vehicles.'

They listened. Yes! The road couldn't be far away. The minister stood up smartly and walked under his own steam. In less than two minutes they burst out into the road, and the moonlight was a thing of joy to each of them as if they had missed it for years. They crossed over to the other side of the road and decided to follow the direction of the vehicle that had passed at the time they burst out into the road. They heard a vehicle coming from behind them. They turned and desperately waved to it to stop. After passing them it took the driver a few seconds to decide to take a risk. He braked to a gradual halt and started to reverse. The minister ran towards it without a word to his friends. His driver followed him, but Zhero went into the forest and stayed there till the car had left. He felt they had looked for him because it took about two minutes before the car drove off.

Zhero prayed: 'Oh God, this forest is very thick. The moon is not shinning through and I have no torchlight to see how the place is. If I sleep off please take care of me, oh God my Creator.'

Trusting absolutely in God he sat down, rested his back against a tree and slept off in less than ten minutes . . . He repeatedly dreamt that the kidnappers were pursuing him towards Lagos, and he was afraid, yet he must go to Lagos in spite of Agbulo pleading with him to stop running, otherwise Naija would shoot him . . . he stopped, swivelled around and bunched his fists — nobody was there . . . Every time he stopped to confront them nobody was there . . . Nobody was there . . . .

When he woke up, the forest was faintly bright. He went to the road and walked towards the direction the car had taken Coles and the minister. He stopped a man on a bicycle and asked him where he could get a vehicle to Lagos. A native of the area who was used to seeing escaped abductees, the man told him he was facing the direction of Port Harcourt; if he wanted to go to Lagos he had to go to the motor park which was about thirty minutes from where they were, but first he had to leave the present spot before the bad people came out. He gave him a lift and dropped him when he saw a motorcycle taxi driver he knew to be reliable. Zhero was speechless. The man told him he knew how he felt and waved the driver away.

The motor park was safe because there were a lot of armed policemen. After paying for a seat on the luxury bus he went to an eatery and ate a hot dish of *eba* and *okazi* soup. The night's experience and the heavy meal sent him into a deep sleep until the bus got to Lagos. He looked at the two business cards Rowland had given him, returned them into his pocket and picked one — the one he would align his destiny with.

As advised by Rowland he asked a young video hawker for direction to the name on the business card. The young man agreed to take him there on condition that he chartered a taxi to take them straight to his master. Zhero was glad to hear that the man he wanted to see was the young man's master. They introduced themselves to each other. It was difficult to get an empty taxi on the side of the busy road in which they were, so Dustan said they should cross the road to the other side. Dustan sharply drew him back.

'My friend, you want to kill yourself? All dese fast cars, how you wan run cross de road? Dis na Lagos o. Come make we take dat overhead. In my village you can take a mat and lie down in the middle of the road from morning to night. People will only gather and look at you — maybe your head is not correct.' They both laughed. 'That's the overhead we are going to.'

The busy overhead footbridge gave Zhero the feeling that in Lagos everybody worked for their food. The swollen stream of humans hurrying past in opposite directions, the pushing and shoving by one or two people who looked to be in a dire race against time, even on the bridge hawkers asking people if they needed a wristwatch, a handkerchief or a video, people bumping against one another and saying sorry or 'Are you blind?', 'Foolish man!' — Zhero liked Lagos, so different from Amabra . . . .

They got a taxi in about fifteen minutes and reached their destination in a little over an hour. Dustan's employer was not happy at the way Dustan barged into his office with a stranger 'who fit be an armed robber sef.' Zhero frowned at him.

'You, what do you want?' Zhero brought out the business card and stretched out his hand to the angry man who thought it was a referee's business card, but it was his own card. He angrily threw it at Zhero. 'I ask you wetin you want you dey give me my card.'

Zhero picked up the card and read out the name: Chief Hezekiah Jerome. The beautiful young woman sitting opposite him laughed then explained the cause of her laughter to the men who looked embarrassed.

'You asked him what he wanted and he said Hezekiah Jerome. So you're the thing he wants!'

Even Chief Hezekiah Jerome laughed.

'Young man, what can I do for you?'

'I want to sell videos, sir.'

'Who sent you to me?'

'Nobody, sir.'

'Who will guarantee you?'

'Nobody, sir.'

'That means on cash-and-carry basis.'

'No, sir. When I sell I give you the money, you pay me commission.'

Chief Jerome laughed again. 'Suppose you sell and run away with my money. Supposing na my enemy send you for come ruin me.'

His belly laugh made Zhero feel that he was standing before a good-natured man. And the two gold rings on the fingers of the left hand with which he had slapped the table while laughing told him that Chief Jerome would not be too concerned about money.

'Impossible, sir. My friend in Port Harcourt sells mobile phones for his master in Owerri and his master pays him commission. He's the one who gave me your card.'

'My friend, I think you are a thief. Get out of my office. And you, Dustan —'

Dustan ran out of the office but Zhero did not move, a footsore traveller at a crossroads in the wilderness. When the woman saw his tears she told him to sit on the couch. She rooted through her handbag, brought out a ₦50,000 bundle, gave it to him and told him to place it on Chief Jerome's table. Zhero did as she said, feeling that she wanted to make a fool of him as he saw her smiling — a woman as beautiful as his mother wanted to make fun of a homeless child in her doorway instead of giving him a gold coin. She continued to smile.

'Rosetta, what is the meaning of this nonsense?'

She ignored her husband. 'What's your name?'

'Zhero, ma.' Because she frowned he spelt it and pronounced it again. 'My name is Zhero, ma.'

'This ₦50,000 is Zhero's collateral. He can always take goods worth less than ₦50,000.'

Chief Jerome stood up and made to pocket the money, she snatched it from his hand, he yanked off her *aso oke* scarf, revealing her long hair whose black sheen Zhero noticed, and they all laughed. That was the day, seven months or so ago, Chief Hezekiah Jerome employed Zhero. He was for two weeks attached to Dustan who showed him the ropes in selling and survival in Lagos. Dustan also shared his room with Zhero until there was vacancy in the twenty-room building, which meant until someone was fired. In less than a month a young woman was fired for embezzlement and her room was allocated to Zhero.

Eating 1-0-1 (one meal in the morning — zero meal in the afternoon — and one meal at night), saving between one and two thousand naira every week in the micro-finance bank, often having enough change to attend a video viewing centre to watch English Premier League and UEFA Champions League matches, life had been rosy for him until the Nigerian Copyrights Commission, gingered by PMAN (Performing Musicians Association of Nigeria) under Charlie Boy's presidency and the Actor's Guild of Nigeria, started to raid the streets and Alaba International Market for pirated CDs and Nollywood videos. In addition the Lagos State Government had recently banned trading in the major streets of the city. But Zhero was not unhappy at all, though. What was most important to him was that he was paying his way in life, and now and then he was able to deposit the occasional one thousand naira in the bank. Also, if he liked he could keep the surplus to himself whenever he sold the videos at above the stipulated prices. But it was unlikely that Zhero would do that.

What he was considering at the moment was not whether or not to keep the surplus to himself but whether or not to switch over to the cash-and-carry basis which was more lucrative . . . He had enough money in the bank, but that meant leaving the free accommodation Chief Jerome had provided him . . . Should he or should he not? Wherever he would be able to afford would certainly not have good toilet and bathroom facilities like his present place . . . He postponed the decision and thought of how he could make good sales in Ajegunle today.

Instinctively he unzipped the bag on his lap and brought out a few videos one after the other admiring the titles and the actors' faces on the cases. The aisle seat and the window seat passengers between whom he was sandwiched were interested in the videos.

'Are they foreign films?' the aisle seat passenger asked.

'No. Nollywood. Only Nollywood,' Zhero proudly answered.

'Are they from Alaba?'

'No oh. I buy them from Happy Life Entertainment Store at No 2 Chief Hezekiah Jerome St, Idi Araba.'

'How much is this one?' the passenger asked.

'Four hundred naira.'

'Other people sell them at two hundred naira. Why is your own four hundred naira?'

The window seat passenger took the one with Patience Ozokwor's photograph on the case and paid for it.

'I know Happy Life at Idi Araba. They sell only genuine films.'

The aisle seat passenger asked him again if they were from Alaba. Zhero did not answer him. He rudely dropped the video on the bag.

Looking at the window seat passenger who was absorbed in Patience Ozokwor's photograph, Zhero discreetly sniffed the air. The rank odour around was from him. Probably he hadn't taken his bath for some days. He too could be smelling after walking and sweating in the sun. He bent his head towards his chest and sniffed himself. He was satisfied that he wasn't smelling. He was relieved when the man went down at the next bus stop.

In spite of the ban and the ceaseless action against the production and sale of pirated videos at Alaba International Market, Chief Jerome and several other people had continued the illegal business there. While Chief Jerome sold only genuine copies of Nollywood, Bollywood, Gollywood and Hollywood films at Happy Life Entertainment Store in Idi Araba, the mainstay of his wealth was the pirate business at Alaba International Market. And Zhero had chosen the most lucrative aspect of the business, the selling of pirate Nollywood videos.

The bus stopped. The bus conductor exuberantly announced, 'Ajegunle! People of the jungle, go down. Ajegunle!'

Outside, Zhero went to a corner and picked the most tantalizing videos he would hold in his hands. A woman came to him.

'Give me that Patience Ozokwor film. How much?'

'Six hundred naira, ma.'

'Wetin! You wan thief? No be four hundred you sell to dat man for inside bus? I no fit stand for this hot sun to price film. You go take or you no go take?' she asked, her voice torn between anger at the boy's dishonesty and an inexplicable liking for a fellow woman's child in a hard quest for his daily bread in the sun.

Zhero smiled, 'Ma, na market naa. You go price naa. By the way, ma, sun get vitamin wey good for a fine woman's skin.' She took the video and threw two two-hundred naira pieces at him. Bending down to pick the money he joked, 'Mama, you dey vex. But remember say you dey pray make your own children become rich people o.'

Laughing, the woman turned. 'I think you too will be a film writer someday. You will make people happy.'

'Amen. Thank you, ma.'

Still laughing the woman went away and Zhero made for a residential area. He preferred door-to-door to street hawking because it was less competitive, though once in a while he hawked in the streets risking brushes with State Government and Local Government Authority officials. In Lagos, unlike in some other states, these officials were wicked — they insisted on implementing the law to the letter instead of taking one or two thousand naira from an offender and warning them not to sin again . . . In truth, the sun was too hot, and he was sweating uncomfortably.

At the risk of being called by shop owners who would beat down his prices he chose to pass through a street he usually avoided. Music was blaring out from almost all the shops in the street. On both sides of the street the gutters were nearly full with waste water flowing or thrown out from houses and shops. Some people also threw solid refuse into the gutters. The stench was so thick that Zhero felt something solid was flowing into his nostrils. He walked fast and held his breath now and then, wondering if life in this place was better than life in Amabra. A girl with a basin emerged from a wooden shack in front of which was a small signboard saying FOOD IS READY and emptied the dish water into the gutter. Zhero ran to avoid being splashed. In spite of the girl's apology two men abused her and the mother she left at home and a woman slapped her hatefully, as if the slight splash of water on her deep green lace wrapper had deprived her of what she left home to look for today. The girl's tears mixed with the sweat on her face.

At Ibiyemi Street he went to a group of housewives sitting between a building and a stinking shallow gutter. A woman waved him away saying no one wanted to buy whatever he was selling.

He smiled. 'Na because una never see dese ones. See dis one.

People think say na only wicked mother-in-law Patience Ozokwor sabi act. Because dem never see dis one before. Any woman wey watch dis one go wan make her daughter marry Patience Ozokwor pikin.'

'Bring am make I see.'

He gave it to her. 'Ma, you sef you go learn how to be a good mother-in-law.'

'Dis boy, you dey craze!'

The housewives laughed and at last they brought four videos. A woman pointed to the ones containing Jackie Appiah and Dakore Egbuson's photographs. Before she could speak he told her they were films no one could attempt to describe.

'Seeing is believing. People wey dey watch Hollywood think say na only white women sabi fine. If dem see Dakore Egbuson and Jackie Appiah inside dese two film, dem go flog dem children anytime de children watch Hollywood film.'

The women laughed.

One of the women asked, 'But Jackie Appiah na Nigerian? She no be Ghanaian?'

'She dey act for Nollywood,' he answered her. 'If not you for know who be Jackie Appiah? White people sef dey come act for Nollywood now. I think you know.' A naked four-year old boy came out of the house. 'Hnh! Future King of Nollywood! The mama wey born you na blessed woman. No shirt, no pant, no shoe, na so one boy for one village be before, but today he is a president.'

The women laughed uncontrollably. A bench tilted backwards and the three women on it nearly fell off. They smartly jumped to their feet and continued to laugh, and they started to sweat even though they were in the shadow of the building and not in the sun. They were happy.

One woman remarked, 'Dis boy don make life sweet for us today. Dis one better pass the local government politics we been dey talk. Video seller, thank you.'

'Dis boy,' another woman said, 'de woman wey born you na lucky woman.'

'Thank you, ma. But to say true, ma, seeing is believing. What a white woman can do, a black woman can do better. Buy Dakore Egbuson and Jackie Appiah video. Watch Nollywood only.'

'As for,' the woman said. 'Na only Nigerian film me I dey watch o.'

She bought the two videos for a bargain, she thought, of one thousand one hundred naira instead of one thousand two hundred naira. They told him to come back at the end of the month, he thanked them, and went away. He stopped at a corner and brought out two videos which he felt would be suitable for young persons. Some metres in front of him a group of young men were playing table tennis in the next street which the youths of the neighbourhood had pedestrianized in defiance of the Local Government Authority and older residents until, they said, the government tarred the street. A car came up to him from behind and stopped. The right back window went down and a man called out.

'Young man, do you live here?'

'Good day, sir, no.'

'But do you know where the primary school is?'

Zhero gave the driver directions and waved to the man in the air-conditioned car who envied the happiness of the boy in the scorching sun.

'Bye, bye, sir,' Zhero said to the man whose silent gaze was disconcerting to him.

'What are you selling?'

'Nollywood videos, sir.'

'Let me see.' He looked at the titles and the photographs on the cases of the two videos. 'Nothing is said about the films.'

'They are good for young people, sir.'

'How much? The truth. Nothing but the truth.'

'Two hundred naira each, sir.'

'Are they genuine? Original?'

'No, sir. Original is one thousand five hundred naira each.'

'Why are you selling fake ones, pirated videos? Videos that won't last.'

'All fingers are not equal, sir.' The man laughed. 'But if you buy the fake the children can watch them, maybe, ten times, then you buy new videos again.'

'I won't buy anyone, but I love your honesty. Take. This is my card. If you ever need help . . . Take it.'

Zhero took the card, genuflecting slightly and said, 'Thank you, sir.'

Zhero stood where he was for a long time . . . He started to walk, thinking for the first time about what he had been doing . . . It wasn't an honest way of life, no, it wasn't . . . .

110

The man's voice sounded like Bazi's . . . Especially when he laughed . . . .

He stopped work early and went home. As he entered the compound he hoped Chief Jerome wasn't at home. He had to pass his bungalow to the workers' quarters. Mrs Rosetta Jerome, who was at the carport, only greeted him back and he went into his room at the workers' quarters. He felt like talking with someone. A little after 8pm he went to Zanzi, a girl he liked because her voice and her smiles reminded him of Daba. She sensed he wanted to tell her something — to say he loved her? — but she shared jokes with him until he fell too sad to laugh.

'Zhero, I know you are not happy. What is it? Tell me.'

He shared his experience of the day and asked her for her opinion about their way of life.

'Zhero, it is better than any other thing I can find now. And a place like this, roof over your head every day and every night, nothing as good as it oh. I no longer sleep in the rain, and I go into the sun only when I like. Zhero, fake videos or not, let us manage life with it.'

While they paused Zhero wondered how come, why a girl like Zanzi should be a street hawker. He decided to ask her.

She smiled mirthlessly. 'I will tell you. I use to be with my mom and I use to go to school. My mom use to be very good, but when she fall in love with one rich man she have no time for me again. All her attention was the man and the money he was spending on her. The man use to behave as if he love my mom very well, but anytime my mom is not at home he use to peep when I am bathing. From peeping he start to force himself on me. When I became tire I have to tell my mom. Instead of being sorry for me she was annoyed with me. She used to beat me with iron rod and say if I repeat it again or tell anyone she will kill me. I beg one of her friend who pity me and took me to her brother at Jos. The man and his wife were very good to me, and they say in the beginning of the next year they will send me to school. The man was like a father to me. I see how good it is to have a father. But when the religious riots in Jos happen and Christians were killing Muslims and Muslims were killing Christians the man and his wife were killed. That day I change my surname to the one am using now.' She shook her head and wept mutely for a moment. 'Plenty people were killed. Two boys and me, we hide in one house that the people burnt. At night we come out and look for

111

food. Some people came with a big lorry and gather boys and girls. They say they will take us to a place and take care of us. They took us to a place far away from Jos. Already there were plenty of boys and girls there before. Some of them, it was when flood finish their villages these people brought them there. Two brothers say is when the mountain at Benue State erupt and they loss their father and mother the people took them and brought them there. In which part of the country we were nobody know. Some people say Western Nigeria, some people say Eastern Nigeria . . . Hey, Zhero! Life is bad oh! I want freedom but now am going to be a slave. They were selling the boys and the girls, they were taking them to Gabon, Libya, Equatorial Guinea, Niger and other places. But me, I was lucky. One man say if I allow him to have sex with me he will help me to escape. I prefer freedom to slavery, so I allow him. After about two weeks he thank me and in the night he take me out and put me inside a bus. That is how I find myself in Lagos . . . Zhero, why are you crying? . . . Zhero, something that happen a long time ago! Please, Zhero, don't cry for me.'

Zanzi's roommate came in and was shocked to see Zhero crying. After a moment she joked about it.

'Zhero, she don break your heart? Zanzi, will you marry me? No, my darling, I do not love you.'

'Lovewari, shut up. Is because I tell him my story.'

Lovewari drew Zhero to the bed where she sat and he sat by her. She placed her right arm around his shoulders. In spite of his sorrow he noticed the sweetness of the perfume she was wearing.

'Zhero, for dis life everybody get im own story o. In fact every life na story. If you see me I dey laugh, is because every story na mixture of tears and laughter. One day you go tell us your own story, then I go tell you my own too. How my father marry another woman not even up to one month after my mother died. The suffer wey I suffer for the hand of my stepmother. Whatever she do to me my papa no go say anything. She say I be witch, na me kill my mama. The day she bring out three old nails from inside the pot of soup and say na me put dem inside, that very minute — I no take anything of mine — that very minute I run away from the house. One day I go tell you how I walk from de front gate of hell through de back gate to reach dis place . . . Zhero, don't cry for us. Don't cry for yourself.'

Lovewari sang, 'Don't cry for me, Argentina,' and the two girls sang Madonna's song of that title, substituting Nigeria for Argentina, tears flooding their cheeks, souls propelled by the undertow of love for life no matter what. At the end they laughed and hugged Zhero, then Zanzi told Lovewari about the business card the man gave him and they both warned him to steer clear of wealthy men and their evil ways of making money. Maybe the man wanted a human being for a Satanic ritual to make him wealthier. Lovewari added that when a rich man asked her for her address she told him 'Chief Hezekiah Jerome St, Idi Araba' before she realized her mistake. She then told him No 99.

'This street that is not up to No 50?'

'My sister, I no want rich people wahala at all.'

At bedtime that night Zhero thought about his mother's frequent saying: It's hard to be a woman . . . .

But about a month later he was happy for a woman. While he was hawking in Isale Street a girl among a group of female students standing by a bus that was being repaired stopped him and hugged him before he recognized her. She did not mind the presence of her teachers and her fellow students' ooh! ooh! ooh! They were both very happy. She took him aside. She was shocked — Zhero who everybody thought had gone with his rich father to the city to attend school, what happened? He told her it was a long story. She told him about Amin: Amin first bought a rickety 15-seater boat which the people of Mabo Waterside laughed at anytime it landed at the waterside, then a 25-seater Yamaha fiberglass boat three months later, and then another 25-seater — Amin had become a rich man. He rented a three-bedroom bungalow. Still she refused to marry him, because of his low level of education. Amin switched to her friend and they married. Though she didn't want him it pained her a little that it was her best friend he chose to marry. In any case she was happy for them. Zhero asked her who brought her to Lagos. She said her uncle who had been in the US for nearly twenty years returned to Nigeria and brought her to Lagos to go to secondary school. Laughing, she said sometimes when schoolwork was tough she wondered if she shouldn't have married Amin — she sometimes missed the freedom of the life at Mabo Waterside. Zhero told her she had made a better choice. She gave him her address and said he must come visit her.

'Zhero, you must, you must come visit me.'

He smiled and they parted. He was happy for Sarah, but he soon thought about his situation. Everybody in Amabra and Mabo

113

Waterside thought he'd gone with his father to the city to attend secondary school but he was only hawking in Lagos . . . Selling fake Nollywood videos . . . Lying to people . . . .

Two cripples, polio victims, sitting on the sidewalk called him. He went to them.

'Zhero, you no look happy, na wetin happen?'

'I never see Zhero like dis before o. Zhero, na wetin happen?' He smiled. 'Your smile sef sad.'

The two cripples shook their heads.

'Make I dey go. Una just call me?'

'No oh!' the two cripples chorused and the first speaker explained that the day had been unusually tough, not one single giver, maybe due to the time of the month, so not even breakfast yet. He gave them four hundred naira, saying it should see them through the day. His smile was brighter when they wondered that he could give in his present mood.

He walked on, forgetting that the goods he was carrying were for sale . . . .

In the night he told Dustan that he would resign from hawking tomorrow — he had made up his mind. Dustan said if he had made up his mind then there was nothing he could say, but even then, should he not get another job before resigning? Zhero said yes, he would get another job tomorrow.

'Dustan, don't look at me like that. I'm not mad.'

They laughed and said good night but for a long time the good night did not allow Zhero to sleep off. It crowded his mind with thoughts: Because of anger I ran away from home and my fellow Izon people wanted me to be an armed robber and a kidnapper. If not for Agbulo they would have killed me . . . Why did I not go with the minister? . . . He would have employed me, or maybe through him I should have met the woman. She would have taken me as her son . . . The police would have forced me to tell them about Ogoun, Agbulo and Naija . . . They would have taken me to Amabra and then to my mother . . . My mother . . . Because of anger I ran away from her. I didn't care how she would feel . . . All these months, how is she feeling now? . . . If they think I am dead, then by now she'll not be sad, she would have forgotten . . . No, my mother can never forget me, she cannot until she dies . . . Maybe I should go back to her . . . I shall go back to her if the man doesn't give me a job tomorrow . . . She lied to me that my father is dead whereas she

114

doesn't know who was responsible . . . But she always told me not to lie, and she would be very angry if I told a lie . . . Why did she lie?

Before 8am the following day he was outside the gate of Yago Enterprises at Bank Road. The gateman said visitors were not allowed into the premises before 10am, and so even though Zhero saw Chief Yago come in in his car a little after 8am, go out about thirty minutes later, and then return around 9am he could not meet him. Visitors were allowed in at 10am and Zhero waited for about an hour before it was his turn to see the CEO.

Zhero showed Chief Yago the business card he had given him long ago and introduced himself.

'Oh! The honest young man. What can I do for you?'

'To give me a job, sir.'

'Are you tired of selling videos?'

'I want another job, sir.'

'You want big money?'

'No, sir.'

Chief Yago laughed, thoroughly delighted. 'A man wants a job but he doesn't want big money!' Zhero looked serious. 'You were happy the day I saw you. While I was asking someone for direction you were laughing with the women. I envied you and the women, so happy the way you were laughing. Why do you want to leave a job that makes you and other people happy? Because of my business card you think there's big money here?' he asked, his amusement still on his face.

'No, sir. Not because of the money.'

'Then what?' he asked, expecting to be further amused.

'When you said I was honest I realized that what I had been doing wasn't honest. Selling fake videos isn't honest. I want a honest job, sir.'

'An honest job.'

'Yes, sir. An honest job.'

Chief Yago instantly phoned for the personnel manager.

'This boy is here to start work today. By the way, what's your qualification?'

'Primary Six, sir.'

Chief Yago stretched out his hand. 'Where's your certificate?'

'It's in the village, sir.' The personnel manager smiled. 'True, sir,' Zhero said to Chief Yago. 'I passed Primary Six, sir.'

'I believe you.'

'Where do you live?' the personnel manager asked him.

'If I start work here, I will pack out of the place I'm living now.'

'Where?' the personnel manager asked.

'The place my master gave me. No 1 Hezekiah Jerome Street, Idi Araba.'

'Your master?' the personnel manager smiled.

'Yes, sir. The man who gives us pirated videos to sell.' The personnel manager laughed. 'I'm not lying, sir.'

'Ariba, employ him. Send him to my office. He'll assist my secretary. I shall take him home. He'll stay in my compound.'

'All right, sir.'

Zhero went down on his knees to thank Chief Yago.

'Get up boy! You're not in your village now.'

Chief Yago and his personnel manager laughed. Zhero was employed and sent to the CEO's secretary, who sensed that he was hungry. She gave him money and directed him to the place most of the staff members went for their meals. He left jauntily in search of the restaurant. In taking the decision to resign from the selling of pirate videos he had been afraid of the future, but now he felt free and relieved, like the mornings after he had slain the monster in his dream. At close of office Chief Yago took him home.

'Teima,' he said to his wife in the living room, 'this is the young man I told you about.'

'Since you merely informed me, he's welcome.'

'Good evening, ma.'

'Welcome, sir.'

Zhero was embarrassed.

'Teima, Teima, I thought you said okay.' She turned her attention to the television. 'Come, Zhero.' He saw his son Joseph leaving the dining room. 'Hey, Joseph,' he said to him, 'who's to clear the table?'

'Naomi is in the kitchen, or will soon be in the kitchen. She'll clear the table, won't she?'

Chief Yago and Zhero were equally shocked as Joseph walked away. And Zhero thought, how he would value a man like Chief Yago as a father! He would love and respect anyone who was his father — anyone . . . .

Yago took him to the boys' quarters and told the housegirl to prepare one of the two vacant rooms for Zhero. After Yago left, the housegirl made Zhero and the driver laugh when she said she would not waste her precious time learning how to pronounce his name but anytime she addressed someone without mentioning his name he should know that he was the one she was talking about.

'So now,' she said to the sky, 'follow me to your room.'

They laughed again, and Zhero felt at home. She said her name was Naomi and the driver said he was Robin.

Naomi corrected him, 'Robin Hood.'

They laughed once more.

'Naomi, you dey look for trouble o.'

'No be you say you like Robin Hood because Robin Hood dey take care of poor people? You, you don watch Robin Hood film before?' Zhero said yes. 'And you like im way of life?'

'Naomi, leave de boy alone o. Make im eat, then we go go to Idi Araba and take im things.'

Zhero took possession of his room, ate *eba* with *egusi* soup in the dining room of the boys' quarters, and Robin drove him to Idi Araba. He avoided Chief Hezekiah Jerome especially because of his pregnant wife Rosetta who liked him so much and often joked that the day she would go into labour Zhero had to be by her so that her son would be like him and not like Hezekiah. He gave Dustan the unsold videos and said he would go to the office and resign the following day. Saying bye bye to Zanzi and Lovewari was painful and bitter, but they encouraged themselves to accept life for what it was and they parted tearfully. However, at No 13 Alabi Atere Street, Surulere, Naomi, Robin, his light and spacious room whose sliding glass window admitted the moonlight, the ice water dispenser in the boys' quarters common dining room from which he took a glass of water to cool down immediately he came back, and the spacious compound within four great concrete block walls soon made him happy and in the office too the following day he was very happy but when he and Yago returned home together and he happily carried Yago's briefcase into the house and left it on a coffee table in the living room, he was reminded that happiness should not be taken for granted. Teima told her son to tell him not to leave the briefcase there.

'Hey Mister follow him with the briefcase!'

Yago heard his son. He was furious.

'Joseph, are you mad!'

Joseph mumbled a rude remark and walked out of the house, leaving his father to think of why he liked Zhero the day he saw him at Ajegunle — a hawker in the sun, so happy, so respectful, so honest

. . . .

Zhero did not look at his face but he imagined it and pitied him. About a month later it was only his voice he heard and he pitied him again, to the point of nearly shedding a tear. Only Yago, Teima and he were at home that Saturday evening and he was to take the clothes the dry cleaner had delivered to him to her. They were in their private living room. He stopped at the door when he heard her usually abusive voice, a sweet feminine voice put to wrong use.

'Your only marital duty is to snore at night. Continue snoring because the great noise makes you a macho man.'

Yago had replied, 'When I work very hard during the day, at night I'm too tired. It's natural. The human body —'

Teima clapped his explanation: 'I love my Biology teacher. He's very intelligent!'

A long pause, then Yago replied in a tearful voice, 'A man makes money, for the sake of his family. A man makes money so that his woman can be proud of him . . . All he receives as reward is insults.'

She might have looked at him contemptuously. 'Louis, why can't you look at me? Louis, when did any scripture say "Money maketh a man"? Manner maketh a man, Louis. Snoring in bed when your woman is sitting up, looking at you, waiting for you is bad manners, my man Louis.'

He knocked and opened the door, stammered out something about her clothes, put the clothes in her room, left the silent couple and went to his room and wondered that in such a wealthy house there was no happiness. Before they went to bed in the night Teima came to the boys' quarters and shouted for Naomi to come out. Involuntarily Zhero rushed out too and he saw madam pounding away at the silent housegirl.

'You foolish girl, you foolish housegirl, you bought me rotten fish, you wasted my money on rotten fish.' She looked at Zhero. 'Wait for me, I've not finished with you,' she said to Naomi and went to Zhero. 'Who called you? You want to fight for her?' she slapped him and pushed him back into his room. 'Where's the foolish girl? Naomi, will you open your door before I break it?' She banged on the door. 'Naomi! Naomi!' It seemed her fist pained her. 'Okay, you can remain there. But make sure you never come out of that room, forever. Witch, you want to poison me with rotten fish.'

When Robin was sure Madam would not come back that night he came out of his room to console Naomi and to advise Zhero

118

never to watch Madam in rage, because she could order Sir to sack him.

The next day he told Zhero more about Madam as he drove Zhero to Yago Textiles and Yago Plastics at Itire to deliver circulars. Nothing illustrated Madam's power as what happened about four years ago when she inspected Sir's petrol stations in Rivers State, Bayelsa State and Abuja. Everywhere she went she found fault with the workers, insulted many and slapped some of them. As she arrived at the petrol station in Port Harcourt — she saw a former classmate of hers nearly at the tail end of a very long queue. She and her friend walked into the petrol station and she ordered one of the petrol attendants to look for a 50-litre jerrycan and go and fill her friend's car with fuel. The girl told her that was impossible because there was no jerrycan nearby and she could not stop attending to the people already inside the station. She shouted at the station manager to sack the girl but he said he could not do that until he had issued her a written query and seen her explanation. When the customers at the station booed her she went away quietly. The next day Sir himself flew into Port Harcourt and sacked the girl and the station manager for publicly disgracing Madam. Since after that incident she had not visited the petrol stations. After a pause Robin added that Madam was not a totally bad woman. 'If she like somebody she like dat person to nonsense, no matter wetin dat person will do.' But the problem was that Madam hated any worker Sir liked too much. He laughed, and then continued. 'Naomi say de day Madam employ am Madam pull her two ears in Sir's presence and warn her to keep away from Sir, because Sir na de only thing she get for dis world and she no dey take am joke at all. De day she suspect her with Sir, dat day hell no go open door for am.' Zhero silently resolved to keep away from both of them as much as he could, although in the office he could be close to Chief Yago.

But about four months later he had to ask Chief Yago for permission to attend evening school. He had added from tips in the office and from his salary enough to his savings at the micro-finance bank in Idi Araba but the problem was that after the office, Madam used him as a houseboy at home. He needed Chief Yago's permission to go to school. Chief Yago said he needed some time to think about it. Madam knocked on his door around 9pm.

'Zhero, you want to go to school —'

'Yes, ma,' he eagerly answered.

'Will you shut up and listen to me! You want to go to school. Who will do the housework? Only Naomi? In this big house and compound? If you talk about school to Louis again, God bless you.'

She walked away.

Since Zhero came to the household he had voluntarily woken up at 5am to sweep the compound before Naomi, Robin and even the night watchman woke up in the morning, but the following morning, as he entered the car, she queried him.

'Zhero, why didn't you wake up early today? Because you rushed to sweep the compound it isn't clean. Next time you do that, God bless you.'

Zhero stammered out an apology and the car drove off.

'Zhero, you sweep the compound? Since when?'

'Since he came, sir,' Robin answered. 'Every morning, five o'clock he has woken up. Me, am still snoring on my bed.'

Chief Yago thanked Zhero and thought about his own son, Joseph . . . He toyed with the idea of going with Zhero to his village, If Zhero's mother is marriageable, divorce Teima, provide for her and her son somewhere, marry Zhero's mother and live happily with Zhero as a son . . . From the boy's character, the mother must be a good woman. The way he genuflects whenever he greets or gives him and Teima something shows very good upbringing. Just like a former girlfriend. In the beginning of their affair she always genuflected like Zhero, until he stopped her from giving him excessive respect. Some religions say marriage is karmic — mine is bad karma . . . .

Last night when they were watching an honours award ceremony she called him Money Miss Road because at his age he had never been given any honour. When he told her he was content with his low profile she called him a selfish man who did not want her to enjoy the glory other women enjoyed when they stood by their husbands while they were publicly honoured. Then as usual she referred to his snoring at night . . . He wondered why she dressed up so early this morning. One after the other, her friends had stopped visiting her and she scarcely went out these days, so where did she want to go to?

Immediately after he left the compound she went to the pastor of the church the family often attended. She had some weeks ago told him about her husband's affection for Zhero, as if Zhero was his son. She had given the pastor many reasons why she suspected that

Zhero was her husband's son and he had advised her to do a secret DNA test. She had come this morning to tell him that the test had confirmed her fear. Pastor Ododo had just finished praying for her and was now counseling her.

'Sister Teima, when you came in here this morning what was the question I asked you?'

'Pastor, I can't remember.'

'I said, have you confirmed it? That's because after you left the other time I prayed and prayed and it was revealed to me that the boy is his son. But what I can't understand is that . . . what wasn't revealed to me is how he doesn't know that the boy is his son. He truly doesn't know . . . Could it be that the boy's mother sent him to his father for a purpose? I suspect she's a woman he had an affair with sometime ago.'

'Is that possible, Pastor?'

'I think it is the case.'

'What do you advise I do?'

'For now don't confront him yet. He might do a paternity test and confirm it himself and accept his son. If you can't be patient till Spirit reveals to me how to handle the problem then find an opportunity to discuss it peacefully with him. Whatever you do, do not attempt to harm the boy. My name means justice. "Ododo" means justice. You must know that by now even though you are not Yoruba. Ododo is my spiritual name. God's justice never fails . . . Harmony, harmony, harmony — these are the first three things a family needs.' There was a long silence. 'Sister Teima, let us pray for patience, love and wisdom.'

She did not take his outstretched hands across the table. She stood up.

'Another time, Pastor Ododo.'

She went back home thinking, Don't harm the boy . . . Don't harm the boy . . . But how about the man?

Naomi came to tell her that breakfast was ready. Without a word to the girl she went to the dining table and started to eat . . . She stopped chewing as she thought: To obey or not to obey Pastor Ododo? . . . As students they were both members of a feared Satanic cult in the university . . . For a thrill they occasionally robbed night travellers on the highway until the night the police killed two members of their seven-person gang and arrested her. While the police were raping her in the savanna the other members of the gang returned, killed some policemen and rescued her. At a religious crusade on the football field some days later a lot of cultists in the university including the members of her gang took part in a mass renunciation of cultism by Christian students. Years after graduation she met him in the church. No longer Louis Araba, but Pastor Ododo. She did not take him seriously until his works of wonder and prophecies convinced her that he was a true man of God . . . .

She swallowed the chewed morsel of toast and spoke out loud, 'Don't harm the boy . . . Don't harm the boy . . . But he didn't say don't harm the man . . . Louis must not know that Zhero is his son.'

While she visualized Zhero and feared some of his unearthly actions he was in an eatery which he had never gone to before even though it was nearer the office than the one he had always gone to.

Zanzi was no longer a hawker of videos. She was a server in the eatery. A number of customers were leaving when Zhero came in. Now he was alone with her.

'So you've left Chief Jerome too?'

'Yes. Jerome tried to rape me in his office. He said because his wife is pregnant he is starving. When I refuse he sack me. And he said if I tell anybody, that day is my last day in this world.'

Zhero shook his head. 'Where do you live?'

'I sleep here. I wake up early in the morning and I bathe at the backyard. Zhero, so you work in Yago Enterprises. Am very glad for you, Zhero.'

Her employer walked in, carrying a big dark frown on her face. Zanzi jumped to her feet.

'Zhero, this is my madam.'

'Good afternoon, ma,' Zhero greeted her.

The way her madam ignored Zhero meant there was trouble for her. Zanzi's heart and stomach lurched.

'Zanzi, you allowed three boys to sleep in this place last night. Why?'

'Is . . . is because . . . of the rain, ma. And thunder and lightning. And they have no place to stay as rain was blowing, where they stand opposite this building, as if they are trying to push the wall with their backs. As human beings —'

Her madam roughly drew her out. The sun was beating down but she made Zanzi look at the sky for some seconds.

'The day you harbour riff-raff in my house again, from that day you will sleep under the sky.'

122

Zanzi went down on her knees and thanked her madam while Zhero apologized on her behalf.

'Thank you, Customer.'

Zanzi did not stand up until her madam had gone out, slowly because her dignity was very heavy.

'Hey, life!'

'Don't worry, Zanzi. It will be good. But, Zanzi, you have lost weight. Is it the work?'

Zanzi looked at her image in the mirror on the wall and shook her head, then she said with resignation: 'Because my madam give me only one meal a day. She say if I cannot use what I have to get what I need then let me starve to death. Not many customer give tip for free. Many customer, they want me to sleep with them. Some of them, even in presence of my madam, they are inviting me to come and spend night with them.' She shook her head at the pitiable image in the mirror. 'Zanzi.'

Zhero comforted her and gave her all the money he had on him. She reminded him that he had not eaten. He said, 'Next time,' and went out, slowly because his sorrow for Zanzi was very heavy . . . .

Because Teima was too busy with the competing ideas in her mind she did not pay attention to anyone or anything in the house until Saturday when Numu, her husband's nephew, visited them. Naomi came into their private living room and announced Numu's presence in the general living room. Even before Naomi had left the room she burst out in anger.

'People won't stay in their houses and stop disturbing other people.'

Yago was surprised. 'It's Numu. She said it's Numu.'

'Therefore?'

'I say it's Numu.'

'Numu, the dissolute.' Yago looked shocked. 'That's what I call him to his face, if you don't know.'

'Why?'

'He says he's a writer, but what good can his writings do to humanity? A man who doesn't practise what he preaches in his novels.' She laughed. 'Since I sacked the housegirl I caught him with he hasn't been here before today. Maybe he has come for Naomi.' She laughed again. 'He says he writes from experience, if he hasn't committed a few evils how would he understand the nature of evil? "The underlying theme in all my novels is evil, human evil." Louis you have some nephew!'

Yago decided not to be annoyed. He spoke calmly.

'There are musicians whose lifestyle isn't praiseworthy, yet their music makes millions happy, raises the consciousness of people against political and social ills —'

'You see why I always say your university education was incomplete because you didn't study Logic 101?'

Yago laughed. 'Teima, leave me alone.'

He fell back on the couch while getting up.

'Is your potbelly now too heavy for you to lift up?' She laughed loudly. 'Lack of exercise! Go to a gym, you won't! If you fall down and die your people will say I've killed their beloved son — as if there is anything left in you!'

He was suddenly very bitter, but he decided to ignore her, and he went out without a word . . . Why would a woman despise her husband so?

'Good morning, Uncle.'

He managed to cheer up, and asked with a lukewarm smile, 'I guess you've come to tell me the happy news.'

'Happy news?'

'I saw your name in the papers last week. Your novel is on the shortlist of —'

'Uncle, those people . . . I don't know what to say about them,' he said bitterly. 'This is the third time a novel of mine has been shortlisted.'

'To look at this thing calmly, Numu, does it take anything away from what you've written? If it's for the money, didn't you say service to life should not be for money?'

'Not the money. Not up to what a Manchester United player earns in one day. There's something good in being recognized as a great writer.'

Yago laughed, 'Just that feeling?'

'A human feeling,' Numu replied, 'a pure feeling.'

'Your friend, U Shettima, does he feel so strongly about literary prizes too?'

'He's never entered for any prize.'

'Why?'

'He says he writes to serve life and not to collect awards.'

Teima came in.

'Madam, good morning.'

She ignored his greeting. 'I eavesdropped before I came in.' Yago frowned. Numu laughed. 'A writer, you must be thinking you're doing a wonderful job for society, and yet no appreciation from society. Go to Broad Street when you leave here. Ask a hundred people, Who's Asa? Who's P Square? Who's Onyeka Owenu? Ninety-seven percent of them would burst out in joy and sing their songs — their answer to your question. Ask five hundred people, Who's Numu? Five hundred and ten of them would think it's a mispronunciation of *nama* — animal — and they would ask you, Don't you know what is *nama*?'

Yago was shocked. Numu laughed — he'd never written anything like this before, the deadpan humour!

'Actually,' he said, when he managed to stop laughing, 'It's Zhero I've come for. I was here last Saturday, you were not at home. I promised to come for him today. That day I heard Odedekoko singing, yet there was no tree around. No trees in Alabi Atere Street, or anywhere in this part of Surulere. I looked around for a cage. No cage but there was Odedekoko singing — Zhero.'

'I guess you want to make him a writer,' Teima sneered.

'Why not?' he asked, loving the sneer on her face and in her tone.

'A writer like you — love thy neighbour as thyself.'

'Teima,' Yago said, 'leave the boy alone. Have you seen him?' he asked Numu.

'He's ready.'

'Just make sure you personally bring him back.'

'I will.'

On the way to the university he promised Zhero he would soon persuade his aunt-in-law to allow him to attend evening school since his uncle was too afraid of his wife. He told Zhero not to be afraid of his wife if or when he married. Some seconds after he thought he should not have said that to the boy he continued.

'I know she treats you cruelly — I mean she doesn't treat you softly, and life may seem to be hard for you. Patience. Turn your suffering into success in life. That's what some writers call noble suffering. Take education seriously. Read. Read. Read. Anything you lay your hands on. If there's something in it, think about it. If it's something bad, reject it . . . . Zhero, do you dream?'

'Yes. Every night when I sleep.'

'I mean, do you think about what you want to become in life?

The good things, the great things you want to do in life?'

'Yes. I want to go to secondary school and university.'

'That's a noble dream. You must live with a sense of quest for education.'

He did not consider if the boy understood everything he was saying. He talked until they reached the university and then went into his office. Zhero liked the university atmosphere. Even on Saturday teachers were in their offices. Several students came into Numu's office and submitted their homework. When a willowy black-skinned girl came in Numu called her name affectionately before complaining. He said he collected the homework in class four days ago but a lot of students were still submitting theirs. Perhaps he should stop giving homework and make it a class test. Aliya was saucy, sweetly to Numu, but shockingly to Zhero — a student talking to her teacher that way! A male student came in, apologized, and went back. Only Aliya knew why he had come in: he was interested in her and had warned her to keep away from Numu, otherwise he would deal with him. A boy she regarded as an emotional coolant, but he was beginning to grow a proprietorial air. A boy with a funny name — Joe Nounoun. Aliya angrily told Numu she wasn't happy with what he was doing to her — every time she came to Numu's office Numu wasn't fully free, and yet as a student whose dissertation was on his novels she should be given enough time to discuss with him. Numu suggested 7pm in his house. Aliya thanked him and went out, banging the door behind her. Numu laughed.

Zhero silently vowed to have a university education.

Numu gave him one of his novels and told him to open it and read aloud from any page. He did and Numu explained what he meant by the myth of hell — how the church invented hell to make humans moral.

U Shettima, Numu's fellow lecturer came in to congratulate him on making the shortlist. When he saw that Numu was not as happy as he expected he told him to listen to what Helen Keller said. He repeated the name — and slowly quoted her: 'The world is moved not only by the mighty shoves of the heroes, but also by the aggregate of the tiny pushes of each honest worker.' Zhero heard every word distinctly but did not understand the meaning of what he had said. Nor did he understand the question the man asked Numu: 'How many award winners do we have in this country, or even in the whole world? Are their books enough for the world?'

Another lecturer came in.

'U Shettima, I've been to your office.'

'Where's it?' U Shettima asked him.

'What?'

'The collection of poems you promised me. I told you I want to use them. Especially your own poem, weird as it is.' The poem he called weird was about Abang's experience. While he was escaping from a group of kidnappers, a car appeared from nowhere and the driver told him to hop in. He did, feeling no fear, only savouring the sense of love from the man to him and from him to the man until the car stopped in front of his bungalow in the university. As his wife and his daughter joyously opened the door of the car he did not thank the man before going out. When he tore himself off from the family embrace in order to say thank you . . . Where was the kind stranger? Where was the car? And how did the stranger know that Abang lived in the university? The gatekeeper swore that he had not opened the gate that night to let in or let out any car. "Oga, na when you come inside?" he asked Abang. U Shettima smiled. 'I say when are you giving me the collection of poems?'

'Unfailingly this evening. I'll take it to your house. Numu, when are we going there?'

Numu turned to Zhero. 'Zhero, I promised my uncle I would personally take you back to the house. I forgot I had an appointment. With this man who takes appointments seriously. We call him The Big Bang. He's a poet. Do you know what, who a poet is?' They laughed. 'That's for another time. But now, can you go home on your own? When you get home tell Uncle I dropped you at the gate and went back.'

'No, don't teach the boy to lie,' Abang seriously said to Numu.

They laughed, and U Shettima asked for the spelling of Zhero's name. He spelt it and they learnt how to pronounce it.

'My name is Umoren Abang. They call me The Big Bang, though I'm an absolute and simple believer in God. This is U Shettima. U without full stop. U is the full name. You know your uncle's name. We are teachers and writers. What do you want to be?'

Zhero said he wanted to go to secondary school, university, and then become a teacher. 'It's a good ambition. In fact you're already a teacher — you teach people to say your name.'

His colleagues laughed and he told Zhero to use the Law of Self-determination to actualize his ambition. He wrote the phrase on a piece of paper and gave it to the boy who felt awed by the gift he did not understand.

'Fix your mind on what you want to be in life. Every day in a quiet place, for some minutes, see yourself as the person you want to be, and one day you will be that person — if you work hard and honestly for it. It's like what Achebe says the Igbo believe in: "If a man says yes, his chi will say yes." Have you read *Things Fall Apart*? No. You will someday.'

'The Big Bang!' Numu exclaimed.

Abang smiled, then said to Zhero, 'The most important advice I give anyone is this: "Honesty is a hard quest." Your uncle will explain it to you.'

Numu smiled, 'Thank you, Abang.'

'Thank you, Numu. We'll cancel our appointment so that you can take the boy home.'

Numu and U Shettima laughed.

'The Big Bang!' U Shettima exclaimed.

'Honesty is a hard quest!' Numu added.

'Instead of "honesty is a hard quest" I would give him these simple lines in your poem titled "The Porter" — "Life is a load/Our attitude makes it heavy or light to carry".'

'Note that too,' Abang said to Zhero. 'Our paths will cross again, even if not physically.'

U Shettima and Abang left and Numu took Zhero back home. He dropped him at the gate with a message to his aunt-in-law that he would come and see her the following day around 4pm.

When he came she was the only one at home, Yago having gone to the beach with Zhero, Naomi and the driver. She admitted him into her bedroom because she was, she said, busy arranging things there. Remembering that she was almost naked she took the red panties on the bed and slipped them on under the primrose skirt she was wearing.

After about two hours they went to the living room where she personally served him for the first time. She opened the bottle of Guinness Stout, filled his glass, took a sip and gave him the glass.

'Don't look at me like that. If your uncle dies can't you marry me? Aren't you African?'

'But you never liked me.'

'I still don't. Only your boyhood . . . Your evil part.' She laughed. 'Don't feel guilty. You've done worse things with your students. I

128

speak from experience — I was once a student of Literature. You are not the only writer who's not true to his calling. Art for art's sake!' she laughed again.

'My sins are scarlet, but my works are read.'

She laughed. 'Anything in life can be defended. Like the principle of double effect someone was defending in a newspaper today.'

'My friend Abang calls it bunkum, but the truth is, sex unlocks my creative reservoir,' he replied half soberly.

She did not laugh at him. 'Then you've found the perfect key today.'

He continued: 'It does for a lot of creative workers. For some writers, musicians, singers, composers, painters, sculptors, dancers, it is alcohol or drugs that release the creative energy. Abang says it's the way of self-destruction. Then, I say to him, we're male seahorses which die after giving birth. We give of ourselves, and then we die.'

'I said you've found the perfect key this day.'

He changed the subject, as if what he had just said was a silly thing he should not have said. 'As I said before, Zhero wants to attend evening school.'

'Numu, don't spoil the good thing we've just started with that matter now.'

'I'm sorry . . . I think I should go before my uncle comes back.'

'Why?'

'Your scent on my body is too loud, and it is a rare one, capable of provoking a jealous spouse to murder.'

She laughed. He complimented her on the shape and absolute whiteness of her teeth, and she laughed again, kissed him and thanked him for loving what she had offered him.

But he regretted what had happened between them when his phone rang at midnight and he saw Mrs Teima Yago on the screen — suppose his uncle heard her talking with him at that hour. He did not answer her. She called again ten minutes later. He fearfully answered her. She said she was in her own room, on the bed she had dedicated to both of them. In any case his uncle was snoring in his room. Did he want to hear the sound? He called her Teima and begged her not to call him anymore. She said because he called her Teima she would sleep peacefully, and she wished him a peaceful night.

For many days his mind was not at peace, he hated women, and many of his female students wondered at his new, unfriendly attitude towards them. Without taking Teima into account he vowed never more to have an affair with another man's wife.

On Saturday she texted him in capital letters to say she would call him in five minutes' time and warned him to answer her call. He did.

'Numu, when I have an affair with a man I memorize every part of his body. For evidence. For example the vitiligo on your buttocks.' He was speechless. 'Tomorrow. 4pm.'

'Ah, this woman is bad karma . . . This woman is bad karma for me.'

He wished a cataclysm would happen in Lagos before 4pm tomorrow . . . .

On Friday after Zhero had taken Yago's briefcase to his private living room following their return from the office he heard Teima telling Joseph in her bedroom to go out of the compound immediately and visit his friends.

'But, Mom, I've just come from outside.'

'I say go out now! And if your dad tells you to eat with him say no. He'll soon be here. Go out.'

Zhero rushed out and ran out of the house. He feared something was about to happen. Why would she warn Joseph not to eat with his father? . . . Even if it meant her sacking him . . . After he calmed his heart he went to the dining room. Yago was alone there and washing his hands preparatory to eating.

'Zhero, you want to see me?'

'Yes, Dad, don't eat this food.'

The order shocked him . . . The word 'dad' surprised him . . . He stood up.

'If you say so, Zhero.'

'Dad, let's give this food to the dog.'

'If you say so, Zhero.' He was trembling. 'If you say so.'

They took the dish of soup outside and gave it to Star, Yago's beloved dog. In less than five minutes after devouring the beef and lapping up the soup, Star writhed in agony.

Yago wept, averting his face from Star's accusing eyes. Teima repeatedly asked Naomi to explain what she put in the soup while the girl repeatedly protested her innocence.

'You will go inside the kitchen and eat the soup you cooked.'

Yago shouted at her. 'Nobody touches that soup!'

She stopped talking and decided to shed tears. Zhero went down

130

on his left knee and started to soothe Star by compassionately stroking its body. Star gradually stopped writhing and only whimpered in response to Zhero's love, more and more softly until it left the body.

Teima pressed Zhero for how he knew that the soup was poisoned. Zhero repeatedly said he did not know why he told Sir not to eat it. (And Naomi, if she tasted the soup after cooking it why didn't it kill her?) Naomi appealed to Ma not to accuse her of wanting to kill Sir, because she was innocent. To prove her innocence Naomi went into the kitchen, brought the pot of soup outside and ate from it.

'If there is poison inside this soup let it kill me now now.'

Everybody waited with bated breath . . . Nothing happened to Naomi.

Teima suggested bringing in the police because only the police could make Zhero and Naomi confess. Yago warned her firmly, and for the last time, not to accuse anybody anymore. And no police — no scandal for people to feast on. She angrily went to her bedroom, fearfully wondered for a long time if the boy was a wizard, and then phoned Numu, she wanted to tell him what had happened. She ended the call because Numu did not speak.

He was trembling in his kitchen. He went to the bedroom and flopped onto the bed . . . If your uncle dies can't you marry me?

'Hey! Evil has walked on two feet into my life. Hey, Numu! See where your writer's cavalier path had led you!'

The writer wept in pity for himself before he phoned his uncle, who told him not to bother to come over.

Yago called Zhero into his bedroom, locked the door and appealed to him to say why he suspected that the soup had been poisoned. Zhero only said something inside him told him the food could kill.

'Okay, you can go . . . No, don't open the door yet . . . okay, okay, you can go.'

He decided not to ask him why he had called him 'dad', which he had never done before . . . Could it be only the served soup was poisoned? By whom? Teima, Naomi, Zhero — which of them would want to kill him, and why? . . . Teima despised his irregular virility but she'd never shown any sign of wanting to leave him . . . Was Naomi a witch? . . . She had to stop preparing food for the family ... Better still, sack her . . . Zhero came together with him from the office — when could he have put poison in the soup? . . . Naomi had to leave . . . Witchcraft had no motive other than itself . . . .

Throughout the night Zhero slept in fits and starts. Awake, he wondered why a woman would want to kill her husband, the father of her only son. To take all his houses and money? Asleep, he saw someone dying, no, it was Star . . . He scrambled out of the nightmare when he saw himself dying. He sat on a chair . . . .

Didn't he hear her correctly? He did, he did, she told Joseph not to eat with his father . . . Could she want to kill him too? . . . He would behave normally towards her so that she would feel he didn't suspect her . . . He tested the lock of the door and went to sleep once more.

The next day, after Yago had gone to the clinic for a checkup, Teima sent Zhero to give Numu an unenveloped note which required him to come over and comfort his uncle whose health had been affected by what had happened, explaining that she had to write because his mobile had been switched off since last night. Immediately Zhero left she called Naomi out of the kitchen.

'Naomi.'

'Ma.'

'How much is your salary per month?'

'Fifteen thousand naira, ma.'

'Fifteen thousand times twelve, that is for one year, is one hundred and eighty thousand naira. Inside this envelope . . . There is three hundred thousand naira inside this envelope. Go and pack your things before the police come for you and Zhero today. I believe you are innocent. Leave Lagos and go to your State. Don't tell anybody you are leaving. Don't give anybody your address. When you reach your state change your phone number.'

Naomi went down on her knees, clasped her madam's legs and thanked her and prayed for her.

'God will bless you, God will bless you. Ma, thank you. So, Sir can think that I want to kill him? A man that I love like my own father all these years.' She started to weep. 'Ma, God will bless you and all your generation to come.'

'I'm going out now, so that I can say I didn't know that you went out. Stop crying, Naomi.'

'God will bless you, ma.' She wiped her face with the kitchen napkin in her hand. 'Ma, God will bless you.'

When Robin discovered that Naomi had run away the household searched no further for who wanted to kill Yago. Naomi's guilty conscience had driven her away. Yago relaxed, but Teima feared and avoided Zhero until the next Saturday.

On Wednesday Zhero had seen Vinko, a boy in the neighbourhood he had been helping with money now and then. Vinko was in a horrible state. His aunt who had accused him of stealing meat from the soup pot had made him rub his right hand with raw pepper and place it closely above a hotplate. When her husband came home and said he was the one who took two out of the four pieces of meat she told him to shut up and she continued to punish Vinko. Zhero gave him money and persuaded him to go to the police. The police took him to Lagos University Teaching Hospital for treatment and arrested the aunt for child abuse, then on Thursday brought his mother from the village to stay with him in the hospital till he was discharged. On Saturday after quarrelling with her younger sister for brutalizing her son Vinko's mother came to No 13 Alabi Atere St to thank Zhero. It was Teima who opened the gate for her and called for Zhero. After thanking Zhero, Vinko's mother explained to Teima that it was for education she sent her son to her younger sister but because of overwork in the house the boy constantly fell ill and missed school. The good mother, Teima, commiserated with a fellow mother but immediately Vinko's mother went out of the gate Teima pounced on Zhero.

'You bastard! You bastard!' she shouted ceaselessly as she slapped him on his cheeks, his head and his shoulders, exasperated by his total silence and unflappable appearance . . . her hands rested on the shoulders of the immobile boy for a moment — she had had an orgasm. She abruptly left him.

At bedtime she wondered at what had happened to her, while in his room he wondered if he had done the right thing in telling Vinko to go to the police instead of enduring his lot and going to school ... What would become of him in the village he was returning to?

When he remembered Numu's advice to him to bear suffering patiently and turn it into success he blamed himself for what he had done . . . His mind went back to Teima's moment of rage . . . a very beautiful woman wearing a smart orange trouser suit and a very sweet-smelling perfume . . . yet there was so much wickedness in her . . . It pained him that she wasn't a happy woman . . . .

She thought about the ineffectiveness of her blows on Zhero, and she thought back to Mamba's initiation in the Siama Valley. He thought he was tough because he had been the leader of a secret cult when he was in the secondary school. During the test of strength,

133

just one blow from her on his tummy, he fell face down into the shallow stream, dead, everybody thought. In those days there was power in her fists, not now — soft living had weakened her hands. Otherwise 'na who born Zhero?' . . . Her mind also went to Eternal who killed people with impunity, protected by his juju charm — he couldn't be shot, butchered or beaten to death. One day her gang bundled him into the boot of a car, took him to a grave they had dug in the depths of the savannah and buried him alive. A month after, they sent a note to his parents directing them to where to recover the rotten corpse . . . She shivered at her past . . . If Pastor Ododo could work wonders in the name of God, then forgiveness was real . . . .

On Monday morning when Zhero was sweeping the compound around 5am Teima looked through her window . . . She admitted to herself that he was a good boy, a boy who, in less than an hour after she slapped him, could go about the compound singing as if he was a bird in a garden of roses . . . Never tired of working . . . Known in the street for his respect for elders . . . Very amiable . . . Even to her in spite of her efforts to hate him . . . And he was so strong . . . so much the opposite of the potbellied person who called himself her husband . . . but he was only a boy . . . .

She laughed at her mercurial attitude towards the boy . . . .

Idleness, she told herself, idleness, that was what was degrading her, and it was Yago's fault — Yago told her not to work, because he had wealth he did not know what to do with. But he went to work and returned home fagged out . . . He might even be having affairs outside . . . .

In spite of her brutality on Saturday Zhero greeted her warmly when he came into the private living room to take Yago's briefcase. Because she regretted her cold response she called him back.

'Zhero?' He turned back. She made to say something, but checked herself. He dropped his face. 'Zhero?'

'Madam,' he nervously answered.

'No, another time, Zhero. Bye,' she said in a slinky voice.

'Thank you, madam,' he said with relief and went out.

She flopped down onto the couch and hated herself for her way of life.

Zhero did not think about Madam's odd behaviour. He only liked her soft tone, her kind look, the way she said bye. He walked with a spring in his step to the carport. In the office he remembered Numu's

134

advice on patience and he congratulated himself on not being angry when she beat him furiously. He felt happy until Zanzi came into the office around 11am. She told Zhero that the beating she got from her madam last night was too much so she had come to the CEO of the company for employment. Zhero told her to wait for the secretary who had gone to the bathroom. She was lamenting her lot when the secretary returned.

'Zhero, who is this? You know her?'

'Yes, ma. I know him, ma.'

'I didn't talk to you, did I?'

Zhero explained why she had come.

'Can she go in?'

'Zhero, is something wrong with you? As she is? Are your eyes open, Zhero?'

'Ma,' Zanzi begged, 'if I start work I will wear clean clothes tomorrow. Is from Second Home, that eating place there, is from there I come.'

Chief Yago came out of his office.

'What's going on here?'

Zhero answered on behalf of the girl who could not speak because her lips were trembling excessively. Chief Yago looked at his Secretary who defended herself.

'I've told her to go away, sir.'

'Young woman, as dirty as you are, you come into my office to look for a job?' Chief Yago said, averting his eyes from the ragged girl who suddenly had been gazing at him as if she had felt a bond in his eyes. He strongly felt like being good to the girl but he feared his secretary and Zhero might call him a weak man. He shrugged off his feeling of compassion and said, 'Zhero, call security to throw her out.'

He went back into his office feeling deeply sorry for the poor girl yet unable to change his decision, and Zhero went with Zanzi to the eatery. She apologized to him for going to his office without asking for his permission or informing him before doing so. It was because of the beating her madam gave her last night for refusing to spend the night with a rich customer. Oh, it pained her heart so much and it made her think about her life the whole night. He told her to stop weeping and wipe her face. She did as he said.

'She always shouts at me to tell her what is wrong in going to bed with a man that will give you big money. But I cannot answer her back. If not, I will tell her it makes a woman to feel like a person that cannot be respected as other human beings. That is what Chief Jerome too wanted to do to me when he try to rape me. A woman who is raped will not like herself again. She will be ashamed of herself. She will feel dirty inside her. She will not be proud of herself again. Even a harlot does not like to be raped. I know, because I have been raped before . . . My madam do not know how I hate her. Sometimes I feel like taking a kitchen knife and stabbing her.'

'Zanzi, you are crying again.'

'I will not cry again. I will wipe my face.'

She did as she said. He paid for a plate of food and while he ate he continued to comfort her, begging her not to hate her madam no matter what. He said his mother told him not to harbour hatred in his heart, because it was the temple of God, and he advised her to practise love too. His mother often said to him that love was better than hatred, it was more powerful than evil, he said to Zanzi, manfully keeping back his own tears in his heart. Before he started to leave he gave her one thousand naira and promised to come to Second Home every weekday for his lunch.

When he saw the tears well up in her eyes again he said to her in a half-tearful voice, 'Zanzi don't cry. And don't give up. If you give up, all your suffering will be for nothing. Someday your own situation too can change, like mine.'

Before Zhero came back that day Teima had changed her mind about him. His qualities which she admired in the morning were the very reasons she should take action urgently, otherwise he would physically displace her and her son from the house. Already he had displaced them from Louis' heart, and Louis who had started to shout at her, bristling at anything she said or did in the house, would very soon shout to her and her son to 'Go!' At 8pm she went to Pastor Ododo, who always feared her presence in his house.

'Pastor Ododo, you don't look happy.'

'I'm sorry if I don't look cheerful. I've had a hectic day.'

'A lie, Pastor Ododo. But I like it — you're human.'

'Teima, I thought we agreed not to —'

'That's not why I'm here. But before I say why I'm here, do you think I can forget the past? Louis, can *you* forget?' She paused then she spoke as if she was reading a screen before her. 'Because of your handsomeness, because you were the toast of student activism, I fell in love with you, then I found out that you were a member of a

136

cult. I had to become a member otherwise your gang leader would have ordered the members of the gang to kill me.'

'I can see my evil past will never leave me alone.'

'Evil or good the past is intrinsically part of the present.'

'Oh! Teima, Teima, I don't know why God created me at all. As a youth what did I know when I joined a Satanic cult? I've been a changed man for years but those few foolish years of my ignorant youth have continued to torment me. A week ago when I was preaching at Tafawa Balewa Square I saw a face in the crowd, I thought it was King Kong and I nearly passed out.'

'If it was King Kong he would have come to you after you finished.'

He continued as if she had not spoken. 'And you, Teima, are my daily torment. My wife believes there's something between us.'

'By the way, how long are your family staying in the village?'

'Oh God! Oh God! Did I ask to be created?'

'As a student of Literature I know that you're acting. As a student of Literature you know that you're being melodramatic.'

He shook his head in self-pity. 'Teima, why are you here?'

'You're the one my husband trusts most. He trusts you even more than me his wife. Pastor, is that good?'

'Please say why you've come.'

'I told you someone poisoned his food.' She stared back at him. 'I don't like the way you're looking at me, Louis.'

'I'm sorry. Please go on.'

'Your job is simple. Invite him, pray with him, tell him what was revealed to you, and pray for him.'

'What was revealed to me? What should be revealed to me?'

'Tell him someone is worming his way into his heart. Already the person has pretended to save his life. After the person gets what he wants . . . then he will strike!'

Hey! Hey!' He paused. 'Who's the writer who said God created humans as playthings to amuse Himself?' She laughed. 'I think it's better to blaspheme and be smitten to death. If only God can strike me dead now!'

'Louis, you made a mistake.' His face requested an explanation. 'Your first day on the pulpit, you should have confessed your past and said you became a changed man the day God arrested you. Then nobody could have blackmailed you. That's the way others do it. If you had done that you would have had more admirers. You would have had more followers, sinners believing that they too can be forgiven and accepted by God. You are a victim of your own mistake, Louis.' They were silent for a long time. 'Time for me to leave. Please see me to my car.' He seemed not to have heard her. 'You're still very handsome, and you still look athletic — no potbelly.' He shook his head. 'The pastor that's always well-dressed — blue trousers, a sky-blue shirt, a blue tie, and a white jacket tonight.' He sighed. 'I say see me to my car.'

He did not get up. Nailed to his chair by the conflict in every fibre of his being he stared blankly at her backside as she went out . . . To confess his past now and be free or to do what she wanted? The tears coursed down his cheeks unchecked, because his mind was on the past . . . The power of the past . . . .

The next day, when Yago told her that Pastor Ododo wanted to see him Teima objected to his going out.

'For what? At this time? After 7pm. Let it be tomorrow. It can't be more than a request for a donation or contribution.'

He told her to shut up, and he went out. When he returned nearly two hours later she feared he might have a cardiac arrest.

'Where is Zhero! Where is Zhero! Where is Zhero!'

He pulled off his *agbada*.

'Louis, what's the matter? What's the matter?'

'Where is Zhero! Where is Zhero!'

As he breathed heavily his potbelly heaved inside his singlet, as if a full-term foetus in the mother's womb was furiously searching for an exit.

'Louis, please calm down. Please let's go inside.'

'Foolish Robin! I say call me Zhero! What are you looking at me for, idiot!'

Robin rushed away. Zhero, who had been to the microfinance bank at Idi Araba in the afternoon to deposit some money, was about to put the passbook in a safe place, but because of the urgency in Robin's voice he put the passbook in the back pocket of his trousers, hurriedly slipped on the moccasins his eyes fell on, and rushed out while putting on his shirt, thinking that there was an urgent errand for him.

Zhero could not understand why Teima, Robin and the night watchman were holding back Yago. Even Numu was there — it must be a serious matter.

'Zhero you poisoned my food! You poisoned my food and said it was Naomi! What did I do wrong? Why do you want to kill me?

Zhero why did you poison my food? You will rot in jail! Zhero, I swear, Zhero, you will rot in jail!' Yago raved tearfully.

Zhero saw that Numu was making signs to him to leave the place. He loped out of the floodlit compound into the darkness of the night.

Chapter Four

Today and tomorrow . . . After receiving her salary tomorrow she would resign. She wouldn't give Alojo the pleasure of sacking her ... Human evil, just because she wouldn't go to bed with him — 'Zera, make up your mind if you want to continue to work here.'

She mentally tried to get up, but the boulder of her thoughts was too heavy for her to shake . . . .

One month's salary, just ten thousand naira. Perhaps she should endure the harassment for one more month? . . . Alojo would probably sack her before then . . . .

She struggled not to look at how she had travelled to be here, but of its own will her mind went back to the day after she returned from Amabra: She accused Bazi of the ritual murder of her son and went to the police. The DPO tried to dismiss her complaint saying that in these days of gender equality when women proudly had children, raised them alone and never cared about the fathers' whereabouts the word 'bastard' no longer had any meaning, it was out-of-date. The bottomline, she insisted, was that Bazi claimed the word sent away her son. When she threatened to take her case to the State Commissioner of Police he arrested and detained Bazi for two weeks. Immediately Bazi came out of police detention he left the country . . . To survive and to continue the search for Zhero she started to sell her clothes and the few jewels Bazi had bought for her . . . Months, no word from Bazi . . . When the rent expired the landlord said Bazi's office told him that since the staff member that occupied the flat before her, for whom the flat was rented, was no longer in the employment of the company, the company would not renew the rent. With the little money she had she rented the present one-room accommodation and moved out of Bazi's flat without any item of his furniture . . . After one month she started selling vegetables at the Mile 1 evening market . . . It wasn't profitable business so she had to go to Kleen Environmental Sanitation Agency for employment as a road sweeper . . . .

Alojo said if she agreed to be his girlfriend he'd make her a clerk and keep her in the office, no more a road sweeper, plus double her present salary . . . A woman's life is a hard experience, she mentally sighed . . . .

When the rich stench from the dilapidated outhouse toilet of the next house rudely intruded into her room through the half-open window she heaved herself out of bed — no, she wouldn't blame Zhero for persuading her to leave Amabra, he only wanted a better life . . . And maybe not totally for Zhero's sake — she wanted release from the life of poverty and hardship in Amabra. She must take responsibility for what was happening to her.

She hurried to the outhouse toilet with her chamber pot and emptied the contents into the toilet before relieving herself. Following the night ten masked armed robbers came into the building when a man opened the back door and went to the toilet, the landlord had compelled all the tenants to use chamber pots between midnight and 5am. That night she was not brutalized by the robbers who said to one another, 'Dis one na poor road sweeper. We all know am.' After relieving herself she rinsed the chamber pot and returned it under her bed. At just over 5am she was the only tenant awake and the bathroom was free, yet she wouldn't wash now, because she washed before going to bed last night, and in any case she would soon start sweating in the road she would be sweeping. She brushed her teeth and only washed her face with a cup of water, bending over the shallow gutter in the frontage. She always avoided using the musty outhouse bathroom unless it was absolutely necessary. She changed into her work clothes, went out and took a motorcycle taxi to Kleen Environmental Sanitation Agency.

Few sweepers were there before her but at 5.45am the first fifty-two-seater bus was full and the sweepers were taken to the various places they were to sweep. Zera was dropped in front of A.P Petrol Station at Aba Road and she set to work immediately, hoping to cover a lot of ground before the start of the dangerous rush-hour traffic when motorists preferred knocking down road sweepers to getting late to their offices.

When she first started road-sweeping she used to avert her eyes from people, giving them no chance to talk to her, but now if someone said 'Good morning, madam,' she happily greeted them back and if they said 'Well done, madam,' she thanked them back. Now and then she even shared jokes with young hawkers . . . .

She staggered as a pedestrian whose eyes were focused on the images in his inner world of problems walked into her, but his effusive apology only made her laugh, and she deftly retrieved his left slipper

141

from the traffic and gave it to him.

'Instead of abusing me you are helping me. Thank you, madam.'

She laughed and watched him walk away — she had walked in those slippers before . . . .

She became aware of the hot sun, her road-worker sweating and her biting hunger. She picked up the black nylon bag she had placed at the edge of the sidewalk, called a beans and stew hawker to a corner of the car park of a two-storey office building and requested for fifty-naira worth of beans without meat. She sat on the ground, took a 150cl plastic water bottle out of her nylon bag and started to glug down the water. The security guard came to where she was. She stopped drinking.

'Madam, good morning. Today, when you finish work you go come sweep dis car park o.' She did not answer him. 'Na dat small beans you wan eat? If you agree to sweep de car park I go tell de girl to add one hundred naira beans and meat.'

She gave the hawker fifty naira and started to walk away. She did not answer the hawker who was reminding her that she had not taken the beans she had paid for. The security guard trotted to her and roughly pulled her by her right arm.

'You common sweeper, wetin make you dey bluff?' he asked her, angry that a road sweeper was behaving with dignity.

As she wept he begged her to forgive him, but as he saw his boss coming out of the building he left her and ran to him. She walked away, wiping her tears.

'Obot, what are you doing with a road sweeper at this time of the day? Very soon you'll say you're broke, you want salary advance.'

'Am not doing anything with her, sir,' Obot said to his boss. 'Nothing, sir . . . True to God, sir.' His boss's attention was on the woman. 'Believe me, sir.'

'Shut up, Obot,' his boss angrily replied, watching the receding figure of the road sweeper. 'Obot.'

'Sir,' Obot quickly answered, expecting the worst.

His boss only shrugged and told him he was leaving for his hotel and would be returning to Lagos by the first flight tomorrow morning.

The next day after Zera finished work she had to go to the tree-shaded corner of the car park in spite of the security guard. She sat on the ground. It was the place she usually stayed in until the agency's bus came to pick her up. She was thoroughly tired and she would have loved to go home on her own but she had given the money she had to a woman who fell off a motorcycle taxi about three hours ago for treatment of her injury in a nearby chemist shop. She was very hungry too. She brought out a plastic bottle from the nylon bag by her side — oh, she had finished the water long ago. Was she about to faint? She breathed in deeply and out several times, opening her eyes wide, and then she coughed loudly. While she was coughing to ensure that she did not pass out, the security guard, who had apologized to her yesterday, came to her and roughly pulled her up.

'You too proud to sweep but you no too proud to use de place!' he scolded her, thinking, if he offered her five hundred naira she'd yield to his authority.

She was staring at him and shaking her head when his boss's jeep drove into the park. Immediately the vehicle stopped, his boss, who had to the driver's utter surprise told him to drive to the office instead of Omagwa Airport, jumped out and rushed to them. Yago and Zera stared at each other. The security guard wanted to do his duty by pushing her away. Yago bellowed at him to go away. Zera's face turned into a River Niger of pain. Yago took her by the hand holding it firmly because he noticed that she was trembling. Without a word they went into his office on the second floor of the building and he told her to have her seat on the couch after using his fingers to determine the cleanliness of the brown leather upholstery.

'Where do you live, Zera?' She did not answer him. 'I recognized you easily because I frequently see you in my dreams. And yesterday something told me the girl I wronged, the girl . . .' He stopped, as if the thing did not complete its sentence yesterday. 'Where do you live?' he asked her again.

'Please only give me transport fare.'

'Please let me take you home.'

'It's not a place you should see. Look at this place. Look at your clothes.' He involuntarily looked at his brown designer suit. 'Look at me.' He observed her well-worn black trousers and dirty oversized Day-Glo green short-sleeved shirt. 'No, you shouldn't go to the place I live in.'

'Ah, Zera, Zera, Zera.' He went down on his knees. 'Please, Zera, I shall take you home. Please . . . please . . . please. There must be a reason we have met again.'

'Okay, you will, you will. Please let's stop weeping. Stand up. The door isn't locked.'

Their weeping increased. After they stopped weeping he pressed the table bell and his secretary came in. When she saw their faces she dropped her eyes.

'Raise your face, Ezahn. We've been weeping.'

'I'm sorry, sir.'

'Thank you, Ezahn.' He started to wipe his face with a white handkerchief. 'Please tell her to wipe her face too.'

Ezahn took some pink tissues from his table and gave to her.

'Thank you, my sister.'

'Thank you, ma,' Ezahn said to the road sweeper she had sometimes seen at the car park but never spoken to before now. The silence was awkward to her. She unnecessarily adjusted the peach scarf around her neck. 'Sir —'

'Ezahn, I may not travel today. I'll call you. Come, Zera, let's go.'

Alone in the office, Ezahn hated herself for her supercilious attitude towards the woman who had once or twice tentatively greeted her . . . In spite of Fr Obot's constant exhortation to the congregation to be good to all humans because everybody was made in the image and likeness of God . . . Last month it was as if the advice was just for her: 'You don't have to be a people person to make people happy. A listening ear if you are approached, a warm "Good morning, how are you?" to the people in your compound, a smile to the person whose face lights up at you in the street — there are many ways to make people happy. Don't say you are not outgoing, don't say you were born shy — go beyond your comfort zone.' She shook her head slowly . . . and resolved to change . . . .

The company driver, who together with the security guard had concluded that the road sweeper must be a woman their boss had wronged in the past, was silently glad that he had never been unkind or rude to her. Partway he asked her respectfully,

'Which street did you say, ma?'

'Ijitoto Street.'

'Thank you, ma.'

'Agogo.' The driver was shocked. 'Agogo.'

'Ma.'

'You're surprised that I know your name?'

It took him some time to say 'Yes, ma.'

'I know only your name, Agogo, because you're the only one who didn't insult me at the car park. I like to know only good people, and remember them only.'

Stamping his foot Yago cried, 'Hey, life!'

'Thank you, Agogo.'

'Thank you, ma.'

No one spoke again until they reached her residence. Once Yago saw the building and the environment which he regarded as a concretization of poverty and human degradation he decided against her continued stay there.

'We shall go to my hotel immediately,' he said half heartedly.

She did not answer him. The street door was open. She entered and he followed her down the dingy corridor to the penultimate room on the left side of the ten-room house. Once he entered her bedsit he begged her to leave the house and go with him to his hotel.

She switched on the light and smiled wanly. 'I told you not to come. You can't even sit down,' she replied after about a minute.

He realized that he had looked at the only brownish white plastic chair in the room and mentally rejected it. He deliberately sat down casually. Looking at the dirty walls with stains of various colours he felt hurt that Zera had been living in such a place. It was difficult to tell the original colour of the walls which had not been repainted since the house was built about fifty years ago. The concrete floor had broken in several places. The room was hot and stuffy like a kitchen the housegirl had closed immediately after cooking because the rain had occasionally swept in through the glass louvre windows. He looked at the wooden window, but she did not open it, because she was afraid that the stench from the neighbouring outhouse toilet might be worse than the heat. She opened the door instead and switched off the 60-watt light bulb.

'Zera, I begged you to come with me to my hotel, you haven't given me your answer,' he said to her, half angrily.

'Because the answer is no,' she replied phlegmatically.

They paused for a long time while they thought about the past. He phoned the driver to bring his briefcase to 'the second to the last' room on the left. When the driver knocked he met him at the door to prevent him from coming inside and took the briefcase. He took out a hundred thousand naira bundle and held it out to her.

'Zera, please take it before I say what I have in mind.' He placed it by her on the bed. 'Let me go to Lagos and come back for you in a week's time.' She was still silent. 'Can you resign tomorrow and not go back to the road?'

'I don't have to resign. If I don't go to work, that's the end of it.'

'Thank you. I'll come back in a week's time to take you to Lagos.'

'You want to put me on top of a palm tree and cut it at the bottom with an axe again?' He felt hurt. 'I'm sorry.'

After a long pause he asked her, 'Where's the child?'

'I aborted it.'

He burst into tears. 'Oh . . . oh . . .'

'Don't cry. That was many years ago.'

'Some hours ago,' he wept, 'as fresh as yesterday.'

For her it was as fresh as today . . . .

'Louis, I'm pregnant . . . Louis, won't you say something? Please, say something . . . I know it's my fault, but I want you to say something.'

'Jump up for joy that I've found a wife?' She was shocked. 'Why did you choose me? Am I the richest one of your boyfriends?'

'Louis! Why would you say a thing like that? Did I say I want to keep it? Am I not a student? Do you think I want to stop schooling?'

'I don't know what's on your mind.'

'I shall abort it. All I need from you is the money.'

'Zera, you won't put your sin on my head, a small girl like you, suppose you die.'

'Louis! You want me dead? It's not dangerous. It's just one month old.'

'Please go and look for the man who impregnated you —'

Reeling from his sight she fell backwards on the bed. He rushed to her.

'Zera, what's the matter? Are you all right?'

'I'll be all right.'

'But the tears on your face.'

'Go away, Louis, go away. Don't touch me! I say go!'

'Okay. I'll go, I'll go. But have you got a phone number?'

She gave him her number and he went out. The driver came back for the briefcase. Without sitting up she told him, 'It's there. Take it and go away, you and your master.'

'Yes, ma, thank you, ma.'

'Agogo.' He came back. She sat up and said affectionately, 'Thank you, Agogo, thank you for your good nature.'

He happily thanked her back and left. She sniffed herself and shook her head. She pulled off her uniform, sniffed at the shirt, then the trousers . . . She shook her head again and wept . . . .

She thought back again to the day he said he wasn't responsible

146

for her pregnancy. Her pain was unspeakable . . . Disdaining to beg such a wicked man, she went out of the hotel, weeping drily, hating herself for the wrong path she had taken . . . .

Yago did not call her. He came back after two days, bruised by his wife's and his son's ill-treatment of him. She had just finished cooking *gbegiri* soup when he came, so she made *amala* and invited him to eat with her. He said it was very delicious but after a minute or so he confessed that he couldn't tell whether it was food or ash that was passing through his mouth.

'What's the matter, Louis?'

He told her about his wife Teima and his son Joseph, and she suspected that he only wanted a serene home away from his abusive home. When she held a basin of water before him to wash his hands he wept wretchedly — when did a woman ever treat him like this?

'Don't remind me of the past, Louis.'

'You must remember the past,' he cried. 'Bring it back, Zera, live it in the moment and shout at me, rail against my evil act, Zera, do it, Zera, abuse me,' he cried pitiably.

She comforted him and he told her the story of a boy who loved him, the boy who saved his life — Zhero loved him but he foolishly drove him away.

She was agitated. 'Zhero?'

'Yes, Zhero. Do you know him?'

She described her son, then she asked him, 'Did he *order* you not to eat the food?'

'Yes, he did. As if I was a child. How do you know, Zera? You frighten me, Zera, speak.'

She laughed. He was offended that she had trivialized his sorrow. She laughed, because her son had been alive.

'You too, Zera!'

'Now, you have lost your son, forever.'

'Zera, if you don't tell me what you mean . . . I feel I'm going to die, but let me hear the truth before I die.'

She told him the story of her life from the day he abandoned her to the day she found him again by his office, and she wept.

'I was just a child when I begged you not to abandon me, a child that needed direction, but you left me to stumble on.'

He wept afresh too and told her of how his father had disowned his mother's pregnancy with him and yet he didn't learn a lesson from it. His own surname too wasn't his father's but his mother's maiden surname, and his mother had never told him his father's name because, she said, it was a word to be hated, and now his own name would be abhorent to Zhero.

She wept inconsolably that she had wrongly accused the man who was good to her and her son of ritual murder, he told her that he too would be good to her, and after finding their son he would be good to both of them too.

For two days they searched for Zhero at the waterfronts in Port Harcourt, the market places, the shanty towns, and even the big refuse dumps. She readily agreed when he suggested that she should go with him to Lagos and search there too, so he phoned his personnel manager to rent and furnish a bungalow in Surulere as fast as he could. The personnel manager called around midday on the third day to say the house was ready but because Zera said she needed some time to get used to the idea of going into another phase of life. They did not leave for Lagos till 11am the next day. The personnel manager and Robin received them at Murtala Muhammed Airport. From the way they looked at Zera it was obvious they admired her, and from their happiness it was obvious that it was not the richness of her Hollandais wrapper or the sheen of her Sample lace blouse they admired but her person. Chief Yago felt proud, he believed himself a blessed man. The personnel manager showed them to the bungalow and handed over Zera's temporary home to her. After he left, Robin told Yago that Yago's parents-in-law were in Yago's house.

'They didn't tell me they were coming. Any problem?'

'Sir, I don't know o. But is like they are vexing for you. Like you have stopped sending them money.'

Yago told Zera to make a list of foodstuffs for Robin to buy before he left. After Robin returned from the market he went home, braced for his wife's father and mother. When he saw four policemen, a man, a woman and Joseph at the gate he feared something serious had happened. Robin opened the gate by remote control and drove in.

'Sir, I lock the gate?'

'No. Don't you see Joseph with them? They have entered too.'

He went to them and asked a policeman if his son had committed a crime.

The woman smiled. 'Sir, let's go in first.'

Immediately they sat down in the living room he asked, 'Where did you see my son? Is he in trouble? And you Joseph, you can't even say welcome to me? When last did you see me?'

The woman smiled again. 'He isn't in trouble. Someone in your house is in trouble. Please call your wife.'

Robin, who was in the doorway, ran to call Teima praying that she should be in terrible trouble . . . for Zhero's sake . . . for Zhero's sake . . . Perhaps Joseph was caught stealing — happy news! Immediately she came in she asked Joseph what he had done wrong? And who bought him the new-looking clothes he was wearing? The boy was silent. Joseph! As she was about to gather rage a policeman told her, 'Sit down, woman.' Yago felt unconcerned about his rudeness. Her parents came in, mentally rehearsing how they would scold their son-in-law, and Yago told them to be seated too. Then the policeman explained why they had come.

A newcomer to the neighbourhood, Mrs Wendoah, a friend of the couple sitting on Yago's right had seen Yago's putative son, Joseph, a look-alike of the couple's son and reported to them. Years ago a clinic had told them that one of their twins had died during childbirth. But when the clinic was recently exposed as stealing newborn babies and selling them, the couple's friend, Mrs Wendoah, who now lived at Alabi Atere Street reported her reinforced suspicion to the couple, who came over and stayed with her. Because Joseph was a friend of Mrs Wendoah's son and frequently came to her house it was possible to do a secret DNA test on him. They did a test and reported to the police that the Yago's had stolen their son many years ago. Mr and Mrs Yago were therefore needed at the police station.

'No need to drag the matter further. When my husband was about to go overseas I told him I was pregnant. I pretended to be pregnant. I bought your son from the clinic.'

'For how much?' the policeman asked her.

'Is that important now?' she replied.

Teima's calmness shocked even the police to whom the heinous crimes humans committed were as unmoving as bloody corpses on Nigerian roads were to frequent travellers. After a long pause Yago found his tongue.

'Robin, go and bring Zhero.'

Teima winced. 'Zhero?'

Yago shouted for Robin who had already left. He came back.

'Robin, I mean Joseph.'

'I know, sir.'

After five minutes or so Robin brought Joseph to the people in the living room who had been silent throughout his absence. Yago broke the silence of astonishment.

'Joseph, this boy is your brother. And these people are your parents.'

Joseph's true mother explained to him what Yago meant.

'Sir, where are you going?' a policeman asked Yago.

'I've just returned from travel. I'm going to rest.'

'You people have to go with us to the police station.'

'How many people?'

The boy he had not loved for years was standing in the doorway. He shoved him aside roughly and went out of the living room. Teima's parents burst into tears and begged the couple to forgive their daughter. The couple, who had resolved before coming here not to be angry, readily agreed to press no charge if Teima would go to the police station and write a confessional statement.

'Robin, you'll take me to the police station.'

For the first time Robin disobeyed Madam. 'Since morning I have not eaten. Am going to find something to eat.'

'Robin, I cannot blame you,' her mother responded, boiling inwardly with anger at her daughter who had just caused the closure of her parents' bank account in this house.

Without a word Robin walked away.

Teima affectionately said to Joseph to go to his room and pack his things. The boy did not answer the woman he had secretly feared since the day his putative father was nearly poisoned.

'Joseph, did you hear me?' He continued to stare at her. 'Joseph?'

His birth mother told him he would take only his certificates and school report cards.

'Come, Joseph,' she said to the boy she had purposely been affectionate towards in Mrs Wendoah's house. He went to her, she hugged him and wept, 'Joseph my son, Joseph my son.'

Only Teima did not shed tears . . . .

Two weeks later Dr Novo, owner of Novo Clinic in the street, visited Yago. After introducing himself he said he had just heard about what happened in Yago's family. Yago silently wondered how that concerned him. After an awkward silence Dr Novo continued. He would have liked to say what he wanted to say in Mrs Yago's presence but unfortunately she wasn't around. (How did he know?) From his nurses, he said, and added, on the street grapevine. Actually

150

it wasn't because of that he had come but because of Chief Yago's son who ran away from home sometime ago. ('My son? You know that Zhero is my son?') Yes. Before the boy ran away Mrs Yago had come to him to help her do a DNA test on a boy she believed a woman had falsely called Chief Yago's son and given to him. The DNA test showed that the boy was Chief Yago's biological son. When he heard that the boy had run away, to salve his conscience he made inquiries and was satisfied that the boy actually did run away.

He thought he had brought exciting news, so he was surprised that Yago behaved as if he had known long ago that Zhero was his son.

'Dr Novo.'

'Sir.'

'You can't be more than forty years old. I don't want to spoil a young man's career. Please, stand up and go out of my compound. Not a word, please.'

Dr Novo stood up and went out, feeling like a newly employed journalist who had brought a scoop to his editor, and the editor laughed — 'This story was published by "NEXT" while you were writing your finals.'

Yago called for Robin and they went straight to Zera. In Robin's presence he narrated what Dr Novo had said, and explained and regretted how he had wronged Naomi and his son Zhero. 'Oh!' he moaned.

'Ma, don't cry,' Robin said, as if he had a proprietary right to weeping.

'While you are weeping for me?'

'The morning after Zhero left, Robin boldly told me that he believed Zhero was innocent. And he called Pastor Ododo a liar! Because he refused to apologize I nearly sacked him, but I changed my mind. Because I didn't want to lose the two employees I loved most at the same time . . . Pastor Ododo made a fool of me. No, I was already a fool. He merely exploited my foolishness.' Shaking his head, 'Pastor Ododo . . . Pastor Ododo . . . I won't bother to go to him. I leave him to divine justice.' He looked at Robin, who dropped his eyes. 'Robin, *you* are wise,' he abruptly said tearfully, the bottled-up emotions since the time Dr Onovo was with him bursting out like hot water from a fully filled and hermetically sealed container that had just been punctured.

'Thank you, Robin.'

'Thank you, ma.'

Yago told Robin to go home and come back for him the next day.

'Zera, we shall continue to search for our son.'

'Yes, we shall.'

'Oh, Zera, how can I make it up to you? Please give me a chance to make it up to you . . . You said you loved Bazi and you regret what you did to him . . . With time you'll love me too, even though your mind constantly goes back to him because, you say, his voice and mine sound alike . . . I'll make it up to you, and you will love me as your only one, Zera.'

'Only because you say so, otherwise I would have said let's remain good friends only. As for what's in your mind, as for marriage, it's impossible until I find my son . . . As a poor student I started a relationship with you just for money. And I was punished for prostituting myself. Now I'm with you again because I'm poor and needy. Oh, a woman's life is a hard experience.' She pulled off her tangerine blouse and threw it on the floor. 'Oh, Zera . . . Zera —'

'Zera, what have you done? You're half-naked, no bra, you're naked, Zera.'

'Am I? Am I? It's too hot.' He went to the door and locked it. 'Thank you. For hiding my shame from the world.' He gave her the blouse and she put it on. She wept again, 'Where are you, Zhero? Where are you, Zhero?'

He wiped her tears and comforted her. At last she stopped weeping, and he said he would open a shop for her so that she could feel independent. She thanked him and he said he was hungry.

Eba and bitter leaf soup?'

'I like it, I like bitter leaf soup.'

'Because bitter leaf is a cut-and-come-again?'

'Yes, I like bitter —' Her irony dawned on him. 'Oh, Zera, why did you say that? I think you'll never be able to forgive me.'

'To forgive is divine; to forget is foolish.'

'Ah . . . .'

'If you'll sigh at my food, I won't bring it.'

'I'm hungry, Zera.'

They went to the dining room, she laid the table and they started to eat in a buoyant mood because they each felt it in their bones that they would see Zhero again. After about two minutes, she wondered what type of food Zhero might have been eating since the day he ran away, and the tears welled in her eyes. He noticed her face. It was heartbreaking. He stopped eating too. She smiled dully, said she was sorry, wiped her face, and they continued eating, no longer happily, though.

After eating they cleaned up the dining room and the kitchen together because he begged her to allow him the pleasure of doing it with her. Then they went back to the living room. After watching the news on CHANNELS TV he said he felt like taking a nap so he went into the bedroom. She changed the channel to SKY TV. A panel discussion had been going on. The host said she would explain the background to the story before showing the clip.

About seven months ago three unmarried policewomen who were kidnapped were rescued by a combined force of soldiers and policemen after a month in captivity. They were raped during their captivity. One of them aborted her pregnancy. When the other two applied for and insisted on their right to maternity leave they were dismissed because they were unmarried. Even though they were raped by their abductors. The policewomen said they kept their pregnancies because their religion did not approve of abortion while the police service insisted that the rules must be obeyed — no maternity leave for unmarried females. Feeling humiliated by the national debate on the issue one of them committed suicide. In continuation of the national debate U Shettima, a writer, university teacher, and activist recently attempted to see the Inspector General of Police who had been silent on the issue. We'll show you a clip of what happened. A bystander who had captured it with his camera phone posted it on the Internet.

The incident happened in front of the IG's office.

'What's your name?' a police corporal asks him. 'Why do you want to see the IG?'

'I want to personally give him a letter.'

'I say what is your name?'

'U Shettima.'

'Who are you?'

'U Shettima. I'm U. U Shettima.'

Infuriated the police corporal slaps him, hits him with his baton. Another police corporal comes in.

'Corporal Shettima, what's the problem?'

'He's messing with me. I asked him what is your name he says he is me Shettima.'

'What did you tell him your name is?'

'U Shettima.'

'What's your first name?'

'U. I'm U. No full stop. My first name is U.'

The policemen laugh. U Shettima leaves them, saying they will hear from him soon.

Zera tuned out the TV discussion. She thought about herself . . . She did not want to abort because she felt it was a sin to take human life. Some of her schoolmates who easily did it anytime they got pregnant persuaded her to do it and not destroy her educational career, arguing that from what the world had become it was impossible for girls not to have sex before marriage, and one consequence was unwanted pregnancies. She agreed to their advice but when she couldn't find the money she changed her mind. She wouldn't commit the unforgiveable sin of taking human life. Already sex before marriage was a sin and her pregnancy was God's punishment for her sin, she wouldn't compound her sin with another sin, she had decided . . . If she had done it she would have saved her educational career . . . Perhaps she should have listened to her friends? But then she wouldn't have known Zhero — a blessing in this lifetime . . . But where was he? She prayed he should meet kind people in the waystations on life's road . . . .

Yago returned to the living room, saying that he could not sleep off. She did not answer him. He looked at her face: the river was in flood. He sat by her and sent out a manly moan.

'Oh! I am evil!'

'Don't cry, Louis, don't cry.'

'No, I'm not crying — oh!'

He realized that she would never be happy unless Zhero was found, so they put more vigour into the search. For two weeks six of his workers daily combed through the low places in Lagos while occasionally Robin drove him and her around the city hoping that the pull of blood would bring their son to them. When he remembered that Zhero used to be a happy hawker of videos he and she went to Chief Hezekiah Jerome's house.

Even though Chief Jerome and his wife Rosetta were not happy that Zhero left them they prayed that no evil should befall such a good boy. Rosetta told Zera that wherever her son went he would be protected by his goodness and she explained his honesty — Zhero always turned over every amount he realized to the accountant whereas if he sold a video at above the approved price he could

154

have kept the surplus to himself. It was after he left she and her husband were told about his honesty. Her husband nearly sacked the accountant for not letting him know. If the poor boy had been rewarded he would not have left the company.

Chief Jerome called for Dustan, who said that because Zhero closed his account in the microfinance bank and because of the way he said bye-bye to him, he felt that Zhero had gone far away from Lagos. Dustan did not tell them the truth because he did not like the man who betrayed Zhero and the wicked woman who was pretending to be Zhero's mother.

The next week Yago and Zera flew to Owerri and stayed in Concord Hotel from which the hotel's car-hire taxis took them around the city separately every day to refuse dumps, building sites, market places, motor parks, big department stores, shantytowns.

Whenever Yago saw people being rude to street hawkers, despising scavengers at refuse dumps or treating touts and porters at motor parks as potential criminals, he would shake his head because he felt society ought to be grateful to them and treat them with compassion, young men and women who had chosen menial jobs to pay their way in life whereas they could easily have carried guns to kidnap and kill for a living, and then he would think of his own son, Zhero, who used to be a porter and a hawker.

On Thursday, a pregnant young woman flagged down the driver. Yago told him to stop and help her. She greeted Yago respectfully as she sat in the passenger seat. When she reached her destination she asked the driver how much her fare was. He told her it was a chartered taxi. She was overwhelmed by Yago's kindness — a man so good? Another man flashed through her mind, a wicked man. As she said 'Thank you, sir' a tear threatened to drop from her eye. She quickly turned away. While she was waiting for the gate of the compound to open and the driver was slowly and sadly making a three-point turn, he told Yago that she was probably going to sell her unborn baby. She would be transported to a maternity clinic in Okigwe and she would stay there until the baby was delivered. Her clothes and other domestic needs must be in that bag she was carrying. She was taking a risk. After delivery they could detain her for a man to impregnate her again, and she would be detained there till she had given birth again. Yago immediately called her back and persuaded her to allow him to help her. No longer caring about life, she shrugged, entered the car with an air of resignation, and they drove to the hotel. They went under a canopy in the garden and he told her he wanted her to keep the baby. She said her intention was to put the baby up for adoption after it was born instead of aborting it. He told her he was going to write her a cheque to enable her to take care of her baby for two years before she looked for a job. She told him her name and he wrote the cheque, then he told her his name, they exchanged phone numbers and he told her what he was doing in Owerri.

'Sir, for the good you have done you shall surely see your son,' she prayed as the tears rolled down her cheeks.

When Zera returned to the hotel in the evening he was careful about his behaviour and every word because she looked to be in a bad mood. But after he said good night to her in her room and went to the sitting room to watch TV she came out of her room and sat affectionately by him. He was impressed by the CNN Heroes, especially Evans Wadongo and Anuradha Koirala. Evans Wadongo the young man who made 1400 solar panel lamps for the use of 50000 people in a rural community in Africa said it was his way of 'turning a dark continent to a bright continent.' He liked Anuradha Koirala, a middle-aged woman from Maiti, Nepal, who had rescued 1200 women and girls from sex slavery and human trafficking in seventeen years. Nominated by a young man and a young woman Anuradha Koirala won the overall CNN HERO OF THE YEAR award.

He thought out loud: He could do a project, get someone to nominate him, and CNN would come to Nigeria and photograph him. He believed there was a dearth of heroes like the ones of tonight in Nigeria. Silently he thought it would pain Teima to see him in glory.

He asked Zera, 'What type of unique project do you think one could do?'

'Can't a person contribute silently, even anonymously, to society?'

'If it isn't brought to the open how would others be inspired by it? The life story of the author is part of the inspiration. Have you ever seen the life story of an anonymous person?'

She silently wondered that at this period of their lives it was personal glory he was thinking of . . . Perhaps his wishes to marry her and to find Zhero weren't pure? Just to expiate his sin?

Without a word she went back into her room and wept. When he came in he was shocked to see her weeping. She shouted at him to go away.

'Hnnh, will this one not be worse than Teima?'

156

'You are comparing me to an evil woman? Louis, are you comparing me to your evil wife?'

'Wife?'

'Have you divorced her? Have you?'

He felt like slapping her, but he checked himself and went into his room . . . He wouldn't give this one the latitude he gave to Teima.

Unable to sleep she went to the sitting room to watch the CHANNELS TV 11pm news broadcast. She tuned out the reports after hearing the headlines until U Shettima's name was mentioned. U Shettima had been bundled into a plane at midnight and deported to his paternal country, Godiva . . . She thought about her son . . . She wondered why U Shettima's story always made her think of Zhero . . . She thought about Zhero's abhorrence of injustice at Amabra.

She was startled to see Yago.

'I'm sorry,' he apologized and sat by her on the two-seater couch.

'I thought you went to bed to sleep. Why aren't you sleeping?'

'Does that mean I can't watch TV with you?'

'Provided you'll do it silently.'

But in less than five minutes he was talking angrily. 'See, see Pastor Amen distributing charity . . . taking the glory alone whereas we moneybags in the church contribute monthly to the church —'

'Instead of thinking of how to find your son, your problem is a pastor's display of charity? Louis! Perhaps you don't even believe that he's your son? But can't you do it for me? A mother is sure of her son's maternity, Louis.'

'Zera, do you think I'm a foo . . .' he checked himself.

Her lower lip tightly between her upper and lower teeth she shook her head — if he had dared!

After thirty seconds or so she started to simmer down and placed her right hand affectionately on his left thigh. He placed his left hand on her right hand and said thank you. She thanked him back, turned off the TV and they went back into their respective rooms. He immediately called his personnel manager, who listened with expectancy, and told him to call him by 8am to return for an urgent matter in the office. The call came when he was in her room and they had to hurry back to Lagos.

For over a week he did not go to her house. On Saturday he strongly felt that she should accompany him to an oil magnate's reception, but he was afraid that she might accuse him of pleasure-seeking while his son was still missing. While he was contemplating on the effective way to invite her Numu visited him. When he saw Numu reading the invitation card he had taken from the coffee table he asked him if his university had taken action against the student who slapped him.

'Joe Nounoun? No. A student slapped me and the university said it was an internal disciplinary matter, so I shouldn't take it to court. The power of money. The son of Dr(Mrs) Julia Nounoun, owner of an oil company, a woman of wealth and privilege. I can see she has invited you to her reception tonight.'

'After the continental award her home town's Development Union is organizing this reception in her honour.'

'A woman who's collecting honorary doctorate degrees from universities every year, such a woman cannot bring up her son properly. Of course, how can she? Because of her character her Haitian husband left her and their business in London more than twenty years ago and married another woman.' He noticed that Yago was not interested in what he was saying, which he had once dismissed as a public slur generated by her political opponents. 'But, Uncle, must you associate with her?'

'For the sake of business.'

Numu shrugged. 'Actually, Uncle, the reason —'

'Before you say anything, I understand Teima visited you last week.'

'I was waiting for an opportune moment to tell you. In fact, that's why I'm here. She wants me to appeal to you to take her back.'

'And what did you tell her?'

His uncle's tone frightened him a little. 'I told her nothing in this world is impossible but —'

'Stop! Don't but. Don't but at all. Nothing in this world is impossible except Louis Yago taking back Teima. It is impossible for Louis Yago to take back Teima. Don't ever mention that evil woman in my presence again.'

After about a minute's silence Yago felt that Teima was more sinned against than sinning. It was wrong of him to call her evil . . . But he preferred Zera to her . . . In spite of Zera's temper.

'For your information, I'll soon marry Zhero's mother.'

'Zhero's mother? Who is she?'

Yago told him the story. Numu was happy for him. For Zhero's sake it was better to marry Zera. Still, he thought, some day he would explain to his uncle why Teima had to steal the baby, how the police gang rape impregnated her and how the induced abortion damaged her womb — she did what she did because she loved his uncle and cherished his love.

The convocation ceremony of a private university was going on on the TV.

Yago remarked, 'Chief (Dr) Juba who was arraigned some years ago for stealing billions. Now the first convocation ceremony of the university he established with his stolen wealth.'

Numu laughed. 'Prometheus stole fire from the gods to give it to humans. No one has ever called him a thief. Rather he's a Greek culture hero. Education is light. That's what Chief (Dr) Juba is giving to the Nigerian children. He's a Nigerian modern hero.'

'I think Teima has a point when she says your works are evil.'

Numu laughed and stood up.

'Uncle, my sins are scarlet but my works are read.'

After Numu left, Yago thought back to how he had to marry Teima: It was a very beautiful and good-natured-girl, Dama, he had intended to marry and she was to accompany him to Britain, where he was going to study textile technology preparatory to setting up a textile factory. When they were to travel to Abuja for their visas Dama came with her best friend Teima and the three of them travelled to Abuja. To be fair to Teima she never showed any sign of wanting him but when Dama was away from the hotel he forcibly tried to make love to her but she struggled vigorously against his attempt, crying sincerely. Dama came in and saw them. Without a word she packed her things while Teima begged her to listen to her. Without a word Dama opened the door to leave, Teima begged her not to abandon her — had Dama forgotten that she had come penniless? Teima was stranded. Helpless, out of anger, she remained in the hotel with him. In the night she was full of fear, and she begged him not to rape her, but he overpowered her, and he savoured his manliness that night . . . In the beginning she was excessively afraid, so afraid that he was momentarily frightened, but after he finished she lay quiet on the bed, looking so relieved . . . then she wept and thanked him for taking away her fear of lovemaking, for giving her a new life, and she thanked him again, and made him promise to love her for ever. He extended his stay in the hotel for a week, and even though Teima complained that he had taken advantage of her poverty she

159

fell in love with him, calling him a rapist — a ravishing rapist, she said, had conquered her heart . . . Before he left for London she told him she was sweetly pregnant for him. To secure her for himself he quietly married her in the registry before he left the country . . . Teima was sweet . . . A very good girl who morphed into a monsters.

On Monday he travelled alone to London and returned nine days after. Because he ached to see Zera he told Robin to take him to her straight from the airport. When he was about five minutes away he phoned her in order to say he was on his way to her house but she did not answer the call. He wondered why.

She was thinking of how her friends at Queens College disappointed her. They had a lot of money but none of them helped her. Especially Fidelia who even showed her the huge amount she had but told her her problem was a matter she had to sort out with her men . . . Her mind went back to her hard life of farming and fishing with Zhero at Amabra . . . and Zhero a porter too, sleeping in the waiting shed at the waterfront . . . then she hated her father who rejected her return to his house . . . How old was she that he couldn't forgive her for her mistake? . . . Wherever he was now, however he was she'd never bother to see him until she died — until *he* died . . . She hated Yago too —

He opened the door without knocking and entered.

'I'm back. Suddenly, because you refused to answer my call.'

'Well done.'

He laughed and picked up the book on the coffee table. 'Odedekoko. You and this Odedekoko novel, when will you be tired of it?'

'Whenever I'm tired of it.'

'I said, read "Rustum and Sohrab", up until now you haven't read it, because of Odedekoko.'

'Must I read what you want me to read? And if I do, do you want to give me a test on it?'

'I think I'm tired — nine days of travelling!'

'Why not? After the long journey, Yago's Nine Quests — more arduous than Rustum's Seven Quests. My hero.'

'Zera, is something wrong? The truth.'

'I loved you once, but right now I don't think I do, until you bring back my son. I hate you the way I hate my father. I don't know which of you treated me more wickedly . . . You may walk out of my life again if you choose to do so — now.'

He feared for her state of mind. To welcome a man from overseas this way — he feared for her state of mind. He put his arm around her shoulders and vowed not to disappoint her again — never again would he ill-treat her, he vowed again.

'Why not, Louis, why not? I've seen poverty, I've stared poverty in the face and there's nothing to fear about it. Don't pity me. As a schoolgirl poverty conquered me for you to abuse. Thereafter it has been powerless over me. I'm no longer afraid of poverty, Louis . . . Louis, go away again. Go on your quest for a happy home. With your shield and your sword, your wealth — countless girls are waiting to be taken.'

'No, Zera, there's nowhere for me to go. For years I searched for love. I've found it and I'm back home. Please don't send me into the wilderness again.'

'When you drove me, a mere child, away into the pitiless forest of life I told myself I had a father. I went to him. He drove me away too. My mother took me to her own village where I turned into a farmer and a fisherwoman, and I ate the fruits of my labour . . . I say go away, Louis, go away again,' she wept.

'No, Zera, we shall marry, and we shall have another child.'

'Is that a proposal?' Abruptly she laughed. 'The hero goes down on his knees and proposes to the woman he had saved from poverty and hunger, "Zera, you must marry me!"'

He was thoroughly ashamed of himself.

Chapter Five

Scavenging at the dumps in Mo Bo was good business for a long time after the Mo Bo City Council Chairman gave the police and the Environmental Sanitation Authority the directive to clear the streets, police stations and even the Council's three pounds of abandoned or unclaimed vehicles at the end of the one month's notice to the owners of the vehicles to remove them from the streets or pay their fines and claim the vehicles from the pounds. The Chairman's directive was due to the spate of bomb explosions in abandoned vehicles in the country.

The main dumps for the disposal of unserviceable vehicles were the Agoa and Tanta dumps. The police and the City Council workers naturally stripped off whatever they considered useful before taking the remains to the dumps, still there was enough for the scavengers to be happy over, and in the heyday of the business from morning to dusk the dumps teemed with boys and young men hacking at metals, tearing out useful vehicle parts, occasionally pushing and pulling a whole vehicle considered to be still useable out of the dump and loading it onto a handcart to be transported to a mechanic's workshop. While some people were happy that a lot of jobless able-bodied young men had found a non-criminal means of livelihood, others blamed the government for encouraging scavenging instead of setting up salvage yards or even a company to relieve people of their unserviceable vehicles and compact the vehicles into lumps to fill gravel pits.

Zhero and his three friends were sitting by the heap of scrap metal they had assembled in the last four days waiting for the scrap metal dealers, motor part dealers and mechanics who might come in the evening to buy in bulk or in bits what the scavengers had gathered. At Agoa Dump, which was well-organized by the self-proclaimed owner of the land, selling and buying at the dump strictly took place from 5pm – 7pm. The alternative was for the scavengers to look for buyers and transport the goods to them but few scavengers could afford to do that now due to a fall-off in the demand for their goods.

Yari was telling the group of four friends some of the atrocities he and his fellow soldiers committed during the Liberian civil war. He said whenever the leader of their rebel group abruptly ran out and forwards naked, signaling a banzai charge, everybody had to follow him that instant shooting every human being on sight, even babies, until the leader shouted to them to stop . . . One day a small number of the group captured a small surviving village, killed the men and started to rape the women . . . The girl he was to rape was the most beautiful girl he had ever seen, she was a virgin, she begged him not to rape her. He pitied her and took her to a place from which she could escape . . . He had barely turned when he heard gunfire. A soldier on the watch had shot her down and was pumping bullets into her body . . . Thereafter he escaped from the rebel group . . . To cut a long story short, he turned a beggar to sustain himself at the age of fourteen, begging in the streets of Ivory Coast, Ghana, Togo; he avoided Nigeria because Nigeria had accepted a lot of Liberian refugees and he was afraid of being recognized as a killer and a perpetrator of atrocities; he did several menial jobs in Godiva because he did not like to be a beggar . . . 'Ma men, today am working in Agoa refuse dump.'

While they paused Zhero silently retraced his own journey from Chief Yago's house . . . That night he secretly stayed in Dustan's room . . . It was Dustan who discovered that in his hurry to escape from Yago's place he'd worn the left moccasin on his right foot and the right moccasin on the left foot . . . Dustan told him the best place to run to was Godiva where Nollywood and Gollywood videos were in high demand, advising him to suppress his honesty, conscience or whatever, make money, whether or not the videos were pirated, make money, then start an honest business . . . Before anyone in the compound woke they left and went to Olu Ajayi Street, Idi Araba where he later closed his account at the microfinance bank . . . Dustan accompanied him to Yaba where he took a Land Flight Continental bus for the three-day journey to Godiva . . . In the last night his wallet containing fifty-one thousand naira was stolen. The kind driver of the bus handed him over to his girlfriend, a food seller at Askee Motor Park in Mo Bo who asked the night guards to allow him to sleep at the motor park at night. He worked in the park as a porter and as a busboy in the woman's restaurant in return for two meals a day until she introduced him to Kings & Queens Supermarket where he was employed to carry customers' purchases to the car park for no pay, given only a uniform and depending on the

customers' tips. That was where he met Ogugo and Matthias . . .
When they found out that scavenging fetched more money than
working in Kings & Queens where they sometimes had to behave
servilely towards the customers they left there . . . He didn't have to
think about selling pirate videos at all, because at the time he came
to Godiva, government officials were arresting the hawkers. Unlike
the KAI (Kick Against Indiscipline) officials in Lagos who were doing
a duty, the officials here seemed to be arresting the hawkers because
they enjoyed beating and inflicting injuries on the video sellers —
they were very violent and wicked . . . He thanked God for giving
him very good friends — Yari, Ogugo and Matthias ...

Yari struggled with his rising anger and hatred for the people
who threw Liberia into a civil war and deprived him of his youth by
killing his parents and his elder siblings and by forcing him to fight
in an adults' war.

Matthias, who had been inspecting his dark-yellowing teeth in
the mirror he had pulled out of a car, burst into laughter.

'So . . . so . . .' he struggled to stop laughing. 'So you used to pray
. . . As a beggar the prayers you used to say for people, do you really
mean it?'

'Sometimes,' Yari replied seriously. 'Sometimes I don't even know
what am praying. But prayer or no prayer God is seeing the heart of
a true giver.'

'You are right,' Zhero said as he was getting up from the flat grey
piece of metal he was sitting on. He went to a woman and her two
daughters who were beginning to leave the side of the dump where
household rubbish was taken and left.

'Madam,' he said to the fair woman, who, to him, looked too
clean for the environment, was too well-behaved to be around some
of the scavengers who did not set great store by good behaviour,
since they had never found it among the things they scavenged.

'Zhero, we dey go. Enough for today,' she answered the boy who
she believed should not have been a scavenger.

'Your sack is not full at all today.'

'E go full next time.'

They laughed. She collected mainly plastic bottles. Since she did
not come to the dump every day it was assumed that she scavenged
only to augment whatever else she was doing for a living.

Zhero joked with her daughters: 'Make una pray make I make
one million dollars today. Tomorrow we go all celebrate.'

164

The woman laughed and Zhero gave the children one hundred Godiva dollars. While their mother was thanking him De Boss, who claimed to be the owner of the land, came up to them.

De Boss always dressed in clothes that he expected would give his six-foot-two height a tough and fearsome appearance, but because his face was very handsome and his voice was like Odedekoko's voice his attempts had never succeeded. Today he was wearing faded blue denim jeans, a dirty blue T-shirt, and a black cap which, though it covered a good measure of his face, could not in conjunction with the jeans and the T-shirt effect the owner's intention, due to his Odedekoko voice.

'Hey Zhero! You and your friends. Hey! All of you come!' Zhero's friends slowly came to him in response to his strained shout. 'Make una listen. From tomorrow, whether una sell or una no sell, una go go dey pay me my money daily. How many days now una never sell, wetin me I go take eat? Una think say I no dey hungry because rubbish don fill my stomach with smell?'

'If we don't sell where do you expect us to find the money —'

'Zhero, na for me you dey speak grammar? Enh, Zhero?' Yari and Matthias blocked his minatory advance towards Zhero, while Ogugo tried to draw Zhero away. 'Zhero, na me you dey talk to like dat? Zhero, you forget whosai you dey?' he asked, looking left and right, as if the question was for everybody in his monarchy, Agoa Dump.

His six bodyguards rushed to the scene from a group of scavengers they were addressing.

'De Boss,' one of them said, 'any problem?'

Another asked, 'Anyone refusing to cooperate?'

'Is dis foolish Zhero.'

As one of the thugs slapped Zhero the woman dropped her sack and quickly enfolded Zhero in her arms, like a hen covering her offspring with her wings.

'Madam,' the thug warned her, 'mind your own business o; if not I go turn my anger to you o.' Like Mother Hen who decided to face the marauding hawk itself she left Zhero and faced him. 'Madam,' he warned as he slowly backed away, 'don't try me o. Madam, you dey try me o.'

'Hey Salisu! Leave de woman alone!'

The thugs were aware of De Boss's interest in the woman. Salisu walked away from the scene.

'Zhero.'

'Ma.'

De Boss had not finished with Zhero. 'Zhero, you bloody foreigner! Na dis work you go do till you die. Instead for make you save you dey give a witch and her two pikin money. Woman wey don kill her husband. Na you be de next person to die.'

The woman and Matthias firmly held Zhero back.

'Zhero,' she pleaded, 'please, no mind am. Na me im abuse.'

The woman understood the reason De Boss hated Zhero — her motherly love for Zhero who loved her children as if they were his sisters. De Boss had several times been mad at her, why should she love a foreigner, a small boy, instead of him who could take care of her? She had simply told him he would love Zhero if he loved God and himself.

De Boss shouted for everybody at the dump to hear. 'Make tomorrow come! I go see which person for dis Agoa wey no go pay daily! Come on, boys, let's go.' He turned to Zhero. 'You Zhero, you go end up as armed robber, like your brother Zero Godiva. Because of woman you go become armed robber, to get money to maintain woman. Zero Nigeria.'

De Boss and his bodyguards sauntered away, glowing with the power they would exercise again tomorrow when the King would return to this part of his monarchy. The woman appealed to Zhero and his friends to do as he said and avoid trouble. To be fair to him, he was doing a fine job in protecting the place day and night and keeping away a crowd from the dump. They agreed with her and she left with her daughters. After thirty minutes or so Zhero and his friends left the dump too, dejected.

In the taxi Zhero thought about the Law of Self-determination which Abang had told him to practise. Almost daily, since he came to Godiva he had practised it, hoping to get a good job but it had only landed him at Agoa Dump . . . Could it be as Pastor Ododo used to say? If one was a good person God might not give him or her what he or she wanted, but surely what he or she needed . . . So Agoa Dump was what he needed? The life of a scavenger? . . . Could it be because he wasn't going to church regularly? . . . And De Boss, what should he do about De Boss? Zainab Shettima says love is a moral absolute, but can he go on giving love to a person who hated him for no reason? . . . .

He slept off till they reached Bondo bus stop at the edge of Bondo, the shantytown they lived in. They made their way into the shantytown following a sinuous path between shacks made of wood, tin, or corrugated roofing sheets to their own wooden shack, a twelve feet long and six feet wide room and a veranda measuring twelve feet long and three feet wide where they cooked and relaxed at night when indoors was too hot. As they entered the room they flopped onto the two mattresses on the concrete floor and thought about the next day . . . .

They had to pay De Boss. If they didn't where would they go to? Tanta? Too many people at Tanta . . . Would they go back to scavenging household refuse? . . . How about carrying loads in market places? Zhero asked . . . After a long pause Yari spoke. Instead of answering Zhero's question he suggested that they should go about and look for buyers of scrap metal instead of waiting for buyers to come.

Someone knocked on the door and came in, stooping slightly because his six-foot-six frame was too tall for the cardboard ceiling. 'Why is your house dark?' he asked. Zhero switched on the light and they saw a very handsome face before them. 'This is why I am here. Your electric bill. You have not paid your electric bill for last month, and this month is about to end,' a very unfriendly voice said.

'Papa Tolbert we shall pay,' Ogugo answered the man some young persons in Bondo said should have been a Hollywood star instead of collecting electric bills in a shantytown, because of his beautiful figure.

Papa Tolbert glared at Ogugo. 'You shall pay. About three weeks late. You shall pay. All small small houses have paid, but you are living in a detached building, and you cannot pay for light . . . If you don't pay tomorrow and I disconnect you it will be forever,' he warned them with emphatic hostility, his fists bunched, as if to prevent the irrevocability of his word from escaping before tomorrow.

He went out after glaring at them one after the other and itching to pounce on anyone who would challenge him. The four friends were speechless for more than one minute. The rain started to fall.

Zhero spoke. 'We shall pay Papa Tolbert this night, and then we shall go and eat at Lick Your Fingers.' His friends laughed. 'Have you finished laughing?' He opened his bag and brought out a new-looking pair of jeans. 'I bought these jeans in Nigeria for ₦10,000, that is G$10,000. How much do you think Godiva Boutique and Stores can pay for it?'

No one persuaded him not to sell his jeans. They were very happy at the prospect of even eating tonight. They went in the rain to Godiva Boutique and Stores, a second-hand shop at Bondo, and after a robust haggling were paid G$3,500. They went to Lick Your Fingers and ate happily. After the rain stopped they went to Papa Tolbert who scolded them for waiting to be threatened before doing their duty and reluctantly issued them a receipt for five hundred Godiva dollars. Zhero mentally converted it to the Nigerian equivalent: five hundred naira from one house. Papa Tolbert must be making a fortune from the people of Bondo. Papa Tolbert called them back and scolded them more abrasively, calling them lazy boys who were living above their means. None of them said a word, so he advised them like a father to pay their bill promptly next month.

'Foolish boys, go well.'

About four years ago Papa Tolbert had provided three transformers for the shantytown and made a deal with the area manager of Godiva Electric Power Authority (GEPA) in Mo Bo to connect Bondo to the national grid. GEPA did not have Bondo in its records — the people of Bondo paid their electric bills to Papa Tolbert.

On their way home Zhero and his friends were happy at the beauty of the night in Bondo: the sinuous paths never drained of people walking up or down even by the rain, voices coming out from open windows distinctly heard by passersby, loud music from radio sets as if each radio set was meant to entertain the whole of Bondo, the familiar stench of blocked-up shallow gutters and small dumps here and there, children playing hide-and-seek, at the video-viewing centre, the cheering and the booing by Nigerians of young men playing football far away, thousands of kilometres away in Manchester — to them Bondo was pulsating with life, life without worries, for they had eaten and paid their electricity bill tonight and tomorrow they would pay De Boss G$1,600, the fee for four days at one hundred Godiva dollars per person per day.

The next day they looked for a buyer before going to the dump. One of their dependable customers promised to come before 5pm. At the dump De Boss's goons were shooing or slapping away the scrap metal scavengers who had not paid their fees up-to-date. De Boss was disappointed when Zhero came straight to him and gave him G$1,600.

While Zhero and his friends were laughing over a joke they saw one of the goons who had emerged from the swamp, approaching them. They braced themselves for a quarrel. He smiled as he came up to them.

'Zero, I just use de road wey you make go inside de swamp. And you even make a small table wey person go go on top and do am into de water. Zero, you get sense o.'

'I hope you been shit well.'

'Matthias!' the goon exclaimed and they all laughed.

Their customer did not come at 5pm but a man from whose truck they had once unloaded disused furniture into the dump came and requested to hire Matthias to work for a few days in a new house he wanted to move into. Matthias looked at his friends. They said it was okay, provided they went with him to know the place and to establish the man's identity. They were afraid of the man. The man was afraid of them too, so he said 'No deal' and drove off in his Mercedes Benz jeep.

Matthias unnecessarily remarked that the buyer they expected had not come, and each of the friends felt as if the man in the receding Mercedes Benz jeep was life abandoning them, they each fondly ached for a miracle to provide them a square meal today.

As a strong wave of stench hit their nostrils Zhero reminded them that they were scarcely aware of the stench whenever they engrossed themselves in work.

'So we for collect more things and add for this big heap? No way,' Ogugo said, 'no way until we sell this one. And since morning we never eat. When I stand up is like the wind want to blow me down.'

Someone rushed to them with bad news: The reason the police and the Environmental Sanitation Authority had stopped bringing vehicles here was that a man had made out a very big place along the Sanka-Mo Bo Road and was paying for the vehicles they took there. And it was there many of the people who used to come to Agoa to buy vehicle parts were now going for their needs. It was a very big place. The man was using machines to do the work, and he had also employed many young men to work for him. The man also had a scrap-metal recycling plant. Instead of abandoning their unserviceable vehicles in the streets many people were taking them to the man for good money.

They had no time to absorb the bad news. While some boys were scrambling for the sacks of refuse a sanitation agency's truck had just brought, one of them slumped face-down on the sack he had just secured. A friend rushed to him. The friend yelled. Azira was dead! Azira's friend explained tearfully as if the reason still mattered: It must be due to hunger. Azira hadn't eaten today. He wanted to make money to buy food.

As the sanitation agency's truck took Azira's body and Azira's friend to the Mo Bo General Hospital several scavengers wailed, more in pity for themselves than for Azira. Some scavengers remembered how Carol died from just a slight cut from a rusty knife in the rubbish. After the bleeding stopped they bandaged his hand and thought he was okay. But on the third day all his body was stiff, he couldn't even open his mouth, and he died. Amusu was bitten by a snake early in the morning as he lifted a mattress someone had thrown into the dump in the night. Amusu died on the way to the chemist shop. How about Demba who was taken to the police station and shot to death because he was carrying a TV set he had taken from the dump? Death, they concluded, was not far away from them.

Before Zhero and his friends left the dump around 7pm, Ekiyor, a young man who liked Zhero, came to him and confided in him that he had saved enough money to buy the West African School Certificate and would soon quit scavenging. Zhero was silent, his mind on his ambition to go to secondary school and acquire the School Certificate. Ekiyor continued. Scavenging wasn't a job anyone should do forever. He wanted Zhero to purchase the School Cert too and both of them could go to the Civil Service for employment. Zhero replied that he would read for the School Cert. He didn't know when, but someday he would, he emphatically concluded, his gaze on the lone bird hovering in the infinite Mo Bo evening sky, as if it was surveying the vastness of its possession.

Zhero and his friends had planned to make a pot of soup if they sold what they had gathered, but their customer did not keep his promise, so they went to Lick Your Fingers for their dinner and first meal of the day, roast plantain and palm oil, then they returned home to listen to the radio music from Ogugo's mobile phone. When a song titled 'Ghetto Boy' reminded them of what had happened at the dump, Ogugo started to blame Azira for his death — his vigorous scrambling on an empty stomach. Matthias' reaction shocked them.

'Please please stop stop! Don't speak evil about the dead! I don't want his ghost to visit me!' he protested vehemently on a half-empty stomach, visibly shaking.

Ogugo switched off his mobile phone and no one said a word until they slept off. Only Ogugo went to work the next day in case someone would come and buy what they had gathered. A little after midday Zhero took a walk outside Bondo . . . He thought of why things were hard for them. They had put together all the money they individually had and paid two years rent for the present accommodation after Ababa where they were living separately was devastated by floods as high as six feet . . . Wouldn't it be better to go back to Amabra? . . . If Chief Yago had reported him to the police, Nigeria wouldn't be safe for him . . . Maybe he shouldn't have reacted to the word 'bastard' and run away from the house? A house that shouldn't be compared to where he was now living . . . The word pained him because his mother had lied to him . . . He should stop looking at the past, face the present and be somebody tomorrow . . . .

He couldn't remember when last he bought a newspaper. He bought a copy of 'The Waves' and went home. Yari snatched the paper from him. Twenty minutes or so later he recounted how a man had gone back to the woman he had abandoned in the hospital about thirty years ago when she gave birth to triplets. He had recently gone back to the woman for financial assistance for him to go to India for a kidney transplant. The woman had forgiven him but the three daughters, who were now very wealthy, had warned their mother that they too would abandon her if she helped their father in anyway. In an exclusive interview 'The Waves' had understood the reason for the children's bitterness: Their mother laboured painfully to bring them up and to give them an education. And she once had an experience that made all of them weep for days: When her rich uncle who used to help her asked to have sex with her they warned her never again to go to him for help. But one day, after they had been out of school for two weeks, their mother went back to her uncle, and he raped her before giving her money. Their mother begged them to forgive her, crying that because their need was urgent and because she had nowhere else to turn to she was forced to go back to her uncle.

Yari sided with the girls while Matthias felt that no sin was too big to forgive. As they argued heatedly Zhero only thought about what he had done to his mother . . . the woman who said she would swallow her pride, she would swallow her bitterness so that he could have a better life — his mother too had sacrificed her dignity . . . .

'Zhero, why are you crying?'

'Zhero, is it because of this story you are crying? Yari, you see what you have done?'

Ogugo returned at dusk with only G$4,000. Actually the buyer had paid G$5,000 for what should normally cost more than G$10,000, and Ogugo had to pay G$1,000 for a van to transport the scrap metal to the man's place. They shook their heads but thanked God it was not worse than that.

When Matthias said that night that he was going to see his girlfriend, Ogugo angrily said that if Matthias went to a prostitute anymore he would stop sharing mattress with him. Matthias went out and came back at midnight.

'Over my dead body!' Ogugo stormed. 'Every time you are scratching because of lice. Buy a mat tomorrow and sleep alone.' A cool breeze started to blow in through the window. Screwing up his face and holding his breath he angrily shut the window to keep out the stench from the too familiar stagnant gutter between the back of their wooden shack and that of a tin shack. Breathing out heavily, 'Matthias should go back to his girlfriend.'

Zhero asked Yari to go over to Ogugo. But Matthias, he insisted, must shave his pubic hair before coming onto the mattress. The friends laughed as Matthias started to shave his pubic hair, now and then cutting his skin and saying 'Yeh!' After he finished he thanked Zhero and gave the others some reasons why he considered Zhero a rare friend, though he was a 'force-ripe guy', because of some of the things he would not do, such as sleeping with girls.

'It's Zhero's wife who would teach him how to do it!' he concluded.

The friends laughed at Zhero who took the joke with a sense of humour — he knew his friends believed him a fool in some respects.

For a long time Zhero could not sleep off. His mind kept going back to the things his mother used to do for him . . . He also thought about her good character qualities . . . She was hardworking . . . She was frugal because she had to save money for his education . . . She never liked to beg for material assistance . . . But her anger made a lot of people fear her, she who always told him to control his temper . . . The day Oguro called him a bastard and he went home and angrily asked her about his father, she shouted, 'I say your father is dead! Why am I not bearing his name? He died before you were born!' She went straight to the house of the boy who had insulted him and slapped him. When Oguro's mother rushed out, his mother lifted her up and threw her down on the ground. The woman couldn't stand up — her waist had broken . . . The treatment cost his mother a fortune. Some members of her age group helped her financially . . .

He thanked God for her love for him . . . .

He smiled — his mother's temper and that of his grandmother were as opposite as fire and water. He couldn't think of anytime his grandmother got angry, even at his mother . . . Whenever his mother was angry his grandmother had a way of looking at her and it immediately quenched her anger . . . To make him laugh when he was angry his mother would call him 'Odedekoko', but his grandmother would call him 'Ekiyor (Wisdom), the one who stole all his mother's possessions except her anger'. . . .

When they went to the dump after three days, someone gave Zhero a message from Ekiyor. Ekiyor had found a permanent job somewhere. Octopus Paul, the carrier of the message, noticed that Zhero did not like what Ekiyor had done — Zhero had shaken his head and then shrugged his shoulders.

'I see say you no like de idea. Me sef. Person wey get only primary six, how much im salary go be? Me, I go stay here. One day I go hit my millions and start my own business.' He noticed Zhero's frown at his marijuana fumes. 'Sorry. You, even common cigarette you no fit smoke. Woman!'

Zhero smiled, because at Agoa Dump, Octopus Paul was regarded as a woman due to his excessive protectiveness towards girls. 'Octopus Paul, go away with your Indian hemp.'

Octopus Paul walked away, the spring in his step forged by the millions of dollars he would collect on Saturday night.

From Monday to Friday, Octopus Paul, the diminutive Wolof from Gambia, worked hard, telling his friends that was his last week at the dump. On Friday night he would stake all the money he had made from the dump in the pools and start drinking native gin and smoking Indian hemp, sometimes on credit, celebrating the millions that would be his at the end of the football matches on Saturday. But every Monday Octopus Paul would be back at the dump with a fresh will to work hard . . . Octopus Paul, now wearing only soiled faded brown boxers which showed off where his buttocks started to part as he bent forward to work.

Zhero withdrew his attention from Octopus Paul and went to join Matthias and Ogugo who were working at removing the engine of a Mercedes Benz 200. Zhero was received into their dream: If the engine they had all ignored could be repaired they would make over a hundred thousand dollars. A good second-hand engine cost about two hundred thousand. It wouldn't cost more than fifty thousand to repair it.

'But from where can we get that kind of money?'

They realized that it would be impossible for them to repair the engine, so they decided that they might sell it at ten thousand, or even five thousand dollars.

Ogugo sang, 'And the rich shall get richer, the poor poorer.'

They laughed and continued to work. Matthias pointed at Yari among about twenty boys, girls and young women who were rummaging through domestic rubbish and explained Yari's decision not to forget the small things that used to sustain them before the boom in motor parts sales. Zhero told them there was wisdom in it.

They wondered about a woman who had erected a tent close to the edge of the swamp. Zhero went to a young man who was probably costing his small collection of plastic bottles and cups, metal pans and pots, two gas cookers, a kerosene stove, and empty drink cans.

'Good day.' The man took some seconds to take his eyes off his wealth. 'Dat woman there, na who she be?'

'Dat woman?' The man laughed. 'I never see her own kind of sickness before o. Anytime, anywhere she dey, piss or even shit dey just dey comot from her body. He don reach three days wey she come here. Na for road she dey beg for money. I no know why she no go beg today. Maybe money plenty for her hand,' he laughed.

They looked at her. She was still. She looked like a huge piece of solid waste someone had walked to the edge of the swamp to dump far away from other humans out of compassion for their senses of sight and smell.

'I hope De Boss didn't harass her.'

'Dat thief, De Boss? Na only de motor part people im dey worry. Dis place wey don give me my daily bread for five years, na who born de person wey go tell me say na im get de land? Na when government begin bring motor vehicle here De Boss appear from nowhere to say dis place na im family land.' After a pause he added, 'Fine boy wey for do something better with im life. I no blame am. Na lack of proper upbringing. When im rich papa and mama no fit control am dem drive am commot for dem house. Na im make he dey behave anyhow.' He paused then continued. 'If he see say you no fear am he go avoid you. Na im make he no dey near me.'

Zhero thanked him and went back to his friends. He thought about the woman until he went home.

Disturbed by the image of the incontinent woman he could not fall asleep at night until he decided that he would *unfailingly* talk to her the next day. He did after she returned to her tent around 6pm.

She told him she had travelled a long way: Her journey started after a very difficult childbirth when she was about thirteen years old. Instead of pitying her, her husband and his relations called her a witch when she was unable to control the passing of urine from her body. They said it was God's way of punishing her so they drove her away and she went without her son to her parents. When the herbalist her parents trusted couldn't cure her they too became tired of her and said if God had decided to punish her this way, then His will be done. So she started going from place to place, driven away from place to place because of the mess and the stench until she reached here . . . after many years. From the way people were looking at her and gesturing she felt here too they would soon drive her away . . . .

She waited for his response but he was silent as he went over her journey, which was recorded in her ragged clothes, her browned skin with blackened patches, and her waypoint — between the refuse dump and the swamp, where she alone would stay at night. She noticed that he was looking at her compassionately.

'Why you no dey spoil your face? I don stop for smell? As for me I no fit know again whether I dey smell.'

He replied with a question. 'Can we go to the Godiva University Teaching Hospital?' She was silent. 'I think they'll give you free treatment.'

'How about how to get there? Which bus or taxi go take me?'

'Tomorrow don't go anywhere. I'll go to the hospital. I think they'll come and take you.'

The next day he went to the teaching hospital where he was impatiently directed from place to place until he saw a respectable-looking man the nurses called Prof. He fearfully went to him and stammered out his reason for coming. Prof was very grateful to him and introduced himself as Professor Kelsey Harrison. He said the woman's problem was VVF (vesico vaginal fistula), a simple thing he liked to treat. Zhero was glad for the woman. Prof called for an ambulance and Zhero took him and a nurse to the Agoa dump where the woman was taken into the ambulance, and it drove off and neared the hospital before the happy Professor Kelsey Harrison realized that the boy who brought the report wasn't with them. Why didn't he come into the ambulance? What was his name? The woman too

175

didn't know. Another time, the nurse said, another time. Professor Harrison thought out loud, 'That boy, this is the beginning of social conscience.'

The mother of the two girls Zhero liked was around that day. She came to him and thanked him. Some of the scavengers wondered what was between Zhero and the woman — was it possible to make love to such a woman? Zhero did not mind them, because, he often said to some of them, they were what they were because they had not found good conduct among the things they scavenged. Some were glad that the woman had gone away with her stench. Matthias, Yari, Ogugo, and a few other scavengers thanked Zhero too. But Zhero's act only confirmed to De Boss that the boy would die a scavenger — using his money to send a stinking witch to the University Teaching Hospital for treatment, how could he leave scavenging? If a person was born to be a scavenger must he die a scavenger?

At home Zhero was happy . . . He thought about Kenitari's story of the gold coin . . . Love was the gold coin . . . He was happy he'd done a good deed . . . He shook his head to clear it of the memory of what he'd done — he mustn't think of reward . . . But he savoured one of the sentences his mother made him memorize from Zainab Shettima's book: 'Even angels wait on the one who gives to life.'

Matthias suggested that they should walk around and enjoy the night. They did, and they were happy as they joked with friends . . . as they sang along with the music from open windows . . . as they saw an old couple fighting seriously while bystanders were laughing because it was just handbags . . . It was when they got to Ayilara St that they realized Matthias' intention of bringing them out — he suggested that they should each take a prostitute. Zhero angrily said no, and Matthias alone went into one of the houses which men were streaming into and coming out from. Ogugo and Yari persuaded Zhero to be patient and they waited till Matthias came out, his beatific smiling annoying Zhero . . . At Diah Street, full of prostitutes too, a video-viewing centre was showing 'Superman'. Though there were many women in the place who looked like prostitutes, Zhero yielded to his friends and they went in to watch 'Superman'.

At home they discussed the film passionately — the feats of superman! His service to society! His triumph over his enemies!

After they trailed off, Zhero's mind went back to Joleen in Amabra . . . Joleen wanted him but he was afraid of his mother . . . Maybe

176

his mother wouldn't have known if they did it? . . . One day his mother warned him, That girl is a total illiterate because she refused to go to school. Remember, you have an ambition. That's why you and I are working very hard — to save money so that you can go to secondary school. If you impregnate that girl you'll be tied to her and low life forever . . . .

To suppress the disturbance between his thighs he shifted his mind to how his mother loved to teach him, using the books she used in secondary school . . . Anytime he made a grammatical mistake she felt that he was wasting her efforts . . . She always wanted him to speak good English . . . She taught a lot of the children in the village A B C, I-T IT and 1-2-3 . . . She also used to teach some of the primary school teachers too, but the local government refused to employ her because she didn't have a teaching certificate . . . His mother loved him extremely . . . .

On Sunday when he was alone at home, out of idleness he took up a newspaper he had bought many days ago . . . On the back page, the man looked like someone he knew, yes it was he, it was U Shettima, what was he doing in Godiva? He read the article. It was on the plight of street children, and children who were hawking in the streets or working at rubbish dumps instead of being at school. U Shettima was blaming the government for neglecting its responsibility . . . He spoke out loud, 'What's U Shettima doing in Godiva?'

There was a commotion outside. He rushed out. Some children were clapping and booing an elderly woman as a young man threatened to strip-search her. A policeman who was passing by stopped, was told that the woman had stolen two thousand dollars in the young man's shop when he went out to buy ice water, and the policeman supported the man's intention to strip her naked. Zhero gave the man two thousand dollars and said the woman should be allowed to go.

'Zhero,' the shopkeeper protested, 'you dey encourage stealing o!'

'Please allow her to go.'

The policeman approved of Zhero's action. The woman thanked him and Zhero walked away. The policeman silenced and drove the children away by threatening to shoot anyone who abused her.

About two hours later Zhero answered the door and saw the woman. She entered before he could speak.

177

'My pikin,' she said in a low voice, 'na bad thing I do. True true, I been thief de money.' Zhero was speechless. 'But na only one thousand. I no fit say na only one thousand because dem for ask me how I know say na one thousand.' Zhero was still speechless. 'Please take, even though e no reach de two thousand you give dat liar, dat thief.'

She put the money in his left hand. The gold coin Kenitari spoke about flashed through his mind.

'No, ma, I no go take am. Make you use am.'

He was going to give her the money with his left hand, but he withdrew his hand, transferred the money to his right hand and gave it to her respectfully. She thanked him tearfully and went down on her knees. 'No, ma, no, ma,' Zhero protested, his eyes shut, and raised her to her feet. When he opened his eyes she told him to wipe his wept face. She too wiped hers, and went out.

He went out too, locked the door, placed the key under the doormat in the veranda, and took a walk away from Bondo . . . What could have made an old woman steal one thousand dollars? . . . Could his own mother do such a thing? . . . He needed university education so that his old age wouldn't be like that . . . but the way things were going would that be possible? . . . .

The old woman's act of stealing reminded him of the day he and his friends went to Ibozi village to watch their annual Amabenimo Ogei. The village turned wild with joy when the chief masquerade wrapped up the occasion with its performance. He and his friends braved the wrath of the gods and went into the forest to peep at the masqueraders undressing in the shrine. It was disappointing, it was sad — the hero of Ibozi, the chief masquerader, was Ebilayefa, an incurable thief who had been sent away from Amabra to his maternal village, Ibozi.

Someone grabbed his left arm, he bunched his right fist.

'Don't blow me o! Don't blow me o!'

It was Ekiyor. Ekiyor said he would have gone to Agoa on Monday to tell him that he was now working in the Ministry of Finance.

'Zhero, you wan die as a refuse man? You free to leave dis way of life o.'

Zhero smiled wryly. 'How free can I be without a good education?'

'Me, am I not a free man?'

'I don't know, Ekiyor, but I don't think that's the meaning of freedom.'

178

They talked about other things, Ekiyor hailed a taxi, and they parted. On his way back to the house, in his inner world Zhero looked at himself, Numu, U Shettima and Abang in Numu's office at the university . . . When Numu was taking him home he repeatedly stressed the importance of education . . . Education, not a certificate . . . .

Yari was at the veranda with a boy. The boy left as Zhero came in. Yari immediately recounted what the boy said the old woman had done.

'Poor woman,' Zhero sighed.

Yari had known a little about the old woman before now: She fished, farmed and traded in the village to pay her husband's university fees. They agreed not to have children until he had finished university. She was very glad when he graduated and waited for him to come take her to the city after working in Shell Oil Company for a few months. But he married an eighteen-year-old girl who had finished secondary school and abandoned the woman because she was illiterate and too old for him.

Zhero shook his head and went into the room . . . Wasn't he as bad as the husband of the woman? He abandoned a woman too, his mother . . . .

Yari announced loudly that he was going out again, and he did. Out of idleness Zhero took an old copy of 'The Waves' in order to look again at a passage he had not understood: 'The story of your life includes what is happening to other people without your knowledge — people whose lives you have affected, people you have been good or bad to, people who have been good or bad to you, people who have affected your life. Your story is part of their stories, their stories are part of your story.'

He thought about it, read it once more and thought again, still he could not understand the meaning — he flung away the paper.

At bedtime the four friends looked at their dwindling business . . . A few months after they started scavenging the massive dumping of unserviceable vehicles at Agoa, Tanta and other places started, and scavenging became very good business. Now that the authorities were no longer bringing vehicles there, should they go back to pots, pans, cups and other domestic stuff? . . . They decided on what they had considered sometime ago — buy handcarts and collect rubbish from house to house at the GRA and other affluent places for a fee . . . But they had a problem: one handcart cost G$10,000. Where would they find G$40,000 for four handcarts? . . . They could start with one. If the motor parts dealer paid them the G$10,000 they demanded for the Mercedes Benz engine they would buy one handcart tomorrow . . . .

All of them woke up early, before 5am, and they laughed at one another for being unable to sleep — because of ten thousand dollars! They restrained themselves from leaving home until 9am. When they reached the motor parts dealer's shop he scolded them for coming so early to his house to wake him up as if he was a debtor. In any case, he would pay them only four thousand dollars. Zhero and his friends were speechless.

'Wetin make una dey look me like dis? If una no like, see, your iron dey there. I never touch am at all . . . Well, I go make am five ... Yes or No?'

They knew Athanasius. If they said no, that would be the end of the deal, no matter how they begged him. Without a word Yari stretched out his hand on behalf of the group. The man looked shocked.

'Bring the five thousand,' Yari said half angrily, half sadly.

'You dey craze? You wan use your left hand to take my money? Dem send you come ruin me?'

'Sorry, sir,' Yari apologized, his ego bruised.

They took the money and walked away without a thank you. Mr Athanasius was not bothered. As long as there was hunger in the land there would be people like them.

Zhero thought back to his Port Harcourt Metropolitan Primary School days . . . sometimes he had as much as five thousand naira in his pocket, and he had no need for it . . . If he wanted ten thousand for clothes, Bazi would be too glad to give it to him . . . .

When they reached Agoa only a few people were there. Dispirited, they extracted from the remains of two cars some of the things that had been neglected before: two bumpers, three slightly damaged front seats, one number plate, and a gear stick before they realized that they had not had their breakfast. They called a hawker, ordered rice and stew and started to eat. When someone else shouted for the hawker to come she demanded for her money.

'Have we finished eating?' Matthias asked her.

'I wan go sell for other people, das why.'

He made to give her the money but took her left hand and held it lustfully. She slapped him with her right hand.

'You dey craze?'

'Hey Matthias!' Zhero shouted at him. 'Don't touch the girl! You got what you deserved.'

The girl hefted her basin onto her head. 'Jero, thank you. I go come back for my money from you.'

Instead of being ashamed of what he had done Matthias said he was a victim of sex addiction, and he regaled his friends with some of his brushes with women. Then they worked happily till dusk, admired their collection for which they would look for buyers the next day, and walked to Agoa Road to take a taxi to Bondo. Because of the stench they were wearing that evening they had to wait for an empty one they would fully occupy. Twenty minutes or so later they got one. When they reached home around 8pm there was a small group of people outside their house and someone was banging at the door.

'Aha! Dem don come, dem don come,' some people said, and everybody turned to them.

'Matthias and Ogugo, una see Solo?' a young man asked?

'Solomon?' Ogugo asked.

'Yes, Solomon. Solo.'

'No.' Ogugo answered. 'We just dey come from work so.'

A woman asked, 'Somebody say two of una, im see two of una and Solo yesterday, true or false?'

Ogugo's brow furrowed in recollection.

'Yes,' Matthias answered, 'yes, but dat na since yesterday morning. We see am. Im say im dey go see im friend dem.'

'Since yesterday! Since yesterday!'

Zhero asked the last speaker. 'Any problem, sir.'

'You dey craze? You think say na play we come play here?'

The man invited the group away.

The four friends stood where they were, wondering what to do. The boy who had told Yari about the old woman on Sunday ran frightfully to them to warn them to run for their lives.

'Dem dey come! Dem dey come with cutlass! Dem dey come with motor tyre and petrol! Zero, dem say una don sell Solo.'

The four friends scattered out of Bondo. Zhero ran as he had never run before in his life. At Sinclair Street a woman standing outside an iron gate opened it and shouted to him to come in. Without thinking he rushed in and panted 'Thank you, thank you' while the woman bolted and padlocked the gate from within. She smiled at his look of surprise at the bold letters on the marquee of

181

the beautiful building: TRAVELLER'S LODGE. She told him he would be accommodated free for the night and she took him to a room on the first floor.

'You were accused of selling Solo?'

'But I didn't do it. We didn't do it.'

The woman smiled. 'I know. Please have a seat.'

'Thank you, ma.'

'Thank you too. This is your room for the night. Room service will bring you food. You may have a bath before you eat. That's the bathroom. Relax. Don't be afraid. You're safe.'

'Good night.'

'Thank you, ma.'

'Thank you too, Zhero.'

The friends met at the Agoa dump the next day. It was when they were recounting their night experience that Zhero wondered at what had happened to him . . . TRAVELLER'S LODGE at Sinclair Street . . . A place he had passed nearly every day, why hadn't he noticed it before? To be accommodated and fed free without asking . . . And he wasn't afraid at all . . . Oh! Oh! The woman, the kind woman even knew why he was running!

'Zhero!' Yari exclaimed. 'What's happening? As if you want to faint.'

'Nothing, nothing.'

'But your mind isn't here.'

'You said you slept under a bridge. Matthias and Ogugo slept in an uncompleted building. Many people sleep there but everybody leaves before daylight otherwise the police will arrest them.'

'How about you?' Yari asked him. 'Where did you sleep?'

'In a hotel.'

The friends laughed wildly at the joke, because even if he had the money, where would he write as his home address in the hotel register? They were satisfied when he said he did not know where and how he had passed the night.

'Yari,' Ogugo said, 'you have not finished your story.'

'Yes. As I was saying I been meet Vincent under the bridge. You know he stop coming here after his *pardie*, Azira, collapse and die here. He say he now goes to Tanta dump. He give me his towel to cover myself when I can't bear the cold when the rain start to fall around 2am. He say he and Azira used to enjoy the night after work. But since Azira die it as if night should never fall, so that he can be at Tanta dump working. He has been living under the bridge for about eight months. He was glad. He thinks I too have come to stay under Lugard Bridge. Many people under the bridge, but only Azira was his pardie.' He stopped and stared at Zhero. 'Zhero, your face is wet.'

'I'm sorry.' Zhero wiped his face. 'Please go on.'

Yari shrugged. 'That's the end of my story.'

At the end of the working day they decided to go to the uncompleted building in which Ogugo and Matthias had passed the previous night but when they reached the bus stop at Agoa Road the rain suddenly started and teemed down for more than one hour. Since they had no home the roofed bus stop could be a comfortable place to pass the night provided many of the people that were sheltered in it went away and gave them space to sit on the floor. As the rain started to sweep the bus stop Zhero told his friends they had to leave immediately the rain stopped. They left as it trailed off.

Yari asked, 'All our trousers and shoes wet like this, how are we going to sleep?'

Zhero answered him, 'You pull your trousers and squeeze out the water. You sleep in your boxers. Tomorrow morning you wear your trousers again.'

They hailed a taxi which took them to Aghogho Street which was perilously close to Bondo, but since they would leave the building at dawn, perhaps it wasn't too dangerous. The building was a six-storey walk-up which was nearing completion when the owner died about twenty years ago, and over which his four wives and their respective children had been engaged in an internecine conflict, burying juju charms in the compound which had scared the family members away after the mysterious deaths of three successive security guards that were sent there by the late owner's lawyer. Some of the homeless of Mo Bo, who did not know why the building had not been completed and occupied, had taken it over for about ten years now, breaking doors from floor to floor and into rooms. The ground floor where Ogugo and Matthias slept last night was fully occupied tonight so they went to the first, and then to the second floor where they found a dank room.

They opened the two windows and the air became lighter after a minute or so. They decided that someone should go and buy a torch, towels, tooth brushes, tooth paste and bread. Zhero volunteered to go, and he did. He was away for a long time and they were beginning to feel concerned about his safety when he returned. He said he had sneaked into Bondo, hoping to take a few things from their house, but only ashes marked where their house once was. They prayed to God to bless Cletus who warned them to run away.

The room they got on the fourth floor the next night was flooded with rain water because one of the windows had no pane. They mopped the water with one of their towels and squeezed the water outside through the window. After about an hour the floor was waterless but extremely cold, yet they had to sit on it with their backs against the walls. At 2am or so Zhero started to shiver, occasionally gnashing his teeth. Every time Yari, who was the only one aware of what was happening, switched on the torch, Zhero controlled his shivering with effort and pretended to be all right. Anxious for daybreak Yari looked out of the window now and then but the darkness of the impassive night was always impenetrable. Zhero was ashamed that he was the weak one who could not cope with their condition, so he continued to hide his shivering. But as they left the building at dawn Yari had to force him to admit that he needed to go to the chemist shop. They stayed with him outside a chemist shop until it opened at 8am. After he ate some biscuits and drank water on the nurse's advice he was given an injection and told to come back for the second dose the next day. Ogugo and Matthias went to work while Zhero and Yari went to Godiva Glory Park and stayed there till Ogugo and Matthias came for them at dusk.

They had come with cheerful news. What they had gathered for several days had fetched them G$15,000. Guess what, guess what — they had also paid G$12,000 for a room at Nze Waterside!

Yari shouted, 'Twelve thousand for one room for one month!'

'For six months!' Ogugo and Matthias shouted in unison.

'I'm well. My malaria has escaped. Let's go there now.'

The friends laughed and went to their new accommodation. As they admired the room and the surroundings Zhero regretted his cowardice out loud — otherwise, he said, he would have gone into the house and grabbed his bag before running away from Bondo that night, and he could have sold the remaining pairs of jeans. Yari told him not to be ungrateful to God.

'Yes, you're right,' he agreed, and he made a mental note of going to Traveller's Lodge the next day to thank the kind woman.

The next day, after taking his injection at the chemist shop and

184

resting at home for about three hours he went to Sinclair Street which he walked up and down two times, and yet no place called Traveller's Lodge. He asked several people — no one had heard that name before. He went to another street and flagged down a taxi to take him to Traveller's Lodge.

'For where?' the driver asked him.

'Sinclair Street,' he replied.

'I know Sinclair Street, but you know where dis your Traveller's Lodge dey?'

He thanked the driver, who looked at him with suspicion and drove off. He went to Godiva Glory Park and thought about his experience . . . Since he knew he wasn't mad he took it that he had had a miracle, and he thanked God . . . He wouldn't tell his friends, because they would laugh at him . . . .

When he woke it was nearly dark. He was afraid his friends would be worried about him. He had to hurry home. He took a short-cut to where he could get a straight bus to Nze Waterside. He stood for a few seconds to admire a white mansion. It was not yet occupied, maybe just completed. 'Someday I too will own a house like this?' He had intended to make a statement about his future but it had ended as a question, as if it was impossible for him to ever own such a house. God forbid! 'Someday I will own a better house than this.' He heard female voices shouting from the uncompleted building adjacent to it. He approached the building gingerly. Two female hawkers were about to be raped by two soldiers. Apparently the soldiers were the ones guarding the white house. The soldiers had pulled off their own trousers and pants and were trying to pull off the girls' tight panties. One of the girls was crying as she struggled with the soldier. She was begging him not to rape her, because her younger sister died of AIDS after the police raped her in their police station after arresting her for hawking. The soldiers' guns were on the floor. Zhero's mind went to his mother who was abandoned by the man who impregnated her. Stealthily he went into the building, took a gun and threatened to shoot the soldiers. He held the gun like a man for whom it was difficult not to kill. The soldiers were terribly afraid — he might be an experienced armed robber, young as he was. In khaki tops only, their suddenly limp penises swaying as they trembled and desperately rubbed their hands, they begged him not to shoot them — in the name of God, in the name of his 'granpapa', they begged him. His great-uncle flashed through his

185

mind, the man he saved, who later feared him as if he was a killer. He warned himself not to shoot. He told the girls to take up their goods and go out. They did so, fearfully and gratefully. The soldiers feared for their lives — they saw a cold-blooded killer in his impassive face, while his mind was on the lot of womanhood. When he felt the girls had gone far he told the soldiers to lie face-down on the floor. Saying 'Yes sir, yes sir' they immediately did as he commanded. He dropped the gun silently, and ran out on cat's feet.

On Sunday, Nicholson, who had left Agoa and gone to the Tanta dump, came with Matthias whom he had met at Ayilara Street. Nicholson was fond of pornographic magazines from America and enjoyed sharing them with his fellow scavengers. Even today there was one with him, and his guests pored over the naked girls. Yari and Matthias conspiratorially noticed that even Zhero was looking at the naked girls. On Nicholson's mobile phone radio they heard the advertisement of a musical show at Hotel Concordia, offering a door prize of G$1million. Nicholson said with conviction he would have attended the show and won the door prize if he had the gate fee. The friends agreed to pay for him on condition that they would share the one million dollars equally. It was a deal, so they went.

When the winning ticket number was announced at the end of the show the friends laughed at their bad luck, but immediately they went out of the hall Nicholson told them they had just won one million dollars. They did not believe him. They went to the notice board where the number had been posted, confirmed it, quietly went out and rejoiced — G$200,000 each! Nicholson promised to go to them after claiming the money the next day.

At home the friends dreamt silently, they dreamt out loud, Ogugo dreamt about the motor vehicle parts business he'd set up, Matthias dreamt about the beautiful girl he'd marry, Yari might think of returning to Liberia, Zhero said he'd buy a handcart and start house-to-house refuse collection at day and attend evening school because two hundred thousand wasn't enough to see him through secondary school.

At bedtime each of the friends knew the others were not sleeping but they were all silent in order to be able to contend with their mental turbulence. Having decided on his course of action Zhero had little to think of, though . . . His mind sailed to Joleen in Amabra . . . but she was an illiterate — marriage to her was impossible . . . Daba didn't complete secondary school and was only a maid, whose

186

mother condoned stealing . . . Zanzi, oh, Zanzi was beautiful, Zanzi who put her arm across his shoulders and wept the night he told her he was leaving Chief Jerome Hezekiah's employment . . . Naomi too liked him, she would playfully fall on him on his bed and shout to Robin that he wanted to rape her — 'Robin Hood, you no go come save your woman?' . . . Robin advised him to be a man and give her what she wanted . . . He thanked God he'd heeded his mother's advice — nothing would stop him from getting an education . . . .

At 5pm the next day Matthias and Yari said they had to go and look for Nicholson and they went out. Nicholson's room was vacant. His neighbours confirmed that he moved out early in the morning. Matthias and Yari went to Hotel Concordia. They were told that the winner collected his one million dollars that night. (Were they sure of what they were saying?) A little angry, the hotel manager said the winner claimed the money about an hour after the show. (Nicholson Wago? Our friend, Nicholson Wago?) Yes, the manager said, pitying them.

After telling Nicholson's story Matthias asked God why he was created? Why was he created with the eyes of an albino for which his wealthy father wanted to kill him for a money-making ritual? He escaped from Kenya to Godiva only to sell rubbish for a living. Why did God create him for such a life?

Ogugo said he wouldn't ever blame God. If he had patiently served his apprenticeship as a motor vehicle parts dealer his master would have set up a shop for him, but greed tricked him to travel under a plane to America where they said there was big and fast money. He was arrested at Ronald Reagan Airport and sent back to Nigeria where he would have been jailed if he hadn't escaped to Godiva.

Yari gnashed his teeth for a long time before he spoke. 'I, Yari, my surname "Doe" even the rebel leader use to fear, I, Yari Doe, the day I set my eyes on Nicholson . . . oh . . . oh . . . .' He looked up at the cardboard ceiling, then left and right at the wooden walls, as if what he should do was inscribed on one of them. 'Oh God of justice!'

Zhero saw only one lesson in what had happened — he was born to work for his food.

Yari looked at him for a moment and walked out of the house, hissing. Matthias followed him, to avoid an outburst at their holier-than-thou friend.

The next day, they did not think there would be much to get from the dump but they reluctantly left home for it just in case someone had dumped an occasional thing or even a vehicle there. They went early but a few people had been there already and they were gathered round something. It was a newborn baby scantily wrapped in brown cloth. Its weak cry drew tears from many eyes.

'Pikin wey some people dey pray for years to get dem no fit get, one wicked woman dey troway her own,' a man remarked.

'Na God go punish am,' a woman replied.

A woman remarked, 'Dem say woman life hard. Dis one, na from de day dem born am im life hard.'

'Why de woman no abort am when de thing never tey for her womb? Na good thing she do so, for put human being inside hard life?'

A woman responded to the man's question: 'Make God no give dis woman pikin until she die. Even her next life sef, make God no give am pikin.'

A woman agreed with the man: 'For TV one doctor say abortion no be bad ting if de woman no want de pikin, and dem do de abortion at de time wey de ting no fit survive outside her womb.'

Zhero immediately suggested that it should be taken to the Motherless Babies Home. Octopus Paul said it would soon die, still he suggested that they should vote for someone to take it there. A few people were surprised at the flood of tears on his face, but he had always been as soft-hearted as a woman. Zhero remembered his mother's advice to willingly serve life and volunteered to do it. Everybody was glad and they generously donated one thousand dollars to charter a taxi. Someone suggested that a woman should accompany him. (A woman? Suppose she was accused of dumping the baby?) They would look at her breasts, wouldn't they?

The young woman who had volunteered to go replied, 'Na only breast? I go even open everything make dem look inside.'

Everybody except the weakly crying baby laughed.

Someone remarked, 'Okponkro, you rotten o!'

The taxi they called charged them two thousand dollars. Zhero urgently told Okponkro to come in with the baby. He would make up the amount. The scavengers waved the baby goodbye with prayers, some of them with tears too. Octopus Paul went to the edge of the swamp and wept.

About two weeks after Nicholson's betrayal Matthias told his friends that his moodiness which they had remarked on several times was not because of what Nicholson had done. He pulled off his trousers and pants and showed them the rashes that had covered his fair skin. They advised him to go for a test without mentioning what they suspected. He said he had done that and would go back for the result in two days' time.

Only Ogugo went to work the following day and when he returned home he waited for an opportunity to speak with Zhero privately. He opened a diamanté case and showed him what were inside: two diamond necklaces, four diamond earrings, four diamond bracelets, and two diamond rings. He found the case in a ladies' handbag in the dump.

Zhero asked him, 'Have you shown anyone else?'

He answered, 'No.'

'What do you want to do with it?'

'Take it to the police. Because I know that's what you'll advise.'

'That's good. Thank you.'

Zhero took the case from him. From the shine in his eyes as he felt and admired the bracelets, the necklaces and the earrings Ogugo wondered if he was about to change his mind.

'They are beautiful?'

'Yes,' Zhero answered, thinking that the necklaces were as beautiful as the one Bazi bought for his mom in Port Harcourt.

'And very expensive too, I am sure.'

'Yes,' Zhero agreed again. 'But they don't belong to us.'

'No,' Ogugo agreed and sighed, 'but while there's life there's hope.'

'Yes,' Zhero agreed.

'Let's go together . . . tomorrow?'

'I haven't felt myself since Matthias showed us his problem. I pray there's nothing wrong with him.'

'I said we should go together tomorrow.'

'Please go alone.'

Ogugo went to Sinclair Police Station the following day. The DPO (District Police Officer) thanked him for his honesty, took a photograph of him and wrote down his name and contact address and promised to announce it on radio, television and in the newspapers. When Zhero, Ogugo, Matthias and Yari heard the announcement on television in an eatery Matthias and Yari joined the other people around in calling the person who took the diamond jewellery to the police a fool from his mother's womb.

Matthias went for the result of his test after a week. When he returned home his friends saw the result on his face.

'Remember what the Ministry of Health says on the TV? It's not the end of life,' Zhero said without mentioning the sickness.

'Zhero is right,' Ogugo sighed, then wiped his tears. 'Zhero is right. The only thing you should do is to take your drugs as the doctors say.'

Zhero advised, 'We'll go to the Teaching Hospital tomorrow, for you to register for free drugs.'

'AIDS is not the end of life. AIDS is only the beginning of the end.'

'No, Matthias, don't say that!' Zhero angrily told him.

'Zhero, you are the only one who doesn't discriminate against me since the day I showed all of you my rashes. If Ogugo and Yari touch me, when they think I don't see them, they wash that part of their body. Since the day I showed them my rashes they don't even drink water at home. They no longer hang their clothes on the nails in the wall because they don't want their clothes to touch mine.' Only Zhero looked at the unused nails in the wall. Matthias smiled ruefully. 'Look at the mats we fold and stand against the wall when we wake up in the morning. They always put Zhero's mat between mine and theirs . . . This is the way God wants to punish me . . . If my father had killed me and used me to make money I would have been useful to someone . . . Why didn't you people allow me to go with that man who wanted to hire me? Maybe he wanted to use my albino eyes to make money . . . Why isn't God equally good to all the human beings He created?'

'My mother told me to love God and not to disrespect God no matter what's happening in my life.'

Matthias thought for a moment. 'You are right, Zhero. One of my secondary school teachers used to say the same thing too. But for me it's too late. Maybe if I abuse God I will not wake up from sleep tomorrow morning. It's better than suffering before dying.'

'Tomorrow I'll go with you to the hospital.'

'Thank you, Zhero.'

When they woke the next morning Matthias was nowhere to be found. Yari interrupted their weeping and confessed: He too had been having sex with Matthias' girlfriend. He used to use a condom because he couldn't afford two thousand dollars per round of naked sex, but one night the woman said she had fallen in love with him, adding that if a Lebanese could do it with her without a condom how about him, a fellow African? . . . 'Hey! Hey!' he moaned.

190

He agreed to go for a test the following day but in the night he was arrested in the brothel when the police swooped on the brothels at Ayilara and Diah Streets. Karachi, their next-door neighbour who had jumped out of a moving police van, delivered the report but could not say which police station the arrested men and women were being taken to.

When they went to Karachi's bedsit for more information he was sniffing cocaine. He raised his head, looked blankly at them for a moment, then continued his heavenly action. They went back to their own bedsit, wondering how Karachi could afford cocaine.

'Zhero, so it's only you and I that are left?'

'They are alive, Matthias and Yari are alive too.'

'Amen . . . Amen,' Ogugo wept aloud.

But about three days later Ogugo woke up weeping from his dream after 2am. Zhero tried to comfort him.

'Hey!' Four friends on a canoe journey, the river took two away,' he cried to the rhythm of the night rain.

Weeping too, 'Don't say so, Ogugo. They are alive.'

'Life has taken away Yari and Matthias from us.'

'Ogugo . . . Ogugo . . . .'

'Buried under the river, no graves for orphans,' he answered, unmindful of the rain drops on his left shoulder from the leaking roof.

'Shift, Ogugo, let me put the basin under the leakage.'

'No, Zhero, let the river swallow me too.'

After they stopped weeping they reconsidered their decision not to go to the police, but they still refrained from reporting to the police because the police were notorious for arresting young men as armed robbers and drug pushers and extorting money from them, especially young men who were not in paid employment.

Ogugo soon returned to his bubbly self but for days Zhero's unhappiness had been discernible to those who liked him. On the eighth day of Yari's absence he was making a supreme effort to be cheerful when the mother of the two little girls came to Agoa. After he noticed for a while that she only sat down and did not collect plastic bottles as usual he went to her. She looked out of place in the environment, a diamond mistakenly dropped in a dump. Zhero respectfully stood before her.

'Ma, you don't feel like working today?' he asked her.

'No, Zhero, I came only to see you.' He was surprised at her

English but did not show it. 'Sit by me, Zhero. You've never minded what De Boss and his men say about us . . . Thank you, Zhero.'

'Thank you, ma.'

'You know my daughters' names, Manna and Chanto, but . . . what's my name, Zhero?'

'I don't know, ma.'

'My name is Chanta.' She paused then continued. 'I sell palm oil at Mile 8 Market. That's why I collect plastic bottles. My customers pay for the bottles too. Sometimes I sell the empty bottles to other traders.' She paused again. 'I came from Makan to sell palm oil in Mo Bo when my husband and I separated. But two days ago he came to have me back, and my daughters and I will go back to Makan tomorrow. That's one reason I'm here today — to tell you about myself.' After a long pause she continued. 'You're so respectful that you won't say a thing unless I allow you to. Zhero, you're a good boy . . . Why have you been unhappy recently?'

He told her about his recurrent dream of his mother at the crossroads, and his fear that she was dead.

Chanta smiled. 'Your mother isn't dead. She wants you to follow her ways. She wants you to follow her advice. Think of the things she used to tell you to do or not to do. Remember her and try to follow her advice whenever a situation requires you to make a choice.'

'Thank you, ma.' He was suddenly uplifted. 'How about Chanto and Manna? They are going too?'

Chanta smiled. 'I have your address. My husband and I, with our daughters, we shall come and see you someday.'

'Thank you, ma.'

'Bye for now, Zhero.'

So she was educated . . . she was educated . . . just like his mother, she was educated . . . picking bottles in the rubbish dump to take care of her daughters . . . Oh, why did he abandon his mother?

He told Ogugo he was tired and went home around 2pm.

In his night dream three days later his mother was waiting at the crossroads. As he approached, she got up and walked in front; he followed her and they walked on, becoming more buoyant the more kilometres they covered . . . He woke up after 6am feeling very happy.

They did not leave home early that day because they had to go to Anthanasius for the five thousand dollars he would pay for some items they had sold to him. Around 2pm as they were going out of Nze Waterside Ogugo called for ice water. As the boy came close to

192

them he abruptly stopped and made to run back.

'Hey, Solo!' Ogugo shouted. 'Stop, Solo.' The boy was trembling. 'Solo, is this you, Solo?'

'Yes.'

Zhero asked him, 'What happened? Why are you at Nze Waterside?'

'The people of Bondo drive us commot from Bondo.'

'Whosai your papa and your mama dey?'

Solo took them to his parents, who apologized hugely for what they had done, explaining that 'the foolish boy, Solo' had only gone to his elder sister's house for some days without telling them. When he returned his family was sent out of Bondo. Solo's elder sister and her husband had to pay the landlord G$50,000 for the house that was burnt down.

'How about our property?' Ogugo asked. 'The landlord was paid G$50,000. How about our property?'

'My pikin, no vex,' Solo's mother begged. 'But una property, de Bondo boys been thief una property before dem burn de house o.'

Without a word Zhero drew Ogugo's hand and they walked away. They chartered a taxi and reached Athanasius' shop before 3pm. They were surprised at his broad, warm, intimate smile.

'Hey, my boys, na good business una been bring for me o.' He pulled out his drawer, took a bundle of ten thousand dollars and gave it to them. 'Please, if una get another supply make una no forget me o.'

They thanked him warmly too and returned home happily. At 8pm they went to a video-viewing centre to watch a star-studded Nollywood film that was advertised on a poster on the wall of the centre. They had come too late for the Nollywood film. It was 'Superman' that was now showing. Athanasius' generosity some hours ago enhanced their enjoyment of 'Superman': Superman's superhuman abilities! Superman's generosity! His honesty! His intelligence! His strength! His courage! His adventurous spirit! And yet his compassion for little people!

They went to bed, or rather, they slept on their mats happily that night with an unexpressed feeling that the hard life was the training ground for heroism.

In spite of their health they went to work the following day. There was nothing valuable around, and they were thinking of leaving when a jeep slowly braked at the edge of the dumping ground. A man in suit came out from the right back door and beckoned on the scavengers to come. All of them except the girls ran to him. First he greeted them and they responded.

'I have a big refuse dump in a very big land I want to develop. A big land,' he repeated, spreading his arms to indicate that though it was 'a land' it was vast. 'I want six strong men to clear away the dump for me.' Nearly everybody's hand was raised as the men shouted to be taken. Slowly backing away from the approaching ragged rabble, afraid of bodily contact with them, he called for silence. 'Can you appoint one person to select the strongest men for me? The pay will be good. Appoint one person.'

'Zhero! Zhero! Zhero!'

The man was surprised that several people pushed forward the only one who had not raised his hand or shouted to be hired.

Zhero selected Ogugo and five others. The man was surprised.

'I said only six men. You have selected six persons, without including yourself. Are you daft?'

Zhero laughed.

'Zhero! Zhero! Zhero, you are good! Zhero, you are my man!' the scavengers exclaimed severally.

The man was touched. 'Okay. Six men. And Zhero is their supervisor.'

The man nearly wept at the happiness of the lowly people. From the bundle of fifty thousand dollars he brought out, he gave Zhero and his six men one thousand dollars each for transport to the address he gave them, and gave the others the remaining forty-three thousand dollars to share.

'Tomorrow. 8am unfailingly.'

They thanked him, he heartily shook hands with some of them and left. About ten minutes after the other persons, including the girls who had not come around, finished sharing the money, De Boss came with three of his thugs. He was furious that Zhero had not set aside some amount for him and his boys. As he approached Zhero he shouted.

'Zhero, you bastard foreigner! I tell you say you no get sense! Na Nigerian foolishness full dat your big head! Zhero Nigeria!' he shouted as he approached Zhero, clenching his fists, his arms stretched taut by his sides as if they were iron clubs. 'Zhero Nigeria.'

Several people were afraid for Zhero, who looked as if he was not aware of what was going on, his mind partly on his mother at the crossroads, then on Chanta's advice. As De Boss made to slap him, Zhero bent low, hefted him onto his shoulders and threw him down viciously. Several young men pounced on the three thugs who were rushing to their boss. The thugs ran away. Some of the scavengers hugged one another, some shook hands, some high-fived, they congratulated one another.

Zhero's mother's wrestling lessons flashed through his mind . . . How to bend swiftly, lift up the opponent and throw him down gently only to make him ashamed . . . How to throw him down and break his waist so that he wouldn't be able to get up and fight . . . She told him never to try to break a person's neck, though she taught him how to do it in case of extreme circumstances . . . .

It seemed De Boss could not get up on his own. He begged for a taxi to be called for him. Octopus Paul called a taxi, two young men helped De Boss into the taxi and he left, silently thanking God that Chanta wasn't around to see what had happened to him. Octopus Paul said since there was nothing more to secure overnight De Boss's services were no longer needed.

Chapter Six

She was sure she'd done the right thing. It wasn't wrong to promise to marry him . . . After they had found Zhero, she would marry him. A woman should marry the father of her child . . . His argument was shocking: What did she need the School Cert for? And the university degree? Was everything he had not going to be hers? . . . If only for self-worth she would get the School Cert, the BA degree, the Master's and even a PhD . . . Vanity, he had said. Yes, vanity. This vanity was healthy, she'd told him . . . Reluctantly he agreed with her, she should get her PhD, and take charge of the Zera Girls Secondary School he was building . . . 'Oh, Zhero, please come back, come back to me —'

Yago knocked and entered. Who had subtly scented the room? He sniffed the air. The scent grew stronger as he neared her. He sat by her on the couch, sweetly enveloped in the scent.

'I love your perfume,' he said as he placed his right arm around her shoulders and wished they would be cocooned together in happiness like this forever.

She smiled. 'Thank you.'

He suspected it was Chanel No 7, the perfume he liked when he was studying in London, Lola's favourite. Lola was a girl he wanted but could not get. He used to buy it for Teima and she used to love it until she knew why he liked it.

'Is Zera the name of your perfume?' She smiled again. 'What's the name?'

'Chanel No 7.'

'S - h -' he lied. She spelt it for him. 'I love it. I'll fill every space in your bedroom with it, ceiling-high.' She sniffed the air. 'You like it too?' he asked her.

'Yes. The sweet scent of the lie.'

They laughed.

'Oh, Zera!' he laughed, a happy man, the object of whose painful quest was a good woman, and he had found her.

'Please tell me what I want to hear.'

'I've paid for the announcement. In newspapers, on radio, on TV. In every West African country.'

'You think they'll do it?'

'It's a trustworthy agency. Starting from tomorrow we can hear the announcement before 'Focus Nigeria' on AIT and before 'Sunrise Daily' on Channels TV. For two weeks. The agency's phone number, yours and mine are the ones to be contacted if there's any information. So wherever you go, let your mobile be with you.'

'How much did it cost?'

'Ten million plus.'

'Ah . . . My Zhero is a missing person!'

'He'll come back soon,' he responded, slightly disappointed that she was not happily grateful to him — he had spent ten million naira.

'You don't believe the prophet?'

'Do you?'

'No,' she lied spontaneously.

'Please don't. Don't be negative about it at all. Be positive.'

'Thank you, Louis, thank you.'

'Tell me about my son — a fisherman, a farmer, a hunter, a wrestler.'

'I remember the day he picked up a snake in the farm. When he became afraid he dropped it, and it bit him on the foot. As the foot swelled on our way back home I thought my son would die. We rushed to the herbalist, who chewed a root and told Zhero to chew it too. After he was healed Zhero said while the herbalist and I were talking he threw away the root — how could he chew what the herbalist had put inside his mouth, a man whose teeth had been browned and disfigured by tobacco?'

They laughed.

'Suppose he died?'

'He said he was sure he wouldn't die . . . Another time fear gripped him was a day he was line-fishing from a canoe. As the fish, which had swallowed the hook, pulled away, the speed of the canoe frightened Zhero. He shouted for me to come and help him, I shouted from the shore, "Leave the line, Zhero, leave the line!" After that incident he feared the river for a long time. I think he was about ten years old then.'

'Fishing alone from a canoe, at an age he should be playing at home.'

She laughed. 'Zhero's hobby was creating new paths on the way to the farm. And people would abandon the old path, saying Zhero's new path was better.' After a brief pause she continued. 'There was a day I thought I'd kill him. He was in primary six then. It was said

197

that Chief Kulokulo had the contract to provide the school desks and chairs but he didn't. One day, when Zhero was beaten for bad handwriting, he told the teacher that should be the last day he should beat him. Didn't the teacher see that they were writing on the floor? Couldn't the teacher go to Chief Kulokulo and demand the school furniture? That Friday, when Chief Kulokulo came from the city, your son Zhero confronted Chief Kulokulo. I was mad when I heard of what he had done. But Zhero turned the tables against me — wasn't it I who told him not to be afraid of fighting injustice?' They laughed. 'Two months after, the school furniture arrived.'

They laughed.

'One irony is that I was the one who led the campaign to reintroduce corporal punishment and moral instruction in the school.'

'It was the wrong punishment he objected to.'

'Yes,' she agreed, 'my son was a righteous rebel.'

They laughed again. Yago was happy, but when she told him of how Zhero saved his great-uncle in the forest he was afraid.

'Zhero can use the gun? That gentle boy? Hey . . . hey . . . .'

'What's wrong with you? My son can't be an armed robber. Is it in your family genes? Besides my Zhero is taprooted in morality. I nurtured the tree with my sweat, my words and my deeds,' she proudly said.

'The Zhero who was with me can't be an armed robber,' he said, to please her, but he felt there was something called 'wind rock'.

'Thank you. When some of his friends became militants and persuaded him to join them he refused. Most of them are now rich. They say they are militants, freedom fighters fighting for the good of the Niger Delta region, but some of them bring a lot of suffering to the very people they say they are fighting for. Zhero told them that if he wanted to use the gun to make money he wouldn't do it in the name of the Niger Delta.'

In spite of his fear he joined her in laughter. Because he was beginning to sweat he turned on the AC and closed the windows. The pause was awkward to him, so he turned on the TV. An English Premier League match was on. She did not like football — she changed the channel to Aljazeera. He suppressed his annoyance. The news was on . . . He paid attention when he heard the Nigerian president's name . . . The president stood at the door of the plane, waved to the waiting crowd on the tarmac, and started to walk jauntily down the steps . . . the president tripped, staggered briefly before the two aides behind him held him.

Yago laughed, 'A youth! They say they want a youth for president!'

Zera did not think it was funny, and the cocoon of their happiness was punctured by her reaction to the story of a four-year old child who was stolen some days ago through the back door of the house by the housegirl when his mother was in the front-yard. As the mother narrated her agony her husband tried to comfort her. Zera wept.

'See,' she commented, 'he's trying to comfort her . . . Her agony is mounting . . . The man can't feel what the woman is going through . . . He's telling her to stop, she's drying her eyes, but can the river stop flowing in her heart? . . . No, fresh tears . . . His arm is on her shoulders now . . . If he enfolds her in his arms, can the emptiness inside her be filled? . . . Why has the world made womanhood a curse?' She consoled the woman, 'May your own child be found . . . But the prophet, the one who sees tomorrow, says mine will not be found alive — Oh, Zera!'

Yago felt guilty . . . After he had just spent ten million naira — he felt she was ungrateful . . . If only he hadn't met her, the first time and this time . . . In the continued silence he thought about Teima ... In truth, Teima's monstrous change developed in reaction to his family members who did not like her, because she wasn't from his tribe, in reaction to the pressure on him to marry a girl from the tribe . . . Teima hated him because, she said, he was too weak to stop his relations from insulting her and trying to humiliate her. She said he couldn't fight for his woman . . . .

'I want to go to the office for something. I'll be back soon. What's available for dinner?'

'Anything I give you, Louis, from my heart. Isn't that enough?'

He liked the idea, but her tone was sad. He went out, suddenly lonesome, and, like an insect just out of its cocoon, not knowing what to do. She turned on the TV, went into the bathroom, wet a towel, wiped her face with it and returned to the living room. She turned on the TV, turned it off almost immediately, and took the book on the coffee table. She put the book back on the table when she thought she heard a knock on the door . . . Yes, someone was knocking.

'Come in! The door isn't locked!'

Numu came in. She admired his simplicity: short-sleeved 'adire' shirt, blue trousers, black sneakers.

'Good day, madam.'

'Numu, good day. Your uncle has just left here.'

'He said so, on the phone. The air smells sweet and your face looks fresh, belying your heart.'

'What did your uncle tell you, on the phone?'

'I'm not as foolish as Shakespeare: "There's no art to find the mind's construction in the face." *I* see your heart on your face.'

They laughed.

'Oh, Numu!' She took the book from the coffee table. 'I like your novel.'

'Thank you. Do you know it's Zhero who gave me the title of this novel?'

'How?' she eagerly asked, 'Zhero?'

'Yes. There was a day I thought Odedekoko was in my uncle's compound. But no tree in the compound, no tree nearby, and no cage. I searched around — it was Zhero singing, just like Odedekoko. I remembered Zhero for another reason while writing it — the way Teima used to treat him so wickedly, yet never a frown on his face. Though it's a slim volume, I consider it my best novel. It's taut.'

'I used to call him Odedekoko. If he wasn't happy and I wanted him to smile I would call him Odedekoko — Odedekoko.'

Numu admired the way she pronounced the word. 'I like the sound of the word from your mouth — your love for your son.'

She smiled. 'Thank you. By the way, your uncle showed me an article about your novels. The newspaper is with him.'

'I've seen it. It was written by my former student.'

'She said your novels are simplistically didactic, and you use cardboard cut-outs — your characters — you use cardboard cut-outs to hammer your themes into the reader's skull. I couldn't find the word in my dictionary. It's your uncle who looked it up in his big dictionary and told me the meaning.'

'Don't mind Aliyah. She hoped to marry me but when she met a woman half-naked in my house she turned into an enemy. Aliyah who praised my novels in her dissertation —'

'Perhaps she lied to pass the exam, now she's telling the truth?'

Numu laughed. 'You're truly Zhero's mother.'

'Thank you,' she said with a warm smile, happy to be Zhero's mother even if he was not around.

Aliyah's encounter with Teima flashed through his mind. He stopped smiling.

200

'Uncle says I'll arrange for teachers for you. They'll come here and teach you. I'll do it whenever you're ready.'

'Thank you.' She opened the novel, closed it and put it back on the table. 'Numu, when I tell your uncle about the things in your novel, especially the many sexual scenes, he just says, "Don't mind that mad boy." Do you, maybe, think he's right? . . . Aliyah, your student, meeting a half-naked girl in your house.'

'My former student.'

'What's the difference?'

'My sins may be scarlet but my novels are read.'

She looked at him suspiciously. 'Red? Are your novels not printed in black and white?'

'Then I'm black and white, a piebald animal.'

'Numu, I fear your uncle's right.'

They laughed.

'Far away all our heroes are alabaster figures, but their close-ups show that some of them have feet of clay. Prometheus gave mankind fire, but how did he get it? He stole it — he was a thief. The image of the foremost mahatma in India has not finished delighting the world, but those who knew him in his ashram said he was a pathetic human groping for truth. Aliyah wrote what she wrote because she has seen my nakedness. The true hero is in Odedekoko. Read my novel. There are millions of heroes in Nigeria . . . A thousand thousand acts of true heroism take place every day in the world not seen by even one paparazzo.' His eyes fell on another novel on the coffee table. He took it and read out the title: 'I Have Loved Glory Too Much'. He fell thoughtful. 'I have loved glory too much,' he mused.

'I'll get you something to chew, and something to drink,' she said, afraid that he might ask her who gave her the novel, and she might have to lie.

She got up, to go into the kitchen. His mind on her beauty, he compared her to Teima . . . He couldn't say who was more beautiful . . . Teima was bad karma for him . . . pestering him for them to leave the country forever . . . 'People say I'm wicked. I want to be good, but I keep on doing wicked things. I love Louis, but see what I'm doing with you . . . I'll be a good woman if we leave Nigeria and marry. Please, Numu, lead me away from the primrose path,' Teima begged him . . . He felt he too was evil, even though he covered the things he was doing with the garb of the writer . . . His mind went back to Zera's beauty . . . .

Zera tried to, but couldn't imagine a female lecturer in Nigeria having sex with her student. She'd read about some cases, but those were in Britain and America.

Tearing his mind from Zera's beauty he jumped to his feet like a suddenly self-aware lotus-eater for whom the journey that truly mattered must continue, and he went to the kitchen. He needed to reflect on his life.

'Madam, please forgive me,' he said to her and lied, 'I've just remembered, I've got to be somewhere in thirty minutes. I'll come another day for a full meal.'

He understood the meaning of her laughter. After he left she went back to the couch and thought about a character in his novel, a professor . . . The professor's explanation to her friend that her many years of anger and bitterness at her parents for giving her out as a maid at the age of ten instead of sending her to school might have caused her cancer or made her susceptible to it . . . .

She felt her breasts for lumps . . . No lumps. In her imagination her lungs . . . her liver . . . her cervix . . . her brain — every part of her body was cancer-free.

She relented on her father . . . He was so full of joy and pride that she was the first girl in the village to get a scholarship, and to attend the prestigious Queens College . . . Whenever she went home on holidays the village called her 'Queen' and he was very proud of her . . . then she injured his pride by dropping out of school due to her pregnancy . . . Maybe she should blame herself instead of being bitter at him?

Her mother flashed through her mind . . . After Zhero was born her mother told her to stop feeling guilty and love her son, and to never blame her father again. Once, when Zhero was seriously sick and she had feared he was about to die she started to curse her father. Her mother was mad at her for clinging to the past instead of moving on. That night her mother made her swear to never talk about her father to her anymore . . . She wondered why she wasn't as good as her mother, she who had religiously taught her son to always love and never hate . . . From where did she get her fiery temper? It must have been from that wicked man, her father. She smiled — even now she was getting angry . . . .

She liked the novel, 'Odedekoko', that was inspired by Zhero. She would read all of it again . . . She was on page 17 when a neighbour in the estate knocked and opened the door.

'Zera,' she said from the threshold, 'I'm idle.' Zera laughed. 'If you're idle too, can I stay with you for a few minutes?' Zera laughed again. 'I mean it, Zera. My husband's wealth is killing me slowly slowly. He says I must not work.'

Going to her, 'Come in, Veronique, please come in.' She took her by the hand and they went to sit together on the couch. Zera felt Veronique's husband was afraid of exposing her mannequin figure to men. 'I'm sorry you're bored.'

'It's the way my husband wants it. If I complain he's wasting my master's degree, he'll reply that it will be useful when we have children. But suppose boredom kills me before the children come?' Zera laughed. 'This is a strange form of spousal abuse, to use Wole Soyinka's words — spousal abuse.' Zera laughed again. 'You're laughing, is that all the help you can give me?'

'Has boredom not flown away? Laughter opens the cage.'

'You're right. Thank you . . . Do you know that my sister lives in the compound from which you came to your husband's estate?'

'Who?'

'Veronica. My younger sister.'

'The university teacher? Dr (Mrs) Veronica Hamza?'

'Yes. She said you always kept to yourself. Just like here.'

'It's because I'm new in Lagos.'

'I'll tell her you're very approachable.'

'Thank you.'

'Veronica is more sensible than me. When her husband said she must not go to work she separated from him. He's stinkingly rich, but my sister says there's nothing as good as work. Any kind of honest work. How can she sit at home and eat only? After six months he begged her to forgive him. She has forgiven him, but she hasn't moved back to his house.' She laughed. 'Perhaps I should do so too?' Zera was silent. 'What do you advise?'

'Dialogue. Patience. Love. No third party.'

'You're a wise woman.'

Zera visualized Veronica — as shapely as a lissom mannequin too.

Veronique said the sitting room was too cold, so Zhera turned off the AC and they both opened the four windows, then Zhera turned on the TV. Prophet Blake was preaching. She thought Veronique would not like a religious programme, so she changed the channel.

'It's Prophet Blake. Please can I listen to him?'

'Sure . . . You know him?'

'Who doesn't know Prophet Blake in Nigeria? I attend his church.'

'A reliable prophet? I mean, do his prophecies come true?'

'Prophet Blake sees the future as if it is the moment.'

'That's good.'

Veronique piled up cases upon cases of Prophet Blake's prophecies that had come to pass, and Zera grew sadder and sadder as Veronique reeled off illustrations of her prophet's divine ability. Uplifted, Veronique thanked her and went back to her bungalow. Zera was sad because it was Prophet Blake who said she would not find Zhero alive . . . .

In her night dream Zhero was dead. She woke up around 2am and sat up thoughtfully on the bed . . . Her mind drifted to the day her father rejected her . . . When she returned from school she told him her school was on holidays, but after two days she told the truth to her mother, who wept, consulted her co-wife, who advised that they should go through his sister . . . Her mother's co-wife feistily defended her, saying any girl could make such a mistake . . . Her father slapped the good woman and she fainted. When people shouted that the woman was dying her father raged, Let her die, and may Zera's baby when it is born die an untimely death too . . . Her mother vowed never to forgive him for cursing an unborn child, took her to her own village Amabra, and never saw her husband till she died . . . Oh, was her father's word coming to pass!

When Yago came at noon he thought a tragedy had occurred.

'What's the matter, Zera, what?'

'They say Prophet Blake's prophecies have never failed. They never fail,' she added in self-pity.

'They. Who are they?'

'A friend.'

'You told a friend? Our secret? . . . Now you've exposed me, you're happy, aren't you?'

'Did I say I mentioned your name? Or even our situation?'

'How can I be sure how well you painted my sin? My reputation means nothing to you, Zera, does it? Answer me, Zera, my reputation means nothing to you?'

'Ask your character, Louis, not me,' she spat out with hatred. 'And the way you raised your hand halfway before dropping it, it's not the first time, I hope you are not thinking of striking me. Because if

204

you do . . . if you do, Louis . . .' she checked herself and sat back on the couch.

He went to his bedroom and flopped onto the bed . . . To leave or not to leave her? . . . Would this one not be worse than Teima? . . . The malignant look in her eyes as she spoke, oh!

He had come to tell her that he, Dr (Mrs) Nounoun with whose company he was to start business, and other business moguls were to accompany the president to China on an economic visit. Now, he wouldn't accompany the president. Let his business go to ruins, he couldn't care less . . . .

He lamented bitterly: 'I can't understand life. You pull a woman out of absolute poverty, you expect her to be grateful to you every day — every second — till she dies, but no. Anytime you are angry with her, she readies herself to attack you physically, forgetting all the good things you've done for her, as if she has lived in wealth since she was born.'

The tears rolled down his cheeks . . . .

For love's sake he had to check his habit of singing when he was happy, because his singing voice, she said, keenly reminded her of Bazi and sometimes slashed at her feelings with a sharp new knife ... He also had to remember not to be too happy while her son was still missing . . . .

She thought about her sudden hatred for him . . . Why? . . . Wasn't she equally evil in a past life, when she, a man then, impregnated and abandoned two young sisters, wasn't that action worse than what Louis had done? . . . As a schoolchild she foolishly and meekly went away when he rejected the pregnancy he implanted in her. Not so this time — she would hold him responsible for the whereabouts of her son —

She checked her rising anger, 'Holier-than-thou Zera, instead of forgiving Louis and moving on, spiritually you are sowing the seed of karma through hatred for a man who's sorry for his own past action. Zera, you ruined two sisters,' she said to herself and felt sorry, as if it was just yesterday she did it . . . .

The next day he travelled to Kaduna and stayed in Durban Hotel. At 4pm or so he felt restless and took a taxi from the hotel's car hire service to drive him around the city. When a girl waved down the car he told the driver to stop.

'Come in, young lady,' he affably said to her and opened the left back door for her. 'You'll go with me to the hotel I'm staying in?' he asked her in a voice that made the driver wonder if he had been driving a teenager all along.

She said 'Yes, sir.'

'Thank you. What's your name?'

'Ama, sir.'

He told the driver to go back to the hotel . . . The girl's respectfulness bothered him, it underlined the age gap between them . . . but what did it matter? After today he would never see her again . . . She walked behind him into the hotel. Inside the lift he wondered why she looked frightened . . . first time in a lift? Anytime he looked at her she dropped her eyes . . . And she looked hungry . . . Her sundress highlighted the beauty of her curvaceous shoulders, but she looked pitiful, about to collapse any moment, needing the support of food . . . .

Immediately they entered his room he changed his mind about taking her, because he felt sorry for having brought the poor girl into a hotel when he saw that she looked extremely frightened. He felt like a weird man who was about to slaughter a chicken with an axe. He apologized for bringing an innocent girl into a place her father would not be happy to see her in and gave her a ten-thousand-naira bundle. She threw the money at him.

'Take your ritual money!' she exclaimed and wiped her hand on her dress, mentally saying 'The devil is a liar', to neutralize whatever satanic substance she might have touched.

He burst out in tears like a child whose parents had just said they would not replace his missing toy, and he said to her, 'You can't understand . . . you can't understand . . .' Then he told her some of his story briefly, concluding, 'I'm not looking for money, it's my son I'm looking for,' feeling a little relieved that a fellow human had patiently listened to his story.

She pitied him but told him to keep his money, and went out, to continue her own quest — for money that would not kill her or turn her into a vegetable.

He wiped his tears with his hands, wiped his hands on the bedsheet without knowing, lay on the bed, and thought about Zera, whose unholy behaviour had driven him into self-degradation . . . .

She too was thinking about him . . . Did she really know the man with whose destiny she wanted to merge her own? . . . Why was Teima so contemptuous of him, and yet he stuck to her? . . . And he told her his own father rejected his mother's pregnancy with him —

was it in the genes? How many bastards could he have scattered about? . . . If she didn't marry him where would she go to? . . . Men could be so wicked — if she didn't marry him he could dispossess her of everything he'd given her . . . She needed a university degree . . . She wouldn't go back to road-sweeping, no matter what . . . .

He thought back to the day he rejected her pregnancy . . . He felt bad that he'd violated his one-woman principle and he once more renewed his vow to not have an affair outside marriage . . . until Wura-Aiye came his way — Wura-Aiye, a ravishing beauty . . . Just after a few months she too said she was pregnant for him . . . The way she easily left when he threatened her made him feel she was truly a gold-digger — a diamond-digger, that was what he called her. But he gave her a lot of money, just in case she was truly pregnant and wanted to keep the baby whose father she didn't know . . . .

He thought about his business and his wealth . . . If he found Zhero he'd give him everything . . . But without Zhero did Zera deserve everything?

At bedtime his mind went back to the casual affairs he'd had . . . the girls he'd taken from the street to the hotel and had never come across thereafter . . . the girls he'd driven away with money for abortion and had never met again . . . when he was a secondary school student, the horrible things he and his friends proudly did, which none of his friends too, he was sure, would now be proud of in their adult life . . . They damaged the lives of women in the name of enjoyment . . . 'Ah, Louis Yago,' he concluded loudly, 'you have sown seeds of suffering . . . seeds of karma.'

Around 3am he woke up and went to the toilet to relieve himself. He sat on the toilet bowl and started to urinate . . . He shook his head at his life . . . He was a wealthy man, a man important enough to accompany the president of the country on an economic visit to China, but his life wasn't a glorious one . . . .

Unable to go back to sleep he decided to read 'The Truth', an evening newspaper the hotel staff had slipped under the door when he did not answer the door at dusk . . . The story of the woman who stabbed her husband to death filled his eyes with tears. She had forgiven him for impregnating their fourteen-year-old child and had agreed to keep it a secret but when he berated her for committing a sin by terminating the child's three-month-old pregnancy — oh, she didn't know what she was doing until their child and their neighbours pulled her away from the dead body she had been stabbing unstoppably . . . The story was titled 'EVIL!'

'Oh, Yago!' he groaned with sorrow for the suffering he had caused women, and he let the tears freely roll down his face . . . .

He went back to Lagos around noon and phoned Zera to come over to his house. She happily said she would be with him before 7pm. She was happy because earlier in the day, before the TV programme, 'Focus Nigeria' on AIT, Veronique had given her hope that even Prophet Blake's prophecy could fail.

When the missing person announcement about Zhero was aired, Veronique who had just come to pass the time with her, had prayed that the boy should be found, for the parents to have peace and joy restored to their hearts. Zera had asked, suppose a prophet had said the boy would not be found alive, would God answer her prayer? Veronique had replied, prophecy or no prophecy God's will would always be done. (Even if the prophet was Prophet Blake?) Veronique had replied that no matter what was prophesied about a good person God could turn it into a blessing.

Zera had broken down and wept. 'He's my son . . . Zhero is my son . . . It's my son that's missing.'

Veronique wept with her. 'If he's your son God will bring him back to you because you're a good woman. If he's your son God will bring him back to you because he's a good boy.'

After they stopped weeping Veronique told her about The Home Stretch, a religious group whose teachings she liked. She said she used to enjoy listening to their discussions on TV some years ago, especially their discussions on love, selfless service, dreams and prophecy.

'Veronique, do you know that when I was in the village some people from The Home Stretch used to come and teach us? But when my personal problem started I forgot everything, nearly everything.'

'Life is like that.'

While they paused Zera thought about what The Home Stretch used to say about prophecy . . . why prophecies often failed . . . why some prophecies were not the truth . . . even if the prophet was sincere . . . .

As she felt more strongly that the prophecy would not come true she grew happier . . . until Yago's call to come and she happily promised to be with him before 7pm.

When the houseboy opened the gate for her around 8pm her

radiant smile made him resolve to present his matter before Chief Yago that night, in her presence. He allowed thirty minutes to pass, and then went to his employer.

'Armstrong, you want to see me?'

'Yes, sir. Good night . . . good evening, sir.'

Zera smiled.

'Any problem?'

'No problem, sir . . . Is about my going to evening school, sir . . .' Zera encouraged him with a smile and he continued. 'Sir, I am a person searching for something. It is education I come to this city to find. If Sir can increase my salary, because ten thousand per month is too small for transport, school fees, books . . . If Sir can add something to the ten thousand naira. If Sir can allow me to close work at 4pm, then I can go to evening classes at Ebute Metta.'

'You want to go to school?' Yago asked with suppressed anger.

'Yes sir,' Armstrong answered eagerly.

'If the houseboy and the housegirl stop work at 4pm, I am to be my own houseboy till the next day? You knew your pay would be ten thousand naira before you accepted it, didn't you?' Armstrong was speechless. 'Free food, free accommodation, and when you're sick it's my duty to buy you medicine, yet ten thousand isn't enough?' He ignored Armstrong's blank stare and continued. 'And the fine clothes you're wearing now, is it with your pay you bought them?'

Zera, who had known suffering, was disappointed. Armstrong apologized and left. After a long silence Zera spoke.

'We'll look at his matter tomorrow, Louis. You're angry now. Tomorrow?' He did not answer. 'The boy reminds me of your son Zhero — his ambition to go to secondary school and then university . . . Whatever he's doing now is because of that ambition.'

'I think I'm not in the mood now. We'll call him tomorrow.'

Armstrong was disappointed that Madam who everybody thought was a very good woman did not put in a word for him. At 6am the next day he left a note on his bed, told the gateman he was going into the world, and walked out of the gate. Zera wept when she read the note around 9am, and she said to Armstrong, wherever he might be then, 'Go well, traveller,' a tear or two dropping on his note. She reluctantly believed Yago's promise that the experience would make him a better person. Maybe he noticed that she did not fully believe him, so he said to her that within one week he would provide mobile phones for all his office and domestic staff. If

Armstrong had a mobile phone he could have called him back immediately.

'Yes,' she agreed, 'and Zhero too, Zhero isn't with us, because he didn't have a mobile,' she added, and wept for her son and for herself.

He comforted her and they ate breakfast sadly because Zhero had no mobile to tell him to come back to his father's mansion.

About eight hours later when she remarked that his attention had not been on anything she said, he replied that it was because he would feel happier in her house. She was glad to hear that, so they left for her house. The true reason, which he did not tell her, was that his mind had been running on Teima since the morning, and he had been thinking about what Numu's friend, Abang, said about the aura of a person lingering around a place the person used to live in. He needed a change of environment.

At Ojuelegba Road there was a gridlock. After twenty minutes or so Robin had to go out and find the cause. He returned in about fifteen minutes to say that the charred remains of two boys — people said the boys could not be more than sixteen years each — their charred remains were on the road, and the large crowd around the remains would not allow the traffic to flow. One of the boys had snatched a woman's handbag as she was about to enter a bus. When she raised an alarm he threw the bag to his friend. Both of them were caught, doused in petrol and burnt by an angry crowd.

'Poor boys,' Zera sighed, 'but why steal? Couldn't they have looked for something else to do, even if it's a menial job?'

'It's the government's fault,' Yago remarked. 'Massive unemployment, yet oil money is flowing like River Niger into private pockets. Like River Benue into private bank accounts,' he said for good measure.

Zera disagreed with him. 'I don't think that's a reason for young healthy people to steal. One can always do something to survive, even menial jobs.'

'Not everybody is as strong as Zhero to be a porter.'

She was highly offended, but she would not show anger in Robin's presence. She only said, 'You're right. Not everybody is as morally strong as my son to do a menial job to survive.'

He knew he had offended her. He decided to be silent. When he thought about her point of view he wondered why he had opposed it. He himself had never justified crime before and he had always said that if the government failed in its responsibilities the individual

210

had a duty to help themselves honestly, to survive spiritually, instead of cheating, stealing, robbing, kidnapping, terrorizing society — his son Zhero was on the right path. He thought about what Numu's friend, Abang once said: 'The so-called non-persons are very important persons in the social fabric.' He agreed with Abang — they were like the sun people cursed on a hot day without giving thought to its usefulness.

He placed her right hand on his left thigh and caressed it. She accepted his silent apology — she caressed his thigh. When they reached her house around 8pm he was beat — he flopped onto the couch in the living room and requested for a glass of cold water. While she was in the kitchen his mind went again to Teima . . . Teima's character didn't match her surpassing beauty . . . but in the beginning of their marriage she regarded him as the best husband on earth, and she worshipped her luck . . . What could she be doing now?

She was in Numu's house. She had, she said, following the missing person announcement she heard on Channels TV and AIT, come to send her regrets through Numu to Yago and to Zhero's mother. She came out of the bedroom barefoot, wearing only diaphanous primrose camiknickers, and sat by him on the settee in the sitting room. She told him to turn off the TV. He said no, he liked Pastor Ododo's preaching though he wasn't a church-goer. She shrugged.

'I shouldn't have treated Zhero like that. A very good boy who never offended me in anyway.' He was silent. 'I like your *adire* shirt. Where did you buy it?'

'Teima, you call me evil. But you're more evil.'

She laughed. 'In the university a friend of mine was fond of saying that the power between a woman's legs is the function of the weakness of the man's head.' She laughed again. 'Because of your love for sex, you were afraid you'd lose me, otherwise you'd have forced me to treat the boy well. I told you never again to talk about his going to evening school, and you obeyed me . . . Whereas you could have exploited my desire for you to make me do the right thing. Who is more evil, Numu?' He could not answer the question. 'You're like your uncle Louis who I once loved so much . . . I had a past I had denounced and I was a truly good woman, a woman who felt close to God at the time I met Louis . . . though he raped me ... but I fell in love with him . . . But Louis couldn't protect me from his meddlesome relations. He was too weak to do so. And I was forced to exhume my past to give me strength against my wicked in-laws. When you returned from London and met a house without a meddlesome extended family you praised Louis, but the credit should be mine.' She took his arm and placed it around her shoulders. 'You, I allowed you to come in and go out as you pleased because I loved you and wanted you.'

'What is this your past?'

'Perhaps I'll tell you someday.' She put his right middle finger in her mouth and chewed on it affectionately for a few seconds. 'Someday, I will . . . For your readers to profit from my life story.' She smiled. 'As you're fond of saying, Your sins are scarlet, but your works are read.'

While he was laughing Pastor Ododo said on the TV, 'Life uses everybody, everything for its purpose.'

He said to her, 'Did you hear that?' He rewound the broadcast and they heard Pastor Ododo again. He laughed and said to her, 'So life is using my works to reach people, evil as I am.'

'Pastor Ododo? You don't know Pastor Ododo, Numu.'

'Life is using him, even as life is using us — you and me,' he replied in a sober tone that made her wonder what had happened to him.

'You suddenly look sad, Numu, why?'

Unaccountably his mind had flashed back to Abang whose spiritual experiences he and U Shettima loved to pooh-pooh . . . And Abang had advised him to stop his affair with Teima . . . .

'Numuh!'

'Louis XIV of France said, "I have loved war too much." He paused then said of himself, 'I have loved sex too much.'

'How about me?' she asked. He shrugged and she said, 'I have loved evil too much?'

A loud knock on the door — they jumped to their feet. He went angrily to open the door — four armed masked men. He did not go back to her on the settee. He sat on the coffee table.

'We are men of the underworld,' one of them announced. 'We demand unalloyed obedience.'

Another one said, 'You cashed three million naira today. As a university teacher, don't lie. True or false? From the university campus branch of Golden Age Bank. True or false?'

'How did you know?'

'Your life or your money?' the first speaker asked calmly. Numu knew the voice, but he mustn't let them know that he knew the speaker. 'I say, your life or your money?'

'That's an ambiguity. What exactly do you mean?'

As the robbers laughed each of them silently resolved to rape his cool and seductive girlfriend before leaving — she would scream and weep for mercy.

The first speaker went closer to Numu. 'You're a brave man, to joke in the face of death . . . Dr Numu, in a country in which some people can't have one square meal a day you have three million naira — cash — in your house. Our consciences are clear.'

Another one spoke. 'How social inequalities turn the youth into criminals. A theme in one of your novels.'

'Do you know how many years it took me to gather that amount, money I want to use to complete the house I've been building for three years?'

'Hey! His girlfriend is texting!' one of them shouted.

Because she continued to text he shot her. She looked unconcerned, happy, grateful. He shot her defiance again, and again, and she collapsed on the settee, like a weary traveller just back home, too tired to recount her odyssey.

Involuntarily urinating in his trousers, Numu told them the money was in the multi-coloured sack in the wardrobe. One of them went into the bedroom and came back with the sack.

'Hey! Alarm! Alarm!' the one who had killed Teima alerted his colleagues.

The alarm had been switched on by a security guard following the gunshots. As the robbers were escaping on motorbikes three of them were shot dead. Two armed security guards who saw Numu rushing out of his house both shot him in error.

A little after 10pm Abang called Yago: Numu and Teima had been killed by armed robbers. Three armed robbers were killed, and one of them, a student of the University, Joe Nounoun, son of the MD of an oil company, was arrested with the sack of money they had stolen. Joe Nounoun was the leader of the most feared student's cult in the university. No one knew he was also into armed robbery.

Instead of responding Yago shouted for Zera to come. 'Come, come hear what I'm hearing, Teima has been killed in Numu's house!'

'How about Numu? Is he okay?'

'They died together. Teima and Numu died together.'

Zera took the phone from him and told the caller that Yago would call back later.

'Hey! Numu dead?'

'They died together, Zera. Teima and Numu died together. At this time of the night what was Teima doing in Numu's house?'

'It might have been an innocent visit.'

He continued as if she had not said anything. 'The way Teima always insulted him, the way he always laughed no matter how strong the insult was, I should have known that there was something to it . . . As for me, my stomach was too big. Couldn't I see how flat my nephew's stomach was? I should reduce my stomach and be strong too . . . When a woman persistently compares her husband to a young man there's something to it, but like all old men I was too foolish to see it. I thought my wealth was a unique selling point.'

'Louis, stop this nonsense!'

'If I do, who would advise my fellow men not to cultivate potbellies?' he asked her, unconsciously placing his right hand on his stomach like a man who wanted to feel the kicking of his unborn child in his beloved wife's womb.

Zera tried hard not to laugh.

A heavily pregnant young woman, shouting for help, ran into the sitting room, pursued by her husband. Seeing Yago, his landlord, the young man turned back, saying he was going to wait for her, in case the landlord didn't marry her and take her to his house and worship her.

The woman apologized, 'Sir, don't be offended. He's talking like that to annoy you, so that you will drive me out . . . Sir, you must help me tonight. Ma knows about my problem. I can't go back to my parents, because they warned me not to marry him. Nothing I do satisfies him — it's beat, beat, beat every day and night. See, as pregnant as I am, he wants me to serve him as a slave. I go to work, he goes to work; I do part-time programme in the University of Lagos on Saturdays and Sundays. During the week I need to study and do the homework the lecturers give us, yet he wants me to do everything in the house. His own is only to watch TV or do physical exercise and go to club house with his friends. Today, because I'm very tired his sister helped me to cook, but he says the food isn't sweet. That's why he was beating me. At this time of the night. His mother is supporting him, that a woman who doesn't cook for her husband isn't fit to be a wife. Ma will tell you about my suffering in this estate . . . Sir, you are not saying anything?' Yago is still silent.

214

'Sir?'

The woman looked embarrassed.

'A tragedy has just befallen him,' Zera said to her.

The woman wailed, 'Hey! Death has befallen me tonight! Hey, my life! What shall I do? Why did I come into this world as a woman?'

Zera tried to comfort her, 'My sister, a woman's life is hard, but it's our only life, so we must use it well.'

The woman's blank look showed that she did not understand Zera's philosophy of life.

At last, Yago spoke. 'Zera, go and tell Oweilakemefa I want to see him.'

The woman went down on her knees and thanked him. Zera went out. Uneasy at Yago's silence the woman went out and stood in the doorway, where she realized for the first time that she was barefoot and in a state of undress — only a pink cotton blouse and a white slip. She shrugged. She was pulling off her clothes when her husband started to beat her . . . because she hissed when he told her to drink the water she had called soup and given him.

Yago had been thinking aloud . . . 'Dr (Mrs) Nounoun, life hasn't been fair to her. In London, her husband impregnated their Nigerian housegirl so they divorced —' He stopped talking when he noticed the woman looking at him . . . .

The woman's mother-in-law reminded him of his own mother . . . The day she cursed Teima . . . .

'I say my son should build a house for my brother in the village you told him not to!'

'Mama, I didn't tell —'

'Shut up! Today I shall curse you.'

As his mother started to strip he ran out of the sitting room, leaving Teima rooted to where she was standing.

'Mama, don't do it o!' he shouted from where he was.

'You, Teima, today I shall curse you . . . All the gods of my tribe, see me, in the purity of the form in which you sent me into this world, I call on you to give effect to my words. Teima, I curse you, I curse you, you shall not have the happiness you are depriving me of. The happiness you do not want my son to give me, you shall not get it from him.'

Fear of the curse sent Teima into hospital for over a week . . . Before she left the hospital her mother and her sister warned him to decide whether or not he wanted to continue the marriage, because their own Teima would not be going back to his house as a docile woman — the gods of their tribe were their witnesses . . . .

Zera returned with Oweilakemefa, who, coincidentally, was wearing a wife-beater. He glared at his wife who had dashed into the living room as she saw him coming, and was afraid because if her musclebound husband decided to drag her out Chief Yago looked physically unable to stop him . . . unless his wife would add her strength to his.

'Good evening, Landlord.'

Yago ignored his disrespectful tone. 'Good evening, Oweilakemefa. Please have a seat.'

'No need to sit down, sir. I promise not to beat her again if she'll agree for us to discuss. Marriage isn't by force. If she says she's my wife she must cook my food, wash my clothes, and so on and so forth. That's what's causing the problem. And she should stop teaching my foolish sister to insult me by saying that in Britain and America the men don't treat their wives as slaves. I'm not a white man.' He glared at the unwifely fair-skinned Nigerian, and then continued. 'I won't beat her again. I'll give her time to decide. I promise you, sir, I'll not beat her.'

Zera had a strong urge to ask if he spelt out those conditions before she married him, but she checked herself and only shrugged. He walked out furiously. Yago looked crestfallen. Mrs Oweilakemefa looked thoroughly embarrassed.

'Come, my sister,' Zera said as she took her arm. 'He won't beat you tonight. There's time to think.' Mrs Oweilakemefa did not move. 'Tomorrow I'll talk to his mother as a fellow Izon woman. Come.'

Zera went out and Mrs Oweilakemefa slowly followed with her two heavy loads — the eight months' pregnancy which was beginning to agitate her womb, and the fear of her marital home. With the flat of her nervous right hand on her bulky stomach which was not completely covered by her pink blouse she apprehensively walked behind Zera . . . .

Despite their own sorrow, for a long time Yago and Zera pricked up their ears at the slightest noise outside but no cry came from Oweilakemefa's house. When Abang called again Zera told him Yago would see him tomorrow.

'Tomorrow, and tomorrow, and tomorrow creeps in this petty pace —'

'Louis, is something wrong with you?'

'In our secondary school we memorized a lot of Shakespeare.'

'Please, don't frighten me.'

'I'm sorry.'

'Let's go to bed. Tomorrow we shall think about Numu.'

'Yes, tomorrow.'

A few minutes before 6am the persistent ringing of Yago's phone woke him. The caller was responding to a TV announcement in Ghana. When he was in Godiva last week Zero and his gang of teenage robbers were arrested while they were robbing the hotel he stayed in.

'Zhero?'

'Yes. Zero: Z-E-R-O.'

'I saw a Private Number on my screen. What's your name?'

The caller terminated the conversation. Yago took it that in Ghana, as in Nigeria, people did not want to be involved in anything that had to do with the police and criminals. Zera watched him looking at his handset. She was afraid to talk. He continued staring at the handset. He was afraid to talk to her too. At last he moaned. She jumped to her feet and hugged him.

'Is Zhero dead? Have they found his body? Louis speak!'

'The caller said Zhero was arrested in Godiva.'

'Then he's alive!'

'A gang of armed robbers were arrested while they were robbing a hotel. Zhero was among them.'

'It's a lie! It's a mistake! Not my Zhero! Not my son!' she shouted, then wept because she feared her son had come to a shameful end.

Yago did not tell her what he saw in his inner vision — Zhero shooting down the men that wanted to kill his great-uncle . . . the teenager who knew how to use a gun . . . the boy who said if he wanted to use the gun to make money he wouldn't do it in the name of the Niger Delta . . . .

'Louis, crying will not solve our problem. Let's stop crying and go to Godiva,' she urgently said to him, as if he was the one who started the crying, and he must get out of the cocoon of self-pity and face life.

He called his secretary to book the first flight after 10am to Godiva for himself and Mrs Zera Yago. When he could not get his accountant on the phone he angrily directed the secretary to tell him to make US$200,000 available before 9am. Then he called Robin to leave whatever he was doing and come quickly.

They had their bath, she packed her travelling bag, and they went to his house for him to pack his things. While waiting for the secretary to call back they encouraged each other to eat breakfast. In the dining room he asked the maid why the table was dusty.

'Let her go, Louis, let the girl go away, let's eat,' she said with a tinge of anger in her voice.

They started to eat because they had a biological duty to fill their stomachs and be strong.

'Oh, my Zhero! At least he's alive. I thank God he's alive.'

'You said we should eat. Please eat.'

'I'm sorry, I'm sorry, Louis, I'm sorry. Let's eat.'

A minute or so later he thought out loud: 'Unless money can't set him free. No matter the cost, Zhero will come back with us.'

'Thank you, Louis.'

'Immediately he gets a visa he'll go to London. Avoid the influence of bad boys.'

She paused. 'I don't believe Zhero did it . . . Do you think he did, took part in armed robbery?'

'I haven't said so, have I?'

She stood up. 'I've had enough.'

'Then I have had too much too. Hunger can't do more than kill a person.'

She took his arm and made him sit again. 'I'm sorry, Louis. I'm very sorry.'

'If you're going to cry then let's go into the bedroom.'

'No, I won't cry,' she said, fighting back the tears, 'I'm not about to cry.'

'Trying times.'

'Yes. It's human, Louis, it's human.'

They managed to finish their breakfast and went out to sit at the porch. The accountant and the secretary came with the money and the flight tickets after 9am. The first flight after 10am was at 12noon.

'Any one before twelve?'

'Yes, sir,' the secretary answered, 'at 10am.' She looked at the time on her mobile. 'But with the traffic . . . I think it's better to go by the twelve o'clock flight.'

'I think it's better to go and wait at the airport,' he said angrily.

'No, Louis, it's too early to leave for the airport.'

She dismissed the staff, who were happy to go away from the boss they had not seen in that mood before.

218

'Trying times, Louis?'

He burst out in laughter. His employees, who had not gone far, looked back in surprise. He called them back.

'Madam said I was angry. Was I?'

The secretary looked at the accountant. Zera told them to lie that their boss was in a most pleasant mood. Everybody laughed, and they said their goodbyes . . . .

She remembered that they ought to have called Abang but decided not to tell Yago. Nothing should interrupt her son's matter. Numu and the wicked woman were dead but her son was alive and needed her help . . . .

Yago too was thinking about Numu . . . that foolish boy was probably having an affair with his wife . . . What could Teima have been doing in his house at that hour? . . . Now she had all of eternity to admire him in hell where it was impossible for men to develop potbellies.

His left hand unconsciously stroked his stomach . . . .

His mind went back to Numu . . . Where would he take Teima to since he didn't believe there was hell? . . . There was something between them — he called her Teima in a text message he sent to her . . . .

The rain was beating down when they reached the Murtala Muhammed International Airport. Yago, who feared flying in bad weather, would have liked them to postpone the journey, but Zera said she would not mind travelling alone — the weather was a test of her love for her son.

The plane left Lagos at 12 noon and arrived in Lagos, the capital of Godiva at 1.10pm. Lagos, the capital of Godiva was spelt the same as Nigeria's Lagos but pronounced 'Lahgohs'. As they came out of the plane he remarked on the hotness of the sun, calling it cruel.

'Shall we go back to Murtala Muhammed Airport where the kind rain is falling?'

They laughed, and she said the Godiva sun and the Nigerian rain weren't clever teachers — they didn't know that no one, nothing could test her love for her son. He did not know what to say to her remark — he only grunted.

They chartered a taxi for the rest of the day and on the way to the five-star hotel the driver recommended for them they made inquiries about the police station in Godiva. He said if it was a very serious case such as murder, kidnapping, and armed robbery it was best to go straight to the IG (Inspector General), but if it was common stealing, rape, 419 scam, assault and battery and so on the DPO (District Police Officer) of the station could attend to it. After they paid for a suite in the hotel he took them to the IG's office and facilitated their admission into his secretary's office.

Just as the secretary was saying to the visitors that the IG was about to leave the office for the day he came out of his office. Yago and Zera stood up and faced him. He looked to his secretary, who jumped to her feet.

'Sir, I have just told everybody that you were going out.'

'It's okay.'

He summarily attended to the four other people in the secretary's office and then invited Yago and Zera into his office. He indicated the settee for them to sit and he sat opposite them.

'Good day, IG.'

'Good day, sir. I sensed you have a serious problem.'

'Yes, sir,' Zera answered.

'What's it, madam?'

Yago explained the reason for coming from Nigeria and straight to his office. The IG was silent for a long time, then he suddenly had an idea.

'What's the name of your son, you said?'

'Zhero.'

The IG frowned. 'Why do you pronounce it that way?'

Yago spelt the name and pronounced it once more.

Zera asked, 'Sir, is he dead?'

'Please, spell your son's name again.' Yago spelt it. The IG felt relieved. 'It can't be your son. The Zero we arrested is spelt Z-E-R-O. And he called himself Zero Godiva. He said he has no father, no mother, Godiva is his parent. Can you imagine the nonsense? Actually no one knew where he came from. He was said to have supernatural powers and he eluded us for many years.'

'But can we see him, sir?'

'Madam, Zero Godiva is different from your son . . . He was arrested in Mo Bo and brought to Lagos. He and six others. He was the gang leader.'

'Can't we just see him?' Zera nearly wept.

'Do you have a picture of your son with you?'

Zera quickly brought out several photographs from her handbag and gave to him. The IG studied them for a while.

'Only passport photos. Not a single full-length photograph. Which is the most recent photograph?'

She took the photographs, then showed him the most recent one.

'Please have your seat, madam. How recent? A month ago?' The IG looked worried. Their faces . . . the colour of their skin . . . 'Is your son strong-looking? Well-built?'

'Yes yes,' Yago answered.

'Even so, the Zero that was killed can't be your son. They were killed while trying to escape from police detention.'

Blake's evil prophecy . . . You won't find your son alive . . . you won't find your son alive . . . .

'IG!' Yago shouted as Zera slumped against his shoulder. 'IG! My wife is dying!'

The IG first opened the door and shouted for his secretary then went to help Yago. The secretary suggested making her lie down.

'I'm alright,' she weakly replied, 'I'm okay.'

The IG offered her a bottle of cold soft drink. She shook her head and requested for water. The secretary gave her ice water and went out. The IG apologized to them — he shouldn't have discussed the matter so brutally.

'IG, when the robbers were arrested, you — I mean the police — should have taken their photographs, and before they were buried their photographs should have been taken again.' Yago thought he had cornered the policeman. 'IG?'

'Part of the myth of Zero: Our two-storey building was gutted by fire a day after Zero was buried. Cause of fire unknown, so it has been attributed to Zero's supernatural powers.'

'So no photograph of Zero?'

'No photograph of Zero — Zero indeed.'

'IG, please can we see the body?'

'No, sir, absolutely no.'

'When was it buried?'

'It doesn't matter when it was buried. Sir, I have to go out now.'

While they paused, Yago gathered courage from the scenario of returning to Nigeria without ascertaining that Zhero had not been killed and buried — how to live with Zera.

'IG,' he boldly said, 'you have been exceptional to us. Please finish what you started. One, my wife and I won't do anything beyond seeing the body. Two, whatever it costs . . . whatever it costs, IG . . . I'm a desperate man, I.G. At the risk of incurring your anger and whatever action you may take against us . . .' He opened his briefcase, took some money and placed it on the coffee table. 'This is US$20,000. For all the expenses of exhuming the body.'

Zera went down on her knees. 'Please, sir, help us.'

'Madam, please get up. You're not feeling well.' He locked his door, came back to his seat and spoke after a long pause. 'I shall take a risk too.'

After putting away the money he called his secretary and told her to take them to a room where they could stay alone until he was ready for them.

'Please give them something to eat. They are from Nigeria.'

'Sir, as I said, I have an urgent business somewhere. Its important. His Excellency, the President gave me an assignment. Two of my boys will take you to where you can see all the seven bodies. Unless there's a problem and you still want to see me I'll say have a nice journey back to Nigeria.'

Zera was very grateful. 'I don't know how to thank you, sir.'

The secretary took them to a very cozy VIP room and ordered sandwiches and cold fruit juice from the canteen for them. She left them, and returned after an hour with two policemen in mufti. At the car park Yago and Zera were taken into the police jeep and their taxi was told to follow the jeep closely. They went to Agon Police Station, where the DPO had been expecting them. Agon Police Station was the place extremely notorious armed robbers and kidnappers were detained until they were arraigned or shot to death while escaping. After receiving the Nigerian couple warmly the DPO spoke with heat in his voice.

'Why should any parent be interested in Zero? A satanic killer who said he had no human parents. Any parent should distance him or herself from Zero, dead or alive. The atrocities that boy committed! Many VIP's in this country were paying him protection money, despite the police assurance of their security, they were paying him protection money secretly. The minister who reported to the police, Zero gave him an ultimatum to resign and leave Godiva. Before the ultimatum expired the man fled Godiva. Should any parent be bothered about the death of such a satanic boy?'

Zera was visibly afraid of what might follow. Yago took her right hand in his left hand and gently squeezed it.

One of the men in mufti corrected the DPO: 'Koba, it's not Zero Godiva they want to see. They have a missing son spelt Z-H-E-R-O. They want to be sure he didn't change the spelling of his name and become a criminal.'

'Oh, I forgot. The IG told me.' He apologized, 'Sir, from the bottom of my heart, I'm sorry. How can the son of a woman like this become a criminal? It's impossible, no matter what.' He paused as if to admire Yago's splendid agbada and Zera's exquisite wrapper, blouse and gele, the sartorial dignity of which bespoke the fact that the son of the man and woman before him could never become a criminal. 'Madam, we have a problem. Because people said Zero Godiva had supernatural powers, we totally destroyed his dead body with a bucket of acid.' He visualized how they poured acid on the living boy after making him watch his colleagues weeping, begging for mercy and cursing him as they were being shot to death. 'It's not a beautiful sight for a mother.'

'Koba,' the man in mufti angrily asked, 'aren't you aware that the IG said no more pouring of acid on corpses?'

'You're in a deep shit, Koba,' the other man said in pity.

'I know,' Koba agreed. 'I know . . . And I have only two weeks to my retirement . . . Zero has poured acid on my forty years of service.'

Yago pitied him — he had suddenly looked wretched.

'ASP Koba,' Yago said kind-heartedly, just let us see the bodies, and my wife and I will return to Nigeria tomorrow. If your colleagues will keep it a secret then it will remain a secret.'

Koba was silent, his left hand on a large scar on his left temple.

'Thank you, sir,' one of the men in mufti said to Yago.

'You are a good man, sir,' the second man said.

Koba addressed Zera: 'Madam, I have a wife too. Sometimes because of the things we do as policemen my wife regrets marrying me . . . Zero and his gang killed over twenty policemen and many civilians during their criminal career . . .' His colleagues nodded. 'Every policeman Zero killed had a wife and children, like me. Six of the policemen were university graduates. Four of them had a BA degree. Two of them had a master's, like me. These two are graduates too . . . Any day, any moment, any criminal can mow us down while we're planting the rule of law. See this scar on my temple.' He stopped — his voice was about to break. He continued after a few seconds. 'Come what come may, time and the hour runs through the roughest day. Let's go.'

'No,' Yago said, 'just a moment.' He opened his briefcase and counted US$20,000 for them. 'A token of our appreciation of your service to life.'

After some seconds of profound silence Koba spoke. 'We thank you, sir. We thank you, madam. Life will return your son to you.'

He locked the money in his safe and they went out. As they passed a burnt storey building Yago asked if it was the one that burnt the day after Zero was buried.

'The Inspector General told you?' the DPO asked. 'Yes. Because of it some people say Zero isn't dead.'

One of the men in mufti laughed. 'Some of them say they saw Zero when the building was burning.'

The second man in mufti said seriously, 'A journalist added a twist to the Zero tale. He said you can wipe out a hundred robbers, you can wipe out a thousand robbers, but you can't wipe out Zero robbers. The title of his article was "They Can't Kill Zero".'

'Foolish journalist,' the DPO said in a dismissive tone, 'a foolish man whose stock-in-trade is silly theories. Says criminals and terrorists are important elements in the fabric of society, and they can't be ignored.' He was about to say something about U Shettima, another foolish man propounding foolish theories, but he felt that his Nigerian hearers were not interested in what he had said. He only said 'Foolish man.'

The taxi driver was told to wait at the police station, and they left, the DPO's car following the jeep in which the officers in mufti and Zera and Yago had come. The police sirens ploughing through the traffic cut a journey of about one hour to less than twenty minutes.

The four cemetery workers wondered why the police had come to bother them about bodies that were buried just three days ago. (Just three days?) Just three days — the mound was fresh. (All of them in one place?) What did it matter?

'Move it!' the DPO shouted at the workers. 'Since when did you start questioning the police? Because you've seen a big man, your ploy to get money?'

'DPO,' one of the men said, 'why do you want to put sand in our soup?'

Everybody, except Zera, laughed, and Yago promised them that the DPO's sand shall be of no effect because the soup would be large and deep. Laughter of all again, except Zera, whose trembling Yago was beginning to feel through her left hand in his right hand.

224

'DPO,' he said out of earshot of the others, 'my wife and I would like to go and wait in the jeep.'

'Come, you'll stay in my car . . . Madam, I'm sorry . . . Sir, do you think she should see it?' Yago could not answer him. 'Sir?'

'My husband can't answer your question. I think you should ask Shakespeare — come what come may.'

The DPO burst out in laughter.

'This is an uncommon woman!'

His remark pleased Zera, and their laughter healed her.

'Let's go back.'

She turned and the men followed her — a woman to admire, the DPO thought; a woman to fear, Yago silently said to himself.

As he remembered that Zhero knew how to use a gun he wished Zero's face was burnt beyond recognition . . . .

Yes, it was. In size none of the bodies could be compared to what Zhero's size could now be, except Zero's body that had been so messily damaged that neither the skin colour nor the facial features could be made out for comparison with Zhero.

Yago looked at the bodies only once and moved some metres away. He didn't believe that the Zhero who stopped selling pirate videos because it wasn't an honest job could become an armed robber . . . But hardship could change human character, and Zhero knew how to use a gun. The thought frightened him. He wouldn't ask for a DNA test . . . Maybe he was in the Niger Delta masquerading as a freedom fighter?

Zera thought, If seven women could lose their children why should any other woman be immune to the loss of children? She looked from one body to the other once more and lingered on Zero . . . She agreed with him that he wasn't Zhero, 'Yes, you're not Zhero.'

'Madam?' the DPO gently said.

'It's enough,' she said and turned to Yago. 'Shall we go?'

One cemetery worker commented, 'Madam, you strong pass man o. You no even spit sef.'

'You dey talk of spit,' another one said, 'she even spoil her face at all?'

The DPO asked them if they were disappointed, and explained to Yago and Zera that whenever the cemetery workers exhumed a body for civilians to inspect they had the medicinal leaves of a plant handy in their hut in case the person would faint. One of them brought out a freshly cut stalk and they laughed. Yago, who was holding his briefcase, opened it and counted US$1,000 for each of the workers. The thank-you's ran on until one of them said if he told his wife how rich he was she would force him to retire immediately, and they laughed.

Another one showed heaven his dollar bills and said soberly like a man who nearly failed in his quest, 'Dis na the thing I dey look for since my mama born me. Now I don find am, time to go home, time to go to my village.' No one laughed. 'Madam, you sef go find wetin you dey look for o.'

'Thank you, sir,' Zera replied.

They said goodbye to the workers. 'As they started to leave, the DPO asked Yago, 'Are all Nigerians as good as you?'

Zera answered him, 'So that others would be good to our son on his journey.'

'Journey?' the DPO wondered.

'The journey of life,' Zera explained.

'Yes,' the DPO agreed, 'the journey of life.' After some seconds he said to Yago, 'Sir, your son's name is Zhero Sai. I shall look out for him in Godiva.'

'Thank you, DPO.'

'Can you promise to let me know anytime you find him?'

'Why not?'

They exchanged names and phone numbers.

When they went back to Agon Police Station the taxi driver took Zera and Yago back to Royal Deluxe, the most expensive hotel in Godiva. After they checked in, the driver politely told Yago that his bill was ten thousand Godiva dollars — for a half day.

'Do you want it now, or tomorrow at the end of your assignment?'

The driver wisely interpreted Yago's smile. 'When I finish tomorrow, sir.'

'Suppose we run away before you come?'

'When I was small my mother used to say every honest service is service to God.' Zera burst out in tears. 'Madam, sorry, I offended you?'

'No, Kamara, that's what I used to say to my son, the boy we're looking for.'

'Then he is not missing. I swear to God, you will find him.'

'Go, Kamara, and be here at 7am tomorrow.'

'Thank you, sir. Ma, I'm going.'

'Thank you, Kamara.'

226

Kamara walked away, thinking of his late mother . . . the office cleaner who sold palm oil in the evening market so that he could have an education, the woman who sometimes went to bed on an empty stomach because she wanted him to ride on a bus to school the next day, but she died before he could make it . . . .

The beauty, the luxury facilities, the exotic souvenirs that attracted tourists to Royal Deluxe meant nothing to Zera and Yago. After having their bath and then dinner in their private dining room they remained at the table for some minutes and went to bed. After about fifteen minutes on the bed Zera spoke.

'I don't know why I'm thinking about Armstrong. We gave the IG twenty thousand U.S$ dollars, the DPO and his colleagues twenty thousand, the grave diggers one thousand U.S$ dollars each . . . Armstrong's pay was only ten thousand naira and he needed a slight raise . . . We didn't treat Armstrong well.'

He did not address the meaning of her comment. 'All for Zhero. I came here with US$200,000. I can give any amount to anyone who tells me where Zhero is. I don't mind scattering what's left in the streets to find Zhero.'

Troubled by the image of Zero Godiva she silently prayed that Armstrong would pursue his quest honestly.

Chapter Seven

For the boys the job was not hard but it was hazardous because even after Dr Faustus bought the 5400 square-metre land about six months back several clinics nearby and one or two sewage disposal companies had occasionally disposed of their waste in the dump which nearly covered 900 sq metres of land despite the NO DUMPING signboard until he paid for soldiers to guard the land. But the health danger was mitigated by his thoughtful action: each of the boys was given a pair of wellingtons, a pair of leather gloves and a mask, in addition to the one thousand dollars he gave each boy every day for transport and feeding. For eleven days the boys shovelled waste into baskets and loaded the four trucks that took the waste somewhere else. Because they were experienced and careful no one was injured, and because of their fizzy spirits the nausea and dizziness Ogugo felt on the third day was easily treated at a chemist shop and Agbarasa's coughing on the last two days was not regarded as a serious thing. When the job was finished Dr Faustus paid Zhero G$15,000 and the rest G$10,000 each.

From the G$9,000 they jointly saved from their daily allowance and their joint pay of G$25,000 Ogugo and Zhero bought two handcarts and rented another room in the building in which they lived, in order to live apart and start separate finances, though still bonded by the will to work hard and achieve their respective ambitions. Ogugo's ambition was to set up a motor vehicle parts shop while Zhero's ultimate ambition was to become a teacher after obtaining a PhD. They woke up early every day and with their handcarts went from door to door in the streets neglected by the Environmental Sanitation Authority for a fee. It was more lucrative than scavenging at Agoa.

Zhero had bought a table, a chair, an electric fan, a bed and a foam mattress, and was fully prepared to start evening school in two months' time. But at the moment, as he was pushing his handcart along Akota Street, he was considering a thought that had suddenly come up in his mind . . . How would his schoolmates feel if they saw him as a refuse collector? In Mo Bo a refuse collector was called a dirty man (with no stress on the first syllable of 'dirty') . . . Should he use a mask as many of the refuse collectors did? . . . But the reason several households had engaged him on a permanent basis was because he didn't wear a mask. Each house paid him G$2000 per month for collecting their refuse two times a week. The cash-and-collect alternative was twenty dollars per bag and many cheats packed the refuse of over one week into one big bag for the same amount . . . .

'Dirty Man, how now?' a woman greeted him as she threw some banana skins into his handcart.

'Not bad, madam,' he replied, his face and his voice not expressing the pain and anger in his heart.

'Go well o,' she said as if to a traveller.

'Thank you, madam,' he replied, again in a calm voice, and his dissimulation intensified the pain in his heart, as painful as a ripe boil begging to be burst.

About five minutes later a woman shouted 'Dirty Man' as she emerged from her eatery. He pretended not to hear her, eager to finish his rounds and leave the sun which he considered very cruel today. As cruel as the phrase, 'dirty man'.

'Dirty Man! You deaf?' she half yelled, frowning, as if the man was awfully dirty too.

He stopped. 'Madam, you see say my vehicle don full.'

'Which kin full?'

She lifted one of the two big refuse bags by the side of the eatery, went to him and dropped it by his handcart, with the righteousness of a woman who had a good intention for her fellow human.

'Madam, na whosai I go put this bag now?' he protested impotently. Without a word she brought the second bag. 'Madam, how I go carry these bags?'

Suppressing his anger he started to rearrange the bags in the handcart. She brought out an assortment of sweat-softened notes from her left bra and held out one hundred dollars.

'Dirty Man, you no see I dey give you money? You dey bluff me?' He took the money from her. 'How many people fit pay you one hundred dollars for two bags?'

'Sorry, madam.'

'Is okay.' She paused to wipe the sweat on her face with the bottom part of her wrapper, bending forward to do so. 'Make you dey come here every day. You know say na food I dey sell,' she mildly warned him, then noisily blew her nose into the wrapper.

'Thank you, madam.'

She blew her nose again and went back to her eatery self-importantly.

He always carried a long rope. After putting her bags on top of some other bags in the overloaded cart he ran the rope under the cart and above the refuse bags several times and tied the ends of the rope, angry at the hot sun penetrating his T-shirt to the skin of his back while he bent forward to do so. When he straightened up he felt a little relief from the sun, and looked at the direction of the woman, with less anger. He did not believe that she would pay so generously next time but he would go to her.

When he reached the Flaniga dump several boys and girls rushed to grab the refuse bags for themselves. He shook his head because he felt that they would not find anything of value in those bags.

A boy hawking chains in a wheelbarrow annoyed him, 'Dirty Man, you no go buy chain? For chain your motor car for night.' He ignored him. 'Dirty Man, go well o.'

He looked at his orange T-shirt — it didn't look too dirty even though when he sniffed it when he wasn't by his handcart he could perceive the smell. He felt all his body was smelling rubbish. After five minutes or so a new-looking Hummer Jeep pulled over in front of him. As he was about to pass it someone came out of it, smiling at him.

'Zero!' The young man continued to smile. 'Zero, is me.'

Zhero, who had stopped, exclaimed, 'Golan!'

'Yes is me.'

'Golan?'

'Yes, is me Golan.'

Passersby were slowing down and looking at them. Golan told Zhero to park his car on the sidewalk. They laughed and Zhero pushed his handcart to the sidewalk.

'Golan, since you left Mo Bo we haven't seen you.'

'I busy. Making money.' He pointed at his jeep, smiling at the difference between their vehicles. 'See.'

'You mean you are not a driver? You mean you own this thing?'

Golan smiled, 'By the grace of God.'

'Are you a businessman? Tell me, I'm interested.'

'Sure?'

'Sure.'

'Keep our secret secret?'

'Trust me, Golan.' Golan mulled over Zhero's trustworthiness. 'I say trust me, Golan.'

He concluded that Zhero was always a trustworthy one. Lowering his voice, he told him he could introduce him to his boss. He would be taught how to use different types of guns, and join in robbery operations. As simple as —

'Golan stop stop!' Golan took a step back from Zhero's instantly incandescent fury. 'How can you tell me such a thing?'

'Am sorry, am sorry, Zero.' Zhero went to his handcart. Golan followed him. 'But remember your promise oh, Zero. My boss is a killer.' He regretted his indiscretion, but then, Zhero didn't know where he lived. 'Zero, is for your own good I warn you.' He'd made a mistake — he didn't ask for Zhero's address before confiding in him . . . 'Well, no problem,' he shrugged.

Zhero pushed away his handcart, shaking in fright and in anger ... After some minutes he was able to push the incident out of his mind — he wouldn't tell even Ogugo . . . .

He looked at the time on his mobile. Why was he so tired? He still had Eastings Street to attend to, four houses . . . He decided to go home . . . He'd never failed them before . . . He'd tell them the truth that he was tired . . . At No 8 the woman always praised him for his dutifulness. He hoped she wouldn't be disappointed in him . . . .

He washed the handcart with the clean-looking but stinking water of a flooded gutter at River Street where several 'dirty men' and motorcycle taxi drivers were washing their vehicles, then went home. He rested for about thirty minutes, had a quick wash in the stinking communal outhouse bathroom, ate beans and fried ripe plantain at a stall several minutes away from his house, came back home and lay on the bed . . . .

To be called a dirty man by one's classmates . . . Maybe he should continue working, save enough money and go to another city to attend school? . . . Dirty Man . . . Even the girls would call him Dirty Man . . . He wiped his tears . . . He'd continue to do the honest job that would enable him to pay his way — far better than what Golan was doing . . . Only four years of evening school to get the School Cert . . . He blamed himself for not telling Chief Yago the truth. Chief Yago would have believed him — Joseph's sudden absence would have been a proof . . . If he went to Numu and told him that he advised Chief Yago not to eat the food because he heard Aunty Teima warning Joseph not to eat the food, would Numu believe him? . . . Even if he didn't believe him would he agree to hide him somewhere and help him financially? . . . Why not go back to his mother? . . . No, he didn't want to see Bazi . . . Golan wanted him to be an armed robber . . . .

When he woke up, the room was dark — after 8pm. He went out. Ogugo's handcart was outside his window. He went to Ogugo's room.

'When I came home you were sleeping,' Ogugo said to him.

'Yes, I was,' he yawned. 'All those chains in your handcart, what are they for?'

'I will sell them,' Ogugo said sharply.

'Those rusty things?'

'I will wash them with petrol.'

'Who will buy them?'

'If nobody buys, I will take them to Manana prison and give to the warders for free.'

They laughed.

Ogugo had bought a second-hand TV, and he often came to his room to watch TV. It was now on Mountain Top View. The announcer invited lovers of Superman to enjoy 'Superman, Our Superman'. An Indian film company showed in detail how Superman's feats were produced. Zhero and Ogugo were sad to see that Superman was an unimpressive young man who was given a makeover. The several times he fell into the shallow water before he steadied himself on the sailboard in the posture of Superman about to zoom off in his super board in pursuit of a speedboat with a female abductee struggling and shouting for help made them laugh at themselves for ever thinking that his sea adventures were real. And when they saw how the illusion of Superman conquering sloppy hills, deep valleys and tall mountains in his quests was created they called themselves 'born fools', otherwise how could they have believed that Superman was real! The friends' reaction to the dashing of illusion was a vow to never watch 'Superman' any more.

Ironically, however, Zhero dreamt that night of going about on invisible wings. He flew everywhere he went, he flew to Port Harcourt in Nigeria, he flew to Lagos and to Amabra, overtaking motor cars and speedboats from above, and the people below did not regard it as strange . . . .

In the morning, subconsciously buoyed by his dream, he jauntily left home at 6am and made for Eastings Street thinking that going there very early was a good way to make up for his failure to collect the residents' refuse the previous day. He chose to take a road he had passed only once before. He enjoyed the way people sidestepped his handcart as he approached in a half run . . . He laughed at himself for thinking of himself as Superman . . . By the foot of the Obadore Bridge something hit his back and he fell down. Several hands grabbed him and started to drag him into the forest. About six men were taking him deep into the forest. Fear paralysed him, he was speechless, but when he saw some bare-chested men dressed in red wrappers he asked God, 'Is this why I was created? Is this the way I am to die? So my mother will never see me again?' Suddenly all the people shouted 'Lion! Lion! Lion!' and scattered away.

He had fallen on his back. He sat up. While gathering strength he looked at where the men in red had been standing under the tree. What he saw frightened him but something compelled him to go near . . . A naked female body! Only blood where the breasts should have been. Her genital area too was bloody. The sight made him retch. He became aware of the stench of the forest, so strong as if it was something solid inside his nostrils. As he started to run away he saw a rotten corpse to his left. A blanket of flies rose from the corpse. The sight and the stench hit him like poisoned darts. His legs failed him. He fell down. He looked at the rotten corpse again. The stench of the forest was stronger than all the rubbish dumps of Mo Bo put together. The wind started to blow from the corpse towards him, pushing into his nostrils as he puffed in terror of the forest until he could no longer take it in and he vomited what had already gone inside him . . . He felt a miraculous relief, he got up and ran out of the forest. His handcart was waiting for him by the foot of the bridge, cars were speeding past under and on the bridge, as if nothing had happened in the forest. He quickly pushed his handcart away.

Ogugo was just leaving when he reached home.

'Zhero! What happened?'

Without saying a word he entered the house, opened his door, went in and flopped onto the bed. His eyes and his behaviour — Ogugo was terrified of speaking to him again. Could he have seen the being carrying a masquerade and could he have been struck dumb? In Nigeria he used to peep at masquerades in the shrine and in Godiva too he wasn't afraid of masquerades.

At last he spoke, 'I tried to pass under Obadore Bridge.'

'Hey, Zhero! Why, Zhero? Don't you know that that place is the most dangerous place in Mo Bo? That place people go to buy human parts. Especially eyes, breasts, penises, and tongues. Thank God you are alive.'

'Yes, I thank God.'

'How did you escape?'

When Zhero narrated his experience Ogugo did not hide his scepticism. He only said 'Thank God you're alive.' Zhero silently wished he had not told him. It pained him that the only true friend he had in Mo Bo did not believe his story . . . Thank God he didn't tell anyone about Traveller's Lodge.

A few minutes after Ogugo left he slept off. Ogugo returned early, in the rain, around 2pm, because though he did not believe the bit about lions it was certain to him that his friend had escaped from the killers at Obadore, and would need someone to help him go through the after effect. He was right. Zhero was shivering in his sleep.

'Zhero!' he shouted and Zhero woke up. 'Zhero, you're shaking ... and your body is very hot.'

'My head . . . and I'm feeling cold . . . It must be malaria. That's the way malaria attacks me when something bad happens to me.' Ogugo laughed. 'Yes, I know my body.'

'Have you eaten?'

'I'm not hungry. But I must eat before I take malaria tablets. Can you buy me one card of Nomalaria and a plate of . . . a plate of rice and stew? But the rain is heavy.'

Ogugo told him to shut up. He said thank you and gave Ogugo three hundred dollars. Ogugo went out and returned ten minutes or so later with the food and the Nomalaria tablets, which Zhero eagerly took because he needed to be well and to go to Eastings Street and Nelson-Cole Lane the next day. But he was too weak to go to work the next day. In the evening, on Ogugo's advice they went to Olumo Chemist shop and were told that the Nomalaria tablets they bought from Sunshine Chemist shop were fake tablets produced in India by Indian and Nigerian businessmen. The nurse gave him an injection and he felt better the next day, but still too weak to go to work. In the evening he was physically well, but he did not look happy. Ogugo persuaded him to walk his mood off and they went out, following the call of loud music and joy in the distance until they reached a neighbourhood celebration of a wedding that had taken place in the registry earlier in the day.

Several people they asked about the newlyweds did not know who they were. Apparently, for them, as for over ninety percent of those at the ceremony, what mattered was not the newlyweds but the *boubaraba* music and dance, and there was a shop at the corner, where anyone could buy what he liked to drink.

The wooden building the newlyweds lived in was so close to the eroding edge of the river bank that Zhero feared for them — an insistent rain storm at night could break the earth and throw the building and its occupants into the river, the way the people living by the river throw their overnight urine and excrement from their chamber pots into the river at dawn.

When rootsy 'owigiri' music started to play, Zhero was transported to the village square in Amabra, and he felt like doing the 'owigiri' steps and waist-wriggling the way they used to do it under the starry Amabra night sky — ah, Joleen, Joleen whose wriggling backside sometimes made the mesmerized singers and drummers lose harmony . . . He wondered if life in Amabra wasn't better than what he was doing in a strange land . . . No . . . Education was important . . . .

They went home when thunder started to rumble. The next day Ogugo volunteered to go with him to clear the bags of refuse that would have accumulated at the four and three houses at Eastings Street and Nelson-Cole Lane respectively. They left home at 6am. When they reached No 8 Eastings Street the gatekeeper told Zhero that his services were no longer needed. When Zhero shouted at him to allow him to see Madam he went in to announce Zhero's presence to Madam. It was her son who came out.

'Good morning,' Zhero greeted the frowning boy who appeared to be much younger than him. 'I've come to collect the refuse.'

'There's nothing to collect.'

'But . . . for some days —'

'We've employed someone else. Try somewhere else.'

'Can I see your mom?'

'I say we've employed someone else,' the roly-poly brat replied. 'Good day, mister.'

'Alright . . . can I see her . . . for the two weeks I've already worked out of this month?'

The woman came out. Zhero was glad to see her. Her son left immediately, happy to return to his breakfast of toast, omelette and hot chocolate.

235

'Good morning, ma.'

'The two weeks you've already worked? How about the discomfort, the nuisance we had to endure? Please go away,' she calmly said to him, torn between compassion for the sedulous boy and the decision she and her son had taken.

'I'm sorry, ma. Thank you, ma. Ogugo, let's go.'

She watched them for some seconds and called them back.

'What's your name?' she asked the boy who before now had come to take away the refuse even if it was raining.

'Zhero, ma. Z-H-E-R-O.'

'You speak good English, Zhero. Why are you not in school? . . . Okay, maybe some other time. As my son said, there's nothing to collect today. You can resume on Saturday.'

Zhero and Ogugo said 'Thank you, ma' in unison.

'Thank you, my sons.'

She went back into her compound, thinking — she could employ him in her company, give him the boys' quarters and enable him to go to school. He'd be a very good influence on her son. She would. She must employ him. The absence of a father in the house was telling on her son. And she, a lone mother, running a business and teaching in the university. Zhero could be a good influence on him. She started to feel that Zhero was her son — a well-spoken boy . . . .

Ogugo was angry. 'Zhero, you are the cause of our suffering.'

'How?'

'See the way the woman's son treated us, as if we are rubbish. If we have sold those diamond jewels —'

'I'm sorry.' Ogugo sighed. Zhero continued. 'No matter what, we shouldn't regret it. It's good to be good to the end, even if we are going to die . . . We won't die. We'll find what we're looking for. My mother used to say to me that a person's survival starts and ends in the mind. The mind. The mind is important. We shall survive, Ogugo, we shall survive,' he firmly said, more to himself than to his friend, shoring up his own mind with the pillars of words and thought.

'But it is hard, Zhero, you know it is hard.'

'Am I not a human being?'

Unknown to them, instead of a positive response to U Shettima's chivvying of the State government over the plight of street children, school-age hawkers, young scavengers, child beggars, child prostitutes, child criminals, the government had ordered the police to clear the streets, dumps, brothels and shantytowns of those persons, and the police had started work at 6am.

They saw a commotion some metres away in front of them. The police were chasing and arresting people. Just hawkers, they told themselves and continued their walk towards No 4. A young man who ran past them from behind shouted to them to run for it. They looked behind. Some policemen were coming. The young man jumped over the fence of a compound.

'Zhero let's run!' Ogugo shouted and abandoned his handcart. Zhero would not abandon his prized possession. While he was looking for an open gate to push it into, the police pounced on him, hit him several times with their batons and took him into their van some metres away. There were other young men and women in it. For many hours loads of boys, girls, young women and young men were taken to various police stations in the city and detained.

In Bansi Police Station where Zhero was detained, the police were having a happy time as people came to bail their relations, friends and wards. The cost of bail was unofficial and negotiable. Zhero had lost his mobile phone in the Obadore forest, otherwise he would have called Ogugo to break the lock of his door and look under his bed for the carton in which he kept garri and money.

At nighttime the large room, on the cold concrete floor of which Zhero and eighteen others were to sit or lie down throughout the night, seemed to have been purposely polluted with stench to punish the detainees for not having been bailed. Even Zhero who was used to various types of stench found the stench unbearable until they saw its source — a commode. When a constable came to take out a detainee they appealed to him to allow them to take out the toilet but he told them to be patient till the next day otherwise they would have nowhere to relieve themselves. He explained that the toilet was usually cleaned every morning but the cleaner did not come to work that day, because she was not well. Zhero decided not to be bothered by the stench.

Some of the detainees still wept, some lamented their fate aloud, while others, like Zhero, silently thought about life. For many hours he did not sleep and he saw through the iron-bar door as the policemen took out a girl or two now and then from the opposite room and returned them. He heard as one of the girls said, 'Remember o, you say you go release me tomorrow o', and the policeman replied, 'Yes, on my police honour, good night', and the girl went back into detention. 'Ah,' Zhero quoted his mother, 'a woman's life is a hard experience.'

On the fourth day those who could not be bailed out were sent to Manana Prison as 'innocent detainees' to await arraignment. At Manana Prison too people came to bail out their relations, wards and friends, but Zhero had no way to contact Ogugo. At Manana boys could buy their freedom without money whenever the Chief Warder, a pederast, was in the mood to sell it to them.

In spite of the drab green walls of the buildings, the prison environment was cleaner and healthier than the police compound and the police detention rooms but the warders were harsher than the police. Zhero felt it was because they had dealt with prisoners for too long. The long interaction with prisoners had also made a lot of them suspicious of even those referred to as 'innocent detainees', as if every detainee was looking for an opportunity to escape. He also noticed the warders' love of power over the detainees. Often they did not tell the detainees to do something, they barked out orders: Hey, all of you! Go and take your bath now! You have fifteen minutes! . . . You! You! And You! Go and sweep the kitchen! You have only ten minutes to do that! . . . Your clothes are stinking! All of you! Here's soap! Go and wash your clothes! Now!

But there was one warder that was very kind to them. Instead of barking at them he would ask a question, 'Are you people ready to have your bath? It's time now,' he would sing . . . 'Hey, boys! How about cleaning the compound? It's good exercise,' he would say, smile and playfully challenge one or two persons to the job.

One day, out of earshot of his fellow detainees Zhero said to the warder, 'Sir, you're not like the others. You're a good man. You're different.'

'Thank you, my son,' the man responded and wiped his teary eyes.

Zhero felt happy — he had given back love to the man who gave them love. Coincidentally, at dusk that day he clearly heard Odedekoko singing in the nearby forest despite the hum of conversation in the male innocent detainees' very large room. Odedekoko in Godiva! He was delighted . . . but gradually the song made him sad . . . and he feared, did it mean he was going to die in Manana Prison? . . . 'No,' he said to himself, 'I won't die in prison. Tomorrow I must tell them to release us. What they are doing is wrong' . . . .

He feared they might brutalize him, but what did it matter? Even if he died he'd have pricked their consciences . . . .

How about his mother? She might never see him again . . . .

He remembered her advice to him to not inherit her fiery temper . . . But she said if he chose to fight for justice he should do so, because it was a good thing, and to die in the course of doing so was better than dying silently from injustice . . . And she said, 'You need courage to cut open a boil. If you fear to cut it then you must live with the pain.'

He discussed his idea with a few persons. They liked it. Each one of them discussed it with a few persons, the idea was spread among all the 'innocent detainees' in the room, and they agreed a resolution: If Zhero demanded for their release they should all support him; if Zhero said they would not do morning labour they should all support him.

The night threw up surreal images of Zhero before his eyes in the dark room . . . He saw Zhero broken and bloody, a grotesque figure, as the warders continued to brutalize him, laughing happily as he begged them to have mercy on him because he didn't want to die, blood spouting from his mouth . . . A warder placed the muzzle of his gun between Zhero's eyebrows and pulled the trigger, and Zhero dropped onto the ground like a not-fully-filled sack of refuse . . . The warders fired into the air and all the innocent detainees ran out of Manana Prison leaving him alone to be beaten by the warders . . . He shook his head — the images were products of his fear. He resolved not to balk at what all the innocent detainees had decided upon . . . But suppose the warders picked him out as the ringleader and . . . and killed him? . . . Then his mother would never see him again . . . Though his mother would be happy to see him alive, if he told her his story, she'd be ashamed that he failed to fight for justice when it was necessary, because of fear . . . unless he lied to her, or omitted to tell her this part of his story . . . If only Odedekoko could sing now as a sign that all would be well with him tomorrow . . . It was night and Odedekoko too was sleeping as all humans were doing, except him . . . All the innocent detainees must be sleeping — the room was quiet . . . He envied his colleagues who could sleep so peacefully in spite of tomorrow morning . . . .

Fear . . . fear . . . he must kill this monster, go to sleep and act tomorrow . . . .

At dawn, after they had relieved themselves and brushed their teeth the male 'innocent detainees' assembled outside the building for their assignments. There was apprehension in many hearts, there was trembling in Zhero's heart as the warder started to reel out their assignments. A thirty-year-old man who dreaded to think of the consequence of Zhero's planned action was about to advise him to be patient and wait for God's time but Zhero took the touch of the man's hand on his shoulder as a cue to speak.

'No, sir, we won't do morning labour again.'

The warder stopped short, and the earth fell silent. After an endless pause of ten seconds or so the warder spoke calmly.

'Did someone say something?'

The warder's words soundlessly ricocheted off the trembling hearts while his stare deepened the silence of the earth.

As he started to open his mouth, Zhero spoke, his heart as calm as the warder's voice 'Yes, sir. We want to be released.'

'What did you say?' the warder asked, calmly again.

Some of the detainees turned their heads around to see if the others were as apprehensive as they were? Had Zhero done the right thing? Where was the safest place to run to?

'We were only working for our daily bread when we were arrested,' Zhero replied. 'We want to be released.' No other detainee spoke. Zhero shouted 'Release us!' and expected his colleagues to shout along. 'Release us!'

Only the warder blew his whistle furiously and then warned them, 'Stay where you are! If you run you will be shot!'

Nine gun-toting warders and four warders with batons rushed to the scene. From a safe distance the armed warders covered the detainees while the baton-carrying warders went to their colleague and asked, 'What happened? What happened?'

Glaring at Zhero, the warder shouted, 'Push out that man!'

'What happened?' one of his colleagues asked again.

'He says we must release them today! He says they are innocent! He calls us oppressors!'

'What!' his colleagues shouted.

'I say push him out! Are you deaf?'

As some hands touched him Zhero voluntarily walked out to the warders who descended on him with their batons while he bravely continued to shout 'Release us! Release us!' and did not stop until he fell down.

'Hey, e don die!'

'Dem don kill am!'

An armed warder shouted, 'No one moves! Stay where you are!'

The warder who had been affronted by Zhero shouted, 'You! You! You! You! Carry him to the clinic!'

The four young men he had pointed at carried Zhero to the white-walled clinic, while the other detainees were returned to their room and locked up till it was time for breakfast. Out of guilt few of them discussed what had happened but nearly all of them prayed in their hearts for Zhero not to die.

The prison doctors and nurses, always detached from the brutality of the warders or the criminality of the prisoners, always put their hearts into their work. At the clinic they battled to bring Zhero back to life immediately he was dumped on a couch, and when he came out of coma they were simply glad that they had saved a life.

As the story of Zhero's visit to heaven spread in the prison it profoundly affected one or two warders and amused many of them. He had told the nurses who asked him where he had been to that he was in a boundless place of shining white light. He was without form but he knew that he was who he was. A presence took him to a place where everybody worked for their daily bread and he was advised to do likewise. He was also advised to practise the Law of Self-Determination. (Law of Self-Determination?) It meant to see himself as that which he wanted to be in life and work honestly to become it, because God had given him the right and the ability to do so.

That day one of the warders who pooh-poohed Zhero's story was involved in an accident on his way to his house. Because he was unable to see clearly in the heavy rain his car had a head-on collision with a truck. The car was a write-off and his right leg was broken. When some of his colleagues visited him in the orthopedic ward of the Teaching Hospital the next day he frightened them. He said his dream pointed to the hand of God in his accident — yesterday he laughed at Zhero's story and said Zhero's heaven was a figment of his imagination, because he said people were working for their daily bread in heaven, which men of God described as a place of eternal rest, eternal enjoyment, eternal bliss.

Following the story from the Teaching Hospital the nurses at the prison clinic asked Zhero to tell them more about heaven. Remembering Numu's novel he invented hell and explained that he was taken there to see the agonizing of the wicked, the unquenchable fire, the howling and the lamentations of the deathless friends of

Satan — he was taken there to be warned to never stop loving God and his fellow humans . . . Fools, he inwardly said of his listeners, if there was hell how could Satan punish his own friends for serving him on earth?

The Chief Warder, who had come to the clinic to see 'what this Zhero nonsense is all about', came to his bed in the middle of his description of hell. At the end he asked Zhero what else he saw.

The previous day when Zhero was supposed to be sleeping he heard two warders discussing the meeting of senior officers that had taken place in the Chief Warder's office at the time he was in a coma. Drawing on that conversation Zhero illustrated the all-seeing nature of the children of God in heaven.

'Shut up! You didn't see what was taking place in my office. Shut up your nonsense! You didn't hear anything. I say shut up your mouth!'

The Chief Warder went back to his office outwardly confidently, but inwardly he was a man sorely worried — did Zhero also see what took place in his office after the meeting? Did Zhero see him taking the boy before releasing him that day?

Zhero was enjoying his importance, but he deliberately looked serious and unwittingly appeared a holy man.

Zhero remained in a light and spacious ward in the clinic for five days because of the aches and pains he suffered as a result of the beating he had received from the warders, and because the nurses enjoyed his presence around them. Anytime Dr Mandawula heard him chatting with the nurses he would say he did not believe that he was a 'Dirty Man' when he was arrested — where did he acquire such excellent English! Zhero would say 'Thank you, sir' and humbly give the credit to his mother.

Before he left the clinic it was decided that he should not be put among the innocent detainees, so after supper at the clinic he was taken to the awaiting trial section of the prison where, the warders hoped, he would be sodomized overnight and feel degraded, unable to raise his head thereafter. He was shoved into a cell occupied by four men. The men screamed and struggled with the warder against the locking of the cell, unmindful of the threats of the second warder who was armed.

'Take am away!'

'We no want am here o!'

'Warder! Warder! You wan kill us?'

'Who are you to tell me what to do?' the warder shouted.

'Then, you,' one of the men addressed the armed warder, 'shoot us now now!'

They pushed open the iron-bar door, pushed Zhero out and closed the iron door back with a clang that rang through the corridor frightening the other inmates one of whom screamed 'Help! Help!' as he banged on the door of his own cell. The warders were surprised. Even after the cell was padlocked the inmates continued to beg the warders to take Zhero away. On their way to the office of the head of the evening shift to report what had happened the unarmed warder told his colleague that the four inmates were among the thirteen men who were arrested at the Obadore forest not long ago. They were caught with the body of a freshly killed woman. Someone had seen them carrying the woman into the forest and phoned the police. Zhero suddenly felt dizzy and, saying to the warders that he needed a rest, sat on the grass verge. Afraid for his health the unarmed warder rushed to the clinic, and two male nurses hurriedly came and wheeled him to the clinic.

Zhero wondered, Did the men recognize him? Or did they see a lion again?

The next day the Chief Warder rushed to the DPO (Divisional Police Officer) of Bansi Police Station and told him what had happened since the day Zhero went into a coma. Both of them had a stake in the well-being of the Obadore Thirteen (the thirteen people arrested at the Obadore Forest) for whose extrajudicial release some powerful persons in the society were about to pay them US$1 million. They decided that the 'innocent detainees' should be released immediately. They rode together in the Chief Warder's jeep to Manana Prison, had a feverish meeting with six senior warders, and assembled the innocent detainees — and announced to them that they were free to go home.

The innocent detainees erupted into joyous shouting. Many of them thanked Zhero, whose name they had known on the day the warders nearly killed him.

'Jero, thank you o!'

'Zero, our saviour!'

'Zero, saviour of the poor!'

'Zero, you be man!'

'Glory to God! Glory to Zero!'

Though Zhero thanked them back he took their gratitude and

joyful noise with detachment, the way he reacted to their silence and betrayal the other day — he had not forgotten his mother's lesson on detachment.

One young woman said to her friend, 'Fine boy like dat, why im mama and im papa call am Zero? Dem no fit find better name? Which kin foolishness be that?' she angrily asked, offended on behalf of the fine boy.

Her friend replied, 'But I like am o.'

'You like de name?'

'De boy, I like de boy. E be like say make I go tell am so.'

Her friend laughed and drew her away from her ridiculous intention.

Amid the joyful noise Zhero asked the DPO, 'Will you people return the money you took from me at the police station?'

The DPO did not take offence at the question. 'How much?' he asked.

Thinking of his need for money to buy another handcart Zhero said, G$20,800.'

Regarding him as a holy young man, they believed his word as absolute truth. They took him to the Chief Warder's office and gave him G$21,000, drawing his attention to the two hundred dollars they had added to the amount he lost. He thanked them, went to the clinic, thanked the nurses and the doctors on duty, and walked out of Manana Prison. Some of the detainees were stranded at the bus stop which was about two hundred metres from the prison. Zhero gave them various amounts. One of them was very sick and needed to charter a taxi home. Zhero gave him two thousand dollars. In the end he was left with G$11,800, enough to replace the handcart he had lost. A handcart cost G$10,000.

He boarded the third bus that came. After about ten minutes the shaggy-haired bus conductor announced to the passengers to have the correct fare ready.

'I no get change o. Give me the exact amount.'

He noticed Zhero frantically searching his pockets, and went to him.

'I'm coming, I'm coming.'

'Where you dey go wey you dey come? Give me your bus fare, my friend.'

Several people laughed.

'I'm sorry,' Zhero apologized. 'I've lost my money.'

244

The driver heard Zhero. He roughly braked to a halt and the shaggy-haired bus conductor contemptuously shoved Zhero out — a lowlife, a liar. A former innocent detainee, one of those Zhero had given some money, was on the bus. He believed Zhero had told the truth, but he kept silent, and shrugged off his guilt at not paying the fare for Zhero. The bus had gone a long way before Zhero realized that the window-seat passenger's hand he felt on his right thigh might have removed the money from his trouser pocket.

He had to walk even though he did not feel so strong. He walked with physical and mental effort because the wind was sometimes too strong for him and wanted to push him backwards . . . When his feet turned heavy he slowed down . . . When he felt like falling he stopped walking and looked for somewhere to sit . . . He was about to sit on the sidewalk when an Nze Waterside neighbour saw him.

'Hey Zhero! . . . You are out?' Zhero nodded. 'Hey, Zhero, am glad for you o.' Zhero's slight swaying and silence bothered him. 'Zhero, you are not well?'

Zhero nodded. Nta held him by his left arm till he hailed a taxi and paid for it to take Zhero home. He reached home in less than thirty minutes. The lock on his door had been broken. He went into his room and looked for the first thing on his mind — the carton of garri at the bottom of which was his life savings. It was nowhere to be found. Ah, the consequence of foolishness! Instead of taking his savings to the bank he said it wasn't necessary since he'd soon use all to pay for evening school — pure foolishness . . . He sat on the bed and said to his foolishness to let him feel the pain . . . He went to Ogugo's room and knocked. A female voice told him to come in. 'Ogugo had got a girlfriend in my absence!' he thought. He entered. The young woman was in panties only.

'I'm sorry. It's Ogugo I'm looking for.' He averted his eyes from her big breasts. 'O . . . Ogugo,' he stammered.

'Who is Ogugo?'

'My friend. He lives here.'

The woman laughed. 'Then you are Zhero. Everyone speaks highly of you. Am the owner of this room now.' He felt guilty as his eyes went back to her breasts. 'They tell me he's a handsome boy. Is he more handsome than you? My name is Esewa . . . Esewa,' she said her name again, expecting him to take the flower she had nurtured for him in his absence

Confused, Zhero went to Oloro four doors from the beautiful

naked woman's door. Oloro told him that Ogugo was arrested when the police raided Nze Waterside for young men who had no known place of work. The tears streaming down his face, Zhero returned to his room without saying a word . . . His life savings gone . . . His best friend gone . . . Nothing to eat . . . No transport fare to Agoa tomorrow . . . .

He went back to Oloro and explained his plight. Could Oloro lend him some money? Any amount. No amount was too small . . . Oloro gave him G$10,000 and told him not to think of refunding it. He instantly dropped down on his knees and excitedly said 'Thank you, Oloro! Thank you, Oloro!' before he remembered that Oloro was not much older than him. He got up, said 'Thank you' once more to the silent neighbour who now regarded the well-liked boy in the neighbourhood as a fool, then left in quieter happiness . . . He would never know that it was Oloro who broke into his room and instinctively knew that a carton under the bed contained more than garri . . . .

His heart full of gratitude to Oloro, he went to an eatery and ate two hundred dollars worth of rice and beans with stew. Then he remembered that when he was on the bus the passengers close to him had sniffed the air, and he noticed that he was smelling. He bought soap, a bucket of water and a sponge and had a wash in the outhouse wooden bathroom without a roof. If the rain fell now it would be a blessing because the bucket of water was barely enough.

At bedtime he was angry with himself, he hated himself, he was sorry for himself —why did he lie that what the police took from him was G$20,800 instead of just G$1,800? . . . How was God looking at him now? . . . A thief, a thief, he was a thief . . . .

The tears flowed as he heard the sobbing of his mother in his heart — Why, Zhero, why did you steal?

Oh, he had failed his mother! A lone mother who believed in her only child!

He consoled himself — if he hadn't lied how would he have helped his colleagues, especially the one who wasn't well?

In the morning the landlord's knock on the door a few minutes before 6am woke him.

'Good morning, sir.'

'Good morning, Zhero. You are out of jail. A short sentence.'

Zhero laughed. 'Landlord, I wasn't jailed for anything. I was arrested for using a handcart in the street and detained. I was —' He stopped because he was getting angry. 'Have a seat, sir.'

'The police has warn all we landlords that we must not harbor criminal. You have to pack out by end of month.'

'But my rent won't have expired.'

'Am not the police. Do you want me to report that I have ex-prisoner in my house? Av warn you. Bye bye.'

Zhero changed his mind about returning to Agoa as a scavenger. If a wealthy family employed him as a houseboy he would live in a good house and a clean environment. He once heard Naomi, Chief Yago's former maid, advising her younger brother on the advantages of serving a rich person instead of working as a tout in the motor park. If he conducted himself well, the people in the neighbourhood would think he was a member of the family. In some families the houseboys and the maids addressed their employers as 'Daddy', 'Mommy'.

A little before noon he was on his way to Linkup Enterprises, a place which found employers for people who had paid ten thousand dollars to register as houseboys, maids, guards, drivers, gardeners etc. He mentally went over the terms he would give the man or woman who wanted to employ him, and saw himself as finishing evening secondary school and doing a part-time programme at MBU (Mo Bo University). Then he'd go back to Nigeria and look for his mother . . . after getting a job so that she'd leave Bazi and live with him . . . .

In the room labelled LINKUP ENTERPRISES: RECEPTION, there were a handful of boys, girls, young women and two men who appeared to be in their early fifties. Zhero sat in a grey plastic armchair. One of the middle-aged men sighed out loud now and then, 'Life.' Some of the applicants regarded him as a strange man, some of them shrugged, some pitied themselves. A young woman asked Zhero if he had filled a visitor's form and he said no. While she was directing him to the secretary's office for the secretary to fill the form for him, a burly man came in. Everybody stood up, Zhero was the last to do so.

'Good day, everybody.'

'Good day, sir.'

'I've seen all your names from the visitor's forms. There's nothing for any of you. The man who will be coming soon is a chief judge. He wants a literate boy, and the boy I intended for him has just called to say he no longer wants to be a houseboy. None of you here is literate. You can come again next week to check up.'

Sluggishly, sighing or muttering, the applicants went out. The CEO noticed that someone was following him. He stopped and turned.

'You, didn't you hear me? Come back next week.'

'I haven't filled the form, sir.'

The CEO laughed. 'As if you can fill the form yourself.'

'Yes, I can, sir, I can fill the form.'

The CEO's brow furrowed in thought.

'Of course you can. Your English says so.'

'Thank you, sir.'

'Follow me.'

He followed the CEO through a door labelled LINKUP ENTERPRISES: CEO's OFFICE. The secretary was busy on the computer. The CEO told Zhero to have a seat and directed the secretary to give him an application form. He went through a door labelled CEO into his own office.

Zhero filled the simple form in less than five minutes and the secretary, who liked his handwriting, told him to go into the CEO's office.

'Have a seat, young man.' The CEO took the form and read Zhero's CV. 'Primary Six. That's good. That's good. But your English is bigger than Primary Six.' They both laughed. 'Address, just Nze Waterside?'

'There are no streets there, sir, and no numbers. The landlords give their houses any names they like.'

The CEO laughed. 'No, you can't say you live in Nze Waterside. No one will employ you.'

'So I can't be employed?'

The CEO was touched that he was about to cry. He cancelled 'Nze Waterside' and wrote 'No 9 Shell Location Road, Mo Bo'. He also backdated Zhero's entry by two months.

'That's where my son lives. Go and fill another form. Take note of the date too. And pay the registration fee. Justice Abramson will be here any moment from now.'

Zhero went to the secretary's office, happily filled a new application form, and asked her how much the registration fee was. He liked the scent of the perfume she was wearing, and her tangerine blouse. His mother had a blouse of that colour too. Bazi bought it for her.

Satisfied with the form she answered his question. 'Just ten thousand.' She noticed his worried look. 'What's the problem?'

He brought out all the money in his pocket. 'It's not up to ten thousand, ma.'

'Then drop the form, come back when it's up to ten thousand.' He shook his head and sniffled. 'You're crying, hey?'

'Sorry, ma.'

He dropped the form on her table and started to leave.

'Hey, come back!' He came back. 'You don't have more than what's in your hand?' He shook his head. 'Have a seat, have a seat.' She counted ten thousand dollars from her handbag and put it in the iron safe. 'I've just lent you ten thousand. You'll refund it when you're paid?' He nodded. 'Promise?' He nodded again. She fought back her own tears as she wrote the receipt for him. 'Wipe your face and go back to the CEO.'

While he was with the CEO the secretary informed her boss that Justice Abramson was around. The CEO hurried out to receive him, and came back with him. Zhero smartly stood up. The CEO was impressed.

'This is the boy for you, sir,' he happily said. After Justice Abramson had sat on the couch the CEO turned the two visitor's chairs at his table and he and Zhero sat, facing Justice Abramson. 'I'm sure you'll like him.'

'If you say so, Odemsa. I'm beat!' he said as he draped his arms over the cushions and stretched forward his legs. 'Background check . . . okay?'

'No question mark.'

'Only one or two commas,' Justice Abramson replied, the deadpan expression on his face frightening Zhero.

Odemsa laughed. 'You can interview him and see for yourself.'

'Tell me the questions you've prepared him for.' They both laughed. Odemsa gave him Zhero's CV and he looked at it for longer than the scanty data required. At last he asked, 'How do you pronounce your first name?' Zhero pronounced it. 'Not Zero. When do you want to start work? Now?'

Odemsa quickly said 'Tomorrow', afraid that Abramson might offer to take Zhero to his house to take his things.

'Why not now?'

'Now that he's been employed we need to say one or two things to him before he reports for duty.'

Abramson looked at the CV again and frowned. 'No 9 Shell Location Road . . . Where's that?'

Odemsa quickly answered, 'Not far from Manana Prison.'

'I hope it isn't a prisoner you're giving me, Odemsa?'

While they both laughed, Zhero's heart palpitated.

'He'll start tomorrow. Your driver can pick him up here.'

'As you like it, Odemsa. How much am I paying?'

'Others pay twenty thousand dollars. But the Chief Judge of the State can pay whatever he likes.'

'Tell your secretary to bring me a receipt for ten thousand.'

The three men laughed and Abramson counted fifty thousand dollars from his briefcase.

'Zhero, give to the secretary.'

'Thank you, sir.'

'Odemsa, I know you. It's the fifty thousand dollars you're thanking, not me.'

The three men laughed and Zhero went out with the money. While the secretary was counting the money they came out.

'Zhero.'

'Sir.'

See you tomorrow. My driver will be here to take you.'

'Thank you very much, sir.'

At home Zhero regretted not spelling out his terms for Odemsa and Justice Abramson . . . Maybe it was good he forgot. He might have lost the golden opportunity . . . If Abramson was so generous with money he wouldn't ill-treat him . . . A tall and imposing man . . . A happy man — very humorous . . . .

As happy as a child in the morning after he had slain the monster in his dream he decided to have himself a nice meal at the most expensive eatery in Nze Waterside. As he stepped out of his room, his landlord emerged from Esewa's room. The landlord stepped back and collided with Esewa, who had been coming out too. She pushed him forward angrily.

'Spencer, are you drunk? Do you want to push me down?' the girl rebuked him.

The landlord was ashamed that his tenant — a small boy — had seen him come out of a prostitute's house.

'Zhero,' he said in mock anger, 'the whole compound have gone to work. What are you doing here?'

Zhero laughed at his embarrassment and went out . . . But that girl is beautiful . . . Why is she a prostitute? . . . Rowland said every human being was a book of stories . . . .

250

In the night Esewa came into his room and entered without knocking. He gazed at her youthful breasts within her tight chiffon camisole while his mother's warning against girls did battle with Esewa's allure. She smiled knowingly and spoke.

'Zhero, Spencer told me your story . . . He said you must pack out at the end of the month. Did you do anything wrong . . . against him?' Zhero shook his head. 'Then why does he hate you so much?'

'I don't know.'

'And you are jobless. What will you do? Where will you go?' Zhero was silent. 'These big men, we get what we can from them, but people like us, let us belong together . . . Can I be of help? . . . Why are you silent?'

'Because I'm thinking of how good you are, Esewa.'

'Thank you.'

'I'm leaving tomorrow. I've got a job somewhere.'

'Oh!!!' She hugged him. 'I thank God! I thank God! Zhero, you are crying, and me too, I'm crying . . . Go well, Zhero.'

She disengaged from him, they wiped their faces, she air-kissed him and went back to her room.

That was Zhero's happiest night at Nze Waterside. Esewa's example of human goodness added to his buoyancy the next day, and Mrs Wama Abramson liked him as she watched him confidently carry out the first assignment she had tentatively given him —the ironing of her rich George wrappers and Swiss lace blouses she feared he might damage. As the months passed for everything she wanted someone to do for her it was Zhero, Zhero on her lips, and yet he never frowned. He never complained that Dahlia the maid was being given less and less to do and even the traditional woman's duty of going to market to buy foodstuffs was becoming his own, even though he did not know that it was because Mrs Abramson had found out that he was trustworthy — the quantity of foodstuffs he bought for ten thousand dollars was sometimes twice more than the quantity Dahlia bought for the same amount.

One morning, as he was trimming the godivabloom plants outside the fence she asked him why it was that everything he did came out beautiful.

'It's because my mother said I should love everything I do.'

'Even as a houseboy?' she asked the boy, full of deep admiration, because every job she had given him was his metier.

'Yes, Mommy, because I'm a houseboy. When I become

something else I'll equally love what I'm doing.'

She also admired him because he had green fingers. Even with fertilizers she had failed to make the plants in the backyard grow satisfactorily, but after he came, without the aid of fertilizers the plants began to bloom. He said his mother taught him a lot of farming skills too.

She would never forget the day she heard him telling a godivabloom to grow like the others, then he said to it, 'I know everybody doesn't grow the same way, but you must grow too.'

After a long silence she sadly said, 'I told Daddy about your request to go to evening school, he said not now.' He stopped working and stared blankly at the garden shears in his hands. 'Will you leave us?'

'No, Mommy,' he quickly answered, sensing her fear of losing him, but beneath his casual manner was the unshared pain of looking at the shards of a broken dream.

'Thank you, Zhero.'

He thanked her back and started to use his bare hands to affectionately brush the sheared pieces off the plants. His action made her regard the godivablooms as newborn babies that needed a gentle touch, and she unconsciously stroked her stomach.

She did not tell him how her husband had shouted at her and called her a foolish woman for bringing a houseboy's request to him — if the houseboy went to school would she do his work? he had asked her.

To take Zhero's mind off his disappointment she said they would both go to market and then he would teach her to cook the Nigerian *okazi* meal. He half happily said yes, but in the market two hours or so later he was like a loving son as he pointed out the things to buy, and in the kitchen he put his heart into the preparation of the meal, enthusiastically telling Mommy what should go next into the pot and at what intervals after the palm oil had boiled for about five minutes — *okazi*, the water in which the beef had been partly cooked before, stockfish, crayfish, salt, pepper, the partly cooked beef, periwinkles and *ugu*.

When Abramson ate the meal in the evening and retired around 9pm without commending her she was worried . . . Maybe he didn't like *okazi*? . . . Maybe he suspected she wasn't the one who cooked it?

Zhero comforted her, 'My mother used to say I shouldn't be

worried that people don't say thank you. The important thing is the love behind what I did.' He silently wished he could say things as well as the way his mother put them. 'Mommy?'

'Yes, Zhero. I was thinking about what you said . . . Your mom was never hurt by what your dad said or did?' He did not answer her. 'Zhero, I think you're tired. Go to bed.'

'Goodnight, Mommy.'

'Good night.'

He left her in the sitting room and went to the boys' quarters. He usually did not lock his sitting room until bedtime. When he entered Dahlia was sitting on the couch.

'Dahlia, what are you doing here?'

'Zhero, since Mommy called you, I have not been able to sleep? What did Mommy tell you?'

'Nothing.'

'How can you say nothing? Zhero, you think am a small pikin?'

'I mean nothing serious. Just the things I'm to do for her tomorrow.'

'You sure? She did not say anything about me?'

'No, nothing about you.'

'Thank God.'

She started to leave.

'What did you do wrong?'

'Nothing.'

'Zhero is the small pikin.'

They laughed and she went with relief to her place, the adjoining sitting room/bedroom. She had been afraid that after she took Justice Abramson's things to his room Mrs Abramson saw him kissing her in the doorway.

Zhero looked around the sitting room which should have been his study if he had gone to school: the couch on which to relax when he was tired, the big table with six drawers that could contain all his books, the armchair with a padded seat and a padded backrest, a ceiling fan, a fluorescent light, screen windows — a place he'd have loved to live in until he finished university . . . but Abramson didn't want to allow him to go to school . . . .

He locked the door, opened the door to his bedroom and went in . . . Thought of the creature comforts he was enjoying made him sad: His bedroom, his sitting room, the bathroom containing a toilet, a shower, a washbasin and a bath — a bathroom which only he and

Dahlia used, so clean that he could have his meal in it . . . If only Abramson would allow him to go to school . . . Just four years, then he could look for a job somewhere else and go to university . . . .

Could it be that Abramson was afraid that if he went to school he wouldn't be able to clean his big house thoroughly every day? But he'd never complained that the house was too big for him to clean — a sitting room, a dining room, a kitchen and a store on the ground floor, four bedrooms and a sitting room on the first floor, on the second floor four toilets and a big hall in which Abramson's town's Development Union sometimes held their monthly meeting . . . If he woke up at 5am he could conveniently clean the house, the whole compound, and do any other things before leaving for school at 4pm . . . .

He pitied Mrs Abramson whose husband always treated her disrespectfully . . . He pitied the ignorant woman who treated Dahlia as a daughter, a girl who was having sex with her husband . . . She took him as a child and was afraid he might leave for another place . . . Poor childless woman . . . Perhaps Abramson was ill-treating her because she was barren? . . . .

In the dream state Zhero flew to Amabra, where Kenitari gave him a bag of gold coins, and he was very happy.

He woke up around 4am and thought about the dream . . . He wouldn't tell anyone about it, because a grown-up flying in dreams was regarded as an act of witchcraft . . . He wondered why the childhood experience of flying had come back into his dreams . . . .

But the dream pleased him. It probably meant he would be rich . . . When he contemplated on it he felt it meant that he should fill his heart with a lot of love — the gold coin meant love . . . He would continue to love Abramson . . . and Teima too . . . .

The next day Mrs Abramson brought up the matter of the *okazi* soup again when he went into her room to clean it, because her husband insulted her in the morning when she mistakenly polished his black shoes instead of the brown ones he had decided to wear.

'Zhero, do you think Daddy didn't like *okazi* soup because it's not native Godivan soup?'

Zhero laughed. 'Mommy, I've eaten *okazi* soup many times in Godiva.'

'Then is he treating me the way he does because I am a barren woman? Sometimes, when he's not happy, he says he and I are two men in the house. He calls me a man because I am barren.'

254

'Oh, Mommy, why are you crying?' Zhero wept. She took the Bible she was reading before he came in and held it to her chest as if it was a baby she wanted to suckle. 'Mommy, God's time is the best.'

She said. 'Thank you, Zhero' and went to the sitting room so that he could clean the room.

Two days later it was her turn to say to Zhero not to weep. She and her husband were silently watching TV in the sitting room when Zhero came in to say if there was no more work for him he would like to go and sleep. She remembered a question he had asked in the afternoon and happily turned it over to her husband.

'Ozoh, Zhero wants to know why female judges are addressed as "My Lord", "His Lordship" and "Sir". Must it be so?'

Abramson, who hated her excessive affection for the boy, answered the question. 'Equality of the sexes. No sexual difference since they do the same job. Like in some houses, no difference between the man and the woman.'

Wama was dumbfounded . . . Zhero did not know that it wasn't his mother that had been brutally humiliated until she took him out and begged him not to weep.

That night around 2am he woke up and started to wipe the tears from his dream . . . His sadness from the dream continued . . . .

His mother had said in the dream, 'Your dad has come back from a long journey but you aren't happy. What's wrong, Zhero?' Then she turned to his dad, 'You, what have you brought home?'

Who was the man? Was Bazi still looking for him? It wasn't Bazi. His voice was like Bazis, but he wasn't Bazi . . . .

On Easter Monday after Mrs Abramson and Dahlia had left for the beach a man visited Abramson. While Zhero was making tea for them he heard the man say he had only come to drop the briefcase with him, and had to rush somewhere. Abramson thanked him warmly and he left. As Zhero brought in the tray of tea he saw Abramson looking out of the window and exclaiming, 'I'm a dead man! My foolish police guard and the gateman allowed them in without approval. I'm a dead man!' Four grim-faced men had entered the compound and were coming determinedly towards the building. Abramson stood paralysed by the window. Zhero grabbed the briefcase, went out of the house through the back door, threw the briefcase over the fence, scrambled over the concrete fence, grabbed the briefcase again and ran out of the bush.

When he returned at dawn the next day he discreetly took the briefcase to Justice Abramson and told no one what had happened. Fifteen minutes or so after, Abramson came into his room to thank him, sitting beside him on the bed.

'Zhero, you saved my reputation yesterday. My hard-earned reputation. Those people were detectives. They turned this compound inside out. When they saw my safe they thought the coffin of my reputation had been nailed. But there was no foreign currency in it. Zhero, thank you for saving my reputation . . . Two things I'll do for you today: Buy a mobile phone with this ten thousand dollars today. This is one hundred thousand dollars. Start school any moment you like . . . Stand up, foolish boy, don't kneel down to thank me.'

'Thank you, sir, thank you, sir,' Zhero repeated as he stood up.

'Do you know how much is in that briefcase?'

'No, sir, I didn't open it, sir.'

'I thought you'd run away with my money, but you're here. Where did you spend the night?'

'Luckily I had some money with me. I stayed in a hotel.'

'Zhero, you're as smart as a crook. Yet why are you so honest? Wama is always praising your honesty.'

'Thank you, sir.'

'But one thing, Zhero. Nobody . . . nobody must know what has happened.'

'Thank you, sir,' Zhero responded, still on his feet.

Abramson got up from the bed and went to Dahlia's room, to be sure she had not come to his room while he was with Zhero. She was not around.

When Zhero told Mrs Abramson that Daddy had given him permission to attend school and he would go in the afternoon to find out when the school would reopen, she danced joyously and waited impatiently for her husband to return from work. When he did she restrained herself until he was at the dining table.

'So what?' he replied when she thanked him. 'Because I said Zhero shouldn't go to school, that's why you never cooked *okazi* soup for me again?'

'But —'

But what?'

'You didn't say you liked it.'

'And *you* didn't see the way I was eating it? As if I hadn't eaten

256

soup since my mother gave birth to me?'

Wama laughed happily and told Dahlia to call Zhero. Zhero fearfully responded . . . But Mommy was smiling . . . .

'Zhero, Daddy said he enjoyed the *okazi* soup you cooked.'

'Thank you, sir.'

'Zhero, don't thank me, cook me *okazi* soup.'

They all laughed, and Zhero happily went back to his room. He was happy to have seen Mommy and her husband laughing together, for the first time in . . . he couldn't remember when last he saw them happy together. Their happiness made his thought of starting school the next day very sweet. He admired his bedroom, then the sitting room — the place wouldn't be a waste, it could make studies easy . . . For hours he thought about his life . . . .

He pricked up his ears . . . Dahlia must be going to Daddy. He allowed enough time, went to the end of the building and peeked. She was walking across the paved distance between the boys' quarters and the main building. Daddy must have switched off the lights. He faintly saw her open the door and go in. Mommy must be sleeping . . . .

Why was Daddy treating her so? Why was Dahlia so wicked to a woman who treated her as a daughter? . . . Should he tell Mommy what they were doing to her? . . . It could backfire . . . He hated Abramson, he hated Dahlia . . . A young and beautiful girl — why?

He went back to his bedroom . . . .

Esewa said people like us should belong together. How could he belong together with people like Dahlia? . . . Dahlia . . . Dahlia . . . .

He could not sleep. He took a chair, went to the veranda and sat. When Dahlia returned she looked at him suspiciously for a couple of seconds before she spoke.

'Zhero, you have seen what you want to see, so what?' He was silent. 'Zhero, I always feel say you are seeing inside me and you don't like the thing you are seeing.'

'Dahlia, leave me alone.'

She sat on his lap.

'If you don't keep your mouth shut, you have put sand in your own garri too.'

'Dahlia, please leave me alone.'

'You sure you want me to leave you alone? What is pressing against my buttocks is different from what you are saying. Tell me am lying. Life is like that, Zhero.' He pushed her away. She laughed

'Not tonight. It must be when am clean and fresh. The whole of the night. And you will use my name to sing the sweet songs you are always singing. Zhero, good night.'

She left him, he went back to his bed, and thought about his mother's warning not to spoil his chances of going to secondary school and then to university . . . .

About three months after he started school, Mrs Abramson firmly told her husband that Dahlia should relieve him of cleaning the big house. Abramson did not object, and Dahlia happily started to clean the house. Zhero was grateful to Mommy, and to Dahlia too.

One Saturday morning after they had finished their morning chores Dahlia gratuitously criticized Abramson.

'Do you know?' she said to Zhero.

'What?'

'That as Chief Judge of this State government suppose to give Justice Abramson many domestic servant — houseboys, housegirls, gardeners, security guards day and night. But he is taking cash instead of allowing government give him domestic servant.'

'If government brings houseboys and maids here, where will you be today?'

'Hey, Zhero! That is true o! This school you are going is making you to be a very clever boy. Is good to go to school. One day one day me too will go to school.'

His aversion to her lessened that moment and in the evening when Mrs Abramson invited them to stay with her till bedtime he liked her anecdotes which made Mommy laugh and laugh. They stopped laughing. For the umpteenth time the photograph of a man who needed G$800,000 for surgery in South Africa had appeared on the screen. He was appealing for charity from his fellow Godivans. While Dahlia and Mrs Abramson were railing at the corrupt Godivan government and the selfish rich people in Godiva, just one of whom could provide the whole amount, Zhero memorized the account name and the account number into which donations could be paid, excused himself and went to his room to write down what he had memorized. If on his return Justice Abramson paid him his salary on Monday he would give the poor man something. When he returned to the women they felt like sleeping. Because Mrs Abramson said the house was too big for her to sleep in alone at night Dahlia had to pass the night there.

On Tuesday Zhero kept his promise. He paid two thousand dollars into the man's account in Coastal Bank of Godiva, and feeling very happy he went into a bookshop along the street to look for a novel or two to buy. His heart palpitated at what he saw — 'Odedekoko', a novel by Numu! The cashier wondered why his hand was shaking as he paid for the book . . . Odedekoko . . . Odedekoko . . . More than half of his mind was on it during the English Language, Mathematics and Religious Studies classes . . . Odedekoko . . . Odedekoko . . . .

Time for study hall, he rushed to Room 1 in Block C and snatched 'Odedekoko' out of his school bag. He felt like finishing pages one to the end in one minute . . . After about fifteen minutes he was disappointed — he did not understand what Numu was saying . . . It was the same thing with the novel Numu gave him in Nigeria. He understood what it said about hell only because Numu explained it to him on the day he took him to the university.

At home he opened the pages at random and read. He could understand some places but many others were beyond his understanding. At the end he went back to a paragraph on page 111 which he understood and liked because of what it said about the main character:

He is cheerful and happy, always grateful that he is alive and can work for his food. He loves the world, admiring the goodness in others and shrugging his shoulders at what he thinks they shouldn't have done. He loves God, he loves his neighbours, he loves everybody he meets along the journey of life.

He thought about the phrase 'work for his food' which he and his mother had taken from The Home Stretch people when they used to come to Amabra . . . He didn't quite understand the meaning of 'shrugging his shoulders at what he thinks they shouldn't have done' but when he shrugged his shoulders twice the meaning became clear, and his mind went to what Dahlia and Justice Abramson were doing — it wasn't his business to report to Mommy; he shouldn't even hate them . . . He felt terribly sorry that he once hated his mother, and he heard her sobbing, For your sake, Zhero, for your sake . . . .

The next day he took the novel to the Literature teacher for him to explain a passage, but before he could speak Mr Bonaventure enthused.

'You know Numu! You know my hero! You are blessed. Please read his novels and you'll be a good man. Get a good education and be like Numu. Perhaps you wanted me to explain the novel to you?'

'Yes, sir.'

'I'll read it. Give me this weekend. I'll explain it to you.'

Mr Bonaventure took the book from him, opened it at random and read some places . . . 'Hnh, Numu! Numu!' . . . He read out the sentences that had delighted him most: 'Heroes quietly serve life, never stopping to receive the applause of the people. There is no end to their quest for more and more of the wisdom, the love and the pure means to serve life.'

Zhero liked his admiration for Numu.

'Zhero, one day you'll be like Numu.'

'Sir, my mother used to tell me I shouldn't think of becoming like any other human being. I should be myself.'

'Your mother is right too, but anyone who follows Numu's footsteps will be a great man. I attended a public lecture he gave in our university when I was a student. I dream of meeting him personally someday. I thought I'd read all his novels. This one must be new. Next week, next week I'll explain it to you.'

'Thank you, sir.'

'Thank you too.'

'Sir,' Zhero said, 'some of the words are like the words in a book my mother bought for me. The book was written by a woman — Zainab Shettima.' Bonaventure looked at him interrogatively. Zhero felt he had offended him. 'Sir, the . . . the . . . words like looking for more love and more wisdom.'

Bonaventure smiled. 'Truth is not the exclusive property of any man . . . or any woman.' Zhero felt relieved. 'Zhero, I like what your mother is doing for you.'

'Thank you, sir.'

'Thank your mother too, Zhero, thank her when you get home.'

On Saturday, before Daddy and Mommy left home to attend a function at Government House, Zhero had told them he would go to the bookshop for about two hours. He had intended to buy two copies of the novel the class would start studying next week, Isidore Okpewho's *The Victims* — one for Estella, one for himself — and another copy of 'Odedekoko' so that Mr Bonaventure could keep the copy with him, but while he was dusting the sitting room in the main building the news of the man who had appealed for G$800,000 had made him sad — only G$567,000 had been received and the man had died. He cancelled going to the bookshop and thought about life; in his bedroom . . . If after all his struggle some sickness would cut short his life was going to school worth it? If —

Dahlia came in. He scrambled to his feet.

'Dahlia, why are you dressed up like this? Did you tell Daddy and Mommy you'll be going out?' She went to the sitting room and told him to come out. He did. She pointed at her travelling bag. 'Where are you going?'

'I have taken enough money from Abramson. This is the key of his safe. I shall throw it away when I leave here. Let me give you my secret phone number.' He was too shocked to respond. She took his mobile from his hand and punched in the number. 'I know you can never betray me, even though you hate me anytime you see me go to Abramson at night and come back. When I tell you I too will go to school, you don't know that I have plan? Zhero, don't pity these big men. We mean nothing to them . . . But I know Mommy will be disappointed. Well, life is like that. And me I don't want to be a woman like her, for man to treat as footmat . . . Zhero, if I don't succeed in life I will not forgive all the men who have use me selfishly.' She laughed. 'Do you know that I was housegirl for a man who use to work in Abramson's office? Because Abramson want me, he send the man to a court in one remote riverine village, and the man sack me, because where he was going he won't have money to steal and live like big man.' She laughed again. 'If I succeed in life I will forgive and forget all the bad bad things men have done to me.' She turned serious. 'Zhero, promise you will not hate me.' He shook his head. 'If they hang me on the cross and people are stoning me, you too will stone me?' He shook his head again and she laughed. She looked at his face. He was shedding tears. 'Oh, Zhero, you small boy, why?' She hugged him tightly and kissed him passionately. 'Zhero, all the hundreds of kisses Abramson and I kiss, not one of them pure like this one I have just kiss you.' She kissed him again. 'Is as if I should pluck out and go with the voice you use to sing in the night when am on my bed listening to you. Especially when you are singing Ebenezer Obey's song, "Àjò kò dàbi ilé".' She smiled. 'Yes, I love your singing, but you are a foolish boy.' She made to kiss him once more but changed her mind. 'You are making it hard for me to leave, Zhero, but like you, me too I have my own ambition ... When you want to judge me, think. For more than five years I serve them, husband and wife, Abramson refuse to allow me go to school, and Mommy cannot do anything about it. You, is because of what you did for him Abramson allow you go to school. You surprise? I hear you people from where I hide and listen that day you return the briefcase . . . Zhero, let me go, if Abramson catch me there will be no key to my prison cell, even though is from a thief I have stolen.'

She left him shedding tears. After a while he deleted her secret number from his mobile so that he would be able to swear that he did not know where or how to contact her . . . He thought, Is this too the journey of life? . . . Go well, Dahlia . . . .

He quickly smothered his incipient sense of guilt about the G$100,000 Abramson gave him . . . The Chief Judge's fruit of corruption, the money in the briefcase, was in foreign currency, not the Godiva dollars he gave him. In any case, he needed a lot of money for his education . . . .

Immediately they returned around 8pm Abramson, whose thoughts had been running on Dahlia, told Zhero to tell her to come quickly, his intention being to tell her to be prepared for the night.

Zhero lied, 'But, Daddy, she said you and Mommy allowed her to travel for one week.'

'What are you talking? Wama!' he shouted and she came rushing from her room to their private sitting room. 'Wama, did you give Dahlia permission to travel? Without my approval!'

'Travel? Is she not at home?'

'No, Mommy.'

'The girl we both agreed that will take me to her hair salon tomorrow.'

Abramson dashed into his bedroom, looked around, tested the safe, frantically looked for the key to the safe and moaned.

'Hey! Dahlia has finished me!' Wama and Zhero rushed to him. 'Dahlia has finished me. I can't find the key to the safe.'

The key was nowhere to be found. He called the CEO of Africa Safes and Security, a personal friend, who came with men and equipment and opened the safe a little after midnight — only a sheet of paper which only Abramson read and shredded insanely, as if he was shredding all the things he had told Dahlia during the nights they were on Venus — his secrets which she could broadcast terrestrially.

'Ozoh, what did she say?' Wama tearfully asked, afraid for his mental health.

'Ask your crocodile tears. Or go to your bedroom and swim in the water.' Zhero flinched at his malevolent tone, his perceptibly offensive sweat that had soaked his white polo neck, his dark frown. 'You Zhero, what are you doing here? If you like, go and cry with her.' Zhero hurried out of the living room. Abramson turned to the CEO, who was reeling as if at a monster that had broken into his safety. 'Dr Uwem-Uyime,' he calmly said, 'I'll see you tomorrow.'

Dr Uwem-Uyime, felt relieved — he was in the presence of a fellow human being, in fact, the Chief Justice of the State . . . Thinking of his own name he shrugged and refrained from passing judgement.

That night Zhero wondered why a man could despise his own wife so much . . . The CEO and his workers pitied her . . . .

From Monday to Friday Zhero did not go to school, because he had to be around Mrs Abramson. Dahlia's action had devastated her and even though the doctor said there was nothing wrong with her she felt that she was very sick. In spite of everything she had loved Dahlia as a daughter, a friend, a sister, a companion — her sudden absence was devastating.

On Saturday night, when Abramson had not returned from the monthly meeting of his town's development union, she told Zhero to read out loud *Things Fall Apart* which she had seen in his hand. It was the novel she had studied for the School Certificate Examination many years ago. She enjoyed it, as if she had not read it before; and his reading, as if he was Chinua Achebe's son, she said, and they laughed. She asked him what he liked best in the novel and he said it was the Igbo proverb that when a man says yes his *chi* says yes. He was about to explain the importance of the proverb to her but when he peeked from the corner of his eye he saw that she was thinking.

She was thinking of where her husband could be at that time of the night. She always feared anytime he went to his tribal meetings because of his people's penchant for juju and witchcraft . . . And the Igbo proverb . . . When she was young she had said the man that would marry her would be a loving man, but how loving was Abramson? It seemed her *chi* had not said yes . . . Where could he be now?

At that moment he was less than ten minutes from home, impatient to confront Zhero. At the end of the meeting Pascal, a warder, had told the story of a boy in the prison where he worked to illustrate the wonderful world humans lived in. Abramson had said he lied, and Pascal was offended.

'Zhero is my houseboy. What are you saying?'

Pascal had reiterated his story and described Zhero's physical appearance and character again. Abramson had hugely apologized. When he reached home he was glad that Zhero was already in the sitting room.

'Ozoh, what kept you so long?'

He wasn't prepared for a question from a woman.

'Welcome, Daddy.'

'Zhero, do you know a warder named Pascal? We are from the same place. Do you know him?'

'Yes. He's a very good man.'

'So you've been to prison?'

'Yes.'

'Ewoh!' Wama wailed. 'Zhero, you too?' she cried as she slouched on the couch, as if the house of love she was building had crashed on her.

Abramson narrated the story of Zhero in Manana Prison.

'Zhero, Pascal said nobody knew why those prisoners were terrified when they saw you. Do you know?'

Zhero told them about his escape from the Obadore forest.

'Wama, you have always wanted to know why this boy is so good. Now you have known.'

She took him into her arms and wept and thanked God for sending Zhero to her — if she had a son she'd call him Zhero.

'Zhero,' Abramson asked again, 'the night the armed robbers were operating in this street and we couldn't get help from the police, remember?' Zhero nodded. 'You met them at the gate when you were returning from school. You said you only told them nobody lived in this house and they went back.'

'Yes, Daddy.'

'With the lights shining in the house and in the whole compound, they believed that nobody lived here!'

'Yes, Daddy.'

'I didn't believe you until this night, after Pascal told us about you. Were you afraid that night?'

'A little. Something told me to tell them there's no one in this house.'

'Zhero —'

'Ozoh, it's enough. Leave the boy alone.'

'I don't know why I'm talking. I think I just want to be sure he's a human being.'

264

They laughed and Wama wiped her face.

At bedtime Abramson thought about the difference between reputation and character . . . It was character, not reputation, that took humans closer to God . . . Zhero might not even know the meaning of reputation but he knew the meaning of honesty, he knew the meaning of industry, he knew the meaning of love . . . Heaven told him to work for his food, and his mother taught him to put his heart into his work . . . .

Wama flicked the bedside switch and looked at the wall clock — 12.18am. She flicked the light off . . . She did not answer the door but it opened and Abramson came in.

'Are you asleep?' she did not answer him. 'Wama, can you hear me?'

'Because Dahlia has left you?'

His heart thumped. She felt his shaking when he sat on the bed. She flicked the light on.

'Ozoh, you're shaking. Are you okay?'

'Yes, yes. I didn't know you knew.'

'Am I not a woman? Because I'm barren you think I'm not a woman?'

She took an envelope from the bedside cabinet and gave it to him. His hands trembling, he brought out a sheet of paper and read it.

He wept, 'You are pregnant? You are pregnant, Wama, you are pregnant?'

'I am a woman,' she replied, the tears coursing down her cheeks.

'Why didn't you tell me you're pregnant?'

'Because the day I got the result, I found out in the clinic that Dahlia had done abortion.'

'Dr Godiver told you? She told you?'

'No. While the nurse was giving me the paper she pointed to a girl going out. She said I was happy that I was pregnant while that girl was happy that she had got rid of her pregnancy.'

Abramson wept.

Chapter Eight

Sometimes, it all seemed like yesterday — the night she hugged Zhero and said if she had a son she would call him Zhero, and when Ozoh came into her bedroom after midnight for the first time in many months, she told him she was pregnant. After they wept and wept that night over the things he had done to her in the past she said to thank Zhero, because he was the one who made her believe that she could be a mother. The boy wasn't called Zhero but as she now watched them playing — the boy saying 'Zeeyoh! Zeeyoh!' and Zhero saying, 'Kick the ball, Zhero Jr, kick the ball like a man!' — she remembered her wish of some years ago, as if it was yesterday. And she was happy that with Zhero around, her son would be raised in a houseful of honesty.

She fondly remembered the day a ring-pull she had removed from a soft drink can and rolled into a ball got stuck in the boy's throat. She and Ozoh were beside themselves with fear while getting dressed and then rushing out to meet their choking and dying son in the car for the driver to take them to the hospital. Just then Zhero returned from school. He put his hand on the boy's shoulder and said, 'Zeeyoh, ha! . . . ha! . . . ha!' The boy did as he said and coughed out the ring-pull. At the clinic the boy was found to be absolutely okay.

Abramson came out and sat by her in the porch.

'The evening breeze is sweeter than airconditioning. Why are you smiling?'

'I remember the promise you made on the night I told you I was pregnant. You agreed that if our child is a boy we'll call him Zhero, but you broke your promise.' He laughed. 'A promise is a fowl's egg, not useful if not broken. Now I'm wiser.'

'That night, the way I felt ashamed of myself, if you had said I should walk from this house to the Atlantic beach and into the ocean I would have done it without looking back.'

'Ozoh!' she laughed.

'Yes, three hours' journey, no looking back.'

'I don't know what I did wrong in my past life. God gave me a liar for a husband.'

They laughed.

'Zhero.'

'Mommy.'

'It's time to leave your brother. Your School Cert exam is knocking at your door. You should go and study.'

Zhero played the ball far away and told the boy to go and bring it. He obeyed, but then he turned back and saw Zhero running away.

'Zeeyoh! Zeeyoh! Zeeyoh!'

'Zhero Jr, come back,' his mother called out.

As if to cancel the name his mother had given him Abramson called out, 'Plato!' and hurried to carry him back, while the boy kicked and cried, 'Zeeyoh! Zeeyoh!'

Wama said to the maid who was coming towards them, 'Lamina, come and take my son.'

She took him from his father. He continued to cry for Zeeyoh. Telling him that Zeeyoh had gone out of the gate she went out of the compound with him. The two non-resident houseboys came from the security house.

'Amama and Oyiko, time to close for the day?'

'Yes, sir,' they answered in unison.

'Then see you tomorrow. But if you don't feel like it, don't come, because tomorrow is payday.'

The young men laughed and left, admiring their employer's sense of humour. Wama liked them, and she was glad of their industry, because since they came Zhero had had ample time for studies. When she saw him joking with them the next day as he was leaving for school she wondered if they too had dreams of education or even a wish to be more than houseboys someday.

In his happiness Zhero took the wrong bus, which stopped at Osoko, and he decided to walk the thirty minutes or so distance to school instead of taking a taxi for fifty dollars. Soon he saw a large crowd around where an uncompleted five-storey building used to stand. He trotted down there. The building had collapsed.

Some people said up to fifty people were buried in the rubble, some said not more than thirty, while a man said the building used to harbour up to a hundred people. Considering the time of day, a woman said, very few people would have been killed. She thanked God it didn't happen at night. It was a house for homeless children and young persons. Since it collapsed about four hours ago only five bodies had been recovered. Some people remarked that it was a good thing the building collapsed, because it used to be a den of robbers, rapists, gamblers and drug addicts who lived outside the laws of the land.

Zhero thought, 'A five-storey house collapsed, only one crane and one caterpillar; people using their hands to remove the heavy blocks.'

The police beat back the crowd who were coming too close to the imaginary line they had drawn between the people and ground zero.

A man said the building collapsed because the owner refused to appease the spirit of the ancient tree that was cut down, a tree that used to be worshipped by the villagers who were dislocated when the government acquired and turned the area into a place for rich people.

Then it was similar to what happened at the North-South Highway, another man said to a small group of people. There the colonial government refused to appease the spirits in the ancient tree which was in the middle of what was to be a dual carriageway.

'If they cut the tree today, tomorrow morning the tree is up again. Three times, overnight the tree will grow. When the DO (District Officer) came he did not say anything to the black workers who were afraid to go near. He just stand under the tree, pray with his lips, then he order the black workers to cut down the fucking tree.' The audience laughed. 'Yes,' the narrator continued, 'he said the fucking tree — my father told me so. As he was shouting at the black people and calling them niggers a black bird from the top of the tree just land on his head — bam! — and drop dead, like that. DO start to shake, saying "Am feeling cold, am feeling cold, cover me with clothes and take me to hospital, pull your shirts and cover me." He die on the way to hospital. That day colonial government pay the owners of the land and juju priests plenty money to beg the spirits in the tree to leave.'

Before the narrator finished, Zhero had felt he heard human cries somewhere. As the small group were laughing at the 'fucking white man' while their fellow blacks were dying under the rubble he did as if he wanted to say something to the police, edged away to where he thought he had heard cries, dropped his schoolbag close by, and started to pull away boulders. A policeman who noticed him shrugged and let him be. When he lifted the fourth boulder the police and the crowd distinctly heard the cries of their fellow humans. Several people rushed to join him and in less than one hour, four people were pulled out. There was jubilation, and there was strong

268

hope for success as two more cranes arrived. As the police beat away the crowd to allow in the cranes Zhero picked up his schoolbag, left the scene and went to school, thinking of what Pastor Ododo used to say: Virtue is its own reward . . . .

At school the teachers told the students that they had started a strike that day because their salaries had not been paid for three months, and advised the students to study on their own. Not in the mood to do so Zhero decided to go to Agoa, just in case Ogugo had returned there.

Ogugo had never come back since they both left, but there were a few old friends around, who were very happy to see Zhero who they thought they would never meet any more. They told him Golan once came in a Hummer Jeep and said he needed to see him urgently, but no one knew his address. Samba went with Golan and had not come back since then. They told him business was picking up at Agoa and Tanta again following the collapse of the salvage yard at Sanka-Mo Bo Road after armed robbers killed the owner and then his wife who took over the business. Then they told him of several tragedies which had happened since he left them. Did he know that Agbarasa died from the cough he contracted at Dr Faustus's dump? After spending all his money to buy different types of cough syrup. Zhero shed tears. And Octopus Paul, Octopus Paul killed himself with a brew of marijuana and native gin when the five draws he had banked on to make him a millionaire failed two weeks ago. Zhero wished he had not come to hear what they had just said.

'Octopus Paul,' he cried, 'Octopus Paul is dead . . . And you, Oja, you now smoke marijuana?'

After puffing on the wrap of marijuana, 'I now smoke, Jero,' Oja answered. 'For house I even boil am with native gin. Zhero, na to give me strength to face life.'

'Why, Oja?'

'Because I no go let life to defeat me.' Zhero smiled wryly through his tears, because he felt life had defeated Oja too — his motor vehicle tyre flip-flops, torn well-worn brown trousers and soot-covered bare chest were life's portrait of Oja's defeat. 'Zhero, na whosai you dey?' When he noticed that Zhero was hedging he came to his help. 'I understand,' he said, 'I no go come make you ashame.'

Zhero gave them five thousand dollars and left, hurting at what Oja had said to him. He went to Agoa Road to take a bus. After ten minutes or so he chartered a taxi . . . Agbulo and Ogoun flashed through his mind . . . When they were porters in Swali Market in Yenagoa they used to talk about helping people when they had made it in life. They talked about making Nigeria a better place. They didn't know that one had to serve life wherever one was, whatever one was. Everybody had something to give. One didn't have to be rich before helping one's neighbour . . . They resisted the temptation to become Niger Delta militants because they didn't like the wicked things some of the militants were doing to their own people . . . But Agbulo and Ogoun became kidnappers . . . Perhaps they were also militants . . . .

Octopus Paul . . . One day, for no reason, Octopus Paul called him aside to the edge of the swamp and told him his story confidentially. His name was Yaya when he was in Gambia. One day three years ago, when he was fourteen years old, when his mother started to beat him wildly the way she had always done, he took a machete and wanted to kill her. She went down on her knees and begged him not to kill her until she had explained why she hated him. When he raised the machete she quickly explained why. Because he was the product of three armed robbers who raped her in front of her husband. Three days after the robbers raped her, her husband drove her out of his house, and three months after, he married a young virgin. The church told her it was a sin to abort the pregnancy, yet when he was born the Motherless Baby Home of the church refused to take him from her. His mother stood up and told him to kill her, but the machete dropped from his hand and he walked out of the house. He fended for himself, first as a pickpocket, then as a bus conductor, and then as an armed robber. One day the police arrested him and his three friends but in spite of his gunshot wounds he escaped from police detention and came to Godiva. He called himself Paul but because of his love for football pools his friends in Godiva called him Octopus Paul after the German octopus that predicted the winners of football matches correctly . . . .

In his heart Zhero thanked his own mother for not hating him ... The best way to thank her was to succeed in life . . . No, the best way to thank his mother was to love her . . . He sent his love to her mentally, and believed that because he loved her and she loved him they'd be together again . . . and she'd be glad he didn't waste her love . . . .

At home he went into the main building in order to say he was back from school. Abramson was angrily talking to his nephew.

270

'The bottom line is the girl you want to marry used to be a housegirl. Your mother has found out. A housegirl before somebody sent her to school. She's now a graduate but she was a housegirl.' Zhero feared Abramson might be insulted. There was contempt on Oludah's face. 'A housegirl — all the men she served would have used her before she became a graduate.' Oludah continued to look at his uncle, as if he was willing the contempt on his face to go slap the foolish man. 'Wama, did you hear my nephew? He's in love with a housegirl.' Wama, who had been thinking about Dahlia, decided not to hear her husband's rich remarks. 'No decent man,' he said to his nephew, 'no decent man, much more an aspiring lawyer like you, will marry such a girl. No —'

'Save your breath. It's because I'm not decent I want to marry her.'

'Then get out of my house!'

Oludah looked at his uncle scornfully and sauntered out, disdaining to argue his surefire case of love. Wama signed to Zhero to go out too. He went out, and wondered if that would be his own lot too — no decent girl would marry him?

He thought about what Dr Eustace once said to his class: 'As hard as it is for some people to pronounce Zhero's name, so it is for the rich and proud to appreciate the humanity of the poor.'

The next day, when Wama learnt that he would not go to school she was happy. They went to Isioko Market together, bought things for *banga* soup, a Nigerian delicacy which he had once taught her to prepare and which Abramson liked so very much, though he said it was expensive because of the fresh fish, returned home and cooked it together.

As Abramson enjoyed the meal she laughed and told him that Zhero had shown her a new route to the market — 'No need for a vehicle, less than fifteen minutes. All these years your drivers never discovered it.'

Abramson admired Zhero too, but he had made up his mind that he would not take him along to Lagos when he was elevated to the Supreme Court of Godiva. He liked the boy too, but not the fact that the boy knew him as a bribe-taker who was nearly arrested by detectives. If he had retained him for so long it was for Wama's sake.

'The other day I was eating *okazi* soup I said to myself, nothing created by God is useless. Do you know that the Sierra Leoneans eat cassava and potato leaves as vegetable?'

'Ozoh, who is the Sierra Leonean woman who cooked cassava and potato leaves for you?'

He laughed. 'You've forgotten that I went to Fourah Bay College in Freetown for a three-month course before I married you?'

'Thank God, you don't have a Sierra Leonean girlfriend somewhere.'

He laughed again. 'Throughout the three months, my fellow Godivans refused to touch the Sierra Leonean vegetables. Me —'

'You found their vegetables as delicious as their women.'

'I was a bachelor then, so why not?'

'Hey, Ozoh!'

As they laughed he started to cough.

'Sorry . . . sorry . . . take some water.'

He drank a little water.

'My bachelor experience helped me to choose a good woman for a wife.'

They laughed again, and he started to cough again.

'Jealous woman, don't kill me with laughter.'

'Plato will follow the footsteps of Zhero, not Ozoh's footsteps. My son won't be a womanizer. By the way, last week the nursery school childminder said when they ask him "What's your name?" he says "Zeeyoh."'

'Hey, Zhero has kidnapped my son!' he laughed.

'Talking seriously, Ozoh, what shall we do about this Krio nursery teacher from Sierra Leone who has influenced the boy's pronunciation of "r"?'

'Don't worry. Very soon he'll leave there.'

'What do you mean? You have a plan to remove him and you haven't told me?'

'Are you the man of the house now? You want to teach me my responsibility?' He noticed that she had turned glum. 'Zhero will unteach him. In case you're thinking the woman from Freetown is my girlfriend, I too will move far away from her. From this night, let Zhero start unteaching the boy.' She laughed. 'Now you're happy.'

She called him a clown and they laughed together.

But when he saw Zhero leaving for school the next day he muttered to himself, 'Why is this president delaying sending my name to the Senate for confirmation as a Supreme Court Justice? He dare not reject my nomination — thirty-five years outstanding service. Only distance can cure Wama of her obsession for this boy.'

Zhero went out of the gate with Daddy's advice to study well to pass well. During study hall when his classmates were enthusiastically discussing Superman's latest feats he strenuously pored over his book. Estella, who would have loved his contribution, mocked him.

'Godiva Television Authority Network News at Nine: All the students of Evening Stars Secondary School, except one, failed the School Certificate Examination this year. The only one who passed, Zhero, made A1 in every one of his nine subjects.'

His classmates gave him a standing ovation, he laughed, and they were happy. Then he told them he stopped being interested in 'Superman' when he saw how it was being produced. (How?) He explained the best way he could, but his classmates said what did it matter? Was 'Superman' not still delightful? If life was like that wouldn't it have been a good thing for humans, a hero helping the poor, the oppressed, the victims of injustice and righting all wrongs? Did fiction not inspire humans to noble deeds? They referred the matter to a Literature teacher who was passing by. He talked about the purpose of fiction, about the willing suspension of disbelief, about the super hero in several cultures and their literature. When he tried to recollect who said the purpose of art was to teach while delighting, someone interrupted him.

'Sir, this film they are advertising on TV, "A Woman Called Godiva", why would someone say our country is a woman?'

Dr Eustace pulled off his blue jacket, draped it over the backrest of the chair, sat down and smiled. 'Godiva was a woman, a noble woman born in 1040. She was the wife of the Earl, a ruler, of Mercia in what is now the United Kingdom. When the people of Mercia wanted her husband to reduce the taxes they were paying because they were poor and they were suffering, Godiva appealed to her husband to listen to the cries of the suffering people. Her husband gave her an impossible condition, in 1057: he would reduce the taxes the people were complaining about if she rode on horseback in the marketplace in Coventry. Naked. Totally naked. For the love of the people Godiva did it. The noble woman rode naked in the marketplace — Godiva sacrificed her dignity.'

'Hnnh!' many voices sighed.

'Wicked man!' two female students exclaimed together.

'Yes, but the good people of the town locked themselves in their

273

houses, except one person, Tom, who did not appreciate the goodness of Godiva, and peeked at her. Godiva's nakedness was the last thing he saw — God made him blind immediately, and he became known as Peeping Tom . . . Some of you are shedding tears. I think I must leave now.' They begged him to continue. There was nothing shameful in weeping. He continued. 'Just as Flora Shaw, the fiancée of Lord Lugard, gave the name "Nigeria" to where the different people the British colonial administration brought together lived, a British female administrator, many years ago, gave the name "Godiva" to our six regions the British brought together as a country. She was a descendant of Godiva. She said the life of personal sacrifices of the women of our regions reminded her of Godiva . . . When you see a woman, her one-year-old child strapped to her back, tilling the soil, think of Godiva . . . When you see a woman who would not eat breakfast because her child has to buy an exercise book before going to school, think of Godiva.' He let them sniffle. 'When you see a woman carrying her small child's desk and seat to school in the morning and returning to the school in the afternoon to bring them back home, think of Godiva . . . When you see women on the thirteenth of next month baring their breasts and protesting in the streets of Lagos against the daily rape of women in Godiva, would you leer at naked breasts . . . or would you think about Godiva?' No one spoke. 'A woman called Godiva,' he sighed, took up his blue jacket from the backrest of the chair and left, wiping his wet face with his right hand, having injected poetry into the history of the motherland.

'A woman called Godiva,' Zhero repeated and thought about his mother . . . .

Tomorrow he'd ask Dr Eustace for the piece he'd submitted some weeks ago. It was a voluntary exercise in creative writing. Dr Eustace had told the class to put down their deepest feelings on paper . . . He'd written about his unknown father . . . .

On his way home Zhero saw Zanzi standing about ten minutes from the collapsed five-storey building. He urgently begged the bus driver to stop and the driver did unwillingly, joining the other passengers to abuse him. He jumped out and ran towards Zanzi, who looked frightened and made to run away from the person coming after her in the lonely street.

'Zanzi! Zanzi! It's Zhero!'

'Zhero!'

She ran towards him, they met, they embraced, each said happy words the other did not catch.

'Zanzi.'

'Zhero.'

'Zanzi, what are you doing in Godiva?'

'Did you come with Chief Yago?'

'No.' He briefly told her how he came to be in Godiva and what he was now doing.

She thanked God she had never had bad thoughts about him even though she felt he abandoned her. She went to his place of work once but the gatekeeper would not allow her in, and when she insisted on seeing Zhero he threatened to call security.

'What are you doing in Godiva, Zanzi?' She smiled. 'Where do you live?'

'Ayilara Street.'

'Zanzi, Ayilara Street?'

'Yes. I am now a prostitute.' Zhero was speechless. 'Is that not what men always wanted me to be?' Zhero shed tears. 'Zhero, don't cry for me. Sometimes we cannot reject what life gives us. When we were selling pirated videos didn't you use to say it is better to do honest work than to steal or beg? I don't have good education, so I am using what I have to feed myself . . . Zhero, you are still behaving like a small boy. Wipe your face . . . Can you come and see me before I leave for Italy?' He was still silent. 'Zhero, if you cry every time you see or hear of suffering you will have no time to take care of your life oh.' She gave him her card. 'Will you come and see me?'

'Yes.' She wiped his face with her handkerchief. 'Zanzi, your English is very good now.'

She laughed. 'I've been to places, Zhero.'

He shook his head and they said their goodbyes. He watched Zanzi, her culottes and her slingbacks flaunting her shapely legs, as she gradually disappeared into the distance, then he chartered a taxi to take him straight to the house . . . Zanzi was right. He had to be strong otherwise life would defeat him . . . Zanzi a prostitute ... But she wasn't a thief, she was taking care of herself, and she was happy — that was very important . . . A prostitute . . . a prostitute ... she could have thought of something else . . . A maid? What was the difference? . . . Chief Hezekiah Jerome started it all when he tried to rape her . . . .

He vowed never to damage any girl's life, and he prayed to God to help him.

At home he did not go to tell Mommy that he was back; he went straight to his room.

After supper he would have loved to be alone, but Daddy had gone out and Mommy wanted him and Lamina to come watch TV with her till bedtime. He went unwillingly to Mommy who happily told him to see, see — the live broadcast of the occasion Daddy was attending. Zhero read out the banner at the back of the stage as if he was told to do so.

THE ICON IS 60!
CHIEF (DR) BETHLEHEM KURO
GIANT OF PHILANTHROPY
GODIVA SAYS HAPPY BIRTHDAY

Wama remarked, 'Chief Bethlehem is really rich. The cost of that banner alone can keep several children in school for six years.'

'But it isn't a waste,' Zhero said. 'Some people would have benefited from it — the sellers of the materials, the artist, the people who put it on the stage, and so on.'

Wama admired Zhero's intelligence and said one day he too would be celebrated.

Lamina enthused, 'Mommy, rich men like Daddy are plenty in this Godiva o! Fine suits, big big *agbada* with expensive material. See the women: what everybody is wearing cannot be less than one million.'

'Hey, Lamina!'

'Yes, Mommy. Don't you see their wrappers? Their blouses? Their necklaces? Their bangles? Some of them are wearing up to three rings on their fingers. Gold. Diamond . . . See that woman . . . that one wearing dark glasses, putting her hand on the table . . . one, two, three rings. One human being wearing three diamond rings. I think she wants people to see her expensive rings — that is why she is placing her hand on the table.'

Wama laughed. 'See, Daddy and Chief Bethlehem Kuro are talking and laughing.'

'He knows that if he does not go and salute Daddy he can go to jail tomorrow.'

Zhero and Wama laughed.

'Hey, Lamina, you will kill me!'

276

'It is true, Mommy.' Lamina replied. 'Do we know how he is getting his money?'

Chief Kuro went to the stage.

'Lamina, let's listen.'

The music had stopped and the MC was reeling out the achievements of the celebrant who was standing on the stage with him: the donation of relief materials anytime there was a disaster in any part of the country; one hundred block houses in his home village; fifty indigent Godivans on his payroll since his fiftieth birthday — how many would be added to the payroll tonight? Fifty university bursaries every year since his fiftieth birthday — what would be the figure tonight?

The audience interrupted the MC with a standing ovation.

Wama remarked, 'Money is good. It's good to do good with it.'

'But can't he do it for God instead of for the clapping?'

Wama looked at Zhero, whose indifferent attention was on the TV. She looked at her husband clapping and felt that he shouldn't have been there.

'Children, it's time to go to bed.'

'Thank you, Mommy.' Zhero stood up. 'Good night, Mommy.'

Lamina said she would not leave Mommy alone, and stayed on until Abramson returned a little after midnight. Immediately they met him at the porch Lamina enthused, 'Daddy we saw you in the telly. Bethlehem went to the place you were sitting to thank you. We saw you, you were laughing with him.'

She held his hand until she realized her embarrassing mistake. Fortunately they were behind Wama. He pulled his jacket and tie and told her to take them to his room. Upstairs he changed his mind and sat with Wama in their private sitting room until Lamina had come out. In his bedroom Wama recounted what they had seen.

'Do you know,' she concluded, 'that when we saw Chief (Dr) Bethlehem Kuro greeting you, Zhero said it's out of fear because you can jail him for the source of his wealth.'

She laughed, but Abramson frowned.

'What type of joke is that? Is every rich man in Godiva corrupt? Very soon he'll tell you that because I'm a judge I shouldn't socialize.'

She remembered that it was Lamina who made the joke but she did not correct herself. Before Abramson slept he told himself, 'This Zhero has to leave this house. How did he know that Bethlehem Kuro would have been jailed for embezzlement of public funds if I hadn't intervened?' In the morning when a driver of the judiciary he intended to assign to Zhero reported for duty as he was about to enter his own vehicle his attitude was cold.

'See Madam. She's in charge,' he told the driver in a the-Chief-Judge-of-the-State-is-not-the-head-of-his-home tone.

She was slightly embarrassed, but after he had left she took the driver to Zhero. Zhero happily greeted her.

'Zhero, this is the driver who will take you to Kumo and bring you back every day. Till you finish your papers . . . What's your name?'

'Edidobiamdudoh,' he spat, and looked as if a piece of yam, not mouth-hot, had burnt him. He repeated it and Wama burst into laughter. Laughing too, he said, 'Madam, don't worry. Me and this my *pardie*, we go get along.'

Wama left happily, not knowing that the driver, who did not like the way his boss had embarrassed her, wanted to make her laugh. Edidobiamdudoh, who told Zhero to call him Dido, every day, for three weeks, faithfully took Zhero to and back from the exam centre at Kumo which was about an hour's drive from Mo Bo. Because the West African Examination Council did not approve Evening Stars Secondary School for the West African School Certificate Examination, Zhero and the other students of the school were registered for the examination at Kumo Secondary School, Kumo.

Wama was happy except once, on the sixth day, when she requested for a vehicle to take her and Lamina to Kings & Queens Supermarket. In Lamina's presence he told her there was no free vehicle. She looked at him aghast.

'Woman, don't look at me like that. Go and take the car you gave to Zhero . . . You can't have your cake and eat it.'

'Ozoh, Zhero is using the car, you are using one, the two other cars you're entitled to are lying idle in the office —'

'I say no car is free — final.'

She left them in the sitting room and went upstairs.

'Lamina.'

'Daddy.'

'I waited for you in the night, you didn't come, why?'

'Daddy, I told you I can't again. Suppose Mommy sees me.'

'When Mommy sleeps, she sleeps.'

'Daddy, I can't. Every time I am doing it with fear. Let's go to a hotel.'

278

'Which hotel in this state? Where is it that people don't know me? I can't toy with my reputation . . . Can I come to your room tonight?'

'That boy Zhero does not sleep at night o. Zhero is a bat.'

'Soon he'll finish his exam and he'll start to sleep like a pangolin, the animal that sleeps eighteen hours a day. She shook her head. 'Let him be an eagle seeing everything from the sky, what can he do?'

'No, Daddy. If he sees us he will tell Mommy. The way Mommy is good to me —'

'Then he has to leave this compound. Is that okay?' She shrugged. 'He'll soon finish his exam. Meanwhile give me a hug and a kiss.'

That day, while they were hugging and kissing, Wama, who had locked herself in her bedroom, wept for Zhero, because she had noticed her husband's increasing hatred for a poor boy that had left his parents in the village and travelled to a foreign land in search of education. At the end she resolved not to use the car until he had finished his exam — she was his mother in Mo Bo, she'd continue to sacrifice her comfort for her son . . . Several times she'd given the money Ozoh gave her for clothes to Zhero to pay his school fees — she'd continue to do so until he finished university . . . If Ozoh had allowed her to work and earn her own money she could have helped the poor boy more substantially . . . No matter, God would help him — God's love was all that mattered . . . .

About a month after Zhero finished his examination, Wama was to go to her home village for two weeks. She requested for Zhero to accompany her for Plato's sake. Abramson said no.

'Why?' she asked, a little shocked.

'Must I give you a reason? . . . If you want one, he's employed to work in this house not to go to your village on holiday,' he replied, silently hoping that she would storm off.

Without saying a word she left him, went to the boys' quarters and told Zhero he would not travel with her. When she returned, he asked her where she had been to.

'To tell Zhero he won't be travelling with me.'

'So you'd already told him he'd travel?' he stormed.

'Because I never thought you could turn down a request from me,' she calmly answered.

She went into her room and thought about his mercurial attitude towards the boy since the day Pascal told him about the prison incident. He turned off the TV and went into his own room . . . There was more to Wama's interest in the boy . . . Take him to the village for what? . . . How many years of marriage, she couldn't get pregnant until Zhero came . . . There must be truth in the traditional belief that even if a man wasn't responsible for a woman's pregnancy if she placed her attention on him during her pregnancy the child would resemble him . . . Nothing was impossible in this world — Zhero's own story was proof of it . . . .

It wasn't a new thought, but he wouldn't do a DNA test . . . She was a virtuous woman, even though Plato only slightly resembled him, the foolish boy who couldn't make up his mind, whether to resemble only his father or his mother. More than that, no scandal should stand between him and his goal — the Chief Justice of Godiva after the old men in the Supreme Court retired one after the other.

Two days after Wama travelled he called for Zhero, and in Lamina's presence accused him of trying to molest Lamina. Zhero felt like saying something, but like a six-year-old who could not shout at the monster pursuing him in his nightmare, he was speechless. Lamina said yes, averting her face from his stunned look.

'You used to be a very good boy, Zhero, and we have been good to you . . . Maybe the School Cert you're expecting is getting into your head. If you pass the School Cert . . . I fear what you'll become . . . I'm sorry you have to leave within forty-eight hours. You should be able to get a place to rent by then. I'll give you this month's pay, plus three months in lieu of notice,' he generously said out of fear of the possible consequences of treating the somewhat mysterious boy too cruelly. 'Go well, Zhero.'

Zhero refused to weep. He left without a word. For some seconds Abramson and Lamina could not look at each other. At last she spoke.

'Daddy, I'm sorry for him . . . When Mommy comes back —'

'I nearly forgot. Call him for me.'

She did not go to call him, she phoned him, and he came back, thinking that Daddy had taken pity on him and changed his mind.

'Zhero.'

'Daddy,' he answered, the gratitude in his heart poised to fly aloft like Odedekoko.

'Give me your phone . . . Let me have it . . . Thank you. I don't want you to phone anyone in this house, even if you have their numbers in your head. Go well.' Zhero left them again. 'Lamina, call me the driver.' She did. 'Jordan.'

'Sir.'

'The room you told me you've found, tomorrow you'll tell Zhero you've found a room. You're not to say I told you. Right?'

'Yes, sir.'

'You can go home for the day.'

'Thank you, sir,' he responded, wondering if his boss was not something else in human form.

Abramson was slightly afraid that he had done an evil thing . . . but he needed to be free to have Lamina.

Lamina left him in the sitting room without a word, went into her toilet, locked the door and wept bitterly, asking God why He sent her into this world as a woman.

Zhero paid for the room the next day and Jordan offered to transport him and his belongings to his new home. When he went to the main building to tell Daddy he was about to leave, Lamina, who was cooking in the kitchen, told him that Daddy said he wanted to have a power-nap. He wanted to say goodbye to her but because she didn't raise her face and didn't look at him he shrugged and went out. He went back to his place and took a last look at the home that had facilitated his studies . . . Outside the compound he looked wistfully at the bougainvillea plants growing on the concrete fence and felt sad that he was leaving the red, white and pink-flowered friends he had cared for for so many years . . . Who would trim the godivablooms? . . . He took a last look at the tree-lined Barthurst Avenue he had felt intimate with over the years as he returned from school at night . . . Barthurst Avenue, ever so breezy . . . He savoured the breeze on his face . . . He regretted not saying goodbye to the bitter-leaf plants at the backyard, the plants whose leaves he had regularly used as a malaria prophylactic.

'Zhero.'

'Jordan.'

'I like the way you are taking it as a man . . . From the things Dido told us, I believe you have not done anything wrong . . . It is because Madam likes you too much . . . Life is like that, Zhero. One day you will forget everything . . . Me and Dido, we will be coming to see you.'

'Thank you.'

'Life is like that, Zhero.'

He agreed silently . . . He prayed to God to bless Mommy . . . Plato . . . Daddy too . . . Lamina . . . Why did she lie against him? he naively thought. Was it because the day he saw her standing in front of the full-length mirror in Daddy's bathroom he told her she was beautiful? . . . But she liked what he said, and she asked him if he could be proud of her as a wife even though she had only the primary school certificate, and he said her beauty was more than a PhD, and they laughed . . . He didn't think she and Abramson wanted him out of the way so that they could be free to have an affair; if that was the case Abramson would have allowed him to travel with Mommy . . . Mommy's love was more powerful than what they had done to him and it would see him through his journey . . . Just before Abramson called him he was preparing to go to Isioko Market to buy a new watering can because the nose of the second-hand watering can Lamina bought yesterday was bad. He would have used his own money because Abramson said he couldn't provide money for more than one watering can in a year . . . He hoped Lamina wouldn't tell Mommy he was the one who bought the bad second-hand watering can . . . .

He went into a second-hand shop and bought a G$500 mobile phone and started to search for a job the day after he went into his new home. Every time the phone came to his attention he feared it was a stolen thing and prayed to God to forgive him. At the Bo Industrial Estate every company, every firm, every factory had a ready answer for the footsore applicants that came around — the NO VACANCY signboard at the gate. At the government ministries, departments and agencies the security guards sometimes threatened to arrest and hand them over to the police. Sometimes he took a break for a few days and then resumed. Once he was sorely tempted to go to a market or a store as a porter. Then an idea occurred to him. With his experience as a scavenger, the Environmental Sanitation Authority should easily employ him. He went there jauntily after doing his spiritual exercise, The Law of Self-determination, and seeing himself as a clerk then as a supervisor in the Environmental Sanitation Authority. It was the same old story — NO VACANCY. When he insisted on seeing the General Manager of the Authority one of the four security guards slapped him. Silently he walked away and went back home.

It was painful to the applicants, they were bitter, they felt unloved by life whenever they heard that in spite of the NO VACANCY notice one ministry, department or the other had just employed 'awaiting-result' young persons. But he must plod on, almost every day.

Whenever he felt too tired to get up in the morning he told himself he wasn't a pangolin, and jumped out of bed.

After one month he despaired of seeing Dido and Jordan who would have at least told him about Mommy and Plato, if they couldn't link him and them up. Probably they had been warned to keep away from him . . . He blamed himself. In his foolish happiness he didn't memorize anybody's phone number . . . If he walked about Barthurst Avenue . . . No; if Abramson saw him he could accuse him of a crime . . . .

For three days he visited the markets he used to go to with Mommy, but no luck. Then one day when the urge was so strong to go to Isioko Market which she rarely went to, he did so. As he opened the door of the taxi, he saw Lamina come out of a taxi. His reaction frightened the driver.

'I'm sorry,' he apologized. 'I've changed my mind.'

'So na where you wan go down?'

The other passengers angrily told the driver not to waste their precious time.

'I'll drop at the last bus stop.'

The passengers laughed.

At home, he despaired of ever seeing the woman who loved him as a son, and her son who took his name . . . .

On the front page of the newspaper he had bought close to the house he saw Justice Ozoh Abramson's photograph . . . Justice Ozoh Abramson had been made a Supreme Court justice . . . He would never see Mommy and Plato again, because they would go with Justice Ozoh Abramson to the capital city, Lagos . . . .

Two weeks later he summoned the courage to go to the house. Immediately the downpour stopped he left home. He would say he had come to congratulate Justice Abramson. When he reached there he stared for endless minutes at the signboard put there by a firm of estate valuers — his former house was on sale. A car dangerously aquaplaned and then came to a stop.

'Zhero,' the man who came out of the car shouted. He was glad to see Jordan. 'Zhero, what are you doing here?'

'I didn't know that they had moved.'

'Yes. Last week. Justice Abramson wants to sell this house. He has one big estate containing ten big houses in Lagos.'

'Do you have their phone numbers?' He brought out his mobile phone. 'Madam's own at least.'

'Number one, I don't have Madam's number. Number two, I have his phone number. Number three, if I give you his phone number, that wicked man, even though he is no longer in this State, I will lose my job.'

'Life is like that, isn't it?'

'Life is like that, Zhero.'

Jordan went back into his car and drove off. Zhero sadly looked at the plants and the flowers he used to trim and water. He mentally told them he was sorry no one had been taking care of them as he ran his hands over some of them. Then he walked slowly to the end of Barthurst Avenue and to the beginning before going to Nzima Road to take a bus. When the bus was close to Koroma Bus Stop he remembered Ekiyor, who lived close to that area. He looked at the time on his mobile. Ekiyor should have returned home. He went down at Koroma Bus Stop and slowly walked for about fifteen minutes to Ekiyor's house. Ekiyor was happy to see him.

Ekiyor's sitting room was superlatively rich. Only the price of his settee could buy everything in Zhero's bedsit.

'Zhero, what will you take? Food, drink, what?'

'Give me a glass of water, Ekiyor.' Zhero drank it as if it was the richest thing. Ekiyor mentally pitied him . . . but he didn't appear wretched. 'I left Agoa long ago.'

'Of course, I can see it in your appearance.'

'In my appearance?'

'Don't you know when you see a person, nobody needs to tell you he's a scavenger?'

Zhero shook his head. 'That's why I'm here. I don't want to go back to the rubbish dump. I need a job.'

'I told you to get the School Cert.'

'This year's results are coming out early. I understand they're almost ready.' Ekiyor did not understand what he was saying. 'I attended an evening school and wrote the School Cert exam.'

'That's good!' Ekiyor was happy. 'Congrats, Zhero!'

'You'll help me get a job?'

'Why not? The Ministry of Housing where I am now, I can help you see the people in charge. It's easy. Your name will be on the payroll the month you give them the amount they tell you . . . Don't look at me like that. I'll lend you the money. Alternatively, you agree to share your salary with them for one year.' Zhero shook his head. 'You don't even have to come to work. You can go to university as I

284

am now doing. Month end you come and collect your salary. School Cert, your salary is less than twenty thousand dollars, but you will be paid one hundred and twenty thousand dollars a month.'

'Forget it, Ekiyor.'

'Zhero, in case you don't know, it's difficult for a foreigner to be employed. They employ very few foreigners in government ministries and departments. Only young people who attended government-recognized schools and obtained their certificates in Godiva. I understand they will stop employing foreigners very soon, and all those who have been employed will have to naturalize. Me, my mother is from Godiva. Let me help you, Zhero, before it's too late.'

Shaking his head, 'No, Ekiyor.'

'As you like it. You are the architect of your own fortune.'

'Let me relieve myself before I leave.'

Ekiyor showed him the bathroom/toilet which was nearly as big as Zhero's bedsit. As he sat on the sparkling bowl without hesitation his mind went to the toilet in the house in which he lived. There were two toilets in the building but almost always they were filled to the brim due to lack of water to flush the toilet after use. Because he was the only one in the building who did not go to work and use an office toilet he was often forced to use a piece of wood to push down the excrement and gradually wash it down with the water he bought from a borehole operator in the neighbourhood. The day excrement from the congested bowl touched his lips as he brought out the end of the word carelessly he spat and spat, washed his face with water and detergent, and spat and spat for more than an hour . . . .

It used to be a humiliating experience to him, a bitter experience, but when he placed his attention on what The Home Stretch said about love and service, cleaning the toilet no longer made him bitter or ashamed of himself — he was giving love to his neighbours, he was serving life . . . .

Knocking on the door, 'Zhero, are you there?' Ekiyor frightfully asked.

He started. He had been sleeping off.

'Yes. Almost finished.'

Ekiyor went back to the sitting room. When Zhero returned he confessed that he had been sleeping — he was tired. Ekiyor remembered aloud that Zhero did not like lying. But he wished Zhero could just for once, just for this once do something . . . something to better his life. Zhero said no.

'Zhero, this big house belongs to me. I acquired it from the Ministry of Housing. The jeep you saw outside is mine. I have two taxis on the road. Plus bank accounts. At twenty-four years old.'

Zhero said no again and left in the sun which had taken over the city from the rain just over two hours ago and was growing bold and hot.

While he was eating in the eatery opposite his residence he saw on TV a team of physically challenged Americans playing basketball with the Godiva team of physically challenged men — on wheelchairs! Very happy men! Like him everybody in the eatery marvelled at the wonder. It was the first time they had seen such a thing. Zhero expelled his self-pitying feeling from his consciousness. After he finished eating he crossed the street and went into his residence and into his bedsit, sat on the bed, and happily thanked God, that he was strong, healthy and capable of walking about to search for a job . . . Energized by his gratitude for life, he went out around 8pm and took a walk in the night . . . .

He loved the starless night in which the street teemed with life, people passing him in opposite direction and from behind, people sometimes bumping against one another and laughing or saying sorry . . . Some young men and young women in pairs strolling along, saying sweet things to each other . . . The discernible figures of a boy and a girl in a corner, the girl afraid that her parents might come out, the boy begging her to stay with him for a few more minutes, reminded him of Joleen and himself sitting on the platform on the riverbank in Amabra enjoying the beauty of the moonlight sleeping peacefully on River Niger . . . Joleen always loved the sounds around. He loved to talk with her but she would tell him to listen, listen to the crickets singing, listen, Zhero, a big fish in the river, *kpata*! another fish! . . . But he didn't tell her he was leaving. There was no need to tell her — he knew he wouldn't marry her, because she was an illiterate . . . .

Far away from his residence, where there were very few houses, some youths emerged from the dark, seized him violently and demanded everything in his pockets. On a night in which he saw the world as beautiful he did not fear that anything could harm him — he said to them that he had nothing for them. The one who had threatened to shoot him recognized his voice.

'Zero!' he shouted.

286

'Who are you?' Zhero asked.

The youth shone his torchlight on his own face. 'You cannot know Vinko again?' he asked, expecting Zhero to erupt in joy.

'Vinko? Vinko!'

They hugged.

'Yes, is me Vinko.'

Vinko's colleagues were annoyed with him. He told them there was no danger, Zhero was a fellow Nigerian. They gave him and Zhero some distance and Vinko told Zhero his story.

'Life is not good at the village. My second aunty brought me to Godiva. Her husband is very worse than my aunty in Nigeria. Every time he insult me that am a bastard, because I don't know my father. As if is my fault. And he also wan make love to me by force, so I run away. Very soon, me and my friends, we will go and visit him. To say good night to him . . . Zero, is a long story on the streets. Those are my friends. One night when the rain was like my village river falling from the sky they pity me and take me to their house, and I became their member . . . Zero, is because there is no job. My friends, they are doing it because police used to harass them when they were hawking in the streets. Two of them even languish in jail for some years before they escape. Man must survive.' Zhero was speechless. 'Zero, you have a place to lay your head tonight? I can help. Am now their leader. Zhero, I say you have a place to lay your head?'

'Yes,' Zhero managed to answer.

'Sure?' Vinko asked, not satisfied with Zhero's cold response.

'Sure,' Zhero assured him.

He thanked Zhero for what he was to him in Nigeria and asked for his address. Zhero gave him a false one, and they parted. Zhero turned back . . . He remembered his advice to Vinko to go to the police and report his aunt for her wickedness . . . Wasn't he responsible for Vinko's situation? . . . If he hadn't misadvised him he might have endured and continued to go to school . . . One had to be careful how one tried to help people . . . .

Something told him the night was getting dangerous, and it added, if anything happened to him in a foreign land who would help him, a twenty-something-year old boy? No parents, he agreed, but he was not afraid, because his single-pointed attention on the object of his quest was his companion on the journey, day or night . . . He would get a job, he would save seriously, then he would go to university . . . .

He saw a taxi and hailed it without thinking and went to Zanzi's place at Ayilara Street. Two prostitutes were inviting him when Zanzi came out, and she hugged him. He did not respond to her warmth. His mind was on the environment men had pushed Zanzi to. The rank odour of the shallow gutter and the frontage of the run-down house perennially wet from the used water the harlots standing at the threshold aimed at the gutter made him feel as if he had taken castor oil — the distaste coursing through his body made him unaware of Zanzi's warm hug. So glad to see him she drew him inside the house and they went to her room. She put a DO NOT DISTURB sign on the outside of the door and locked the door.

'Hey, Zhero! You have travelled too. And we are together again.'

'Life has brought us together again, Zanzi,' he replied in the tone of a traveller who had been to many places, seen many things, and now took life for what it was.

'Zhero, you are talking like an old man.'

They laughed . . . while gazing at him Zanzi pulled off her blouse to show off her breasts, and she offered herself to him, like balm for a weary traveller. Zhero slowly said no. She lay on the bed and begged him to take her, her belly and her bosom moving up and down as she said to him that sex — not the one for money, the one from the heart — was a divine expression of love, of gratitude to the only one who used to give her money and asked for nothing in return, she begged him to come to the bed and take her, assuring him that she had no HIV — she tested negative before she got the Italian visa. Remembering his mother's warning not to impregnate a girl and thereby abort his ambition, he said to Zanzi that it was a matter of principle, not out of fear of AIDS, and he told her how his mother was abandoned by the man who impregnated her. Zanzi wept for him, she wept for all women, and told him he was lucky he wasn't born a woman — a woman's life wasn't easy . . . .

On the eve of her departure for Italy he visited her again. After they had eaten together, in the presence of the man she said was sponsoring her and her friends to Italy, she gave him an oversized shirt she had bought for him during the day.

'Zhero,' she apologized, 'I'm sorry it's too big for you, but very soon it will be your size. From the way you're growing you'll be a superman one day. Zhero, even if we don't see again, wear this shirt on your wedding day and feel that I'm with you.'

She took his phone number and promised to call him regularly.

288

He left her, neither happy nor sad. At home he thought about her for a long time, from the first time he knew her to the moment she gave him the oversized orange shirt and told him to feel that she was with him the day he would wear the shirt she bought out of love, and he slept off while praying that no evil should block her way, from Godiva to Italy . . . .

He was woken by a knock on his door . . . Could it be Zanzi? He didn't give her his address. Vinko? Impossible. He gave him a false address. After the pause the person knocked again. A little fearfully he opened the door. It was his next-door neighbour, a tall and handsome but taciturn middle-aged man.

'Good morning, sir,' he greeted him.

'Good morning, my son.'

'Please come in, sir.'

The man entered. 'Thank you.'

'Please, have a seat, sir,' Zhero told him, pushing the only plastic chair towards him.

'My son, let me not waste your time. Can you help me? I have no transport fare to go to work today. Can you lend me one hundred dollars? When I reach office I can sort out myself.'

'Okay, sir.' He brought out a note from his trouser pocket. 'Sir, it's a two-hundred dollar note. I don't have change.'

'Give it to me like that. I will refund two hundred at the end of the month . . . Thank you, my son. Sorry I disturbed your sleep.'

'Thank you, sir.'

The man went out and Zhero thought about life, concluding, Everybody is richer than someone.

He had not thought to go out that day, but having woken up so early, he brushed his teeth, had a bath, dressed, and went out to search for a job. He walked for about thirty minutes to the bus stop and boarded one going to Bo Industrial Estate . . . He thought about his finances . . . If he didn't get a job he'd be broke in about a month . . . The problem was that all he had wasn't enough to take him back to Nigeria . . . He had practised the Law of Self-Determination religiously yet life had refused to be smooth for him . . . Maybe he wasn't doing it well? . . . Maybe God had a better plan for him . . . He resolved to put more faith in the spiritual exercise.

He went down at Mogadishu Bus Stop and walked for about five minutes to the factory in the industrial Estate he had in mind. The NO VACANCY signboard was still there but the gatekeeper told him the Environmental Sanitation Authority was employing refuse collectors . . . A refuse collector? If he told them he was awaiting the result of the School Cert exam they might give him a better position . . . Or, get the job, be a refuse collector for a few weeks, and when he got his result ask for a clerical post . . . .

At the Environmental Sanitation Authority office he only saw the security guards driving away angry young men. He slowly went to the bus stop which was about five minutes away. A bus came after twenty minutes and he went in sluggishly, to the annoyance of the girl behind him who asked him why he was so lazy at his age. If her elder brother behaved that way she'd flog him. Some passengers laughed. He did not answer her. He languidly dropped onto a seat and slept off while thinking about what Abang said about life — a load the porter's attitude made light or heavy for himself. He was angrily woken up about fifteen minutes later by a woman who had come in at Garrison Bus Stop. He looked at her vacantly.

'Shift make I siddon. Dis early morning able-bodied man dey sleep for bus. You be pangolin?'

He was the type, she said, her people, the Yoruba in Nigeria, called età, a pangolin, the animal that slept almost all day. Zhero meekly shifted to the window seat. A man remarked that she was the type of wife that would flog her husband.

'Why not? If I marry a man like this, who will put food on the table for my children?' Many people laughed, and she continued to thrill her audience. 'The rain poured, Pangolin slept on, and the flood carried him away.'

More people laughed. Zhero raised his head from the backrest of the seat in front of him and sat upright. It pained him that a fellow Nigerian had enjoyed humiliating him, but he did not say a word ... Abramson called him a pangolin the only day he did not wake up before 6am . . . Abang said life was a load the porter made heavy or light for himself . . . At the next bus stop a news vendor held out a newspaper to him: WEST AFRICAN SCHOOL CERTIFICATE EXAMINATION RESULTS OUT. A happy headline — he hurriedly paid for the paper and with a fast-beating heart read it. He went down at the next bus stop, searched for a computer centre, saw one adjacent to Twenty-Four Seven Supermarket, went in, feverishly paid two hundred dollars, gave a computer operator his registration number and the examination year and she checked for his result online . . . An excellent result! He shouted his thanks to God, the staff rejoiced with him, and he paid two hundred dollars for the result to be printed out for him. The proprietor of the supermarket and the computer centre, who was walking by, came in. Why were they making a noise? They apologized and showed him Zhero's result.

He looked at it for about a minute and said, 'A1 in English Language, C3 in eight subjects. Young man, have you got a job?'

'No, sir,' Zhero replied, his heart beating faster.

'Do you want a job?'

'Yes, sir,' he answered, trying to breathe normally.

'Then you've got a job. Can you start tomorrow? At the Supermarket.'

'Yes, sir. Thank you, sir.'

They shook hands and the proprietor left, impressed by Zhero's behaviour — respectful, grateful, happy, but not servile. Zhero looked for a restaurant — he had not eaten since morning and he had felt slightly dizzy when he loudly rejoiced at his result. As he was about to eat he remembered Gabriel Okara's poem, 'The Call of the River Nun' and softly said, 'O incomprehensible God!' The man opposite him at the table thought that was his grace, a strange way of saying grace.

Zhero struggled hard not to show his joy on his face. He felt like shouting out that he was a secondary school graduate and in a matter of years would be a university graduate. Happiness did not allow him to enjoy the meal but he finished it anyway. He paid his bill, five hundred dollars, and tipped the waitress one hundred dollars.

Outside, the happy sky told him that life was beautiful . . . He smiled, that was pathetic fallacy — he'd attributed his mood to the sky . . . To go home, and probably sleep, would waste the day of joy . . . He wished he could meet some of his former colleagues and show them his West African School Certificate result — nine papers at one sitting! . . . Mrs Abramson would have been so glad, the woman who often gave him all the money her husband gave her for clothes, she would have been so glad that her self-sacrifice wasn't a waste . . . For her sake he thanked God that Plato would easily have a good education. He prayed the boy should make good grades throughout his educational career . . . Teima who didn't want him to go to school, how would she feel if she saw his excellent result? . . . Numu would be so happy . . . Chief Yago would be ashamed of himself . . . Oh, his mother! He had not thought about his mother! The woman who should take a lot of the credit, if not all of it . . .

Maybe he should go back to Nigeria and make her happy? . . . Even beg Bazi to forgive him, and go to university without tears? . . . He postponed the decision and went home.

At bedtime he realized that he did not know how much his salary would be . . . Well, the man saw his qualification; he should know that he was highly educated and qualified.

The next day he was at the Supermarket before 7am. He wondered that a supermarket called 'Twenty-Four Seven' was not open overnight. A salesgirl who was going to the back of the building explained to him that they stopped being open beyond 10pm since last year due to frequent raids by armed robbers. The doors opened at 8am. He went in and saw that all the workers were already inside, prepared to attend to customers. Apparently they had all gone in through the back door.

The proprietor came around 10am because he had an appointment with Zhero. He called for the supervisor and told him that Zhero was starting work as a store detective.

'Any previous experience?' the supervisor asked Zhero.

The proprietor answered, 'He just passed his School Cert yesterday. Attach him to Abraham for one, two or three weeks, depending on how intelligent he is. Zhero, show him your result,' he proudly directed.

Zhero showed him the computer print-out. The supervisor did not take it.

'This is not a certificate.'

'He'll bring it when it's ready. Zhero, your pay will be fifteen thousand dollars a month. You like it?'

'Yes, sir.'

'It's better than being jobless. Any day you don't come to work, minus five hundred dollars. You work Monday to Sunday. Morning shift, 8am – 3pm. Evening shift, 3pm – 10pm. You have started to make a living, Zhero. Congratulations. Supervisor, take him to Personnel for letter of appointment.'

'Thank you, sir,' Zhero said to the proprietor.

'Come, let's go.'

He followed the supervisor to the personnel manager, who did not mind that the proprietor neither consulted her on Zhero's employment nor personally told her that he had employed someone. She took from Zhero what the proprietor regarded as his certificate and issued him a letter of employment before noon.

292

When, at noon, Zhero told the store detective he was attached to that he was hungry the detective told him that he should always eat before leaving home or come very early and eat before the doors were opened at 8am. The supervisor, who heard them, took Zhero to a nearby restaurant and bought him a plate of rice with stew and chicken at five hundred dollars. Zhero was afraid — that was his one day's pay. He told the supervisor so. The supervisor told him it was a welcome treat. At closing time, 3pm, the supervisor frightened him more. He gave him twenty thousand dollars to help him through to payday. A welcome treat too, the supervisor told him, and he unwillingly took it. And he chartered a taxi to take him home instead of waiting for the rain to stop, then walking to the bus stop — he was loaded.

The next day the supervisor called him into his office and asked him if he liked the job.

'Yes,' Zhero answered. 'But from my house to this place and back is two hundred dollars a day. So what's left is three hundred dollars a day, nine thousand dollars a month, not up to the pay of a primary school-leaver in a good place.'

The supervisor smiled. 'Which means this isn't a good place?'

'I'm sorry, sir, I'm sorry, sir, that's not what I meant.'

'Relax, Zhero. This is a friendly conversation, not official. Wherever a person is, he can make it heaven or hell for himself. Just do what Abraham tells you. He's your trainer, your immediate boss for now.'

The supervisor stood up and they went out. Alone, he considered what the supervisor had said and agreed that he was right: 'Wherever a person is, he can make it heaven or hell for himself.' The supervisor was right. Because of his reaction to a simple word he ran out of Bazi's house. When he should have told Chief Yago that he heard his wife warning Joseph not to eat the food he kept silent. And so he was now thousands of kilometres away from his home country ... 'Wherever a person is, he can make it heaven or hell for himself.' It was never too late — he'd make this place a heaven for himself.

At 11am Abraham asked Zhero if he was able to eat at home. Zhero said no and was allowed to go to the restaurant for one hour. But he came back just after fifteen minutes, and did not know why Abraham was not happy at his early return.

Eight days later, he discovered a sharp-practice and reported to his trainer: some customers were paying for unusual quantities of goods to only two checkout assistants, and the receipts and the bulky quantities of the expensive goods did not tally. He suggested to Abraham to personally observe them and arrest the checkout assistants and the customers. Abraham observed them and said he would tell the supervisor so that they would have policemen around when they would descend on the dishonest checkout assistants and their collaborators. (Why not immediately? The establishment was losing loads of money!) Abraham advised him to be patient. Sweeter to arrest them when the enjoyment of stolen wealth was entrenched in them. A store detective must know the virtue of patience.

At home Zhero was happy at his achievement, but around 7pm Abraham and the supervisor knocked on his door. He was surprised. He was ashamed of his very humble bedsit. He was mortified when, after the supervisor had sat in the brown plastic armchair, his trainer had to sit on the bed — he, Zhero, that was known in the office for his excellent School Cert result.

'Zhero, Abraham told me that you have sharp eyes.'

'I said a sharp mind,' Abraham corrected him.

'The more proud I am of him — a sharp mind. Before three months you will move to a more befitting house.'

'With soft furnishings,' Abraham added.

'We are proud of you, Zhero,' the supervisor smiled.

'Thank you, sir,' Zhero happily said.

'We are to thank you . . . You know Mrs Johnson and Mrs Goldeni?' the supervisor asked him.

'They are the two checkout assistants, sir,' he eagerly answered.

'Yes.' The supervisor paused for a long time. 'Whatever they do, remove your eyes. Don't see anything they do. Right?' Zhero was speechless. 'If you do as we've told you, here's fifty thousand dollars a month . . . Take it.' Zhero shook his head. The supervisor smiled sagely — the boy just didn't want to appear eager. He repeated the offer avuncularly, 'I say take it, Zhero, and keep our secret secret.' Zhero shook his head again, emphatically this time. The supervisor was shocked. 'Then don't come to Twenty-Four Seven again.' Zhero winced at his malignant voice. 'Don't let Chief Araki ever see you again.' He signed to Abraham, who went out and returned with two muscle bound men wearing jeans, black T-shirts, and cow boy boots, whose faces flaunted their love for why they had been brought here. Zhero strongly felt that they were killers. 'Boys,' the supervisor said, 'take a good look at the bastard foreigner. Whenever it is necessary

294

you won't mistake his face.' After a long pause during which the men unblinkingly fixed their bloodshot eyes on Zhero, he asked, 'Zhero with the sharp mind, will you cooperate?' Zhero wanted to say no but could not open his mouth. 'Then farewell, foreigner.'

Zhero rushed to the toilet immediately he felt they had left the building and urinated copiously. From the toilet he went straight to Mr Egudo who he once lent two hundred dollars. Mr Egudo frowned, thinking that he had come to remind him of the repayment which was long overdue, but Zhero immediately told him what had happened.

'My son,' Mr Egudo advised him, 'if it is possible do not only leave this house, but also leave this city. Remember, this is not your country. If a man wants to die let him die where his people can find his bones.'

Zhero thanked him for the advice, went back to his room, dropped on his knees beside the bed and prayed for God's protection, weeping at the turn his life had taken. Then he decided that if he did not get a job within two weeks he would return to Nigeria while he had enough money for transport fare. He had enough money because of the twenty thousand dollars the supervisor gave him on the day he started work . . . Fifty thousand dollars a month and to allow their dishonesty to go on . . . The solution was to get a job very fast, and he'd use the twenty thousand to rent a room somewhere else . . . .

At bedtime when his thoughts focused on his hardships he felt that life had been too wicked to him . . . Then he remembered the experience of Traveller's Lodge . . . the happy days at Agoa Dump . . . how he used to play with Plato . . . the hardships in his life and how he surmounted them were happy experiences too, they made him happy, they made him proud of his abilities . . . those hardships gave him strength, courage and a loving heart . . . oh, his escape from Obadore Forest ... 'God is with me, God loves me,' he said out loud in appreciation of life . . . .

He woke very early in the morning to have his bath before the other tenants would wake. The bathroom was excessively stinking because he had not washed it since he started work. He hurried his bath and decided to go to the room to towel himself. He saw Mr Egudo coming out of his room.

'Mr Egudo, good morning, sir.'

'I think, I thought you were inside the house.'

'Any problem, sir?'

'No, don't worry.'

Zhero went into the room and started to towel himself. He noticed that his trousers, which he had placed in the middle of the bed, were almost dropping to the floor. He took them up, the lightness confirmed his fear. He anxiously searched the pockets. He hurriedly wore the trousers and went to Mr Egudo's room and banged on the door.

'Who's that?' Mr Egudo shouted. 'Who's that?'

'Open the door! Open the door immediately!' Zhero shouted back as he continued to bang on the door.

Several other tenants rushed out of their rooms. Mr Egudo came out.

'Zhero, what is wrong with you?'

'Please, sir, give me my money.'

'What are you talking, Zhero?'

Zhero grabbed his neck and made to strangle him. The others begged him not to do it as they tried to release Mr Egudo from his vice-like grip. At last he released him. Several people asked Zhero what happened. Zhero told them what had happened. Mr Egudo swore to God that he had only twenty thousand dollars in his house and brought out the bundle.

'You're a liar, sir. It's because I told you someone gave me twenty thousand.'

A man asked, 'Zhero, what is the proof that this twenty thousand dollars is your own?'

Everybody was surprised to see Zhero smiling.

'Please, ask him, is he sure that this bundle is twenty thousand dollars?'

'I swear to God,' Mr Egudo said, 'it is two-two hundred dollars pieces. One hundred pieces.'

Zhero smiled again. 'He's right. But there are also ten one-thousand dollar pieces. The total in this bundle is thirty thousand dollars. The one-thousand dollar pieces are in the middle of the bundle.'

Zhero was right. The money was handed over to him and Mr Egudo's co-tenants booed him.

'Mr Egudo, when will you stop this stealing?' a young man asked him.

'Is it his money?' Mr Egudo angrily countered. 'After all, the person who gave it to him stole it. You, Zhero, you think you can disgrace me? Because of the two hundred dollars you gave me one day? Wait and see. Before the end of today, if those people don't come after you, call me a bastard.'

His audience did not understand his rant. They booed him again as he went into his room, banged the door and locked it.

Zhero went into his own room and decided to leave Godiva. He remembered Ebenezer Obey's song which Dahlia loved very much, and he sang 'Àjò kò dàbi ilé' as he packed his tote bag. 'Yes,' he said to himself and translated the words. 'A foreign land is not like home.' When he was sure that everybody had left for work he quoted Wole Soyinka to himself, 'Traveller, you must set out/At dawn.' Then he went out and hailed a taxi to take him to Askee Motor Park, hoping to spend some hours with the first woman that was good to him in Godiva before taking the night bus to Nigeria . . . He thought back to what Abang said about honesty in Numu's office — 'Honesty is a hard quest.' He didn't quite understand it, but he had come to know that if one wanted something in life honesty could make it difficult to get . . . but the experiences along the way enriched the seeker spiritually.

When he got to Askee Motor Park it looked like a place he had never been to before. All the ground had been concreted, there was only one big richly furnished restaurant. After looking around in amazement he asked about the woman he thought to say thank you to before leaving the country. A driver told him Madam Beauty left Askee Motor Park even before its management was privatized. She went to her home village, Makan, after her husband died in a motor accident in Nigeria. He went back to the waiting room and wept drily, blaming himself for not coming to see the good woman when life was rosy for him in Justice Abramson's house.

At 10 o' clock he decided to go to the restaurant to eat. Outside the waiting room he called a news vendor and bought a copy of 'The Waves'. The restaurant, which was being operated by a Nigerian, made him feel he was already in his home country because of the mouth-watering native Nigerian dishes on the list. And a Yoruba track was playing: 'Ìrin-àjò ni mo wà' (I am on a journey). It was a revelation — even in Nigeria the journey would continue. 'Zainab Shettima is right — the journey never ends.'

While waiting for the *afang* meal he had ordered he opened the pages of the newspaper and looked at the headlines . . . He gasped at U Shettima's obituary: U Shettima was dead, shot dead in his bedroom by three men who did not steal anything . . . How would Numu take this sad news? Maybe he was already aware of it? . . . He would take the newspaper to Numu . . . .

Chapter Nine

He couldn't go back to sleep. Just after four. Too early to have his bath and dress . . . He went to the toilet, relieved himself and came back to the bed . . . His mind went back to the journey from Godiva to where he was at the moment, an interesting one — the journey of life . . . .

The bus had arrived in Lagos around 5am. At dawn he took another bus, hoping to see his mother before noon, but due to the unimaginably poor state of the Benin-Ore Road the bus arrived in Port Harcourt a little after midnight. He slept at the bus station and at 6am hailed a taxi to take him to Rt Hon Westwood Avenue . . . trembling imperceptibly as his heart preceded him to No 13 Rt Hon Westwood Avenue, he apologized out loud.

The driver heard him. 'You dey go back to your mama wey you been offend?' he asked.

'Yes,' he answered in a tone that forbade conversation.

It was the driver's turn to be hostile when he couldn't recognize Westwood Avenue. The two-lane avenue had been turned into a six-lane avenue that had swallowed many houses, and No 13 was one of the houses that were no more, and his mother was nowhere to be found. Daba too was nowhere to be found because her street too had been expanded and many houses had disappeared . . . The beauty of Westwood Avenue with its admirable sidewalks, drainage system and the green plants in the median hurt his heart . . . The driver angrily called out to him to come remove his bag from the car. He went back into the car and told the driver to take him to . . . .

'Where?'

'I don't know. Anywhere, anywhere.'

The driver intended to return him to the bus station but when the tailback at Ikwerre Road stopped moving for more than thirty minutes, he told him to get out, just get out without paying a kobo so that he could turn back. He went out, walked to near a petrol station and thought of what to do . . . He said to himself he wouldn't go to Amabra even if his mother was there. While he was thinking of going to Mile 1 to buy a small backpack and dispose of his big bag and some of the things in it, he noticed the signboard at the petrol station — WANTED: Petrol Attendant. Apply Within . . . The hand of God once more in his life — he started work that morning, and together with two other petrol station attendants slept in the small office at night on condition that he too served as a security guard at night . . . But after two months he couldn't stand the workers' dishonesty any longer, even though he had refused to share in the proceeds of their dishonesty. They manipulated the pumps and dispensed less petrol than a customer paid for and at the end of the day they happily shared the total that had accrued from their sharp-practice. Jonah, who liked him a lot, advised him to provide for his future, saying that he had already built two houses. He refused to join them. After he got his second month's pay he had a strong feeling to leave the work . . . Without saying a word to anyone, without taking his bag from the office, he walked away . . . .

He kept walking, stopped in front of a workshop to admire a bare-chested young man sweating profusely but singing and obviously enjoying his arc welding, the young man stopped singing when he noticed him, they both smiled then he continued walking, and when he came to Wings & Will Supermarket he went inside because the name looked and sounded artistic in virtue of the alliteration and the ampersand, asked for the manager, was shown to the proprietor, and he requested for employment . . . She looked at him for a minute or so and seemed to change her mind about what she was about to do or say. He answered her questions truthfully: his qualification, the jobs he had done before then, why he left Twenty-Four Seven in Godiva, and why he had just walked out of the petrol station. After remarking that she too knew the petrol station as a dishonest place she employed him as a Store Detective, drove him to the petrol station to take his bag, probably to confirm his story, and then gave him his present accommodation, the boys' quarters of her house . . . .

Some of the things that had happened to him, if he wrote the story of his life, some of the things would be like fiction . . . The day Dr Eustace was talking about the use of improbabilities and exaggerations in folk tales to his class he had the urge to use himself as an example to tell him that the supernatural wasn't always far-fetched . . . .

Bazi's company was no longer in Port Harcourt, and his residence too had yielded to road expansion . . . .

He did not know when he slept off. The alarm of his mobile

300

phone woke him at 6am. Remembering his reminiscence before he slept off, he thanked God for his present circumstances and got out of bed. He went to the toilet/bathroom and brushed his teeth. While in the shower he decided that he'd had all the basic things he needed . . . except a TV . . . In two months' time he should be able to buy a TV, and then serious saving should start . . . He needed a TV — he should stop going to her house to watch TV . . . .

At 6.30am he went to the carport and waited by the car till she came out of the house a few minutes before seven. 'Good morning, madam.'

'Good morning, Zhero. Ready for work?'

'Yes, madam.'

'Then let's go,' she said cheerfully.

He usually waited for her to go in before he did. In spite of the severe harmattan she turned on the AC. He flinched at the cold air as he came in.

'Sorry,' she said, 'because of the dust I can't open the windows.'

'Thank you, madam.'

Because the gatekeeper did not pull back the right half of the gate fully the right back door of the car was slightly scratched as she was going out. She pointedly ignored his huge apology even though she was not angry.

'Zhero,' she said, after they had gone some way, 'do you know that there may still be dishonest people among the workers?'

'I don't think so.'

'Why do you say so? After the two cashiers you caught, one would have thought no one would do anything dishonest any more. But last week again you caught two cashiers and four customers. Imagine! Printing their own price tags and attaching them to the items they want . . . they want to steal! And on the most expensive items.'

'I don't think anyone will dare do it again.'

'Vigilance, eternal vigilance, Zhero.'

He laughed. 'I will, madam, I'll be vigilant.'

'Thank you, Zhero,' she said feelingly, tapping his left thigh affectionately.

At Ada George Road she saw her boyfriend and braked roughly. The vigilant driver behind her spewed out all the venom he could produce as he came level to her door: 'Nincompoop! Idiot! I go drive myself!'

She was sorry but she considered his insult as her verbal apology.

She only pressed a button to unlock the right back door and expected her boyfriend to open the door and come in. After some seconds she pressed a button to open the passenger window.

'Come in, Osborne, what are you waiting for?' she asked with a tinge of anger in her voice.

'For Jero to come out.'

Zhero ungainly opened the door, scrambled out of the car, saying 'Sorry, sir,' and went to the back.

'Nami, good morning,' her boyfriend greeted her as he came in.

She hated the proprietorial note in his gravelly voice. She took several big breaths and drove off. No one said a word. Zhero feared what might happen to him — Achebe said, 'When two elephants fight, it is the grass that suffers.' He noticed that she was beginning to sweat in spite of the AC.

The sight of a man trimming the plants outside a compound momentarily took his mind off his problem. He used to enjoy trimming the godivablooms, and Mrs Abramson used to admire him . . . .

He remembered Naija, his kidnapper, when his eyes fell on a huge chain hanging on the back of the tailboard of a truck . . . If that padlock was opened the chain would drop to the ground. All his life it was the key to the padlock he had been looking for . . . He visualized Naija shouting as if it was yesterday . . . Chains of poverty! Chains of illiteracy! . . . Naija, his own cousin . . . .

At the car park he felt very awkward. He stood back until they had gone into the building. Then he went in, and while waiting for the supermarket to open to customers at 8am he absently exchanged greetings or bantered with his fellow workers, his mind on the major matter in his life — Osborne in his employer's office. About thirty minutes after the supermarket opened only a young woman came, went to the jewellery section, asked a sales assistant questions about wedding rings and went out, leaving his mind free to worry about Osborne in his employer's office. After Osborne came out alone from her office, scowled at everyone in his path and went out of the building, he waited with bated breath when she called for the accountant who was also her assistant . . . to endorse his sack and to pay him off? . . . He didn't feel she could do an unreasonable thing . . . but she could sacrifice him for her happiness . . . Why did Osborne hate him so much? . . . Why did he enjoy humiliating him? . . . Where had they met before? . . . The evening he went into Nami's living room and saw her and Osborne roughhousing. Osborne

302

made to throw a pouffe at him and shouted at him to go out — 'You bastard, you have the audacity to come in without knocking!' The word 'bastard' rankled with him till the next day.

He noticed that he was sweating slightly despite the harmattan coldness of the morning. The accountant came out and went to his cubicle. Then she came to personally invite him to her office. He took a deep breath.

'Zhero, I said I want to see you,' she spoke again, the anger from Ada George Road still visible on her face.

Rousing himself, 'Yes, madam,' he answered and followed her.

In her office she laconically told him, 'I'm going home,' then stood up, took her handbag and signed to him to go out. 'Zhero?' she called him back. His eyes fell as she gazed at him. 'You know I'm sorry, don't you?'

'Thank you, madam,' he answered, as her strangely affectionate tone raised his face to the level of her blinding gaze. His eyes fell again.

'Thank you too, for what you are.'

To his surprise she came back around 9pm and when the shop closed at 10pm they left for home together. On the way he reminded her of his suggestion to her to consider opening on Sundays too as many other shops did.

'I will, Zhero, I will. But money isn't the most important thing in life. I don't know what it is, but not money.' After a pause she continued. 'You people work from 8am to 10pm. That's human exploitation. If we are to open on Sundays too then you have to work shifts . . . Zhero, I don't know how I came about using people from 8am to 10pm, Monday to Saturday . . . It has made me rich, but I'm not a happy woman . . . When I call myself a woman I feel so old, a rich old woman . . . What do you say, Zhero?'

He was confused. 'I think we can open on Sundays too, then give people off-duty days.'

'Zhero is harping on money,' she sighed, like a mother at her intellectually challenged child.

He laughed, she joined in, and they were happy till they got home. Four men who had been waiting for Zhero for over thirty minutes angrily approached them at the gate. Zhero recognized them. He went to them and tried to draw them away from the gate, but immediately she parked the car she came out and listened to them. Zhero was pleading to be given a few more days. He would pay them at the end of the month. Her heart pounded in her chest — were they sellers of goods stolen from her supermarket? She went to them for an explanation.

'Ask your husband na,' one of them angrily replied, intending to create a scene to compensate themselves for the long time they had stood in the harmattan cold. 'See light — yaah! yaah! — inside your compound,' he gestured at the opulence of electricity in her compound. 'You think say light na free?'

Zhero explained: They were men from the electric power authority office at East-West Road. A month ago when he went there to complain about the long power outage at Halley Street they said they had applied to their Mile One office for cables. When he went to Mile One they said they had applied to their Trans Amadi headquarters for money. When he went back to East-West Rd two weeks ago these men told him it would cost only ₦60,000 to restore power to Halley Street and the adjoining areas. He gave them ₦40,000 promising to pay the balance at the end of the month, and that day power was restored in the night. His promise was for month-end but they had come before the end of the month.

Nami's response was not the torch the men expected to set the tinder-dry night alight. She calmly asked the gatekeeper to bring her handbag from the car. He did. She took ₦100,000 bundle from the handbag and from it gave them ₦20,000. She thanked them, and they left without thanking her back.

A few minutes after she went into the house she called for Zhero. She felt he was trying to upstage her. She was angry.

'Zhero,' she said immediately he came into the sitting room, 'That twenty thousand is to be deducted from your pay. So you are left with ten thousand.'

'Thank you, madam,' he replied, sincerely grateful that she had saved him from embarrassment.

'By the way, why did you think you should be the power supplier in Mgbuoba?'

'The day I told you, you said who would believe me if I told the households at Halley Street to contribute the money? I told you it was cheaper than using the generator but —'

'Shut up, Zhero! Did you tell me you were going to pay from your pocket? Answer me!'

'No, madam. I'm sorry.' His face buckled under the glint in her eyes. His eyes fell. 'I'm sorry, madam.'

She laughed abruptly. 'Now that you've taken your salary in advance, how are you going to manage? A little sharp-practice in my shop?'

He was highly offended, and she saw it, but he spoke calmly. 'Since I have free transport no problem. I can buy food on credit.'

Her maid came in. 'Madam, food is ready.'

'Thank you.' The maid went out. 'Zhero, what are you eating tonight?' she asked, to pacify him.

'I ate in the afternoon.'

She was shocked. 'In the afternoon!'

'Yes, madam.'

'Come, let's go and eat. Every day Orah will bring you your own meal. Whatever I eat you will eat, Zhero.'

'That would be impossible.' He corrected himself, 'That would be difficult . . . It would be difficult for me.'

'Then take back what you gave to the men.' From her handbag she offered him what was left of the bundle from which she had given the men twenty thousand naira. He shook his head. She threw the money at him. The notes scattered on the floor. 'You want to humiliate me again? Go away!' He started to pick up the notes. 'Go away from me!' she shouted again and started to cry.

'Madam, please, I'll eat the food. Please. But let Orah bring it to my place.'

She wiped her face. 'Thank you . . . No, take the money too.'

He was overwhelmed. She stood up, went into her bedroom, and thought about her past . . . then she said to her bedroom, 'He's less than twenty-five . . . twenty-two if he's a day . . . but he looks more than man enough for any woman . . . A person is as old as their hard life experiences . . . I shall have this one for myself and I shall love him with a pure heart.'

She thought about her fruitless relationships with men . . . A year after she had Yagood, she met William Kanom and felt their relationship would be forever even though he was married. After establishing Wings & Will Supermarket, and a fat bank account for her, he died in an air crash . . . She wanted a man to be good to . . . .

At bedtime he warned himself to be careful about her — she might be volatile . . . He'd thought he was in the Home Stretch, but from what had happened tonight . . . oh, why? Why? . . . He needed patience, humility and endurance, otherwise all his years of suffering would be a waste — no, he wouldn't waste his suffering . . . .

His dream of flying to Godiva and back to Port Harcourt made him happy when he woke up, though he did not understand what it meant . . . If he was with his mother he would have shared his experience of flying in his dreams though the people of Amabra regarded some dreams as acts of witchcraft.

Two weeks later Nami's friend, the proprietor of Princes and Princesses Primary School in Abuja, brought Yagood to her mother, Nami, for her to spend the one-month holiday in Port Harcourt. Yagood had a sharp mind and a sharp tongue. The first day she met Zhero she said to her mother she liked him.

'I'm glad you like him.'

'But he's always thinking and he doesn't like to laugh.' Zhero laughed. 'So you can laugh?' Zhero laughed again and they became friends. 'I like you.'

One Sunday when Zhero was reading the story of Cinderella to her in the sitting room to the delight of her mother, Osborne came in and interrupted them. When she requested Zhero to continue, Osborne took the book from him and started to read.

Yagood giggled. Her mother told her to shut up.

'But, Mommy, his pronunciation is crude.' Nami looked at her daughter in surprise then erupted into laughter. 'Yes, Mommy. Our teacher calls it a fisherman's pronunciation, straight from the canoe.'

Osborne bristled at the insult. 'You are a spoilt shild. Your mother hasn't brought you up well. You want to compare me, a university grazuate, with a sop — a shop — assistant?'

Nami was shocked.

Yagood asked her, 'Mommy, where's my daddy? You said my daddy can read better than Zhero.'

Osborne sniggered. 'Your daddy. Yes he can read better than all daddies. When — if — you find him.'

'Mommy, where can I find my daddy?'

Zhero pitied the girl. Nami shouted for Orah to come and take the girl away. Then she calmly addressed Osborne.

'You will leave my house now.' Zhero immediately went out. 'It's goodbye forever, Osborne.'

'Nami —'

'Out of my house!'

Zhero heard her distinctly from the window. He slowed down, in case he needed to go back to protect her. Osborne came out and charged towards him. Zhero dodged his right fist and headbutted him. As he fell on the concrete floor Nami shouted from the window.

'Zhero, please don't touch him again! Please Zhero! I say don't touch him again! Zhero!!!'

Zhero looked at her direction, shrugged, looked at Osborne on the ground, then walked away, as if from a rubbish heap containing human waste too. Nami, who was looking out of the window, and Orah and the gatekeeper, who were close to the scene, were afraid that Osborne had passed out. At last he was able to get up and walk towards his car, his left hand on his forehead. The gatekeeper quickly rushed to open the gate, and Osborne drove out of Nami's life.

That night Nami found her wakefulness sweeter than sleep, because it was made of Zhero's manliness, and she savoured it.

The following Sunday, after Nami and her daughter had gone to church, Zhero told Orah that he was going to Boro Park, and went out. When Nami returned home she rushed a meal and went to Boro Park too. She found him out and sat by him on a concrete seat.

'Let me see. It's "Odedekoko". You said you know Numu. Someday you'll tell me about him.'

'He's a very nice man.'

'You said "Odedekoko" is a quest story? The quest for happiness?'

'It's about love and evil. The power of —'

'Not now. Not now.' He smiled. 'Talk about Zhero.' He smiled again. 'His dreams . . . His fears . . . Yes, his fears — why he wouldn't laugh as often as, as much as my daughter, Yagood, would like him to . . . Can Zhero be afraid of happiness? . . . Because happiness is transient?'

'Madam, I don't know what to say.'

'What is Zhero's quest? Won't you go to university?'

'Someday I must,' he answered gazing into space as if the object of his quest was in the distance, out of reach only because he was resting.

After a long pause, during which she adventurously decided to reach for the object of her own quest, she said unabashedly, 'I want you to be highly educated for both of us.' For both of us! A bolt had struck him, but she had not finished. 'You don't have to marry me now. After university, if I'm not too old for you, if I'm not too low for you, if you want to marry me, then we shall . . . After you finish I may go back to university and get a degree too.' She was annoyed at him for his silence. She stood up to go but when she saw his face she was alarmed, she sat down. 'Don't say a word, don't say a word.'

He nodded, breathed deeply three times, and she made him place his head on her shoulder. 'Oh Zhero.'

After a while she stood . . . He stood up too, and they went towards the car park, silent like persons who had just woken up in bed and were consciously redreaming the pleasant experience they had during sleep.

In the car he asked her, 'You aren't afraid that a man can disappoint you? Suppose after he gets his degrees he leaves you?' She said nothing. 'In Godiva I knew a woman who was abandoned by the man she sent to university.'

'Can you do it?'

'Any man can.'

'I would have given back to life only a little of what it had given me abundantly.' She noticed his tears. 'Zhero, why are you weeping?'

'I'm happy, I'm happy that there's so much goodness in this world,' he answered, overwhelmed with joy that he had found the object of his quest only a stretch of his arm away . . . She reminded him of Godiva. His mother too was like Godiva. More women were like Godiva than not. 'Thank you, madam.'

'Stop weeping, Zhero.'

'Thank you, madam,' he said again, wiping the tears that issued from his spontaneous memories of the hard quest.

'Thank you, Nami,' she corrected him.

'Thank you . . . Nami,' he hesitantly accepted the correction.

'Yes, even in the office. But if you can't, then no address form.'

She saw a young man hawking gold-coloured chains in a wheelbarrow.

'Zhero, those chains are fine,' she said as she braked and pulled over. 'The one on my gate is too rusty. Go out and see how he's selling them.' He went out. She rolled down the window. 'Just one.'

Zhero shouted, 'Hey! Aboki!' The man turned and came to the car. 'How much, these your chains?'

'One-one thousand only.'

'You no go take five hundred?'

'No. E no like am for pibe hundred.'

'Zhero, take one.' She gave him one thousand naira. 'Pay for it and come in, Zhero.'

The hawker thanked her happily. Zhero paid for it, went back into the car and she drove off.

'It's beautiful, isn't it?' He smiled. 'You like it?'

'Yes, Nami.'

She was glad he said Nami. 'Thank you, Zhero.'

In Literature, she thought, this would be regarded as an improbability . . . Incredible, but real, it was happening in her life — she had just told a man to marry her . . . .

He thought of how it would be between them the next day. To address her without 'madam', to say 'Yes, Nami, no, Nami', would that be easy, even possible? He postponed the decision to the next day in the office, but on Monday he told her he could not go to work, because he had not been able to sleep in the night. She smiled and happily went to work alone.

Still unable to sleep, restless like a quester until he had found the object of his quest, he told Orah he was going out for a short walk and he left the compound . . . Next week he'd go to Rivers State College of Arts and Science at Rumuola to find out about their UME programme. Oyinkuro said they were very good at preparing candidates for the University Matriculation Examination . . . .

Five minutes or so later he spontaneously took a taxi to University of Port Harcourt at Choba. At the time he reached the area of the lecture halls he saw young men and women coming out of or going into the lecture halls, holding books or bags of books, some of them looking serious, some of them happy and chatting with their friends. He smiled — maybe for some life was a heavy load. He decided against going into a lecture hall because he had no books — he might be regarded as a criminal. When he remembered some of his classmates at ESSS (Evening Stars Secondary School) he smiled. They would pretend to be undergraduates and chase the female students at the university. At ESSS they called it 'imposture'. By the way, he had never looked up the word in the dictionary. He'd do that today . . . In front of the building in which admission matters were treated he gazed at his future, and he was happy at his letter of admission for the BA degree in English . . . At last he left the place . . . Some people were taking transport to the residential area, others were walking . . . He admired the people wearing jeans, even girls ... In jeans too he went along with those walking in the tree-lined avenue, and continued to soak up the atmosphere . . . .

At noon Nami called Orah to know where Zhero was, why wasn't he answering her calls? Orah told her Zhero had gone out since morning, and she panicked. She was about to leave the office when her mobile rang. He was sorry that he hadn't heard her so many missed calls, that was because he'd been strolling about in Port Harcourt. They laughed and she was happy.

He was happy too. He bought a newspaper and decided to go home and read it and sleep. A little after he went into the house Orah brought him a meal of fried rice, fried chicken and sauté prawns. He thanked Orah, called Nami to thank her, said grace and started to eat with gratitude to life . . . He smiled when he remembered the day he said 'O incomprehensible God!' before eating and what followed a few days after that. After eating he washed the plates, which surprised Orah when she returned for them and found that he had washed them. Even Bamida, the gateman, had never washed the plates — he sometimes washed his hand into the deep dish and then covered it back! They laughed, he thanked her and she took the plates after remarking that gratitude was his second nature. He thanked her again and she went out, slightly disappointed, because the receiver of her kindness did not know that gratitude had a better door than thank-you into the heart of a giving woman.

'Ah,' he said as he remembered a phrase Dr Eustace was fond of using, 'my dream is coming up roses . . . Dr Numu will be proud of me . . . Dr Numu asked me, "Zhero, do you dream?" My dream is coming up roses — I will be a teacher.'

On page 9 of the newspaper he had bought he saw thirty names shortlisted for the Naija Hall of Glory. Ten winners would be admitted into the Hall on October 1. Chief Yago was on the shortlist. He had established a boarding school for girls, providing free qualitative education, free accommodation, free uniforms, free textbooks, free meals, pocket money. Chief Yago described his project as 'man's offering to womanhood'. Zhero did not think about the phrase but he felt that if there had been such a school his own mother wouldn't have followed the path she did . . . The newspaper criticized the inclusion of two security guards who had retired from the civil service after thirty-five years of honest service. In the office in which they had worked they had once found an accountant's door and safe unlocked, and because the safe contained millions of naira they had stayed in the office overnight to secure it. The paper did not like the fact that the men had worked for thirty-five years in the civil service without improving themselves educationally. To work for thirty-five years in the civil service and not grow beyond the primary school leaving certificate, the paper believed, was not a good example for the Nigerian child. Zhero could not say whether or not the paper

310

was right.

Nor could his friend, a porter who worked in a wholesale soft drinks store adjacent to Wings & Will. In the end they agreed that honesty was good, so also was education. Before they parted Oyinkuro, the porter, spoke about himself to Zhero, and Zhero admired him.

Oyinkuro concluded, 'I am not suffering for nothing. This work is very tiring but I am managing to do a part-time programme in Rivers State University of Science and Technology. No work elsewhere, that's why I am a porter, even though I already have the West African School Certificate . . . If a man works as a porter until he is too old then he has suffered for nothing. He has even wasted the long life God gave him.' He looked at his calloused hands. 'God forbid.' He spat drily. 'God forbid.'

Zhero remarked, 'Any honest worker is minus one criminal in society.'

Oyinkuro asked, 'If a person is too old and he has not saved for his old age, is he not a liability to society?'

That Tuesday, at bedtime Zhero thought deeply about Nami's offer of a university education . . . A woman who wanted university education for her husband meant well for him . . . Not a woman who wanted to dominate the man . . . Perhaps because of the way Osborne used to treat him she wanted him to have university education too, so that she could be proud of him? . . . To abandon the woman who paid for one's education, could he for any reason do it? . . . Would the fear of ingratitude not bind him to her even if she turned impossible? . . . He thought about his mother who would do anything for him without expectation of reward . . . .

He would have liked Nami to go back to university and get a degree too, but the problem was the supermarket — who would take care of it? He had to be careful — she was a little annoyed when he said education was very important . . . From her English, anyone would think she was a graduate . . . .

In the morning on their way to work he told himself not to fear ... yes, he wouldn't fear to call her Nami, he would call her Nami and see his colleagues' reaction . . . her reaction too . . . .

'Zhero?'

'Yes, Nami.'

He called me Nami, he called me Nami!

'Do you want me to turn off the AC?'

311

'No. It's okay.'

'Sure?'

'Yes,' he said even though she had seen him pulling down the sleeves of his deep green jacket.

'Zhero, my friend's wedding in Lagos I told you about, you'll go with me.' He was silent because he immediately saw himself running away from Chief Yago's house the night he was accused of trying to kill him. 'You're silent, but you're going with me. If you say no, I'll make it an official order.' He was still silent. 'When I want you by me I must have you, or I'll break down and cry. Like a child — till I find my missing toy.'

They laughed.

'I don't like to see a woman crying. I don't like to see a woman suffering.'

'Why?'

'Because of my mother.'

'Then she must have suffered.'

'Yes, for my sake,' he replied and wondered where the person who loved him most could be this morning.

'Where's she?'

'In the village,' he lied, then said to himself that he hadn't lied — the village was where he felt she would go to after waiting in vain for his return.

'When we come back from Lagos, the first thing we do, visit your mother.'

'No. Not now.'

'Why?'

'I'll tell you. Before we go to Lagos.'

She caressed his left thigh.

'I have a story to tell too — the beloved child of a struggling woman.'

Stories, he thought, the story of his life was expanding.

He unconsciously closed the AC vents in front of him. She decided not to make any remark. In the long silence that followed he saw himself as a scavenger in Godiva, pushing a handcart in the streets, collecting rubbish from house to house . . . He was arrested, thrown into the stinking cell in Bansi Police Station, then taken to Manana Prison . . . The brutality of the warders at Manana Prison: warders shouting at them, kicking them, slapping them, spitting at them, not giving them enough time to finish their meals, stripping some chained prisoners and leaving them in the sun or in the rain, and the female warders laughing at them . . . The day some armed warders forced two prisoners to scoop up excrement under the almond tree with their bare hands!

He needed education to put a distance between him and such experiences . . . .

He heard Pastor Ododo's voice in his inner world: 'God says yes to pure goals. My dear brothers and sisters in Christ, if you have a pure goal it will pull you through all conditions in life. It's like a football match. The players are scrambling for the ball in the box, then someone would kick it through the legs of the others into the net. Nothing can stop a goal that must be scored.

His goal was education. It would pull him through all conditions, and he would get it . . . Nami was a good woman . . . Oyinkuro was a porter and was attending university part-time . . . Nothing as good as paying one's way . . . .

She read out loud a newspaper headline: 'JUDGE ASSASSINATED FOR SENTENCING KIDNAPPERS'. She looked at him, intending to tell him to call the vendor, but he was absorbed in thought.

'Did you say something?'

'I wanted us to buy a newspaper, but the vendor is far behind now. Later. It seems the people who said the courts should not sentence armed robbers and kidnappers any more have started to carry out their threat. What's this country turning into? Why would a human being live by armed robbery or kidnapping? Instead of doing something, no matter how small, to survive.' She looked at him for his reaction, but he was silent. 'Zhero, what are you thinking of?'

'The red light!' he warned.

It was too late. The traffic warden at the Wimpey/Ada George junction who wanted to stop her jumped out of the way as she stepped on it.

'Nami!'

They laughed — the traffic warden had no means of pursuing them.

They reached their office a little late. As early as 9am the supermarket teemed with customers because some government ministries and departments had paid the salaries of their staff on Monday and Tuesday. There were not enough shop assistants to cope with the number of customers, so Zhero mostly helped the customers in locating what they wanted or even carrying their shopping baskets to the checkouts, instead of watching them. Even then he spotted a young woman who loaded her shopping basket with items from the provisions shelves then went to the jewellery section to pick some items. She felt uneasy in the long queue before one of the checkout assistants. As she noticed that he was approaching she changed her mind about the jewels and returned them.

'Madam,' he said to her as she was returning to the queue, 'you don't like them?'

'Just necklaces and . . . er . . . Next month. I can manage till next month.'

He laughed and she laughed uneasily. After taking a customer to a shelf and showing him the Susan Cocoa Powder he wanted he looked at the young woman's queue again. She was not there, and no one knew when she left the queue. He told a shopping assistant to remove the basket.

At midday he needed to go and eat. He went to the accountant/assistant manager who gave him just thirty minutes to do so. He first went into the cloakroom, the cubicle in which the workers left their jackets, handbags, wrappers etc before the start of work. He took some money from an inner pocket of his jacket and went to the restaurant.

About thirty minutes after he left, the accountant and the female store detective went with fury into Nami's office, the store detective carrying a deep green jacket.

'What's the matter? Uriah?' she asked the accountant. 'And you, Tariebi, what's wrong with that jacket?'

'Madam,' Uriah said sorrowfully, 'since morning Tariebi has been watching Zhero. When Zhero came to me and said he wanted to go and eat, I and Tariebi, we should have searched him at the door because we have been suspecting him for some time. But he went into the cloakroom for some time before he went to the restaurant. When Tariebi and I searched his jacket, see, see the things we saw.'

'Four gold rings!' Tariebi exclaimed.

Nami burst into tears.

When Zhero was called into her office he met her crying and his mind jumped to Yagood — if Yagood should be dead . . . .

'Zhero . . . Zhero . . . who owns this jacket?'

'It's mine, Na . . . madam.'

'What's in that green jacket, Zhero, what's in this jacket, Zhero?'

314

'It's less than ten thousand naira.'

'How about these things?' She pointed at the gold rings on her gold-rimmed oval glass table. 'These things, Zhero, these things were found inside your jacket . . . Ah, Zhero . . .' He was still speechless. 'When I had a hunch that there were still dishonest people among us it was you I told to be vigilant.'

She cried afresh and Uriah and Tariebi joined in, three innocent humans who could not understand why such evil should exist in the world — it pained Zhero that the cause of their sorrow had been attributed to him.

Uriah asked, 'Why, Zhero?' Zhero could not answer him. 'Because of this thing you have done, you that Madam liked more than her blood relation, because of you Madam will not trust any human being again.'

'Oh!' Nami wailed. 'Not even my own self . . . Zhero, go home, take your things and leave my house. All of you, please leave my office, leave me alone,' she cried impatiently because love had eluded her again.

Uriah and Tariebi went out, leaving their sorrow-flooded faces for all to see and drown their hearts in. Zhero was rooted to the spot.

'Nami.'

'Sh!' Her forefinger on her lips warned him not to pollute her name.

'Madam.'

'That's better.'

'Please, madam, don't let them disgrace me.'

'After you've disgraced yourself, what's there left for someone to disgrace?'

'Please, madam, please . . . investigate this matter . . . Suppose someone wants me out of the way?'

'Who's your enemy here?'

'I don't have any enemy.'

'Definitely not Uriah and Tariebi, two people who have worked with me for years . . . And they are of your tribe. So why would they lie against you?' When she saw his tears she wailed again. 'Oh, Zhero! Zhero!'

'Madam, please don't send me away,' he begged, thinking that she was relenting, and he dropped onto the chair in spite of her deep frown — his legs were too weak to carry his sorrow.

'You sent yourself away.' As he made to speak she continued. 'No wonder you had sixty thousand naira to restore power to Nigeria — my sixty thousand naira.' He shook his head, deciding to be silent — he would never defend himself. 'Zhero, that's the door. Walk out of my life . . . Do you hear me, Zhero, or do you want me to call security?'

'You once said you would never doubt my character.'

'Your character!' she sniggered.

'Have you forgotten?' he lamely asked.

'Out of my office before I call security!' she shouted, as if his reference to his character was insufferable. 'Your character! What do I know about you? You showed me a computer printout of a School Cert result and I foolishly employed you — no questions, no nothing. That's your character, isn't it?'

He shook his head — is this how life is? 'Madam —'

When she lifted the receiver of the phone on her desk he jumped to his feet and went out without a further word, in deep sorrow because love had too quickly turned into hatred. Immediately he reached the house he told Bamida and Orah what had happened, and they both swore that he did not do it.

Nami came home around 6pm. After Orah told Zhero she had finished eating, Bamida accompanied him to her.

'Bamida, why are you here?'

'Madam, I come with Zhero.'

'You old man, if you know what's good for you, out! Now!'

'Madam,' Bamida replied in surprise, 'na Zhero na.'

She got up from the settee and slapped the middle-aged gatekeeper.

'Out of my compound! I've finished with you too.' She pushed him with both hands but the six-foot-four hulk from Chad wouldn't budge. 'Tomorrow come to the office for your pay,' she panted and then shouted, 'Orah!' Orah!' Orah rushed to her. 'Orah, lock my gate after this foolish man leaves my compound . . . Orah!'

'Yes ma! Yes ma!'

'Go and wait for him at the gate! Foolish girl!'

Orah rushed out, saying 'Yes ma! Yes ma!'

Bamida was too shocked to speak. Zhero begged him and forced him out of the house. 'Sir, just go to the gate and stay there,' he said and gently drew him out.

When he came back to her he stood before her, speechless, as if the tongue that had sweetly said 'Nami' in the morning had been pulled out of his mouth a minute ago by sorrow.

The silence was searing her heart. 'Just yesterday I told you of the day I forgot to take a bag containing ten million naira to the office. At midday I flew back to the house. My bedroom was locked and Bamida said Orah had gone to the market. A girl I employed just four days ago — I nearly collapsed. Just then the poor girl returned and said the money was in my bedroom.' He was still silent. 'A primary-six-certificate girl can be so honest.' She looked away from his eyes, two jagged knives slashing her heart. 'Many times I've deliberately left huge sums carelessly around, but Orah is still with me.' No word from him. 'Now I wish she would steal the money and go and better her life.'

At last he found his tongue. 'Nami? I don't want to leave you, no matter what, Nami.'

Her name on his lips — she wept, 'I thank God you didn't say yes when I begged you to marry me. Now I see why, I see why — you only wanted to ruin me and move on . . . A porter before, a hawker before, a scavenger before, a houseboy before — you, Zhero, *you*? How can *you* have been all those — *any* of those? Love-drunken fool, I couldn't read the fiction.'

She was provoking him to tell the truth about himself. She believed he was too good to be the things he said he had been. She needed to know who he was, what he was. But there was no other truth about him, and it pained her unspeakably that he had selfishly refused to admit that he had lied to her.

'I've never begged anyone to pity me before. It's because it's you I'm begging . . . If I must go, can you give me one month? Just one month, Nami. Not for Zhero, but for your fellow human . . . Nami, I'm not ashamed to go down on my knees. Nami, don't look away, see, see me on my knees. Just one month.' She stood up and started to leave. 'Nami? Oh, Nami, for Yagood's sake,' he cried, as if he was Orpheus and Euridice was about to disappear forever.

Without turning she said, 'Okay, just one month,' and continued to leave him . . . because he was a thief.

In her bedroom she thought, He said for Yagood's sake . . . For Yagood's sake she must be good to her fellow human . . . No, no, Zhero must go . . . .

From where she was after pretending to run to the gate to wait for Bamida, Orah had heard everything . . . So Madam wanted to marry Zhero? . . . It would have been so good for her — she deserved a good man like Zhero . . . .

Shortly after Zhero came to live in the compound Nami had seized and burnt all Orah's slinky clothes and given her ₦200,000 to buy 'respectable' clothes. Orah now knew why: Madam didn't want Zhero to fall for her!

In his room Zhero lamented the unfairness of life . . . He felt like a lone fisherman on a boat who had suddenly seen a harbour in the distance after endless months of being adrift on the dangerous seas, but just as he clasped his hands in prayer to thank God the undertow carried him back out of sight of land . . . Suddenly he blamed himself for crying — Zanzi told him not to cry. He must stare at life eyeball-to-eyeball. He rejected the victim consciousness — he would blame no one, nor would he carry a load of guilt on his head. What was happening to him was a challenge. He must continue to appreciate the hand of God in his life . . . .

When he remembered the story of Orpheus he concluded that life had not been unfair to him — even though he was the product of a woman's error, or a man's wickedness towards her, he was to blame for how he had come to be here tonight. But unlike Orpheus, he vowed, he'd not fail in his quest . . . Thinking about the stories he had read he wondered, could a seeker give his all to the quest and not find his object? . . . He'd not fail in his quest . . . .

Every morning he waited for her to leave home before going out and at night would only come back to the house when he was sure she would have retired. Orah begged him to allow her to sneak him food because she felt he was losing weight, but he firmly said no. She offered him money, went down on her knees and begged him to take it and eat well. He took the kindness in her heart but not the money in her hand — he only hugged her and said thank you. Once when he was going out Bamida offered him his own breakfast but he only smiled at the Chadian and shook his head at the goodness of the human heart, then said out loud outside the gate, 'There will be time, my friends, there will be time for full gratitude.'

On the thirteenth day Nami heard that Oyinkuro had introduced Zhero to the proprietor of the place he worked in. With hatred for the man she subconsciously loved most she went to the proprietor, who admired the deep green skirt suit she was wearing. She said thank you, and told him that Zhero was a thief. When Zhero returned the next day he was seriously warned to keep away from the store, and in his presence Oyinkuro was warned by the proprietor.

'You, Oyinkuro, for the first and last time, the minute I shee you with Jero, that minute you are fired.'

Zhero thought of appealing to their tribal kinship . . . No need, the proprietor already knew that they were all Izon. Sadly he went out of his fellow Izon man's office, wistfully glanced at the direction of Wings & Will, the poetically named supermarket, and walked away in opposite direction . . . He was at a crossroads — to go to Amabra or back to Godiva and explain to the proprietor of Twenty-Four Seven why he left? . . . To go to Amabra as a failure? To return to Godiva at the risk of his life? . . . Should he accept the primary school's offer of five thousand naira a month to teach English? He told the proprietor that five thousand naira was just enough to rent a room and he begged her to make it ten thousand a month but she said no, her highest paid teacher earned eight thousand naira a month. To go back and accept the offer? Then how would he feed? How would he transport himself? Nami paid him thirty thousand naira a month! He wept drily — he was getting tired of the load of life.

At home that day he remembered The Home Stretch teaching: 'God is not interested in your tears. He is waiting for you to dry your tears, to see His help at hand.' The Home Stretch also says: 'Life is life. It is what you make of it — sweet or bitter, heaven or hell.' Yes, he agreed, like Odedekoko's song . . . He smiled at the analogy he had drawn between life and Odedekoko's song, his smile gave him a second wind and he vowed to leave Nami's house before the end of the one month — he would find a job, even if it was scavenging, and he would rent a room. He would collect only plastic bottles. He had seen a place where plastic bottles were being recycled, and plastic bottles littered Port Harcourt daily.

When he was in Godiva he had bought a copy of The Quran and read a lot of it. He looked for it, read the statements he had asterisked in Sura 7 (The Heights) and contemplated on them:

We never charge a soul with more than it can bear . . . .

And a voice will cry out to them, saying, 'This is the Paradise which you have inherited with your labour.'

He resolved never again to complain about life's challenges, nor would he despair anymore — he should thank God for giving him the ability to face life's challenges . . . He thought about the sweetness of rest after the day's labours . . . He would do any honest job to survive.

It pained him that he had to leave her soon, but he had to — oh, Nami! Nami!

He would continue to love her. Not sexual love, but divine love. The woman who employed him within a few minutes of meeting him, the best thing he could do was to be forever grateful to her . . . .

His thoughts went to his fellow workers at Wings & Will . . . One after the other, he joyed in their good qualities . . . Especially Adaku, whose beauty, he used to tell her, was put together by the goddess of River Niger from the offerings of all the girls of Onitsha to her from their beauties. A very kind girl too . . . He sent her love Soul-to-Soul . . . and gratitude too for her courtesy to customers . . . Because he called her Daughter of the River, Adaku said he must go with her to the bank of the Niger at Onitsha someday. But that was not to be. She averted her eyes as he was leaving Wings & Will — Adaku too regarded him as a thief . . . .

Tears of pain, shame and self-pity rolled down his cheeks . . . .

The day he bought a newspaper around 5pm and read about Pastor Ododo's brutal killing by a lone gunman called King Kong, who said he would tell the court, not the police, why he killed the so-called man of God, he returned to the house immediately to mourn the death of God's beloved pastor, the one who always settled disputes impartially saying 'My name is Ododo — justice'. He went home immediately, not minding if Nami would see him.

Unknown to him she peeked through her bedroom window and watched him disappear into the boys' quarters, and she collapsed on her bed, a living-dead frame, because her heart was inside him. The next morning he did not wait for her to leave home before he went out. She told Bamida to lock the gate, went to his room and opened the door with the spare key in her possession. She wanted to look for evidence of his having made more money than his pay. She searched the desk drawers . . . his box . . . his bag . . . the wardrobe . . . even under the bed . . . .

She went back to the wardrobe and stared at the contents . . . She shook her head — only three pairs of trousers and four shirts. His deep green jacket, his only jacket, was still in her office. She examined the new-looking oversized orange shirt she had never seen him wear and shook her head again.

She pulled out the top drawer of the desk again and looked at the sheets he had written on . . . She read a poem titled

'ODEDEKOKO':
Odedekoko
Singer of happy songs
Singer of sad songs

Your songs are happy
The same songs can be sad
Sing on, Odedekoko
Singer of life experiences

The second one was titled 'HALLEY'S COMET'.

~~Bright like a comet~~
~~Swift like a comet~~
~~Our love~~

Swift like a comet
Shining like a comet
Nami and Zhero's

This was a work in progress. She read 'Odedekoko' again . . . She lay on his bed, clutched his pillow to her breast and wept . . . She got up, took another sheet from the drawer and read aloud what he had written, 'Nami, my harbour after the buffeting by life.' She groaned, 'Oh! Oh!' And the tears erupted afresh in her heart, rolled through her eyes, and down her cheeks. She lay face-down on the pillow — let the water drench Zhero's pillow. She sat up, the room was reeling, she wished it was time for her to go — 'Halley's comet, come take me along!' She thought she heard footsteps. She listened. 'Zhero, Zhero, oh, Zhero!' she wept, as if he should reward her with his presence for sweetly pronouncing his name.

When she went to work around eleven, dressed in her deep green skirt suit, a female worker who had been moved by Zhero's hungry and tired appearance the previous day when she saw him tramping the street followed her into her office, dropped on her knees and confessed. When Tariebi was called in she took a look at Adaku and confessed too — it was Uriah, it was Uriah who engineered Zhero's disgrace and downfall.

'How long has your dishonest practice been going on?'

'A long time, madam,' Adaku confessed. 'But when Zhero came

he spoilt business for us. Madam, sack me, but please call back Zhero.'

'Let's see if he'll come, let's see if he'll come.' The tears flowing down her cheeks she slowly lifted the handset, which was weighted with the uncertainty in her heart, and asked, 'Zhero, is that you?' He immediately said yes, madam. 'Zhero please come to my office. Now. If you love me the way I love you. Please come before my heart stops,' she cried with relief.

Fearing for her health he chartered a taxi and flew to Wings & Will in about twenty minutes. Some of the workers sniggered as he walked apprehensively to Nami's office. He knocked, opened the door and went in. Tariebi fell on her knees and begged him in their native language to forgive her. He was baffled, but was relieved that Nami looked well, though she appeared to have been crying. She told Adaku to repeat her story and she tearfully did, her eyes averted from Zhero.

Tariebi cried, 'The love of money has spoilt the Izon tribe — Tariebi and Uriah engineering Zhero's downfall. Zhero, for God's sake, please forgive us.'

Word had gone round long ago that after Tariebi and Adaku's long stay in the proprietor's office Zhero had gone into the office too, so Uriah was not shocked to be invited to the office, to see the gloomy faces in the office, or to hear the young women's confessions. And he did not contradict the confessions.

He only shrugged, 'Eh, àkpí . . . àkpí . . . .'

Adaku was afraid. 'Tariebi, what's he doing? Is he invoking juju?'

'No,' Tariebi answered, 'àkpí means life.'

'Is that all you have to say?' Nami asked him in a tone that was divided between anger and disgust.

'I only need Zhero's forgiveness. Let him forgive me for tarnishing his reputation. And Madam to forgive me for betraying her love and trust. Then do what you like with me . . . It is sweet when we are doing it, for many months, then just one day, no, one second, and everything turns bitter . . . very shameful.'

Nami's simple decision was to sack them but Zhero advised her to invite the police and take them to court — it was the only way to deter others. A security guard went to the police station which was a stone's throw from Wings & Will. The policeman, a sergeant, arrived and the three criminals were invited back to the proprietor's office. As the policeman entered the office Zhero, who had barely spoken with Nami while they were waiting for him, screamed to 'Agbulo!.'

'Zhero!' They hugged. 'Hey, Zhero!'

'Madam I'm sorry,' Zhero apologized after he had recovered from the shock of seeing Agbulo as a policeman, 'this one is more than a brother to me.'

Agbulo returned the compliment, 'Zhero is more than myself to me.'

Nami smiled, then shook her head.

'Agbulo? Zhero said.

'Zhero,' Agbulo responded in a life-is-like-that tone.

'Business first. Miss Nami Ogo is the owner of this Supermarket. She invited you. She'll tell you why. Madam, please tell him.'

'Adaku.'

'Madam.'

'Tell the officer everything.'

After Adaku recounted what they had done, Agbulo said he would take them to the police station.

Uriah pleaded and said there was nothing else to investigate. After the sacking of the four cashiers some months ago only he and the two girls had continued the 'fraud'.

Adaku cut in, 'The reason why those cashiers didn't confess is because Uriah made us to swear juju. I want everybody to know, if anything happens to me Uriah should be responsible. If I die Uriah is responsible.'

'Accountant, is that true?' Agbulo asked. 'This case is more than stealing.'

Uriah replied in his native language, 'Ah my own Izon man, don't forget that we are one oh.'

Agbulo was affected by the appeal to tribal kinship but he half shouted, 'Get up, let's go. Madam, we shall lock them up, freeze their bank accounts, and arraign them to court. They must be jailed.'

Tariebi and Adaku said they had only a pittance in their bank accounts — how much was Uriah giving them?

Uriah prostrated on the tiled floor without distaste since the floor was higher than his moral level. 'Madam, I have only one account. I have only thirteen million inside. My salaries too are inside the thirteen million. Madam, my family will be put to shame in the village. My village people are planning to make me a chief next month. Arrangements are in top gear . . . Oh, what a shame.'

'How much is your salary per month?' Agbulo asked him.

'Fifty thousand per month.'

'How many years have you worked here?'

'Three years, sir.'

'Fifty thousand times twelve is equal to six hundred thousand naira a year — Get up, get up — Six hundred thousand times three equals one point eight million.' Agbulo laughed, 'Oh, my Izon brother!' Nami could not help laughing too. 'Madam, let him keep two million and refund eleven million.'

'But I do other businesses too.'

Agbulo laughed, the gap made by the two front teeth a criminal knocked out of his upper jaw last year giving a quaintly happy quality to his laughter, he laughed again, then spoke to him in Izon, 'You will close your mouth and take anything I am going to tell her to give you. Once we reach the police station my hands and my feet are no longer in this case.' He reverted to English. 'A thief have no choice. Madam, you can't say how much they have stolen. And if this case go to court it may take a long time. At the end they will jail him but you may not be able to get the money. That is why plea bargain is better than making case. So let him write you a cheque of eleven million. You issue him a receipt of eleven million naira jewellery.' He looked at her. She was silent, her mind on a higher thing than money and jewellery. 'You can look at it as the jewellery he has been buying on credit, or as the jewellery he has been helping you to sell.' Agbulo laughed. 'This life, there are many things to make human beings laugh!'

Nami shook her head, and there was a long silence.

There was a long silence.

'Zhero.'

'Madam.'

'What do you say?' Zhero was silent. She wished he would say yes. Her childlike desire was to be free of worldly matters in a Nami-Zhero universe. 'Zhero?'

'It isn't bad. But let him bring a bank draft. The bank into which our salaries are paid is less than one minute from here. Is that where the money is?'

Uriah said yes and agreed that Agbulo should go to the bank with him. He went to his cubicle with Agbulo.

Agbulo told him, 'I hope you know that I know that you have other bank accounts, but I don't want the police to investigate?'

'My own Izon man, let me give the foolish woman eleven million and go to my home village to rest.'

'Then you will see me later?'

'Of course, I will, I must.'

'Give me your phone number.'

Uriah wrote his phone number and residential address on a piece of paper and gave the paper to Agbulo. Then they went to the bank where he got a bank draft for eleven million naira in favour of Wings & Will Supermarket and they went together to Nami's office. He was issued an appropriate receipt, and the security saw him, Tariebi and Adaku out of Wings & Will.

In her office Nami asked Agbulo, 'Officer, how are we to thank you?'

'Because of Zhero I cannot say give me this or that amount. Anything from your heart.'

'Then Zhero will advise me. Zhero?'

'I'm thinking, I don't want Adaku to be sacked. An Igbo girl who loves me more than my fellow Izon people.'

'Zhero is right, Madam. How do we reward people like that in society?'

'Suppose she continues to —'

'No, she cannot. People like that become the most reliable. Ask Zhero. He know what am saying.'

Nami phoned Adaku to come back to work the next day, but Adaku said no, not because of shame, but because she needed to start a new life somewhere else. Nami told them what she had said.

'She is a woman,' Agbulo said unfeelingly, 'she can always take care of herself.'

Zhero shook his head. Nami waited for his response. At last he spoke.

'Madam, I want to go out with my friend. It's a long time we last saw.'

'Zhero . . . you'll come back?' she asked fearfully.

'I'll go home from there.'

'Zhero?' He looked at her. She pointed to his deep green jacket which she had draped over a chair since the day he was first regarded as a thief. She smiled to him to take it but he did not respond. She stood up, went to where the jacket was, took it up and gave it to him. 'Please wear it, Zhero.'

'Is it not your own?' Agbulo asked his friend, a little impatiently.

'It's clean, Zhero. I've dusted it every day, except today.'

Agbulo, who did not understand their language of love, urged his friend impatiently, 'Do as Madam say, let's go.'

Zhero forced back his tears with a dull smile.

'Thank you, Officer,' she said with relief to Sgt. Agbulo.

'Thank you, madam,' he replied and went out.

As the friends were leaving the supermarket Zhero's colleagues thanked him, shook hands with him, and prayed for God to bless him, bless him, God would bless all his children yet unborn, and his children's children too, and punish his enemies with everlasting hellfire. Zhero smiled instead of saying amen.

Agbulo and Zhero decided to go to Zhero's house and they did. Bamida, who had let them into the compound, quickly went to inform Orah and they both fearfully went to Zhero's room. Zhero laughed and assured them that Agbulo was a childhood friend. They went away and Agbulo told the story he had been bursting to let Zhero hear.

'After you and that minister escape we went for big operation. By the way, that night, after you people escape, police came into the forest that night and many of our people died, remaining only Naija, Ogoun and me because I woke the two of them quick. We joined with another group and went on mother of operations — broad day bank robbery. Everybody was killed. Out of twelve of us only me escape, every other person killed, because three police APC's came. That day I vow to stop being a criminal. After two years, when I was running short of money, I join police force. After all, nobody alive know I was armed robber and kidnapper . . . I got the School Cert somehow and joined police force . . . Is the gun, the pull of the gun which made me to join police force . . . Zhero, life is full of wonders. Me, Agbulo, fighting crime, killing armed robbers, killing kidnappers — life is full of wonders.'

'Yes. That's why you saved my life.'

'Zhero, not to mention. If it is to mention, I will not leave your house till tomorrow, if I start mentioning the things you use to do for we all. Ah, in those days, Zhero . . .' He shook his head. 'Zhero, if not for you, I will have died of tetanus . . . You spent all your money to treat me.'

'Agbulo, it's enough.'

Zhero thought back to their days at Swali Market . . . Yes, he was generous, but only to his few friends. Now he knew how to give to all life . . . .

Agbulo broke the silence. 'Zhero, I know you will keep my secret

secret, that's why am not even asking you to do so. I know you, Zhero.' After a long pause he continued. 'Zhero, you are the youngest among us, but the way you think is different from all of us.' He paused again then continued. 'Zhero, do you still think about life? The way you use to do in those days.' Zhero smiled. 'How about me killing armed robbers now, shooting kidnappers?' Zhero's face was expressionless. 'That's why I use to say I can't understand life.'

Zhero inwardly answered that he too didn't understand life — why did life show him things he shouldn't know?

Orah came in with two covered dishes on a metal tray.

'When Madam phoned me and said I should tell her when you come home, I told her you were already in the house with your police friend. She said I should make food for you, that she is coming very soon.'

Agbulo opened the dishes. 'Thank you, beautiful girl.'

'Thank you, sir,' Orah replied and went out.

'Zhero!' Agbulo happily said. 'This food is sweet — jollof rice with beef and fat fat prawns . . . The way you have chosen is the right way. Me, I have changed, but any moment it can be good night for me. That's why I won't marry. I won't have children.' He paused while he ate with a relish that Zhero admired. He continued. 'Everywhere am posted to they like me. Because of my braveness ... my bravery. Especially against armed robbers . . . Hey, Zhero, this food is sweet. How did that girl prepare the meat?' With the spoon he turned two pieces of meat over several times, as if he wanted them to reveal the girl's culinary secret. Zhero laughed. 'Because of my braveness — bravery — they always include me to go against armed robbers . . . But I know, one day, just one bullet will fell me ... But I will fall like a hero. And police will bury me a hero.' They laughed, then ate silently till the food had finished. After licking his lips Agbulo spoke again. 'Zhero, don't ever regret the way you have chosen. Whatever a person is looking for, if he has patience he will find it. We, is lack of patience that pushed us into the things we did . . . I think it is your fault too. If we were together at Swali Market we won't change. But you left me and Ogoun and went to Mabo Waterside . . . Patience, Zhero, patience is very important in life,' he nodded sagely.

'Thank you for the wisdom.'

'Hey, Zhero!' he exclaimed characteristically light-heartedly. 'If Ogoun has not died, three of us to meet together, it would have been very sweet . . . Anytime I go to Amabra, your home village, I use to think is only me that's left, not knowing that you are alive doing fine.'

'What do you go to do there?'

'The secondary school. Every month-end, when I was in Yenagoa, I use to lead a group of us to guard the principal from the bank to the school to pay teachers.'

'There's a secondary school in Amabra?'

'Yes. Is new. Shell built secondary school for your village.'

'I am glad,' Zhero said in a cold tone. 'I am glad,' he repeated without appearing to be glad, his thoughts on Chief Kulokulo . . . .

When Nami returned around six she went straight to Zhero's place in the boys' quarters — her second time in his bedsit — and had her meal there. Orah told Bamida what was happening and they were both happy.

Five minutes or so after the meal, Nami asked, 'Zhero, shall we go to the main building?'

'I'll be with you later.'

'Then I'll stay the night here.' He laughed. 'Yes, Zhero, trifle with my feelings. I deserve it.' He was silent. 'Zhero, I too suffered. There was no peace in my heart until the moment Adaku restored your reputation . . . You don't believe me?' She pulled out a desk drawer and showed him his poems. She answered his interrogative eyes. 'In your absence I came in here to weep. I read "Odedekoko", I clasped it to my breasts, and I lay down on your bed and I wept ... I wept more than you're doing now . . . Zhero, it shall be the same again with us?'

He wept more as he saw the stains of her violet lipstick on his pillow, evidence that she had truly been here in his absence, he wept more, and then told her, 'If you can mistrust me once, you can mistrust me one-hundred-and-once more.'

'But you can still love me?'

'I have always loved you. Especially that night you turned your back on me when I was on my knees —because of the love in your heart you couldn't look at me.'

She hugged him. 'Then it shall be the same again?' she asked, hoping that he would push her down onto his bed and follow in a dive. Because he was silent she disengaged from him. 'Talk to me, Zhero, it shall be the same again?'

He told her it would be hard to forget . . . A man once disappointed

328

him and he had carried the pain in his heart for years . . . Forgiving was easy, but forgetting was . . . .

He shook his head. 'What you did to me pained me in a way I can't describe. It pained me more than what Chief Yago did to me.'

'Who's Chief Yago?' she asked, her heart pounding with fear.

He told her his story of Chief Yago. At the end he sighed, 'That's my story, Chief Yago's story,' wiping his eyes with his right hand.

She took his right hand and stared at it, saying, 'Louis Yago . . .' as if she could see Louis Yago in his palm.

'You know him? Who told you his first name?'

'I shall be happy to reconcile you with him.'

'Now it's your turn to trifle with my feelings.'

'No, my Zhero, it's because the pain in your heart is the pain in his heart too.'

She stood up abruptly. 'Zhero, please come to me, otherwise I'll come back here to spend the night.'

She went to her room . . . .

The next morning she told Zhero to wait for her at home while she went to the airport to pick a dear friend. His attention on her deep green trouser suit and the aqua scarf around her neck he said okay. She came back with her friends around 11am and invited Zhero to come and say hello to them.

A woman gleefully jumped up from the settee as he entered the sitting room, dashed to him and hugged him tightly as she repeatedly exclaimed his name, she hugged him tightly and more tightly as she chanted 'Zhero! Zhero! Zhero!' as if the transcendental moment had come when mother and son should merge together into joy.

When they disengaged he heard Chief Yago's voice, as if it was from another world. He looked. Chief Yago was here! He was baffled — Chief Yago and his mother in Nami's house!

'Zhero.'

'Sir.'

His mother happily corrected him. 'Say "Dad". He's your dad.' She laughed happily. 'Have a seat, my son, then you'll understand. Come sit by me,' she said, happily like a stigmatized woman whose reputation time and truth had restored.

He sat by Nami, who was silently glad and grateful to him.

'Zhero, I'm your father. Zera, please tell him everything.'

Zera told their story, from the day Yago declined responsibility for her pregnancy to the moment they received Nami's phone call, and she thanked God for giving her the strength for the hard quest for vindication of her decision against abortion.

Nami told her own story too — from the day Yago saved her unborn child for her to the moment Zhero mentioned him. Zhero was shocked that she was going to sell her unborn daughter, but he did not show it, nor did he condemn her, he only blessed his mother silently — selling him never crossed her mind.

'Where's the girl?' Zera asked her.

'She's gone back to Abuja.'

'What's her name?'

'Yagood,' Zhero answered.

'Yago's good deed,' Nami explained. 'That's the meaning of the name I gave my daughter — Yago's good deed.'

Yago was overwhelmed by her sense of gratitude and he thanked God for it in a teary voice. When he was able to compose himself he asked Zhero when they should come back for him. After some thinking Zhero delivered part of a piece he had written in Godiva and given to Dr Eustace to edit.

'Not tomorrow. Humans don't fall from the sky and accept the first man who says I'm your father as their father. A father is the man you knew even before your baby eyes could see him. Some people knew their father when they were in their mother's womb: as he caressed the woman's stomach he heard the child kicking in the womb, while the child heard his laughter, the song of joy from his heart, his gratitude to God for the coming child. When my mother caressed her stomach and sang to me it was the pain in her heart I felt in her womb.'

He was word-perfect but sounded and looked spontaneous because every time he said those words they were fresh from his heart and poignant, reminding him that the man that impregnated his mother abandoned her and he was therefore a bastard.

His mother cried, 'Zhero, don't be cruel to me again.'

Nami left the sitting room in tears and joined Orah in the kitchen to prepare a meal for her guests.

'Zhero, one thing is certain. From your language and the wisdom in your words, one thing is certain — you have had a good education.'

'From the school of life,' his mother added.

'Yes,' Yago agreed. 'We've each brought something home from the years — love and wisdom.'

330

'And the quest continues. For more love and more wisdom,' his mother said.

Zhero smiled — his parents had internalized Zainab Shettima's ideas.'

When his father dangled before him secondary and university education anywhere in the world he said he needed time to consult with Nami, and added that he already had the West African School Certificate. In her happiness his mother said her ambition was to have a university degree too; already she had got the GCE (O. Level). Now that she'd found him it was time to go to university.

'Thank you, Mom, thank you, Mom,' he nearly wept as he embraced her.

'Thank you, my son.'

'I love to see Uncle Numu.'

'Numu is . . .' His father hesitated.

'One of my strong influences,' he completed his father's sentence. 'His words and his novels also gave me courage to face life. Whenever the days were too hard I thought of Mom, and then Uncle Numu, especially the promise I made to him — to succeed in life like him.'

Yago hated his nephew afresh. 'Zhero, Numu is dea —'

'Dear to me too,' his mother cut in quickly. Yago shrugged. 'Zhero, I have one of his novels I like.' She brought out two books from her handbag, put back one and showed him the other. 'See, it's "Odedekoko".'

He smiled. 'I have it too. What's the title of the other one?'

'"Rustum and Sohrab".'

He had never read it before, he said, though at school they had been told about the man who killed his own son in error. Yago felt guilty, while Zera happily told Zhero that it was his father who, ironically, had bought it and forced her to like it. He was happy. He thanked his mother for her reading habit.

'So, Auntie Teima had left?'

'Yes, Zhero,' Yago answered. 'She has left. Forever.'

'Has she remarried?'

Zera quickly replied, 'Your dad will tell you the full story someday.'

A very beautiful woman, he silently said, and visualized the day she beat him after Vinko's mother had left . . . A woman often angry, yet even while she was beating him he was only thinking of her beauty in the trouser suit and the sweet perfume she was wearing ... And the way she sometimes said his name as if she was his mother — even if she didn't love him all the time she wasn't a totally bad woman ...

Yago thought of the day Teima asked Numu if he wanted to make Zhero a writer. He felt love for Numu was already turning the boy into a writer. He shrugged.

While the four of them were relaxing and watching TV after eating, Zera suggested to Nami to go back and complete her university education even if she did not need the degree for economic purposes. She answered that she would consult with Zhero before making a decision. Zera looked at her son, who did not answer the question in her eyes in anyway. But before he retired Yago persuaded Nami to accept an invitation on behalf of Zhero to visit his Asokoro home in a week's time.

That night mother and son spent joyous and tearful hours together telling the stories of their lives to each other, concluding with what the Holy Bible says, "All things work together for good."

For hours Orah too did not sleep . . . Chief Yago was the man who took her to Durban Hotel in Kaduna and offered her ten thousand naira, but he didn't recognize her, maybe because she told him her name was Ama . . . It was true, it was his son he was looking for, so it was Zhero he was looking for . . . She would never tell anyone ... For Zhero's sake it would be a secret till she died . . . The way he wept that day, she felt he was telling the truth, and after she left the hotel she prayed to God for him to find his son . . . Perhaps her own father who abandoned her mother in the hospital the day she gave birth to quadruplets would someday come back too? . . . She'd like to see him, to know what he looked like, but she and her three sisters would never forgive him for calling their mother a witch who wanted to ruin his life with four female children at a time. Her mother said he went to Gabon and married another woman . . . .

She shuddered at the thought of the night a man was arranging with some people to kill her . . . After she escaped from his house she vowed never more to prostitute herself, no matter how bad the condition was — better to starve to death . . . .

She remembered Jide who wanted to marry her, but his mother said no, because she was a housegirl . . . Maybe it was good, because if he had married her, then if he knew about her past, it would have been a very serious thing . . . Maybe no, if he truly loved her?

The tears running down her cheeks she spoke out loud, 'If a bad woman repents, can God not forgive her? If a bad woman changes, can a good man not marry her?'

She went down on her knees and prayed, as she had done for years, for God to forgive her . . . .

Joy, thoughts and memories took the place of sleep in Zera's head . . . Like bitter leaf but very useful, the hard experiences of life . . . She used to lament that other girls had followed men and got on in life but the same thing she had done only briefly had been the cause of sorrow for her for so long, until she came across The Home Stretch and the teachings started to sink in . . . then the Silent Voice said to her, You are not the other girls, you are you . . . Another time, the Silent Voice said to her, The journey of life is a unique experience, no two persons travel the same way . . . Zero too had only travelled his own unique way — she didn't have to collapse under a load of guilt.

As she prayed for Mrs Wama Abramson the tears coursed down her cheeks . . . Louis said they would go with Zhero to Godiva to thank her . . . She too would be good to parentless children in need — oh, she would!

After his parents left, Nami half hoped Zhero would reject the invitation, but he accepted it and they went to Abuja on the due date. For the first time Zhero travelled on a plane, for the first time he felt that the genuine Niger Delta militants were right to take action against the neglect of their region as his father's driver proudly told him to observe the beauty of the tree-lined ten-lane Airport Road, the Abuja City Gate, Churchgate Towers built of sky-blue glass, not mud, NNPC Towers, Sheraton Hotel in the distance, Wuse residential and commercial area countless times the size of Amabra, the Three Arm Zone consisting of the Presidential Villa, the Supreme Court, and the National Assembly . . . for the first time Zhero understood why people worshipped wealth when he saw the opulence of his father's mansion in Asokoro . . . then he laughed at life — the price of his father's mansion could buy all the structures in Bondo and Nze Waterside several times over.

The houseboy told him that his mother had gone to Maitama for something and his father was having a nap as he showed them to the exclusive section of the house they were to stay in, which consisted of two rooms, a sitting room and a toilet/bathroom. While they were both admiring the place out loud Nami made a remark.

'I fear,' she said, 'the purpose of this weekend with your parents — this weekend in Asokoro — is to help you decide whether or not to marry me.' His suppressed anger at life started to rise. 'The power of wealth,' she continued as she sat by him on the couch in his room, 'yes, the power of wealth . . . No matter what, I'm eternally grateful to your father.'

Without saying a word he went downstairs and told the driver to drive him around the city. About thirty minutes later she called him to come back for her.

'If I come back to you now we must go back to our own house ... in Port Harcourt . . . immediately.'

'Hey, Zhero! Zhero, how do you want to present me to your parents?'

'Then let me drive about until my anger is off.'

'Zhero, did I offend you?'

'No, Nami, I'm not angry at you. I am angry at . . . you should know why I ought to be angry, Nami . . . Nami, I love you.'

'Please don't keep long.'

He told the driver he wanted to buy newspapers. The driver pulled up near a newsstand and made to go down. Zhero quickly went out.

'Do you have any Port Harcourt paper?'

The owner of the newsstand laughed. 'Something wrong with you?' The man laughed again, as if he was proud to show that he had lost two of his upper teeth. 'Rowland? Rowland!'

'Jero! I laugh because I am happy the kidnappers did not kill you. Jero, I cry that night o. I cry for many days. Why should God allow kidnappers to take a good boy like you away? How many years now, Jero? You still know me!' he laughed again, the great gap between his front teeth as jolly as Agbulo's, Zhero thought.

Zhero had become the cynosure of the people who were reading the papers at the stand without any intention to buy any papers, and he felt embarrassed.

'Rowland, give me your phone number. We'll talk later.'

He took three newspapers and discreetly gave Rowland five thousand naira. Rowland was overwhelmed by his generosity.

'Hey, Jero, na you get dat jeep? See the way you dey speak English.'

'Rowland, give me your number.'

While they were exchanging phone numbers he vowed to use his changed situation to help Rowland to do whatever business he loved to do at a higher level — provided it wasn't selling pirate videos, or anything dishonest. He told the driver to take him back home. Rowland's rather ragged appearance had melted his anger . . . He had achieved so much since he parted with Rowland . . . Rowland's mother didn't know who raped her, and she told Rowland so, yet Rowland was a happy man . . . He smiled at a thought that often made him sad in Godiva: In drumming chastity into his head his mother had never told him not to make her own mistake, because that would have suggested that she regretted the offspring of her mistake . . . No matter what Chief Yago had done wrong, Chief Yago, his father, genuinely loved him, no matter what he'd done to him and his mother . . . His ex-wife Teima, without what she did he couldn't have been so rich in experience . . . He laughed — Teima ensured that he attended the school of life seriously!

The driver looked at him.

'I'm sorry, Ndidi.' His mind went back to Teima . . . He thought of the day she swore that he would never be more than a houseboy. He laughed again. 'Ndidi, don't mind me.'

He decided to bury his mind in a newspaper . . . He liked the editorial comment of 'The Fourth Dimension' on the Naija Hall of Glory nominees. Objecting to the upcoming glorification of the two former security guards, the paper wondered if the organizers of the Hall of Glory had ever heard about Kimani Maruge, the ex-Mau Mau fighter who went to school at eighty-four. The paper described him as an inspiration to the African child, and advised the organizers of the Hall of Glory to adopt him as a Nigerian and give him a posthumous honour, if there was a dearth of heroes in Nigeria . . . Zhero silently praised himself . . . On second thought, must everybody be highly educated? How many highly educated people were happier than Rowland? . . . He wished the two former security guards hadn't been nominated for the Hall of Glory. The exposure had only humiliated them . . . .

When he reached the house Nami and his mother were sitting together on the couch in Nami's room. Each of them took a newspaper from him. His mother shouted at what she saw on the front page: Prophet Blake was dead!

'Do you know him?'

'Yes, Zhero, I know him.'

Zhero read the news and gave her back the paper. She stood up and went to Yago with the paper.

'Zhero, who is Prophet Blake?'

'I don't know. The paper said he was walking up and down the aisles in the church and prophesying about the coming elections in

Nigeria, then he collapsed on the floor and died.'

Nami changed the subject. 'Zhero, since the day you knew Chief Yago is your father you haven't been happy . . . like . . . like a boy who has found his father.'

'That's because I never searched for him.'

'Even then, meeting Chief Yago again, the man you said loved you so much —'

'Perhaps if he hadn't turned out to be my father.'

'Let's listen, let's listen.'

She pointed to the TV. A medical doctor was being interviewed on Africa TV on IVF (in vitro fertilization).

'Can the Ethical Committee approve IVF for unmarried women? Is it ethical?'

The doctor smiled. 'It's not unethical. It's the woman's choice. The Committee has not started to approve it for unmarried women in this country, though. There are countries where they can easily get it.'

'How about the cultural attitude to children born out of wedlock, children without known fathers?'

'In many countries there's no longer the negative attitude we hold in this country. In any case, if the woman has the courage, it's her choice.'

'It won't be easy in this country where the word "bastard" still rankles. My people, the Yoruba would say "Ìmí àle — bastard!"'

The doctor laughed, laughed as if he was in his sitting room. 'Until a few seconds ago, I can't remember when last I heard those words. And you a woman!'

The interviewer laughed too. 'Prof! As if you're not Yoruba.'

Nami called the interviewer a foolish woman and said, 'Thank you, doctor. My own Yagood is not a bastard.'

Zhero felt the doctor was laughing at him. He tuned out the TV discussion. His mind went to and stayed on Bazi for hours that day, and a week later in Port Harcourt, after Nami had gone to church his mind went back to Bazi and refused to leave him . . . .

At that hour Bazi was at No. 13 Alabi Atere Street, Surulere, Lagos. He told Zera that when one of his workers called him to say that she was a road sweeper he had instantly flown back to Nigeria and to where she had been seen in Port Harcourt. She could not say a word, the image of herself as a road sweeper choking her. When he told her that he had seen her go into a jeep outside Union Bank and trailed her to her house on Friday, she thanked him for all the pains he had caused her over the years and told him to go away, because she was now a happy woman. (Then she had found Zhero?) She told him to go, just go out of her life forever. He replied that that was impossible — all he wanted was to live the rest of his life with her in Amabra, where once she canoed him across the river. In spite of her anger she erupted into laughter — how ridiculous men could be! Yago came into the sitting room. She told him the visitor was the Bazi she had told him about before. Instantly remembering that she had told him that she loved Bati Bazi so much, he told the rival for his love to go away as the lady had said. His loud and angry voice invited his mother to the sitting room.

'Mama, we are sorry we disturbed you.'

She did not answer Zera. She was musing on Bazi's face. Zera and the two men felt embarrassed.

'Mama . . . .'

'Zera, I'm coming.' She said to Bazi, 'You look like a son of Bazi. Your face is like Bazi's face. Bazi in Ghana.'

'My name is Bati Bazi.'

'Bati! Come! Come embrace me!'

She pulled him up and embraced him. His father was the one who impregnated her in Ghana and denied responsibility for the pregnancy. At that time she lived in the same street with Bazi and his wife, Bati's mother. She left Ghana, pregnant with Louis.

'Mama, your name is Gloria?'

'My name is Gloria, my son. Where is Bazi now?'

'He's still in Ghana.'

'He was a man I loved so much. I believed everything he said about my beauty. Bazi too was handsome, that is why you are handsome . . . Ah, Bazi was a handsome man,' she repeated wistfully. 'I believed him when he said he wanted me as a second wife, but when I happily told him I was pregnant Bazi called me a fool.' She laughed. 'You look surprised that I laughed. It is because if Bazi had not called me a fool I would not have succeeded in life. After Bazi I no longer depended on any man. I no longer listened to any man's sweet words. I expected nothing from any man, alone I brought up Louis. It's good he called me a fool.' She laughed again. 'When a man tells a woman you are beautiful she loses her head — is she not a fool? I stopped men from praising my face. I slapped those who insisted on doing so, for thinking that I was still a fool.' They all laughed. 'Let us laugh, my children. There is more beauty in this world than a woman's face.'

'My father has several times regretted his action. He's always reminding me that if I see you in Nigeria I should apologize on his behalf and tell you that he's always thinking of his child. My mother told me she didn't know what he had done until after you left. She said she liked you so much because of how you used to make her laugh. And she too wants to see the child.'

'Your mother Ajua was very good to me. That is why when Bazi did not want to marry me as he promised, I left Ghana quietly. Better Ajua did not know. Hey, Ajua wants to see the child!'

'Yes, Mama.'

'See, look at him opposite you. That is your younger brother. Haven't you noticed that your voices sound alike?' Zera burst into tears. 'Zera instead of being happy, you are crying. What is wrong? Zera . . . Louis, is anything wrong?' she asked, about to be angry, for the first time, at the young woman she had loved as deeply as she had hated Teima.

Bazi went to Yago. 'Louis, let's embrace as brothers. We are African, so we are brothers, not half-brothers.'

Yago stood up and they embraced.

'Louis,' his mother said. 'I still want to know why Zera is crying.'

'Louis, Bati,' Zera tearfully said, 'tell Mama everything . . . Louis you do it . . . now.'

Yago told his mother the whole story. She was not shocked. She only said to them, 'What has happened has happened. Life only requires you to move on.' To their surprise she laughed. 'Only God knows what you people did to one another in a past life.'

Only Zera did not laugh — the truth staggered her, the validation of her recurrent dream experience of the dashing young lawyer who impregnated two sisters and abandoned them.

Bazi was happy that Zhero had been found. He requested for his phone number and address — he was bursting to meet Zhero. Zera inwardly said no instantly. Though she loved Bazi more than she loved Yago she would not trust her child to him again. She said she would take him there. Yago did not want her to travel alone with the man she loved so much — he said he too would go.

Zera called her son and told him she was aching to see him. He laughed.

'For laughing at me I'll be with you tomorrow. Tell your wife I'm coming, this time tomorrow.'

They heard his happy laugh on the phone.

Bazi was surprised. 'Zhero is married?'

'It's a joke,' his brother answered.

But around noon the next day what Bazi saw was not a joke. As Nami, who had left her office with trepidation to come home and meet Zhero and his parents, entered the sitting room she felt dizzy as her eyes fell on him. His breathing turned rapid, he squirmed in his seat. Zhero and his parents were baffled. Nami sat by Zhero. When at last she spoke it was to Yago.

'Sir, why have you brought this evil to my house?' Yago was baffled. 'This man is an incarnation of evil.'

'Nami!'

'Ma, this man is an evil man. I don't want to see him again . . . You, you lied to me about your name and identity. After I told you I was pregnant I didn't see you anymore. You changed your phone number . . . Sir, how come you are with a man like this? You're too good to know him.'

'Nami, we met for the first time only yesterday. Bati is my half-brother.'

'Nami laughed. 'What's his name?'

'His name is Bati Bazi,' Zera answered.

'So, Zhero, this is the Bati Bazi you told me about? I knew him to be Jerry Frimpong.'

'Nami,' Zera fearfully asked, 'is Yagood the child?'

'Yes, my beloved Yagood is the daughter of an evil man.' She laughed. 'The brother of the evil man saved my child, and she's called Yagood — Yago's good deed.'

Zera explained her statement to Bazi, and then to Nami how the two brothers had met yesterday. Zhero's parents were inwardly glad — if Bazi married her their son would be free for them to take away.

'Nami, where is the girl?'

Nami laughed scornfully. 'Even now he can't say "my daughter"!'

He wept. 'Twenty-something years of marriage, I was childless, because I stuck with a barren woman . . . but I have a daughter somewhere. Nami, my German wife left forever for her home country because of her fear of kidnapping in Nigeria. I went there to persuade her to come back, but we divorced. If only —'

Zera's phone rang. It took her some time to decide to answer. 'Hello . . . Good day, Oweilakemefa.' She listened to Oweilakemefa, then replied. 'Oweilakemefa, because I'm very happy today I now promise to help you. But I'm in Port Harcourt right now. I'll call you when I get back to Lagos . . . Bye for now.'

'Foolish man,' Yago remarked.

Zera explained to the others: 'It's a man who was encouraged by his mother to beat and ill-treat his wife till she ran away a few months ago. When his mother brought him an illiterate girl from the village they fell apart. He now says he can't leave the mother of his daughter and marry another woman. So he wants me to accompany him to her and beg her to have him back.'

'Foolish man,' Yago said again.

'Nami.'

'Ma?'

'Can you and Bazi excuse us?'

Nami looked at Zhero. 'Only Zhero can answer that question.'

Zhero told his parents he should be given time to think, and they agreed to come back with Bazi in a week's time.

He added, 'I think you should all go back today, otherwise Nami's emotional upset will increase.'

Bazi was not surprised at the boy's adult behaviour — he had always been like that. When he calculated the time, he was sure he could not have been to university — there must be another reason his English was so good, and he was wiser than his age.

They took the boy's advice and went back to Lagos that day. After they left, Zhero told Nami that he wanted to walk off the shock. She felt he was cruel to leave her alone but she did not say a word — if he liked he could walk to Asokoro.

At Shell Location Road a jeep braked roughly and pulled over in front of him. Someone jumped out —Ogugo!

'Let's not shout, let's not shout, just come in.'

They both went into the back. Zhero greeted the driver.

'Olomu.'

'Sir.'

'This is my best friend in the world.'

The driver greeted his boss's best friend once more. Ogugo directed him to take him back to the house and then called someone to say he might come late. They went to a street Zhero had not known before and drove into a compound containing a big building and a boys' quarters. As they climbed the stairs Ogugo told Zhero that he, Ogugo, was the owner of the building.

'My tenants live in the ground floor and the first floor. I, Ogugo, the landlord, live in the second floor.'

The friends laughed. Immediately they entered the sitting room Ogugo called out for the maid and told her to serve Zhero whatever drink he wanted.

'Give me ice water.'

'Zhero! You are still like that? Me, I have changed a little. It is necessary to socialize.' After he had taken the ice water Ogugo asked him, 'Zhero, you were walking in the sun. Any problem?' Zhero smiled and shook his head. 'You sure? That heavy sun. You were preparing yourself for hellfire?' They laughed the way they used to do in Godiva anytime they had money to feed for a few days. 'Seriously, Zhero —'

'No problem at all, Ogugo.'

'I mean financial problem, Zhero, because if there's problem you will not tell anyone.'

Zhero smiled to reassure his friend, and Ogugo told the story of how he escaped from the police at Nze Waterside, lived in the streets until something told him to go back to the police station he had taken the diamond jewels to. When the DPO said they had been announcing for him to come he said that was why he had come. The DPO gave him back the jewels and he signed a statement to that effect. To cut a long story short, he sold the jewels to a Syrian in Lagos in Godiva, came to Nigeria, bought a place at Obigbo close to Port Harcourt and became a 'building materials merchant.' After a pause he continued sadly. 'Zhero, do you know that when I went back to Godiva last year to thank the DPO, do you know that they told me he has been killed when he and his men were fighting armed robbers in a bank?'

'Hey! What a life.'

'But I looked for his wife. She has three children, the oldest one about ten years old. You should see where she is living, wife of a police officer who sacrificed his life for the people of Godiva. If you see the place, you will say is better not to be alive . . . By the end of this year I'll go back to see her.'

'Thank you, Ogugo.'

'Thank me? Are you not the one who made me so? Before I met you do I know how to do good?'

'You're now a good man, a giver. Thank God.'

'Thank you too. Zhero, am many years older than you, but your

341

ways are better.'

Zhero changed the subject.

'I looked for you, and for Yari too.'

'I too, Zhero, I look for two of you. At last I was just sure that nothing will happen to you. Because God can't abandon you. As for Yari, anytime I think about him, I still feel sad.'

'Ogugo —'

'By the way, Zhero, that woman, Chanta, she came to the house, before I was arrested at Nze Waterside, she came to the house with their two daughters. She wept and wept and wept when I said I don't know where you are. She gave me fifty thousand dollars and her address for you. But as I was arrested and I run away from the house I don't have her address. As she cried and cried that day and said poor people should be good to poor people her husband start to cry too.'

After a long pause Zhero said, 'I've got the School Cert and I shall go to university. How about school, Ogugo?'

'Zhero, I tell you I wanted to make money. Now, am making money. Zhero, at the watersides we use to live in, there are people with School Cert, people with university degrees but no jobs. Some of them are pool-betters, some are drunkards, armed robbers etc; some of them, we are better than them.'

'You're right.

'Zhero, when I say am making money I mean money. The massive development that is going on in this Rivers State, business is good for hardworking people like me. That boy Amaechi is doing a lot for the State. Some other governors are doing well too, but I like him. He is my State governor. I like what he is doing. Roads, bridges, and especially schools. The primary and secondary schools he is building, even in riverine villages, are better than many Nigerian universities. Many boarding secondary schools too for that matter. So if Amabra had been in Rivers State, your people too will by now have a good secondary school. Development everywhere, Zhero. When government spend money well, they create jobs for the citizens, instead of armed robbers and kidnappers. That boy, only God can fully thank him,' Ogugo enthused.

'Ogugo, you call the governor of the State a boy?'

'How old is he? He's not too older than me, though he's doing well for the State.'

'Isn't it because he has a good education?'

342

'I know Zhero will boil it down to education. But the governors in some states, are they not educated?'

'Maybe they don't have the right type of education?'

'Now you talking!' Ogugo exclaimed triumphantly. 'There is education that is good, there is education that is not good. Instead of not-good education let me be happy with my primary six.'

The friends laughed, their way of agreeing with each other's point of view when they were in Godiva.

'Zhero, the girl I shall soon marry is almost a master's degree owner. She is waiting for the convocation of Rivers State University of Science and Technology. All our children will go to school. To make you happy.'

They laughed again and Zhero said it was time for him to leave. The maid came to the sitting room and said, as if to Zhero, that food was ready.

'Thank you,' he replied. 'What's your name?'

'Cynthia, sir.'

'In which class are you? . . . Cynthia, in which class are you?'

'Zhero, she will soon start school. To please you.'

They laughed, Zhero said he would eat Cynthia's food some other day, and she went out.

'Zhero, let me give you Chanta's fifty thousand.' Zhero told him to keep it. 'No. Any day you see her you must be able to swear I gave you her gift of love.'

Zhero received the gift and passed it on to Cynthia, saying it was from God through him to her. Cynthia dropped on her knees.

'Thank you, sir.'

Ogugo smiled in admiration. 'Thank you, Zhero.'

'Thank you, sir,' Cynthia repeated. 'Goodbye, sir.'

Cynthia's simple joy haunted him until Ogugo dropped him at the gate of his house, and he invited Ogugo to visit him in two weeks' time to hear his own story. Nami welcomed him back coldly, thanking him for avoiding the problem they ought to have solved immediately.

'Nami, let's think about it for some time.'

'Think? What's there to think about?'

'Nami, tell me the truth. Do you love Bazi?'

Unaccountably she felt angry that a subordinate was about to interrogate her, but she checked herself and said something milder.

'Are you suggesting that I parted my legs for him for the sake of money? You may also say I made my wealth on my back since you know about my late boyfriend.' When she saw his face she immediately went down on her knees and begged him to forgive her. 'I deliberately wanted to hurt you because your question wasn't fair.'

'In any case it's not about your love for Bazi; it's not about your love for me; it's not about my love for you; it's about our love for Yagood — its about what is good for Yagood. I'll stand by your decision.'

Without a word she left him and his mind went back to Cynthia ... a small girl . . . where were her parents? . . . If there was one thing he needed from God it was the power to keep families together . . . Osborne laughed at Yagood when she asked about her daddy . . . He loved Nami . . . A woman called Godiva — sacrifice was the noblest human quality . . . He would sacrifice his happiness for Yagood . . . .

He remembered what Numu said in 'Odedekoko': Divine love transcends romantic love whose essence is sexual . . . .

He and Nami never mentioned the matter again until the day Bazi called her.

'Who gave you my number?' she had asked him angrily.

'Zhero's mother.'

'Why have you called me?'

'Our daughter's school is close to my house at Asokoro in Abuja.'

'Who's our daughter?'

'Yagood. Yagood, our daughter.'

While he waited for her response the image of himself and Zera on the river flashed through his mind . . . but for Yagood's sake he'd beg Nami until she married him. At last she spoke.

'Bati, don't you go near my daughter, Bati, don't dare do it!'

'That's why I've called you. To have your permission to see her. But if you say no, I won't.'

'Absolutely no!'

'You prefer a small boy to the father of your daughter?'

She switched off her mobile and went to Zhero in the boys' quarters.

'Any problem, Nami?'

'You gave my phone number and my daughter's school address to Bati without telling me?' His silence was infuriating. 'Answer me, Zhero!'

'I'm sorry. I didn't know that's why my mother asked for them,'

344

he answered calmly even though he had noticed that she had raised her right hand and checked herself.

'Your mother! What right . . . oh, Zhero, I'm sorry, I'm sorry.'

At bedtime she said to herself, 'Nami, Zhero's parents don't want their son to marry you.' And she thought about Bazi's subliminal question: You prefer a young boy to the father of your daughter? ... She persuaded herself not to forget that Zhero was also a former porter, hawker, houseboy and scavenger . . . .

A porter, a hawker, a scavenger, a houseboy . . . .

For long Zhero's own mind was on Orah. Like him, she too just walked into Wings & Will one day and Nami employed her . . . If she got a good education his mother wouldn't say no . . . Orah was a teachable young girl. She had once or twice told him how she'd like to go to secondary school . . . He was sure she loved him too. Today when he thanked her for all she'd done for him she replied, 'Is it the things I do for you that you love?' He wished he'd told her it was herself he loved . . . She once said the woman she served before she came to Nami loved her very much, but when her son said he'd love to marry her the woman sacked her, calling her a 'non-person in society', and then she sent her son away to London . . . 'A non-person,' he said . . . and sighed . . . and wondered at the consciousness of humans . . . .

His thoughts went to Evening Stars Secondary School . . . Estella loved him and wanted him . . . He remembered the day the boys in his class blamed Eve for the downfall of mankind and the girls said Adam was a fool, a weak-head who couldn't zip-up. He said he didn't believe the forbidden fruit was sex, because if it was, with whom did Eve have it before she tempted Adam to have it with her? Estella seized him and kissed him passionately. And the girls called him Adam that day . . . Estella pestered him, to visit him at home, but he couldn't let her do so, because he didn't want her to know that he was a houseboy . . . .

The tears coursed down his cheeks and onto his pillow as his thoughts went back to the way Nami treated him when he was thought to be a thief . . . a person she'd volunteered to send to university . . . My sixty thousand naira, you used my sixty thousand naira to restore power to Nigeria . . . But Bamida and Orah trusted him . . . .

Esewa . . . May God guide her to a better livelihood . . . .

On the day Zera, Yago and Bazi returned to Port Harcourt only

Zhero was at home. Nami had deliberately left for the office.

Zhero's mother asked him, 'Zhero, have you made up your mind?'

'She'll tell you her mind. I'll stand by her decision.' He silently said, 'God's will be done.'

Bazi silently wished the boy was his son. He had admired him since the day they first met at Mabo Waterside . . . the boy who saved him from being kidnapped . . . a listenable voice too.

'Zhero, can we go to her office?' Bazi asked him.

'Yes, Da . . . yes, sir.'

They went to her office. Zhero opened the door without knocking and they saw her talking to a woman. 'Wura-Aiye, all of us must help you to save your daughter from hanging. I know the law authorities in Libya are wicked, but they love money more than our own officials here. I'll do what I can to help, but not that kind of money — from where will I get that kind of money?'

Wura-Aiye was shocked to see Yago. 'Mr Yago, what have you come here to do?'

Yago was shocked to see her too. 'Nami, do you know this . . . this thing?' Nami was shocked. 'This thing who put me in the family way and called me a harlot? Mr Yago the daughter I was pregnant with is facing the death sentence in Libya for drug trafficking — fifty wraps of cocaine in her stomach. They say one Italian mafia reported the girls' entry to the Libyan authorities because the Nigerian mafia using and trafficking the girls refused to pay their dues to the Italian mafia.' She wept. 'I failed my daughter. When she told me the fraudulent man who wanted to marry me was raping her I didn't believe her, I thought she was jealous of my happiness, so she ran away. And I never saw or heard about her until I was told last week that she was arrested for drug trafficking and she needed money to regain her freedom. And my daughter has changed her surname to Alainibaba — fatherless.' Zhero sat with a thud on the floor. 'Alainibaba — fatherless.'

'Madam, what's her first name?'

'Is it her first name that matters? Who are you? Oh Zanzi, Zanzi, come see the thing who calls itself a human being. Come and see —'

'Oh Zanzi! Zanzi!' Everybody was shocked. 'I know Zanzi . . . I know Zanzi, the waitress at the eatery by your office in Lagos who came to you for a job, and you told security to throw her out . . . because she came in rags to your office.'

Yago wept.

346

'Zanzi Fatherless?' Wura-Aiye wept. 'Zanzi Motherless, Zanzi Very Motherless . . . Oh, Zanzi, when we were in Burutu your friends called you Odedekoko because of your voice — it was neither the voice of a woman nor that of a man. Odedekoko, your voice is sweet . . . Odedekoko, let all good mothers like me, Wura-Aiye, let all good mothers like me hear it and rejoice in their mothering skills . . . My parents named me well — Wura-Aiye: gold of the world.'

'Oh Yago!' Yago groaned.

'No, Odedekoko,' Wura-Aiye continued, 'no, Libya can't kill you — your song will live forever.'

Yago momentarily thought, 'If this story gets out my reputation as a candidate for the Hall of Glory will become a national joke.'

Nami noticed that Zhero was limp on the floor. She yelled and bent down over him.

'Zhero! Zhero!'

Some customers and her staff who heard her yell wondered what was happening. A security guard ran to her office.

'Call the driver! Call the driver! Zhero can't die!'

Ogugo, who was in the supermarket, asked the checkout assistant he was about to pay to, 'Which Zhero? Zhero Sai?'

'Yes, you know him?'

The money dropped from Ogugo's hands. Yelling 'Zhero! Zhero!' he ran to the proprietor's office and burst in. 'Zhero! Zhero!'

'Who are you?' Zera asked him.

'Zhero and me came from Godiva! Bring Zhero! Bring my only friend in the world!'

He helped to raise Zhero, they took him into his jeep, Zera and Nami climbed in too and he told Olomu to 'fire off' to Uchechi Clinic.

While Zera and Nami wept, Ogugo repeatedly addressed his friend.

'Zhero, is a lie. You didn't die in Godiva, is not in Nigeria you will die . . . Zhero, is a lie oh . . .' He laughed mirthlessly. 'We say we will find the thing we are looking for. Me, I have found my own. You too, will find your own . . . .'

Between his assertions to his friend he called and told the nurses to be ready with a stretcher at the car park . . . he told Dr Ogonda to be personally present . . . he told Dr Ogonda he and his friend would be at the clinic in less than five minutes. In less than five minutes they were by the entrance to the building.

As Zhero was being wheeled to the emergency room Ogugo

assured Zera and Nami that Zhero would be okay — since his friend Dr Ogonda established the clinic nobody had died in it. Zera and Nami felt relieved. A nurse showed them where to wait. Zera thanked her but Ogugo looked at her contemptuously.

'You don't know me?'

He followed Zhero into the emergency room where Dr Ogonda, another doctor and two nurses were waiting. When he started to tell Zhero it was impossible for him to die, the second doctor compassionately told him to go outside and wait. He did not mind the doctor but when Dr Ogonda nodded at him to go out he obeyed and stayed outside the door to continue to tell Zhero he must not die.

Where she was sitting with Nami, Zera prayed out loud to God not to allow Prophet Blake's prophecy to come true, not to allow Prophet Blake to take her son along on his journey of doom. Nami feared for her sanity and felt it would be better for her if Yago and Zera went away with their prized son. She had pretended not to know that Zhero preferred to go with his parents, it was painful to accept the fact, but she must give him his freedom, and forgive him . . . for the sake of Yago's good deed . . . Thinking about how he would have depended on her if he hadn't found his father, she said to herself, Because the goat scratches his sides on the wall people think he has no kin.

After thirty eternal minutes or so Dr Ogonda came out and was surprised to see Ogugo by the door.

'Dr Ogonda, you can't understand how close we are. In any case how is he?'

Dr Ogonda smiled. 'He's okay. No, no, no, *you* can't go in now. They'll take him to a ward, then you can see him later.'

'Special ward, special ward.'

Dr Ogonda smiled. 'I'll see to it.'

'Dr Ogonda, let's go and see the women who came with me.'

They went together to the visitors' room. Zera and Nami jumped to their feet on seeing Ogugo and the doctor. In answer to their interrogative eyes both men smiled.

'Who are they?' Dr Ogonda asked him.

'Actually I don't know them. Is only my best friend Zhero I know.'

'I'm Zhero's mother,' Zera answered.

'Ma, you are Zhero's mother!' Ogugo shouted as if he were at the Agoa dump. He embraced her. 'Ma, like Zhero, I too have no father

348

but I love my mother. Zhero loves his mother very . . . too much!'

Zera smiled while Nami shook her head.

Zera added, 'Thank you.'

'Ma, Zhero is okay. I have not seen him but the doctor say is okay.'

'Yes,' Dr Ogonda said. 'But I can't allow my friend Ogugo to go in and see him yet. If Zhero hears his shout he'll go into a coma.'

They all laughed.

'Can wee see him?' Zera asked.

'In a few minutes. I'll be here to take you to him.'

'Thank you, doctor.'

'Ogugo, let's go to my office.'

In Doctor Ogonda's office Ogugo gave the records clerk who came in Zhero's full name and his own address as Zhero's.

'Sir, your deposit is fifty thousand naira.'

'Special ward?'

'No, sir. Special ward is one hundred thousand naira.'

'Go. After I go to my car I'll bring one hundred thousand.'

'Dr Ogonda nodded his assent and the young woman left. About fifteen minutes after Zhero had been taken into a private ward Dr Ogonda decided to take Zera, Nami and Ogugo to see him, warning Ogugo on the way not to be emotional, not to shout, not to try to embrace him, not to shed tears.

'I agree with you, Dr Ogonda. Is the way we grow up. Let me go and pay the deposit.'

Only Zera and Nami went with Dr Ogonda to see Zhero. He was on a drip, otherwise he looked well.

'It's because he hadn't eaten since after breakfast yesterday.'

His mother was alarmed. 'Zhero, do you want to kill yourself!'

'Zhero, because your mother forgave your father and her heart is at peace, I too shall forgive.' She paused then added, 'For the sake of Yago's good deed.'

Her words suddenly extinguished the bitter memories in his mind . . . for the first time his mind flashed back to the moment Chief Yago firmly told Ariba to employ him, and after office hours he took him home without being asked . . . his face brightened.

Dr Ogonda saw the beauty of a newborn baby's face.

The tears welled up in Nami's eyes . . . When she stood up from the bedside chair Zera tearfully hugged her, saying 'Thank you, Nami, thank you, Nami' and stroking her back. Then she sat on the bedside chair. Her right hand on her son's chest she cooed affectionately, 'Odedekoko.'

He smiled.

She cooed again, 'Odedekoko.'

END